Only In My Dreams

Only In My Dreams

RIBBON RIDGE BOOK ONE

DARCY BURKE

AVONIMPULSE
An Imprint of HarperCollinsPublishers

Excerpt from *Yours to Hold* copyright © 2015 by Darcy Burke.
Excerpt from *Various States of Undress: Georgia* copyright © 2014 by Laura Simcox.
Excerpt from *Make It Last* copyright © 2014 by Megan Erickson.
Excerpt from *Hero By Night* copyright © 2014 by Sara Jane Stone.
Excerpt from *Mayhem* copyright © 2014 by Jamie Shaw.
Excerpt from *Sinful Rewards 1* copyright © 2014 by Cynthia Sax.
Excerpt from *Forbidden* copyright © 2014 by Charlotte Stein.
Excerpt from *Her Highland Fling* copyright © 2014 by Jennifer McQuiston.

EPub Edition FEB 2015 ISBN: 9780062389305

Print Edition ISBN: 9780062389299

AM 10 9 8 7 6 5 4 3 2 1

For my daughter, Quinn.
You teach me every day that
the best things in life are unexpected.
I love you!

Chapter One

January

SARA ARCHER TOOK a deep breath and dialed her assistant and close friend, Craig Walker. He was going to laugh his butt off when she told him why she was calling, which almost made her hang up, but she forced herself to go through with it.

"Sara! Your call can only mean one thing: You're totally doing it."

She envisioned his blue eyes alight with laughter and his dimples creasing, and she rolled her eyes. "I guess so."

He whooped into the phone, causing Sara to pull it back from her ear. "Awesome! You won't regret it. It's been waaaaay too long since you got out there. What, four years?"

"You're exaggerating." More like three. She hadn't been out with a guy since Jude. Easy, breezy, coffee barista Jude.

He'd been a welcome breath of fresh air after her cheating college boyfriend. Come to think of it, she'd taken three years to get back in the game then, too.

"Am I? I've known you for almost three years and you've never had even a casual date in all that time."

Because after she and Jude had ended their fling, she'd decided to focus on her business, and she'd hired Craig a couple of months later. "Enough with the history lesson. Let's talk about tonight before I lose my nerve."

"Got it. I'm really proud of you for doing this. You need a social life beyond our rom com movie nights."

Sara suspected he was pushing her to go out because he'd started dating someone. They seemed serious even though it had only been a couple of weeks, and when you fell in love, you wanted the whole world to fall in love too. Not that Sara planned on doing that again. If she could count her college boyfriend as falling in love. She really didn't know anymore.

"I was thinking I might go line dancing." She glanced through her clothing, pondering what to wear.

"Line dancing?" Craig's tone made it sound as if he were asking if she was going to the garbage dump. He wouldn't be caught dead in a country-western bar. "If you want to get your groove on, Taylor and I will come get you and take you downtown. Much better scene."

No, the nearby suburban country-western bar would suit her needs just fine. She wouldn't be comfortable at a chic Portland club—totally out of her league. "I'll stick with Sidewinders, thanks."

"We wouldn't take you to a gay bar," Craig said with a touch of exasperation that made her smile.

"I know. I just don't want company. You'd try to set me up with every guy in the place."

"I'm not that bad! Taylor keeps me in line."

Yeah, she'd noticed. She'd been out with them once and was surprised at the difference in Craig. He was still his energetic self, but it was like everything he had was focused on his new boyfriend. She supposed that was natural when a relationship was shiny and new. "Well, I'm good going by myself. I'm just going to dance a little, maybe sip a lemon drop, see what happens."

Craig made a noise of disgust. "Don't ass out, Sara. You need to get laid."

Sara's fingers froze on the edge of a long-sleeved silk blouse. She'd had precisely two partners—her college boyfriend, the douche, and Jude, her rebellion boyfriend after she'd moved away from Ribbon Ridge, her small hometown, and her large, overprotective family. Some of whom still saw her as the little girl with Sensory Processing Disorder who had public tantrums and got overexcited in certain situations.

She jerked herself back to the phone conversation. "Very funny, Craig."

"I'm serious." He exhaled loudly. "Though the thought of stepping foot inside Sidewinders gives me hives, Taylor and I will come along and be your wingmen."

Her fingers landed on a shirt she'd never worn, a sexy, sleeveless aqua top that would flash some cleavage. It was one of those items of clothing she'd bought on a whim, on Craig's insistence, actually. "You don't need to sacrifice yourself for me," she said. "I'm probably just going to dance a bit and come home. Boring."

Her skin itched at the thought. She didn't want boring or expected. Not tonight.

"With that sort of attitude, you're going to have a blast." His sarcasm dripped through the phone. "Listen up. Where's that shimmery aqua top we bought last fall?"

She smiled as she pulled it off the rod and hung it so she could see the front. "I'm looking at it."

"Sweet. Now, get your Rock Revival jeans. You look hot in those, and you hardly ever wear them."

She went to the opposite side of her walk-in closet and picked out the jeans he was talking about. She hung them beside the top. "Please don't ask me to get a pair of heels. I can't dance in them."

He sighed. "Pity. But you have awesome ballet flats. Wear the silver."

Good call. She pulled them from her shoe shelf and dropped them to the floor beneath the jeans. "What else?"

"Jewelry, of course. I'm not completely sure what you have, but some big silver hoops would be good. And a long necklace. Do you have something fun? You are kind of a jewelry whore."

She totally was, and she had the perfect necklace. It was silver with pearls and aquamarine-colored crystals. She'd consented to buy this shirt because it would go with the necklace.

She straightened her spine. "Okay, you've dressed me up, now what? I haven't picked up a guy in…oh, never mind. This is a terrible idea. You're a bad influence."

"NOT even. We've been friends a long time. Have I ever steered you wrong?"

"No." He was always supportive and honest.

"Get yourself dolled up and go dance. Guys are going to flock to you like hummingbirds to honeysuckle. Taylor and I will come with you, if you want."

"That's nice of you, but it's not necessary." It was one thing to talk about picking up a guy, and another to make an actual commitment to go do it. Plus, guys didn't usually pay attention to her. But then she never tried to get their attention, either. "This isn't going to work."

"It *is* going to work. You're gorgeous, and if you wear what I told you, you'll look hot. The question is, can you let your guard down long enough to invite a guy in?"

She transferred the phone to her other ear. "I don't know. Craig, I don't really want a relationship." She was still too focused on her business, on growing Sara Archer Celebrations into *the* premier event-planning firm in town.

"I know; that's why you're going to have a one-night stand."

"I don't *do* one-night stands!"

"It's one time, and it'll be good for you. No, *great* for you. That settles it; I'm coming, and I'm going to make sure you get laid."

"I don't need a pimp."

"Ouch. Okay, I won't come, but I'm serious. Why not let yourself go? Just see how the night goes. You're smart;

you'll protect yourself. All I'm saying is if the opportunity presents itself, you should go for it."

His belief in her and the fact that he never belittled her abilities gave her courage. She looked in the full-length mirror hanging in her closet. She *was* smart, and she *did* deserve to have some fun. "I'll try."

"There is no try, Sara. You can do it. You deserve an amazing night."

"I do. Thanks, Craig."

"Text me if you need help. I'll be on standby. I can be your wingman from afar."

She chuckled. "Bye, Craig."

"Call me tomorrow—I want details!"

She shook her head and hung up.

After setting her phone on a shelf that held her sweaters, she took a deep breath and set about transforming herself into someone else. Someone who was self-assured, knew what she wanted, and wasn't afraid to go after it. Wait, was that really a transformation? Wasn't that the person she'd become after leaving home?

Once she'd changed her clothes and freshened her makeup, she contemplated herself in the mirror. Talking to Craig and coming up with a plan—albeit a somewhat sketchy one—filled her with angsty anticipation. Instinctively, she went for the edge of her sleeve before realizing she didn't have long sleeves on. She returned to the jewelry box on her bathroom counter and slipped a half-dozen bangles on her arm. The knock of the metal against her skin would feel good as she danced, and they gave her fingers something to do when she needed to fidget.

Not processing sensory input the same as most people meant adopting what others might consider odd habits: fiddling with the edges of her sleeves or with bracelets, squeezing her arms together—sometimes until her face flushed a little bit—but she'd long ago learned to do that only in private or simply by avoiding certain scenes, such as crowded country-western bars.

Maybe tonight wasn't such a good idea.

No, it was Thursday. It wouldn't be too hard for her to navigate, and she'd become very accomplished at removing herself if a situation began to overwhelm her. She had to be. Learning to manage this completely on her own was one of the reasons she'd moved away from her huge, meddling family.

Pushing them to the recesses of her mind, she slid a pale pink, sparkly gloss over her lips, took a final inventory in the mirror, and left before she could change her mind.

Sidewinders wasn't far—maybe ten minutes. She hadn't been there since before Thanksgiving, but it never changed. Peanut shells still littered the floor of the bar, and the clack of billiard balls sounded from the loft overhead. As she moved farther inside, the music overtook almost all other sound. Blake Shelton's voice surrounded her, and she smiled as her body began to thrum with the rhythm.

Her pockets filled with her necessities—driver's license, debit card, phone, car key, and lip gloss—she was hands free. She'd even left her jacket in the car, reasoning that she'd be too hot to wear it anyway.

Normally she would've beelined for the dance floor, but she had a different objective tonight. Maybe. Either way, she wanted to take her outfit for a test drive. Summoning a confidence she wasn't sure she completely felt, she attempted a sultry walk to the bar and popped onto a barstool. A dark-haired bartender maybe two or three years younger than Sara approached with a smile. "What can I get you?" she asked.

"A lemon drop, thanks."

"Cute top—that necklace goes great with it," she said, before taking off to make Sara's drink.

Sara looked down and smiled. So far, so good. Now if only a guy paid her the same attention.

"Here you go." The bartender delivered her lemon drop. "You want to keep an open tab?"

"Sure." Sara slid her debit card across the bar. After sipping her drink—and nibbling at the sugared rim, which was often the best part—Sara turned her barstool toward the dance floor. She doubted she'd recognize anyone, but stranger things could happen.

The music had her foot tapping against the stool while her gaze drifted from the dance floor to the tables she could see. A trio of attractive men sharing a pitcher of beer drew her notice. No way could she invade that knot of testosterone. She was about to continue her scan when recognition sparked. Though she hadn't seen him in years, she knew one of those guys. And holy wow, Dylan Westcott was way hotter than she remembered from high school. Which was saying a lot since he'd been unbelievably good-looking back then.

Dylan laughed at something the guy next to him said. Dimples accentuated his lean cheekbones as his face settled into an easy, sexy grin. His dark brown hair was thick, but cropped short on the sides.

His gaze connected with hers and Sara nearly spilled her drink. Caught staring, she abruptly turned back to the bar. Maybe this had been a terrible idea. She didn't know the first thing about how to be alluring or how to tempt a gorgeous guy like Dylan-freaking-Westcott.

Finish your drink and go home, she told herself.

"Hi."

The greeting came from behind and to her left. Afraid she knew who it was, she slowly turned her head. Yep. Disaster. He'd come over to talk to her.

His brows pitched low over his amazing gray-green eyes as he scrutinized her. "Sara Archer?"

Butterflies crowded her stomach and a slight euphoria permeated her brain. "Yeah. Hi, Dylan."

"You remember me." He sounded surprised.

Sara smiled. "Well, you remembered me, too."

He cracked a smile in return. *And she'd been worried about a downtown club being out of her league?* "Hard to forget a television star."

"Ha. Right." She and her siblings—the "famous" Archer Sextuplets plus their younger brother, Hayden—had starred in their own reality series during their tween years, well before Derek had come to live with them. "That was a long time ago. I can't believe you'd recognize me from that."

"We went to high school together, too."

"You were three years ahead of me. You didn't even know I existed."

Unlike Sara, who had been ultra-aware of him. He'd been quarterback and captain of the football team and senior class president. He'd also been spoken for and had later married his high school girlfriend, though Sara had heard they were now divorced.

"I'm hurt. You make me sound like a self-involved jerk." He smiled self-deprecatingly and lowered his voice. "I'm pretty sure I was." He gestured to the bartender and pointed at his nearly empty pint glass. "One drawback to Sidewinders—no Archer beer."

"True." Her family owned nine brewpubs, which sold their beers exclusively. "It's how we draw you in."

He glanced at her, but his gaze lingered just long enough for Sara to wonder if he was interested. A shiver raced down her spine. "How long has it been? You look fantastic, by the way."

Mission accomplished. She quashed the giddy feeling that threatened to make her giggle like a college girl. "Thanks."

She took a sustaining drink of her lemon drop, sneaking a look at his rugged jaw and lips that could curve into that bone-melting thousand-watt smile. If she was going to flirt with Dylan Westcott, she needed all the help she could get. "This is incredibly cliché, but do you come here regularly? I thought you lived in Ribbon Ridge." Which was a good forty-five minutes away.

"I do live there, but some friends invited me to meet them here tonight. How about you? Are you still in Ribbon Ridge?" His mouth cracked into that self-deprecating smile again. "Sorry, it's not a huge town. I should probably know that."

"It's big enough to miss those kinds of details. But no, I left a few years ago. I live near here."

He glanced around. "And are you here alone?"

She hated that she felt self-conscious. "Yep. Just needed to get out for a bit."

His gaze dipped down briefly as if he were registering that she wasn't exactly dressed for a quick jaunt to the local bar.

She rushed to add, "I came to dance."

"Awesome, let's hit it." He slid off his stool and held out his hand for her.

Her heart pounded in her chest. When she went out—which was rarely—no one ever asked her to dance. It was why she preferred line dancing, because she didn't need a partner.

Craig's voice sounded in her head. *If the opportunity presents itself, you should go for it.*

Just then the music changed to something a little bit slower. Couples paired up on the dance floor. It was precisely the kind of song that usually drove her back to the bar or, even more likely, home. But here was a man—a sexy, *interested* man—asking her to dance.

Sara took his hand, and when she slid her fingers between his, a burst of heat snaked its way up her arm and settled into her chest. The look he gave her as they walked only intensified the feeling.

When they got to the dance floor, he swept her into his arms. He was more than a good head taller than her, probably six-one, with broad, muscled shoulders draped with a sexy black button-down shirt, and lean hips encased in worn jeans that fit like they'd been tailored for him.

She loved the press of his hand around her waist and the touch of his palm against hers. She closed her eyes briefly and let herself be carried away. He smelled fresh and masculine—not from cologne, but from whatever soap he'd used. Rosemary and pine. Northwestern and scrumptious.

Too soon, the music picked up again, and she forced herself to move away from him. They broke into lines, and it became evident that while he was a good dancer, he didn't know the steps. He tried really hard to keep up, but at the end of the song, Sara took pity on him. "Should we go back to our drinks?"

He grinned at her as relief flooded his gaze. "Yes, save me. Please."

She wouldn't tell him that her suggestion had also been selfishly motivated. If she danced too long her senses would wind up, and she wanted to stay in control tonight. She didn't want to have to bail to pull herself together. Not when the night was going so well.

A warm glow spread from his arm, which he'd situated at the small of her back as he guided her toward the bar. "How about we move to a table?" he asked.

The flutters in Sara's belly picked up speed. "Sure. Over there?" She pointed to a table in the corner. It was cozy. Dim.

"Perfect." The way he said the word and the way his gaze caressed her made Sara wonder if he was talking about the table. But no, guys didn't look at her like that or flirt with her so outrageously.

She made her way to the table and settled herself on the bench against the wall. A couple of minutes later, he came toward her, carrying her unfinished lemon drop and his beer. He handed her the drink and clinked their glasses as he slid onto the bench beside her. "To old friends."

She drank, peering at him over the edge of her glass. Her stomach fluttered as she watched him. This was the closest she'd been to a guy in a long time.

He set his nearly empty pint glass on the table and turned his head toward her. "Okay, Vegas Rules."

She blinked at him. "What?"

"You know, 'What happens in Vegas stays in Vegas.' You can't tell anyone how badly I suck at line dancing."

She laughed. "Deal."

He looked relieved, but only briefly. Then he frowned. "Uh-oh. Now you have a secret you can use against me. It's only fair if you give me one, too."

"A secret?" She instantly thought of the heat pooling in her belly because of his proximity and decided sharing that would be *too* revealing.

"Make it something good."

She arched a brow at him. "Really? Not being a very good line dancer is hardly a 'good' secret. I think that gets you something along the lines of my being a bit clumsy. If we'd kept dancing, you would've seen it."

He shook his head. "I don't believe it. You're a great dancer. You're making that up."

"I *am* a great dancer." She shot him a *so there* look. "But I'm still clumsy. It's my—never mind." She'd been about to say it was her sensory processing disorder, but why bring that up? Breaking free from her family meant she didn't have to be the girl with SPD. She wasn't embarrassed or ashamed, but she'd wanted to keep tonight light.

"Hmmm, you're very intriguing, Miss Archer."

She turned her head and saw that his gaze held an underlying glint. Curiosity. Interest. Confidence flowed into her from that look. She could do this—flirt, attract, *seduce*. "So far these secrets are lame. You owe me another one. And make it good." She narrowed her eyes in what she hoped was a coquettish way.

He chuckled. "I do? Let's see." He tapped his finger against his lower lip, drawing her attention to his mouth. Which in turn forced her thoughts to what it would be like to kiss him. "You should run screaming in the other direction. I'm bad news."

The way he lowered his voice to deliver his warning made her toes curl. "Why? You can't drop a bomb like that and not explain it." She finished her lemon drop.

He eyed her empty glass. "Another round?"

She hadn't planned on more than one drink tonight, but she could handle one more. Besides, the evening was becoming far too interesting to bail now. "Sure. But talk."

He signaled for the server who came and took their order. Exhaling, he leaned back against the wall. "You seem like a nice person. I'm...just a fun-loving guy looking for a good time now and again." His gaze was guarded, but seemed to smolder anyway.

"So you pick up girls in bars a lot?"

He smiled enigmatically, his eyes never leaving hers, as he picked up his glass. "Occasionally."

She ran her fingertips along the smooth stem of her glass. "Is that what you're doing tonight?"

"I hadn't decided until now. But I guess it's ultimately up to you." The look he gave her as he set his empty glass on the table nearly ignited her into a ball of flames. No guy had *ever* looked at her like that. Like she was something good enough to eat. She shifted in her seat and wished she had the guts to do what Craig had recommended— Dylan had all but suggested it. So why not? Why couldn't she have a hot one-night stand with Dylan Westcott? She knew him—enough anyway that he wasn't some random stranger. Honestly, it was the best-case scenario. And he definitely seemed interested...

The server brought their drinks. Sara took a long sip to bolster her courage. She cocked her head at him and gave him a questioning look. "Vegas Rules?"

"Of course." He took a pull on his fresh beer and set it back down.

"I had a massive crush on you in high school." She cringed, waiting to see if she'd totally blown the mutual attraction they seemed to have going.

His lips spread in the most captivating grin. "Really? I had no idea."

The dormant sixteen-year-old inside her silently squealed. "You had a girlfriend. A pretty serious one too—you got married later, right?"

He gave a short, dark laugh. "Yeah, and you can see how well that turned out."

Sara was sorry she'd brought it up and sought to lighten the mood again. "I'm sure it was all her fault."

"Absolutely." He shook his head then leaned toward her, bending close to her ear so his breath tickled her flesh. "Not true. I told you I'm bad news."

A shiver, both from his words and his nearness, shot through her. Had he cheated on his ex? He'd intimated he was a player. Hesitation dampened her excitement, and that pissed her off. She was here for a good time, damn it. She slid out from behind the table. "Thanks for the disclaimer. Come on, Bad News, time to learn some line dancing."

He got to his feet. "Be gentle."

She speared him with a look she'd never dared before—it was hopefully both seductive and sassy. "I don't think that's what you really want."

His eyes narrowed, and sparks seemed to ignite between them. "You *are* dangerous. Perhaps you're the one who needs a disclaimer."

A part of her knew it was all playful banter and might go nowhere, but she'd relish the thrill of his attention for as long as she had it.

Chapter Two

AFTER HUMILIATING HIMSELF for a good half hour on the dance floor, Dylan guided the petite and lovely Sara Archer back to their table. What the hell was he *doing*? Sara was a nice girl with several brothers. Large brothers who would probably kick his ass if he picked her up in a bar. There was a reason he conducted his extracurricular activities away from Ribbon Ridge—he preferred no-strings-attached hook-ups. Sara Archer was about as far from that as he could get. Yet here he was, flirting with her. There was no harm in flirting, was there?

He hadn't known who she was when he'd approached her. He'd seen a cute blonde who'd been alone, and he'd made his move. When he'd gotten up close, recognition had socked him in the gut. Though he'd recovered quickly, he'd been too entranced to make some excuse and retreat. Which had brought him to his present conundrum: flirting with someone he knew as opposed to the much safer—and much preferred—woman he didn't know.

He slid onto the bench seat beside Sara and took a long drink of his beer, thirsty after their dance floor exertions. She studied him over the top of her lemon drop as she sipped. Her eyes were blue with just a hint of gray, and when they did that slight narrowing-thing, she exuded a saucy, sexy air that jolted him with electricity. Like they were doing right now.

"You did better out there," she said.

"You're talking about the slow song. I think I can manage a form of hugging and swaying."

She laughed. "Yes, you can. But I meant all of it. You're a good sport."

"You're a great teacher." It could've been a cheesy, flirty line, but he meant it. He'd had fun out there with her. While she was definitely sexy, Sara Archer was the sort of woman he could be friends with. Which made her *not* the sort of woman he'd pick up. Time to bring this evening to a close.

"Thanks." She finished her lemon drop.

"You want another?" So much for concluding things. He needed to get a rein on himself.

She was quiet a moment. "Two's my limit. If I want to keep my wits about me. And since you're bad news, I think that's probably best." She pulled her phone from her pocket and looked at the display. "It's getting late. I should go."

He nearly exhaled with relief. "Can I walk you out to your car?" There was no harm in that, and even though he didn't like strings, he was still a gentleman.

Her gaze flickered with surprise. "Sure, that would be great." She flashed him a smile that stirred his blood with anticipation. For what? He was walking her to her car and then coming back inside to really get his evening started.

He got to his feet and held his hand out to help her up. She slipped her fingers into his, and the connection rocked straight to his gut. He dropped a twenty on the table to pay for the beer and lemon drop and put his hand at the small of her back to walk her out.

She took a few steps then stopped. "I need to stop at the bar to settle my tab."

"Let me."

"You already bought me one drink. That's enough." She gave him another smile that sparked a physical response he ought to ignore.

He watched her walk to the bar, appreciating the curve of her hip encased in jeans that looked tailored to her. He'd noted she wasn't wearing ridiculous heels. She'd come to dance and had donned footwear accordingly. Practical *and* sexy. She was dangerous, all right.

He went toward his buddies' table to grab his coat.

"Dylan," Josh called.

Dylan nodded at Josh and Noah and the two women who'd joined them.

Josh stood up to join Dylan and turned him away from the table. And toward the bar where Sara was talking to the bartender. "You leaving?" Josh asked. "She's hot."

"Just walking her out. I'll be back." A sense of disappointment settled over him. He suspected his shot at a great evening would diminish as soon as she left.

Josh gestured toward Sara. "Dude. She's smokin'. And she seems into you. What's the problem?"

"I sort of know her family." Or, at least his brother knew their family. "Cameron is good friends with her brother, Hayden Archer."

Josh's eyes widened briefly. "As in the brewpub Archers with the six or seven kids? Great beer. And dude, that family's loaded."

Dylan was well aware of the Archers' wealth and fame. They'd lived in Ribbon Ridge since it was a tiny prairie town, and through real estate development and smart investments, they'd become one of the richest families in the state. "Which matters...why?"

Josh shook his head. "It doesn't. But I get that she's a little too close to home for you. Bummer."

Yeah, bummer.

"Here's a radical suggestion," Josh said, smoothing a hand over his close-cropped head. "Why not get her number and maybe take her out on a real date?"

Dylan narrowed his eyes at his friend. "Very funny."

"I'm sort of serious. It's been three years since your divorce. Are you going to spend the rest of your life having one-night stand after one-night stand?"

Maybe not the rest of his life, but that was a long time to plan. For now, he was fine with it. No, for now, that was all he could manage. It wasn't like he led women on. He was always up front with what he wanted.

Sara turned from the bar and scanned until she saw him. She smiled and headed his way.

Dylan elbowed Josh away from him. "Keep your advice to yourself. You're not exactly a role model."

Josh laughed. "True."

Sara reached them, and Dylan performed the requisite introductions. They said good night, and he escorted her outside.

As soon as they hit the night air, she shivered. "Do you have a coat?" he asked, already turning to go back inside to get it.

"I left it in my car."

"Here." He took his jacket off and wrapped it around her shoulders.

She smiled up at him. "Thanks. My car's over there, the blue Audi."

As they walked to her car, she pulled her key from her pocket and hit the unlock button. He opened the door for her. "Thanks for a great time."

She turned to face him, standing in the crook of the open door. "I'm sorry it has to end." Her features tightened very briefly, as if she regretted saying that. Then she lifted her chin and gave him a direct stare. "It doesn't really have to. Vegas Rules, right?"

Holy shit, she was going to hit on him. And why not? They'd flirted all night. Only he was going to be an asshole because he couldn't go home with her. Not Sara Archer. "I'm not sure that's a good idea."

"It's a great idea. Let's take Vegas back to my condo." Her eyes narrowed again in that sexy, provocative way. "But here's the thing: I'm only interested in tonight."

Had the parking lot just disappeared beneath his feet? That was his line. The player had just been played.

She lifted her hand to her mouth. "Oh no, I've offended you. I'm so *bad* at this."

No, she was actually quite good. His brain screamed at him to run back inside, but every other part of him was hot and ready. Eager.

"You admit this is odd for a woman," he said, still trying to make sense of it. And maybe offering her an out in case she'd spoken in haste.

She moved her hand to her cheek. "It is, isn't it? I'm cool with it. I've always been a little odd." She winked at him, her eyes darkening to full-on winter storm, and he was completely sucked in.

He took her hand away from her mouth and pressed a slow, deliberate kiss to her palm. He wanted her to know exactly what she was getting into. "You're not odd, and you're not bad at this. *I'm* bad news, remember? Just so long as you know that." He speared her with an intense look, again giving her a chance to run if she wanted to.

She nodded, mesmerized.

He slid his hand around her waist to steady her. Never breaking eye contact, he pulled her against him. He went slowly; he didn't want there to be any regrets tomorrow. She put her hand on his shoulder, curled it up to the back of his neck, and pulled his head down. It was all the encouragement he needed. He swept his mouth over hers.

Hot desire rushed through him as their lips met. Her fingers curled into his shirt and pulled him closer.

He gripped her tighter and opened his mouth over hers. She met his tongue, and then everything exploded. Sensations—light and dark and absolutely dizzying— cascaded over him. She tasted and felt like heaven.

Just when things were spiraling to the point that he wanted to press into her, she pulled back. She dropped the key into his hand. "You drive."

Hell, she really was new at this. He shook away a tinge of hesitation. He returned the key to her palm and shook his head. "That's not how it works. I'll follow you."

Her eyes widened slightly. "Oh, sorry."

Damn it, what was he *doing*?

He circled his fingers around her wrist. "Look, Sara, maybe we should just call it a night. I don't want you to have second thoughts about this."

"I'm not. I get that I'm a bit of a novice here, so if that's a turnoff for you, fine." She spoke flatly, sounding like a completely different person.

He turned her and backed her against her car, settling his lower body against hers and slipped his hand along her neck, beneath the soft fall of her hair. "Let me be clear about one thing: I'm pretty sure you couldn't turn me off if you tried. Okay, two things. If you can go into this with your eyes wide open, then let's go. Just understand that there will be no follow-up phone calls, no dates, no repeat performance. If you're good with that, I'm driving that dark gray pickup over there and I'll follow you. What's it going to be?"

Her amazing eyes stared up at him for a long minute. His cock had hardened against her, and he silently prayed that she hadn't changed her mind. Her eyes slanted and she licked her lower lip. "Let's go."

She pushed against him and got into her car. He had to shake himself to move. He hadn't been this turned on in a long time. He hoped she didn't live far.

"I'm close—maybe ten minutes," she said. "There's a security gate, but if you drive in right behind me, it'll be fine."

He nodded before turning toward his truck. Once he was settled in the cab, he quickly texted Josh that he was headed out.

Josh responded with a cocky, *I knew it. Noah has to pay up.*

Dylan shook his head as he started the engine and pulled out of the parking lot behind Sara's Audi. He'd thought he would cool off on the drive, but his brain was crowded with the smooth glide of her tongue, the feel of her trim waist, and the heady scent of her perfume and whatever she used on her hair that smelled like citrus and spice.

She pulled into her development and stopped at the security gate. He watched her punch in a code and the gate slid open. As instructed, he followed close behind her then turned right as she led him to her place.

The last garage on the right slid open and she pulled inside. Dylan parked his truck on her driveway. He jumped out and went into the garage. She was just stepping out of her car, which drew his attention to her fabulous legs. They were ridiculously long for a woman who couldn't be more than five-six.

She shot him a quick glance, but said nothing before leading him around the car and up a short set of stairs to the door.

He trailed her down a hallway, which opened up into the main entry. She turned toward him and shrugged out of his coat, then hung it on a rack of hooks set beneath a mirror. "I'm clean and I take shots."

He reached out and snaked his arm around her waist. He drew her forward until she knocked into his chest. "I'm also clean, and I bear condoms."

She slid her arms up his chest. "Thank God, I was wondering if you'd have to run down the street to the convenience store."

He chuckled, glad to know she would've waited rather than call the night off. "I would have stopped on the way."

"Good to know." She pulled his mouth down to hers, and the passion that had ignited between them in the parking lot sparked into flame once more.

This kiss was deeper, hotter than the first. He didn't bother holding back—not now. Her body tucked into his, bringing her breasts, her thighs, all the best parts of her flush against him. She tasked like lemons and sugar, delectably sweet. He couldn't get enough.

And her citrus spice scent was driving him mad. He moved his mouth to her jaw and licked a path to her ear where he tugged at the lobe with his teeth. She arched her neck, and he took the cue, spreading kisses along the slender length.

"Would you mind kicking your shoes off?" she asked.

He didn't mind at all. They were boots, so he worked his feet out of them while keeping a hold of her. "Anything else I can remove while I'm at it?"

She pulled her chest back from his and ran her hands over his shoulders. "Why not? Your shirt seems really extraneous."

"Agreed." He went to the top button, but her fingers were already there. He dropped his hands to the bottom button and flashed her a grin. "Meet you in the middle."

Her answering smile was both demure and enticing at the same time, which was a first in his experience. Damn, this one could be *very* dangerous.

But there was no going back, not when their fingers met and her hands were already pushing the front of his shirt apart. He shrugged out of the garment, and she tossed it behind her.

Her brows knitted adorably as she focused on his chest. "This T-shirt is also an impediment." She tugged the hem up, and he helped her pull it over his head. It joined his button-down and boots on the floor of the entry.

She splayed her hands over his flesh, her fingers digging into him slightly. "You must have a trainer."

He chuckled, low and deep. "No. I work with my hands."

She gave him a look that was pure seduction. "Really? Show me."

His blood fired. "Bedroom?"

"Upstairs."

"One more kiss." He lifted her up and turned, pinning her against the wall that ran beside the staircase.

Their mouths met in a tangle of lips and tongues, heat and need.

She wrapped her legs around his waist. His erection nuzzled perfectly between her legs. Damn, she felt good, even with their jeans between them. Her fingers tugged at his hair while her tongue did crazy things to his mouth. Then her lips were on his jaw and his neck, driving him absolutely insane.

He turned with her. "Hold on." Carefully, but with fierce intent, he carried her up the stairs. There was a landing at the halfway point. He couldn't resist the wall trick again and another kiss. Her legs squeezed him tighter as they kissed, and he considered doing the deed right there. Good thing they hadn't completely stripped downstairs. In fact...

He tore his mouth from hers and looked down at her reddened lips, her lust-glazed eyes. "You're wearing more than me. Not fair."

"True." She kicked her shoes off, and he heard them drop to the carpet. "Better?"

"Hell no."

She traced her finger down the side of his cheek and over his lips. "What do you want?"

"The shirt. And the bra."

She put her legs down, keeping her gaze locked with his. She lifted the necklace that dangled over the front of her sexy top

"No, that stays." He had a wicked vision of her wearing that sparkly thing and nothing else. "It goes with your eyes."

She blinked, and for a second he worried that he'd broken the magic going on between them. But then she tucked it into her top and carefully lifted the shirt over her head.

He ran his hands up her arms, helping her—oh, who was he kidding? He wasn't helping so much as appreciating. She was toned and beautiful, and he couldn't keep from touching her. He kept his hands on her wrists over her head and gave her an inquiring look. She answered by kissing him again. Her nearly bare flesh against his was torture. Or would've been if he didn't know exactly where this was going.

Her bracelets jangled against his hands as her body pressed into his. She angled her head, deepening the kiss. He took her shirt and threw it somewhere. He twined his fingers with hers and brought her arms down to her sides. He pulled her away from the wall and found the clasp of her bra. With a flick of his fingers, it came free between them. She grabbed it, and he had no idea what happened next because the feel of her breasts against his chest sent him into overdrive.

He kissed down her neck. "So soft," he murmured. "God, you're beautiful."

He drank in her pale perfection and cupped her breasts. They fit his hands like she'd been made for him, which had to be the most ridiculous thing he'd ever thought. There was no such thing as Fate or Things That Were Meant to Be. There was only the moment, the sensation, *this*.

He flicked her nipple, felt her shiver, and grinned. Oh, this was going to be a night to remember.

SARA REGISTERED HIS mouth closing over her breast, his tongue licking her nipple, his hands kneading her flesh, but she wasn't sure she could process it. She might've thought her senses were overstimulated—and she supposed they were—except she didn't feel overwhelmed or panicked in any way. She felt...spectacular.

Yes, it had been a long time since she'd done this, but it had been *never* since she'd felt this incredible. Every touch, every kiss, every word was better, sexier, hotter than anything she'd ever experienced.

Dylan made her feel like she was amazing, like she was in control.

"Are we going to make it to the bed?" she asked.

He paused—very briefly—in his sucking. "Not if you don't want to."

Yes, he made her feel in total control, and that's what would make this night perfect.

"The bed might be nice." She'd never had sex anywhere other than a bed. Maybe she should try something new? No, the one-night stand was unusual enough, she decided.

His head came up, and cool air brought her nipples into even stiffer peaks. "Let's go." He slid his hands under her ass and lifted her.

She scissored her legs around his waist and held on to his neck. And because his mouth was so close, she kissed him again. It took her breath away in its intensity, like they hadn't kissed a dozen times already.

He turned with her and made his way up the rest of the stairs.

"Go right," she said against his mouth before licking along his lower lip.

He groaned softly. "You're going to kill me."

"Oh, don't say that. I'm not done with you yet."

He laughed low in his chest. "Thank God."

"The door's straight ahead."

He carried her over the threshold and stopped abruptly, his mouth freezing on hers. "Wow, it's pink. Really, really pink."

She felt a blush creeping up her neck. Yeah, it was really pink, not like a little girl's room or anything, but she liked pink. A lot. "There's some brown." In a few accent pillows, in the curtains.

"So there is." He smiled at her, his eyes crinkling at the edges. "It's adorable."

Uncertainty invaded her sexual fog. Adorable wasn't sexy. She didn't want to be adorable. She was tired of being the cute younger sister. Back in the parking lot, she'd been sure he was about to call things off. He thought she was maybe in over her head. And yeah, she probably was, but damn it, that was her choice. And she was so sick and tired of everyone trying to protect her or thinking they knew what was best for her. *They didn't.*

She pulled her legs from his waist and stood. "You think I'm adorable?"

He tightened his hold on her. "Hey, I didn't mean anything. Adorable is good." His brow furrowed. "Isn't it?"

She turned him around and walked forward, which forced him to edge back into the room. When they were close enough to the bed, she pulled away from him and pushed him onto the mattress. Or tried to—her pillow-top mattress made the bed very tall.

Instead he teetered against the edge, but didn't quite fall back.

She pursed her lips. "You were supposed to fall on the bed."

"Oh, sorry." He made a show of sprawling backward.

She almost laughed, but she was trying to make a point. A sexy, unadorable point. "Adorable is good for little girls with pigtails or puppies. Does adorable do this?" She reached for his waistband and flipped his button open. "Or this?" She pulled his zipper down and slipped her hand inside his jeans.

His cock was thick and ready. She slid her hand down over him, shocking herself with her actions.

"Probably not," he croaked.

She removed her hand to tug his pants down over his hips. She pulled them off and threw them toward the wall. His socks followed.

All that remained was his boxer briefs. Should she take them off now? Could she? Her fingers found her bracelets and stroked the smooth silver. It calmed her, reminded her that she was a grown woman and she was having a night to remember.

Shaking off her hesitation, she leaned forward and slipped her fingertips in the top of his waistband. "And does adorable do this?"

She slowly drew the briefs down his hips. He was absolutely gorgeous, his hips lean and tapered. Then his cock rose free and she seized her inner vixen, which she never even realized existed until tonight. Without bothering to finish removing his shorts, she licked the tip of his erection. Salt and heat rushed over her tongue.

His loud intake of breath filled the room. She opened her mouth and sucked him inside. His fingers wound into her hair. Her necklace dangled over him. He was right, there was something ridiculously sexy about it.

She took him as deep as she dared, running her tongue along the underside of his cock. His breathing came shorter, and his fingers dug into her scalp. She pulled back and plunged forward again with controlled movements—yes, control. She was absolutely in charge of this situation, and it felt *divine*.

"Sara." His desperate plea only fed her power.

She wrapped her fingers around the base of his shaft and slid her hand up to meet her mouth. Then back down. Up again. His hips rose to meet her while he cradled her head.

"Sara, if I promise to never, ever call you adorable again, will you stop?" He sounded strained—pained even.

"What's wrong?" She swirled her tongue around his tip while working her hand along his cock. "Am I too much for you?" She smiled before sucking him in again.

His sexy groan filled her with need. "If you don't stop, this is going to be a much faster escapade than I'd hoped."

She understood. And she'd made her point—to herself, which was the most important thing. With a final lick, she stood back and looked down at him. His eyes were slitted, his hands now fisting the coverlet. He sat up, his abs flexing with the movement. Sara was, quite simply, speechless at his beauty.

He reached out and pulled her toward him. He spread his legs and settled her between them. "You're one tough taskmaster. But I think pink is now my favorite color. Especially since it makes me think of your lips." He kissed her, his tongue exploring her mouth with a brief ferocity before he moved south. "And your nipples. Mmmm." He suckled one and then the other with slow, seductive strokes of his tongue.

He undid her jeans and slid them, along with her underwear, down her legs. "Shall I see what else might be pink?"

He pushed her pants down to her calves. She stepped on one leg to work it off and then kicked the garments to the side. But he'd already moved on. His fingers found her center and he deftly slipped one inside. His head bent. "Pink. And lovely." He grinned up at her. "And very, very wet."

Sara closed her eyes as his fingers worked their magic, alternately stroking and pressing and thrusting. In a swift move, he'd scooped her up and set her on the bed.

"That's better." He spread her legs and buried his mouth against her. His tongue found her clit, and she gasped. Sensations bombarded her. The bracelets fell over her hand, and she slid them around her thumb so that she clutched them in her palm like she was holding onto a tether. And maybe she was. She was certain that she was about to float away.

But she didn't. His mouth and his fingers grounded her, kept her captive until she had to relinquish the control she'd fought so hard to gain. Only she didn't care.

Blinding pleasure crept over her, threatened to take her somewhere she'd never been. He sucked on her clit hard and thrust his finger deep inside of her. She bucked, a savage cry erupting from her mouth as an orgasm plunged her over the edge of a mountain she'd only glimpsed the top of before and into a dark, warm abyss.

After her shudders subsided, he left her. A moment later he touched her hand. "Here, let me take these." Her bracelets. She was still clutching them with a death grip. She felt a moment's panic. Could she let them go?

She opened her eyes and looked at him leaning over her. Holy wow, he was handsome. His chest was so muscled, with just a light dusting of dark brown hair between his pecs. He'd said he worked with his hands...and he was certainly an expert, in her opinion. He'd taken excellent care of her so far.

She slid the bangles off and handed them to him. "Thanks." He set them on her bedside table. When he turned back, she gave him a sultry smile. "I'm still wearing the necklace." It was half question, half provocative statement. There was something deliciously naughty about wearing it—and nothing else.

"And it looks great on you." He lay down on the bed beside her, propping his head on his hand. He lifted the necklace from her with the tip of his finger. Then he dragged the chain over her nipple, sending shockwaves through her. Desire ramped up again, as if she hadn't just orgasmed a few minutes ago. He leaned over and drew her breast into his mouth while he moved the chain back and forth over her other nipple. Sara cast her head back against the bed and gave herself up to the sensations. She'd felt a bone-deep satisfaction when she'd come. It had been a sensation she wasn't sure she could compare to anything else—and over the course of her life, she'd spent a lot of time thinking about how she processed sensory input.

Still riding the heady wave of empowerment, she rolled to her hip, dislodging him from her breast. She pushed him back on the bed and gestured for him to rotate so his head was on the pillows.

His gaze was sexy-lazy, but he situated himself as she directed. "Am I where you want me?"

Lust pulsed through her at the suggestion in his tone. "Yes." She straddled him, pulled the necklace between her breasts, and leaned forward so it grazed his chest. "Am I?"

"Hell yes." His thumb massaged her clit, and he stroked his hand along the underside of her breast. Then he traced his finger up and around the nipple, finally pulling gently on the peak.

She sucked in a breath and rotated her pelvis against his hips. She edged forward so that his cock brushed her sex.

"Condom," he said. "In my wallet in the back pocket of my jeans."

Right, the condom. Damn, she'd almost forgotten. *Dumb move, Sara.* "Be right back."

She climbed off the bed and found his jeans on the floor. Normally the clutter of their clothing would drive her somewhat mild OCD nuts, but she actually didn't care just then. She pulled his wallet from the pocket and withdrew a condom—he had a few. Which went with what he'd said at the bar—this wasn't atypical for him. That she was simply one woman among many gave her a moment's pause.

She glanced at the bed to find him on his side watching her.

"It's always good to have backup in case the first one breaks," he said, answering her unspoken question.

He was a thoughtful planner. She liked that. A lot. Too bad she was resolved to make this a one-night stand only. Yes, *she* was resolved. His history—and future—were none of her concern.

She went back to the bed and tore the condom open. "I haven't ever put one of these on." Her other partners— the whopping two—had always done it.

"Really? I'll help. It can be kind of fun if you do it right."

"I bet." She pulled the condom from the package and set the wrapper on the nightstand. "Roll it down?"

"Yep." He brought her hand to the tip of his cock. "Start here—obviously." He smiled wickedly. "Then just pull it down. The slower the better."

She brought the latex down over his flesh. His hand stayed with hers, which made an already sexy activity completely erotic.

When they were done, he closed his eyes briefly. "If you have to wear a condom, that's the way to do it." He looked at her, his gray-green eyes intense. "You still want to be on top?"

She echoed his answer. "Yep. Let's do this." She strad-dled him again.

He chuckled. "You're fantastic." His fingers stroked her folds. Then he reached up and curled his hand around her neck. "Come here." He pulled her down for an open-mouthed kiss. His tongue clashed with hers, exploring her mouth while his hand held her head captive. It was the most erotic kiss she'd ever experienced.

His other hand had stayed between her legs, play-ing with her clit and gliding along her flesh. She ground down against him, wanting more. Then the head of his cock nudged her opening, and he slid into her.

Oh. My. God.

She really couldn't say whether she thought the words or said them out loud. She only knew that already, lit-tle lights were flashing behind her eyes. It wasn't a full orgasm like before, but the sensations and pleasure were incredible.

Then his hands were on her hips, pulling her down onto him and lifting her back up.

Oh. My. God.

She couldn't think, couldn't process, couldn't do any-thing but feel him rocking into her again and again. His mouth was on her breast, sucking and pulling on her nipple, intensifying everywhere they touched.

She was pitched forward so that his cock stroked into her against her clit. She moved faster, seeking the pin-nacle right before her. So many times she'd gone after it only to fall short. But this time she knew—she *knew*—she'd get there.

As if sensing her quest, he put his thumb on her clit, and she exploded. She was aware that he continued to thrust, registered the extreme pleasure radiating from her core.

He rolled her over so that he was on top, his cock driving into her. "Sorry," he muttered darkly, "I just needed to…"

She pulled his head down and kissed him as he'd done to her. He groaned into her mouth. She widened her legs and wrapped them around him, drawing him in deep. She clasped his back and moved one hand to his ass. So muscular, so tight.

He pounded into her a few more times and then shouted. She lifted her hips to meet him, giving him, she hoped, the ecstasy he'd given her. At last, they slowed.

He brushed her hair back from her face and smiled softly. "Damn, Sara."

It was the very best thing he could've said. Her lips spread into a wide grin as exhaustion washed over her.

He withdrew from her and left the bed. She heard the bathroom door close.

She tossed some of the pillows away and pulled back the covers. Crawling between the sheets, she didn't think her bed had ever felt so deliciously good. No, *she'd* never felt so good. Sleep was typically an elusive beast, but not tonight.

Swiping the necklace off—she'd never look at that the same way again—she tossed it on the bedside table. She curled to her side, closed her eyes, and fell instantly asleep.

Chapter Three

Three weeks later

SARA STARED AT the tabletop in the gathering room of her childhood home. It was the first time they'd all sat here since Alex had died two and a half weeks ago. As usual, the sides were uneven—four chairs on one, three on the other. But it wouldn't be in the future. There were only six of them now, and the chairs would be equal on both sides. That symmetry would appeal to Evan, but glancing at her brother, she knew he'd trade it in a heart beat to have Alex back.

"Thank you for coming, as Alex requested." The crisp, business-like tone of Alex's attorney, Aubrey Tallinger, filled the room and drew Sara back to the present. The cold, depressing present.

Next to Sara, Mom blew her nose and lowered the tissue to her lap. Her eyes were red, and her blonde hair appeared lackluster because she'd stopped spending much time on it. Instinctively, Sara reached out and touched her shoulder. Mom turned and gave her an appreciative nod just as her fingers closed over Sara's for a quick squeeze. Though Mom moved her hand to her lap, Sara kept a hold on her shoulder. Sara needed that anchor right now to calm her overstimulated senses.

"Get on with it, then," Dad said, his voice perpetually darkened with unshed tears. Where Mom's face was blotchy, Dad's was a bit gray. It matched the strands of hair on his head that were overtaking the dark brown at a seemingly faster rate in the past two weeks.

Aubrey, standing at the end of the table where Mom usually sat, opposite Dad, smoothed her shoulder-length, wavy red hair behind her ear and gave a small nod. Sara didn't envy her. Being the focus of attention at the best of times was enough to wind Sara into a knot, but on a day like today, when her insides were threatening to erupt into some sort of breakdown, it was all she could do to simply sit still.

Be calm, Sara. Focus on what's happening. You can be here. She squeezed her mother's shoulder to ground herself. Mom had always been the strength at the heart of their family. But how would she do that with a piece of her heart gone? At least that's what Sara imagined it must feel like to lose a child, even a twenty-seven-year-old one.

Aubrey gently cleared her throat. "Alex set up a trust last year." *Wait, how long had he been planning to kill himself?* Sara's insides churned. "The beneficiaries are his siblings: Liam, Kyle, Tori, Evan, Sara, Hayden, and Derek."

As she said each name, Sara looked around the table. Her brothers and sister filled her with joy and angst—blessings and curses all rolled together. She only wished she could find the joy and the blessings. Lately, they were like dreams, intangible and fleeting.

"What are we benefitting?" Hayden, the youngest by just over a year, sat directly across from Sara. His light brown hair was ruffled, like he'd tossed and turned all night and hadn't bothered to tame it. His mouth was pressed into a grim line, making him look a million miles from the lighthearted, affable brother who made them all laugh and put himself before pretty much anyone else.

"A property." Aubrey clasped her hands in front of her. "Alex used his inheritance from your grandfather to purchase the old Ridgeview Monastery. He wants all of you to come back to—or stay in—Ribbon Ridge and convert the monastery into a premier hotel as part of Archers' entertainment brand."

Liam held up a hand. "Whoa. What does that mean?" He glanced around the table before pinning Aubrey with a dark stare. He hadn't cried once that Sara had seen, but then he'd always been the strongest of them, the leader. He and Alex were supposed to look identical, but they'd never seemed that way to Sara. Liam was healthier, more vital, more confident. She'd expected him to lose a bit of his swagger, and she supposed he had. But he still didn't look weak. She wasn't sure he could.

Aubrey cocked her head to the side. "He wanted you all to reunite in Ribbon Ridge to oversee the transformation of the monastery into a hotel and restaurant."

"He just expected us to drop our lives and come back here?" Liam growled, his blue-gray eyes dark with pain and anger. He'd already complained about having to spend so much time away from Denver the past couple of weeks, though he'd flown back and forth twice since Alex's death.

Dad shot Liam an irritated look. "What's wrong with that?"

"Nothing, I guess, for some people." Liam's gaze shifted from Kyle, who was directly across from him, to Sara at the opposite end of the table. She got why Liam had looked at Kyle, but at her? Was it because she lived only forty minutes away?

Sara's defenses kicked up. She let go of Mom and put her hand in her lap. "Why are you looking at me?" Agitated, she fingered the edges of her sleeves. The tiny ridges of the cuff of her sweatshirt stroked across the pads of her thumbs and fingers. She focused on the small detail, using it to soothe her inner turmoil before she spun up into a rare sensory meltdown.

Liam shrugged, but it was the kind that carried a chill, as if he could barely be bothered to be here. "It's easy for you to come home. You practically *are* home."

She looked at him sharply. "But I'm not. Like you, I run a successful business." Not as large as his real estate empire, but Sara Archer Celebrations was nothing to scoff at. "I can't just pick up and move home."

Liam's eyes narrowed but he quickly looked away. Sara bit her tongue. She wanted to rail at him—at all of them. Emotions she'd buried for so long bubbled up, but she swallowed them back. None of them realized how hard it had been for her to move even forty minutes away or the sense of accomplishment that gave her.

Coming back to Ribbon Ridge would interrupt the life she'd built for herself and thrust her back into a situation where she was labeled and coddled and...*forget it*. Her muscles tensed.

"Shall I continue?" Aubrey asked quietly.

"Please," Mom said with an edge of frustration.

Aubrey gave a subtle nod. "Like the pubs your father's company owns, the hotel will pour Archer brews, and its restaurant will also offer five-star cuisine under the direction of Kyle."

Everyone's gaze snapped to Kyle, seated at the end of Sara's side of the table. Despite his tan, he looked washed out, as if he carried the weight of the world on his shoulders, not at all like the carefree beach bum who'd run to south Florida nearly four years ago. His blue-green eyes found hers and he shook his head, his jaw clenching.

Sara wanted to kick him. An opportunity was falling into his lap, and his reaction was to act like he didn't want it? It shouldn't have surprised her given how he'd ditched town, but it still hurt. She peered at him around Mom and Tori, who sat between them. "You should consider it."

He showed no sign that he'd heard her.

Mom clasped Sara's hand. "Your sister's right. I hope you'll at least think about it."

When Kyle still didn't respond, Aubrey coughed delicately. "You'll each own one-seventh of the property and the businesses on the property, which Alex envisioned as a hotel and restaurant at a minimum. He set aside specific roles for each of you."

Liam shook his head. "I already have a job."

Kyle crossed his arms and glared across the table at Liam. "Because your life is so much more important than anyone else's. It's fine for me and Sara, and probably everyone else, to come home, but not you?"

"I didn't say that, but as long as you mentioned it…" Liam leaned forward and set his elbows on the table, fixing Kyle with a probing stare. "Just what's keeping *you* from coming back here and honoring Alex's wish? Your *über*important bartending job? The roots you haven't put down in Florida?"

Kyle's eyes flashed. "Don't make assumptions."

"Am I wrong?"

"You're an arrogant prick."

Liam shrugged, but the tense set of his shoulders said he was anything but nonchalant. "An arrogant prick who's apparently right."

"Boys." Mom's voice quavered, but it earned everyone's attention. "I know we're all hurting. Please don't take it out on each other."

Tori blew her nose, which was red from crying. Without makeup and with her long, straight, auburn hair pulled back in a ponytail, she looked young and vulnerable, a word she'd hate to be used to describe her. Tori was as type A as people came. She turned her head toward Aubrey. "You said Kyle is supposed to manage the restaurant. I assume Alex wants—wanted—me to design the hotel?" It made sense because she was an architect at a firm in San Francisco that designed high-end hotels and restaurants around the world.

Aubrey nodded. "Yes. Liam would oversee the entire project; Evan, the technical aspects of the business; Sara would establish the property as a premier entertainment space; Hayden would manage the hotel; and Derek would work the financials."

Hayden linked his fingers together on the tabletop. His lips pressed together in annoyance as he glanced at Liam. "We *all* have jobs. I can't just stop working for Archer Enterprises to manage this hotel."

Liam nodded in agreement. "Exactly. I sure as hell can't walk away from my business in Denver."

"You've made that pretty clear." Evan's deep voice drew everyone's notice. He bent his head back toward the table where his fingers were systematically taking a pen apart and putting it back together again. He hadn't cried either, but he kept everything to himself for the most part, which made it hard to determine what he was feeling, if anything. Sara never pressed him—she alone knew what it was like to be so overwhelmed by your surroundings that you simply couldn't process anything.

Aubrey looked around the table. "Alex knew you'd be resistant. He wanted me to remind you that he's never asked anything of any one of you, and while you were off pursuing your dreams, he was stuck here, hooked to an oxygen tank and visiting doctors on a weekly basis. He hoped you would pull together to try to rebuild the family you once had."

Is that how Alex had seen it? Sara glanced at Derek, whose face was stoic but who had nodded while Aubrey spoke. His dark blue eyes were a bit bloodshot, likely from all the hours he was putting in at Archer Enterprises. Work soothed him, or so he said.

Derek made no secret that he didn't understand why they'd all left home. He'd come to live with them after being orphaned at seventeen. Though he'd never been formally adopted, he was as much a part of their family as any of them. "You should all come, even if it's only intermittently as your schedule allows. Every single one of you can make that happen," he said quietly. "You're a family, and you should feel damn lucky to have each other."

"Except we can't ever be that family again," Tori said softly. "Not without him."

Derek's eyes lit like a fire had been stoked behind them. "Even more reason to do it. What else will it take for you to appreciate what you have?" His gaze lingered on Kyle—they'd been best friends before Derek had joined their family and up until Kyle had left. The precise reason for their rift was unknown to anyone but them, and it was clearly as wide as ever.

Sara wanted to crawl out of her skin. The anxiety and tension building inside of her were reaching a fever pitch. If she didn't move, she was going to freak out. She leapt out of her chair and walked around the table to the windows.

Without turning to look at the table, Sara knew every single one of them had watched her get up. A few might even be tempted to come after her to offer help. She hoped they wouldn't.

"Sara?" The question came from Aubrey, and Sara's shoulders sagged with relief. She didn't want to be coddled, but she knew she was breaking down. Damn it, she thought she'd moved past all of this.

"She's fine," Mom said. "She needs to get up and move around."

Sara turned back toward the table. The only person still watching her was Kyle. Unable to make eye contact, Sara crossed her arms and tried to disguise the clenching of her muscles. Hopefully this infernal meeting would be over soon. She didn't know how much more she could take.

Aubrey cleared her throat. "I know this is an emotional time, and you can certainly think about—"

"I'll do it." Tori sat straighter in her chair and pressed a kiss to the back of Mom's hand. "I'll take a leave of absence from work and come home."

Mom smiled at Tori, though a tear tracked from the corner of her eye.

Aubrey relaxed, and a small, relieved smile broke over her. "You will?"

Tori looked around the table. "Yes, and I expect the rest of you to come with me. Liam, you can take a leave too—you have capable people working for you, and you can certainly have a foot in each place. Just fly yourself back and forth for heaven's sake." Tori turned to Kyle, who was seated on her right. "And there's absolutely no reason you can't come home. Consider it your chance to make up for your sudden, inexplicable departure four years ago." Then she looked across the table at Hayden and Derek. "You're both already here. You'll help, right?" She looked up at Sara. "And you're pretty much here already."

No question for Sara, just the same assumption Liam had made—that she'd never really "left" in the first place. Which wasn't true. Sara *had* left, and coming home would feel like a massive step backward—probably because deep inside she felt like she needed it. *No, I've overcome this. I am not the same girl they grew up with. I am successful and capable, and I don't need them.*

Derek turned to Evan on his right so that both had their backs to Sara. "What about you, Evan?"

Evan didn't look up. Sara knew he was listening, but that he might be a beat or two behind—and he wasn't likely making an effort to keep up. The pen came apart again in his skillful fingers.

Tori frowned at Derek. "Evan can do his tech stuff from home."

Evan lived in Washington, about two hours from Ribbon Ridge, but he rarely left his apartment. Coming down here a couple of times a year was about all he could handle. He worked from home and was content to be alone most of the time. Typical Tori to give him a pass and no one else.

After a long, strained moment, Aubrey clasped her hands and looked expectantly around the table. "Who else is in?"

"Not me." Liam's response was quick and definitive.

"Me neither." Kyle's came on the heels of Liam's.

Mom's shoulders drooped. "I'm disappointed in both of you."

Hayden looked down the table and shook his head at Liam and Kyle. "You're a couple of tools. You've spent the past five years doing whatever you damn well please while I've been here helping Dad with the business and helping Mom with Alex. You can't manage to get your asses back here for even six months to get this project off the ground?"

"You know it wouldn't be six months," Liam said.

"It could be, just to get it started. My point is, you aren't willing to offer *anything*."

Liam turned in his chair and leaned around Evan to look down at Hayden. "Listen, I'll do what I can from Denver. Maybe I can come back now and then if you guys need some direction."

"I think we can handle it fine." Derek's tone was frigid, and though Sara couldn't see his face, she imagined he looked as cold as he sounded. "Really. Don't trouble yourself."

"So far that's Tori and Sara, plus Derek and Hayden who are already here?" Aubrey clarified.

"Sara didn't actually say," Kyle interjected. His gaze was supportive and reminded her of years gone by when he'd been her chief advocate. She wanted to be happy about him sticking up for her, but she was too wound up.

She avoided looking at any of them, instead fixating on the refrigerator. "I'll come."

She hadn't been completely sure she was going to say it until the words left her mouth. And now, as they echoed in her head, she felt a surge of panic. She'd built a successful event planning business and the momentum she could lose by stepping away...Rationality fought for traction in her brain—she had a great assistant who would watch over things while she helped out here. Six months maximum. It was a temporary thing. She could do it for Alex and for Mom.

Mom's head came up to find Sara near the windows. She mouthed, "Thank you." Her appreciation and relief soothed Sara's turmoil. Mom had been such an integral part of her life—and still was—Sara felt a pull to be here for her.

Liam got up from the table. "I need to get back to Denver. Can I refuse my portion of the trust?"

"You can't, actually." Aubrey's eyes narrowed slightly. "The trust is set up so that any of you can come back and claim your share at any time. Alex expected some of you might not jump on board immediately."

Liam resolutely crossed his arms. "I won't change my mind. Is there something I can sign to transfer my share to the others?"

"No. Alex worded his will very specifically. It's yours whether you want it or not."

Hayden waved his hand toward the other end of the table where Evan and Kyle were seated. "So the three of them can just sit back and enjoy the profits that the four of us work to generate? That's shittastic."

Liam scowled at Hayden. "I don't want it." He turned his scowl toward Aubrey. "Figure out a way for me to give it to them."

She pursed her lips. "That won't be possible. Alex wanted all of you to contribute. I don't think he wanted to make it easy for you not to."

Derek shook his head. "Can't you all see that Alex wanted you to recapture your sense of family?"

"I'm disappointed you won't come home." Dad's authoritative voice took hold of the room. "Evan, there's no reason you can't relocate here. You don't have to live in the house—I'll find you a place. Liam, you could very easily carve time out of your schedule to participate. You're the boss, for Christ's sake. And Kyle." His tone turned even darker. Sara couldn't help but cringe, even though she was also disappointed in Kyle. "You've no excuse whatsoever. You think you do, but you don't. I know it. You know it."

Kyle didn't look at him.

Evan finally glanced up from his pen, but he didn't make eye contact with anyone, which wasn't a surprise. "I'll think about it." He wouldn't.

Aubrey turned to the chair behind her and pulled two envelopes from her bag. "There's one last thing. Alex wrote each of you a letter." She walked behind Kyle and Tori and handed a manila envelope to Mom, then she skirted Sara's chair and gave another to Dad. "Mr. and Mrs. Archer, Derek, he wanted you to have your letters immediately. The rest of you will receive yours in due time." She delivered the third envelope to Derek, who set it in his lap and stared at some distant point behind Tori's head.

Tears leaked from Mom's eyes and her hands shook as she looked down at the envelope. Dad was stone-faced, his palm flat atop his envelope, which sat on the table in front of him.

An apprehensive tremor ran through Sara. What would her letter say? Right now, as unsettled as she felt, she wasn't sure she wanted to read it and was relieved she didn't have to.

"I want my letter now," Tori said, emotion coarsening her voice.

Aubrey's eyes shone with regret. "I'm sorry, but it doesn't work that way. Alex was very specific about when each of you would receive your letter."

"When?" Liam's muscles clenched. His gaze was furious.

Aubrey didn't move from where she stood beside Dad. "I'm not allowed to divulge that information." After a tense moment, she looked away from Liam. "So, Tori will manage the design aspects, Sara will be in charge of the event space, and Hayden and Derek will oversee the project?"

"Sara won't—" Tori started then abruptly closed her mouth. "We'll work it out."

The frustration Sara had contained throughout the meeting surged over the banks of her control. She stalked forward, stopping a foot or so behind and between Evan and Derek so she could see Tori across the table. "I won't what? Were you going to say I can't be in charge of the event space?"

Tori dashed the tissue across her nose and looked away from her. "I wasn't."

"Bullshit," Kyle said. "That's exactly what you were going to say. Sara runs her own business, or haven't you heard? Even I know that, and I'm clear across the god-damned country."

Again, Sara wanted to appreciate his sticking up for her, but it only reminded her that he'd abandoned her to do that for herself. And she'd learned quite well. "I don't need you to fight my battles, Kyle. Tori, you have no idea what I can do. But maybe you don't care either. More for you to control and to allow you to bask in the limelight, right?"

It would be so easy for Sara to bolt. She wanted to—every part of her was screaming to get away from this oppressive environment—but that would only fuel their belief that she was somehow less capable than them. Instead she turned to Aubrey and lifted her chin. "Tell us what we need to do."

Aubrey's gaze was warm and encouraging. It gave Sara a much-needed boost of support and helped calm her spiraling senses. "I'll put a meeting together early next week for everyone involved. We'll talk about big-picture plans."

Liam shifted his weight and folded his arms across his chest. He glanced at his siblings but directed most of his irritated stare at Aubrey. "You'll need to think about schedules and permits and hiring contractors."

"Yeah, we'll manage, thanks," Derek said, his voice tinged with sarcasm.

Liam sent him a sharp look to which Derek only lightly shrugged in response.

Aubrey straightened her jacket. "I'm confident things will be well managed."

Tori tucked her hair behind her ear. "Agreed. It'll take me a few weeks to finish up some things at work, but I can be here working on plans by mid to late March."

"Sounds good," Hayden said. "Liam, Kyle, Evan, I'm sure we'll be well underway by the time you bother to come home again."

Liam gritted his teeth before going to Mom and dropping a kiss on her cheek. "I'm out of here. Bye, Mom."

Mom's posture sagged. Sara went and set her palms on Mom's shoulders, giving her the same reassuring pressure that had grounded Sara for so much of her life. It felt so different to be the one providing the support, but she was glad to do it—and glad she'd agreed to come home.

Thoughts swirled in her mind…She needed to call Craig and talk to him about the business. She'd need his help to make this work. A thread of panic worked its way into her gut. No, she *could* make this work. In the face of her siblings' doubt, in the hour of her mother's need, and in the wake of her brother's suicide. She didn't have any other choice.

Chapter Four

April

DYLAN LOOKED UP at the gunmetal gray sky through his windshield. When he'd left his house ten minutes ago, it had been blue with patchy clouds. Now it looked like hell was going to rain down. Welcome to spring in Oregon.

He glanced at the clock on his dash and applied his foot to the gas pedal, speeding up the dirt and gravel road as fast as he dared. He was cutting this close. Which shouldn't surprise him since he'd sort of dragged his heels. Something about your livelihood depending on a job working for the family of your last one-night stand.

He suddenly realized Sara *had* been his last one-night stand, and damn, that was over two months ago. No action whatsoever in February *or* March, and he'd just now noticed. He shrugged the thought away.

Bidding on the Archers' monastery renovation project a few weeks ago had given him a moment's pause—but only a moment. He needed this job and was damn glad that Hayden Archer had suggested to Cameron that Dylan bid on it. Running a successful general contracting firm was Dylan's goal, but when he'd gotten out of the army six years ago, construction had taken a nosedive. Undeterred, he'd started by doing odd handyman jobs and steadily built Westcott Construction, tackling residential remodels and builds, and in the last couple of years, a handful of commercial remodeling gigs, though nothing close to this scale. Putting this high-profile project on his resume would finally make him competitive in commercial construction.

Most important of all—his guys needed this job. If he had to work with the family of the one-night stand whom he still thought about but figured he'd never see again, then so be it.

Thinking he'd never see her again was foolish. He was bound to run into her at some point, whether this job had come up or not. The question was, how would it go? She'd walked into their one-night stand with her eyes wide open, had been the instigator, in fact. He had to assume she'd be professional, and he meant to be the same.

Things had changed since then, he reminded himself. Her life had been turned upside down not even a week after their night together when her brother had killed himself. Dylan imagined that even if it hadn't been a one-night stand, any relationship that might've sparked that night would've been crushed beneath the weight of grief.

He shook Sara from his mind and gripped the steering wheel with tight resolve as the old monastery came into view. Today's interview was only for phase one, a small house they were renovating into a wedding-event space. They were taking it from a mid-twentieth-century ranch to a two-story countryside Craftsman cottage that could handle a three-hundred-person exterior and seventy-five-person interior event. The project was totally doable for Dylan and his crew, but he wanted the bigger fish: phases two and three, the restaurant and the hotel.

Interviews for those wouldn't take place until later next month, but Dylan would start his hard sell today. They might not think he was ready for such a large commercial job, but he absolutely was, and he would prove it to them.

He was ready with a great presentation, and he was going to win them over with the fact that he and his crew were Ribbon Ridgers. Screw whatever larger firms they might interview next month. They couldn't do better with cost, accountability, and delivery than Dylan and his guys.

He pulled his work truck into the parking area, which was little more than a large dusty square. He stepped out with his laptop and materials just as the first fat raindrop struck his truck. The second one landed squarely on his forehead.

There were two other cars. Hayden and who? Damn, he really hoped it wasn't Sara. Seeing her again would be fine. But seeing her for the first time at a crucial business presentation with her brother in the same room, not so much.

Dylan jogged to the wide oak front doors of the main building, which somewhat resembled a stone church. As he pulled one of the doors open and stepped inside, the rain began to fall in earnest. He'd cut it close in more ways than one, apparently. But a glance at his watch said he still had four minutes to spare.

With a smile that suddenly felt like dried mud on his face, Dylan froze. The cavernous room was mostly empty, save a long, folding table with a handful of chairs scattered around the perimeter. Seated behind it were three people: Hayden Archer, a woman he was pretty sure was Hayden's sister Tori, and Sara.

Shit.

She looked great. Her blonde hair fell against her shoulders and framed her face—a face that was bent down toward the table. She appeared to be perusing some documents. Or maybe just avoiding his gaze.

Double shit.

He swallowed anxiously as he stepped forward. "Good morning."

Hayden stood and came around the table to shake his hand. "Hi, Dylan. Do you remember my sisters, Tori and Sara?"

One of them better than Hayden would probably like. "Yes." Dylan went and shook Tori's hand. "Good to see you." He moved to Sara, who looked up at him, her eyes inscrutable.

She held out her hand. "Good morning." Very formal. Very unlike their last meeting.

He was so screwed.

Or maybe not. She was trying to be businesslike, right? He could absolutely do the same. He shook her hand and masked the jolt of desire that raced through him. Maybe they shouldn't touch.

She snatched her hand back and put it on her lap where he couldn't see it. Yeah, definitely no touching.

"Thanks for coming up here today," Tori said. She tucked her straight auburn hair behind her ear. "Have a seat." She gestured to the chair on the opposite side of the table.

"My pleasure." Dylan took the seat while Hayden moved around to the other side of the table. "I'm excited to be considered for this project. This old monastery is part of the local landscape." Careful to avoid looking at Sara, he glanced up at the beamed ceiling with the dull, round pendant lights and let his gaze wander to the high, arched windows against which sluiced thick rivulets of rain. The windows and beams would be striking design elements to work around. He envisioned an elegant space with chandeliers and gleaming hardwoods. "I'm so glad someone is finally going to put it to use again." The monks who'd inhabited it had vacated the premises nearly a decade before.

Hayden smiled. "Alex had quite a vision for this place."

Dylan realized he'd been half holding his breath, waiting to see if they would mention their brother. He was glad Hayden had so that he could say something without having to awkwardly bring it up. "That's great that he'll have this tremendous legacy. I'm just sorry it came about the way that it did." He couldn't help but look at Sara, but she kept her head bent.

"Thanks," Hayden said. "It's tough some days to work on this without him here, but we know it will be worth it."

Tori touched her brother's arm and gave him an encouraging smile before looking to Dylan. "Looks like you brought a bunch of stuff with you today."

"I did." Dylan opened his case and withdrew his laptop as well as the presentation he'd put together. It included the phase-one proposed construction schedule, letters of recommendation, and before-and-after photos for a handful of his projects, some of which were commercial and some residential.

He booted up his laptop and handed the hard copies over to Tori since she was in the middle. She glanced over them briefly before passing them to Hayden. "After going to the University of Washington, you were an engineer in the army, right?"

"Yeah, I was ROTC at U-Dub. Then I did four years in construction engineering."

Tori made a face. "Demerits for being a Husky."

Hayden gave Tori a sidelong smile then looked at Dylan. "I'll give you bonus points for *not* being a Duck." He was a Beaver from Oregon State, a chief rival of the Ducks from Tori's alma mater, the University of Oregon. He was apparently willing to forgive Dylan for being a Husky since it meant he wasn't a hated Duck. Hayden continued, "No combat engineering?"

Dylan shook his head. "No, nothing that sexy." Bad word choice. His blood heated and he fought not to glance at Sara. "Just boring construction—building barracks, repairing stuff, total snoozefest. But I'll take that over serving in combat. I mean, I would have if it had come to that, and it almost did given the timing. It was a great opportunity to serve my country in a necessary job in my chosen field." He'd spent most of his time stationed in craphole bases stateside, which his ex-wife had hated.

Dylan pulled up his presentation on his laptop. "You guys ready to rock 'n' roll?" He looked at each of them in turn, but Sara still didn't make eye contact. That was good, he told himself. Yeah, it might be a little awkward, but at least she wasn't glaring at him.

He flipped the computer around so he could talk them through the slides outlining his proposal. "I've reviewed your plans for the cottage, and we'll have no problem meeting the August deadline for the wedding." They'd informed him their brother-from-another-mother, Derek Sumner, would be getting married there. "In fact, my schedule puts the end date right around the first of August."

Hayden studied the hard copy of Dylan's schedule. "Looks great."

"I also included a mock-up of a schedule for phases two and three." All three pairs of eyes looked at him in surprise. "I know you aren't hiring for that yet, but it doesn't hurt to get a leg up on the competition, does it?" He smiled, his gaze lingering on Sara, who quickly averted her eyes to his laptop.

"Very enterprising of you." Hayden nodded. "We'll take a look, thanks."

"We're really only hiring for phase one right now, though," Sara said, the familiar tone of her voice gliding over him.

"I get that, but think of how smooth things could be if you hired us to do all of it. We'd be here from the beginning, and we'd know all the ins and outs."

Tori took the presentation back from Hayden and flipped to where he'd run hypotheticals for phases two and three.

"Since I don't know exactly what you have planned, I just made some estimates," he explained.

Tori glanced up at him. "We don't know what we have planned yet either. I've been focusing on phase one. I'll start drafting plans for phase two, the restaurant and brewpub combo, after we start demo on the house."

They were converting the church portion of the property into the restaurant. Dylan's schedule was built around that renovation and also adding on the brewing facility to the small chapel that, in his vision, would be a great expanded bar for the restaurant—a sort of hybrid brewpub. "Well, my schedule is adjustable. I just wanted to show you that we can handle larger, commercial scale."

Hayden smiled at him, seeming impressed. "Great to know."

Tori nodded in agreement. She flipped back to the front of the book. "This phase-one proposal looks great. I think you've got a terrific grasp on what we're trying to do, and it certainly looks as though you have the right team to deliver the project. Plus, you're under budget, which is most attractive of all."

"If you were awarded phases two and three, would this be your first large-scale commercial project?" Sara asked. She glanced at him, but for the most part kept her gaze fixed on his laptop.

"It would, yes," Dylan said. "We've done several smaller build-outs, as you can see, but this will be my first job as general contractor over a large project."

"I see." Sara sounded doubtful.

Dylan wondered if her skepticism stemmed from his lack of experience or from their one-night stand. No, that wasn't fair. She wouldn't judge him because of that. It had been mutual *and* her idea.

"I understand your hesitation," he said slowly, trying to choose the right words to win them over. "You might get a more qualified and experienced bid, but you won't find a crew who will work harder or people who will care about this project the way you do. This is our town, and this property will be a signature location. We'll do everything to deliver superior work."

"A very compelling argument," Tori said. "I love that you guys are local. You know Ribbon Ridge and how to make this part of the community."

Sara gave a slight nod, but any other reaction was impossible to read.

Hayden watched her for a moment then turned to Dylan. "You've given us a lot to think about. Thanks for coming. We'll be making a decision—on phase one— very soon."

Dylan shut his laptop and slid it back into its case. "Great, thanks again for the opportunity. Talk to you soon."

He would've shaken their hands, but he didn't want to touch Sara. That wasn't exactly true. He did want to touch her. But knew it wasn't a good idea, not if they were going to be working together.

With a final glance at Sara, he strode outside, where the rain had ceased and the sun had broken through the clouds again. He climbed into his truck and set his laptop on the passenger seat.

Instead of firing up the engine, he stared at the monastery, or at least the church portion where they'd held the meeting. The presentation had gone as well as he could've hoped, despite Sara's presence. But really, why did her presence matter? They'd had a mutually agreeable one-night stand. Couldn't they also be coworkers?

Except they wouldn't be coworkers. She'd be his boss. *Holy hell.*

He ran his hand through his hair. He was overthinking this. She wouldn't hold the one-night stand against him. She might, however, deem him unqualified. Of the three of them, she'd seemed the most skeptical, the most concerned with his lack of experience, at least with the larger phases two and three. Maybe he should've worked harder to convince her.

Yeah, he should do that. He climbed back out of his truck and started toward the monastery, his shoes squishing in the soft mud and making him wish he'd worn his work boots. The door opened and Sara walked out toward him. They both slowed, blinked at each other.

Unlike him, she was dressed for their surroundings: knee-high black and pink rain boots—of course; dark blue skinny jeans; and a long, khaki sweater belted at her waist. She came toward him. "Hey."

"Hey." He turned, taking a couple of steps until they stopped a few feet apart. "I wish I'd known you were going to be here today."

She tipped her head to the side. "Would that have affected your presentation?"

"No. It was just a surprise to see you."

"Sorry, I didn't mean to ambush you. I figured you knew. Hayden's been handling the communications aspect with the bids." She fiddled with a pair of bracelets that fell over her hand, reminding him of the bangles she'd been wearing that night at Sidewinders. Which in turn reminded him of the necklace…Damn, he needed to clear those thoughts right out of his head.

"It's fine," he said, now wondering why he'd climbed out of his truck in the first place. To convince her to hire him. Right. "Listen, I wanted to come back and tell you that I'm the best guy for this job."

She nodded slowly. "We still have another presentation tomorrow, but you're a great candidate. For phase one."

He gritted his teeth in frustration. "Are you even going to consider me for the other phases?"

"I don't know. We're not quite there yet."

"Listen, I don't want what happened—"

"It won't." She cut him off, color highlighting her cheeks. "Any decision I make won't be personal."

He was relieved their…indiscretion wouldn't affect her judgment. But it didn't change his resolve to win her over. "You'll have our undivided attention. I can guess who else will bid, and while they have proven track records, they'll be slower because of their infrastructure. They're going to promise you eighteen months and stretch toward two years. I'm promising fifteen months— depending on your schedule—and I'm going to deliver. My guys and I will work the extra time, put in the added effort, we'll give a whole level of attention and commitment those firms won't—or can't. Plus, we're here. If there's a problem, I'm only a five-minute drive away."

Her nose scrunched up forming a little pleat at the bridge. "You live that close?"

"Off Sebastian Hill Road."

"I didn't realize. You *are* close."

"I could walk, in fact." He glanced up at the sky. "Though I think I'd get drenched. Rain's coming in again."

She looked up. "I better get back inside."

He tried to read her expression, but she didn't give a thing away. "Did I sway you at all?"

She twirled a bracelet around her hand and then ran her thumb across the flat side of it. "A little." She smiled. "You're very passionate." The color returned to her cheeks, but this was a deeper pink than before.

"I want this job." With the same ferocity he'd wanted her that night—a night that should've faded in his memory. His conquests—and he had no problem admitting that's what they were—were always one and done. Not like Sara. He wasn't going to be able to file her away or forget about her completely. She'd be in his face, tempting him. And, damn, he was tempted.

She returned his stare, maybe sensing his desire—both for the job and for her. "My dad always says to be careful what you wish for."

A plump raindrop hit her nose, galvanizing her into action. "Ack! I need to get a file from Tori's car and get back in before it pours again. We'll be in touch soon." She turned to go.

"Sara, wait."

Pausing, she looked back at him over her shoulder.

"I was really sorry to hear about Alex."

She averted her gaze. "Thanks."

There was nothing else he could say. Nothing else he could do. Except he sort of wanted to pull her into his arms and hold her, just for a moment. But he didn't. The rain started falling, and she raced to her sister's car. After she retrieved the file, she tossed him a lingering glance before going back inside.

Dylan retreated to his truck. By the time he buckled his seatbelt, the rain was pelting hard and fast. Puddles were already forming in the mud.

His back pocket vibrated. He pulled his phone out and saw the text from his mom: *We still on for lunch tomorrow?*

Lunch. *Right.* Mom liked to see him a couple of times a month, which shouldn't have been difficult since she only lived thirty minutes or so away, but Dylan didn't love spending time with her and knew that made him sound like a complete jerk. Out of a sense of guilt, he scheduled a lunch with her every few weeks, but often had to cancel if a job came up. Work always came first. However, since he didn't have anything scheduled for tomorrow, he supposed he should confirm. He texted her back: *See you at 12:30.*

He started the truck and swung it around toward the road, windshield wipers at full tilt.

As expected, there was no response from her. No "Can't wait" or "Looking forward to it." There was never any sentimentality or warmth. Mom was as no-nonsense as they came—forthright, tell-it-like-it-is, don't-expect-any-gushing. About anything. Most mothers cherished everything their kids made, and he supposed she did—in her own way. But she hadn't bothered to keep even one of the Mother's Day presents he'd made for her in school. Sure, she put them on the mantel for a few weeks, but then they disappeared. Later on, she'd admitted that she'd tossed all of them because she hated clutter.

He suddenly thought of the Archers. He bet their mom kept all of their stuff, even though there were so many of them. He also thought of the good-natured ribbing between the siblings. Dylan had three half-brothers and a half-sister, and he loved each of them, but he wasn't really a part of either family. His dad, stepmom, and brothers were a unit, and his mom, stepdad, and sister were another unit. He'd always felt like a fifth wheel. It was hard to join in on jokes you'd missed or share memories of things you hadn't done because you'd been with the other family. Dylan was just Dylan.

And that was fine by him. He'd tried the family route when he'd married Jess and failed spectacularly. He was firmly in the solo lane, and he liked it that way. No expectations. No disappointments.

His contracting firm was the most important thing, and he was going to make damned sure he got this job.

SARA BRUSHED THE raindrops from her sleeves as she went back inside.

"Raining again?" Hayden slipped Dylan's presentation folder into his laptop bag.

"Yeah." Sara handed the file folder she'd retrieved to Tori. It was from the guy they were interviewing tomorrow, another smaller firm like Westcott.

Tori smiled up at Sara. "Thanks for getting that. I would've gone."

Yeah, but then Sara wouldn't have seen Dylan. "It was no problem."

"You were out there for a bit, and I just heard Westcott leave," Hayden said. "Were you talking to him?"

Sara nodded as she took her seat. "He really wants the whole enchilada." Which meant she'd see him all the time for months and months. So much for the one-night stand, never-have-to-see-you-again scenario.

Tori didn't lift her focus from the file folder she'd laid out on the table. "Yeah, I got that."

Hayden exchanged looks with Sara. "It's not a bad idea."

Sara lifted a shoulder. "I don't know. He doesn't have the experience." He didn't, but was that really what was worrying her? Or was it her fear of having to work with him when he'd done things to her no one else ever had?

Tori looked up. "True, but I like his hometown approach. Call me sentimental, but that really appeals to me."

"Just like Dad," Hayden said, leaning back, "he almost always goes with the local guy."

"This firm might work, too," Tori said, thumbing through the papers in the file. "I really liked Dylan's aggressive attitude, though."

"Me too." Hayden stood. "I need to get back to Archer for a meeting. See you guys here at ten tomorrow morning."

Before the door closed behind him, Sara watched him sprint toward his car in the downpour. "He's not coming to dinner tonight?"

Both she and Tori were temporarily staying at home—at their parents' house. They'd kept their residences, Sara near Portland and Tori in the Bay Area. Hayden lived in his own house in Ribbon Ridge and periodically came to dinner, which was a welcome respite from the doom and gloom of their parents, who were—understandably—still struggling with Alex's death.

"Guess not." Tori looked up from the file. "Do you blame him?"

"No." Sara sat beside Tori and rubbed her hands over her upper arms. The monastery was drafty, and the space heater they'd brought didn't provide much warmth. "I doubt Dad will be home either." He spent a lot of time at the office or out cycling.

Tori closed the file and sighed. "Probably not. Thanks again for getting the proposal from my car. Did you offer so you could talk to Dylan? Didn't you have a crush on him in high school?"

Sara stared at her in the way that sisters stare at each other when they're being pains in the butt. "That was a decade ago. Totally irrelevant."

The one-night stand? Not so much. But it *should* be irrelevant. She wasn't going to let it color her decision on awarding the job. And she sure wasn't going to tell Tori about it. It had, however, been difficult to ignore the flutters in her belly when Dylan had walked into the monastery. And then outside, the sun shining down on him from between the angry clouds, highlighting the gray-green of his eyes as he'd looked at her in that clothes-stripping way…

Get ahold of yourself, Sara. He wasn't mentally undressing you. He was fighting for the job.

"Well, he's still totally hot. And ex-military." Tori watched Sara's reaction.

Sara shook her head. "Uh-uh. I'm not biting. Let it go."

Tori exhaled and tossed her a small smile that signified the end of her goading. "Just as well since we'll probably be hiring him for phase one."

"He's your first choice?"

"For the cottage, definitely. And his attitude today only sealed the deal for me. You seemed pretty hesitant about even considering him for the other phases though."

She *was* hesitant, and if she thought about it, not for the right reasons. She couldn't let their one-night stand and any lingering attraction, which she absolutely felt, influence her decision. "You're not?"

"Maybe a little, but I'm inclined to give him a chance." Tori sat forward and waved a hand. "We're putting the cart before the horse here. I need to work on the plans before we consider anything, and I can't focus on that until we get underway with this cottage. You're sure you're up for overseeing that phase?"

Sara frowned. The last several weeks had been tough as she'd transitioned management of her business to Craig, and half-moved home to help with this project and provide support to Mom. Craig had eagerly agreed to help out—he'd been great actually. Mom, on the other hand, was a basket case. She'd started seeing a therapist but was still incredibly depressed. Dad was keeping everything bottled up and was pulling further and further away emotionally. It was like he just didn't want to deal with Alex's death at all.

All of that had combined to create stress, and Sara's sensory regulation had been all over the place. So much for proving her capability if she couldn't keep herself from having meltdowns every couple days. Granted, it wasn't quite that bad, but it wasn't as good as things had been the last few years. Which made Tori's question all the more grating, even if it was well intentioned.

"I can do it," Sara said. "I know you think I'm struggling, and I suppose I am, but we all are. I just look different doing it than you." That was the crux most of them didn't understand. Yes, she was different, but she was okay with that. "The cottage is my baby anyway." No way they would stop her overseeing it.

Converting the ranch-style house at the edge of the property into a wedding-event space had been Sara's brainstorm when they'd first toured the property several weeks ago. The idea had come to her after she'd talked with Derek's fiancée, Chloe, who'd been concerned about getting married at the Archers' house given Alex's suicide and the overall aura of depression. Moving the wedding to this new space would take the pressure off Mom. Plus, Sara could totally envision the place as a premier event destination. Once the hotel was operational, it would be in high demand.

"You're right, it is your baby," Tori said. "But I'm still your sister, and it's my responsibility to watch out for you, even when it's annoying." Her gaze softened. "Really, Sara. I know I can be overbearing sometimes, but you know my heart's in the right place."

"I do. Although I don't always appreciate it, I understand it."

Tori crossed her arms over her chest. "What are you going to do when that part of the project is done? Go back to your condo and your event-planning business?"

"That's the plan, yes." They'd discussed the need to hire a team to run the hotel and restaurant—none of them believed Kyle would ever come back to do anything. While she, Tori, Hayden, and Derek had consented to bring Alex's dream to fruition, they didn't see it eclipsing their current jobs permanently.

Sara's cell phone vibrated on the table. Glancing at the display, she saw it was her assistant—funny since she'd just been thinking of him. She shot Tori an apologetic look. "I have to take this." She swiped the phone up and stood. "Hey, Craig, how's it going?"

"Terrible." He sounded stressed. "Kristy is really unhappy that you're not here."

Sara rubbed her forehead between her eyebrows. "I know. I've explained to her that I was on a leave of absence and that you're fully capable of helping her plan these details." Kristy was a classic Bridezilla. "I told you she'd be difficult. You just have to manage her with a soft but firm hand. She'll come around."

"I don't know." Craig sounded doubtful. "I think she might be ready to walk. She said she's talked to another planner."

Sara walked to one of the windows. A patch of blue sky was trying to overtake the dark clouds dumping their rain. "It's an empty threat. She wants Archer beer for the reception and I'm the only one who can make that happen."

Craig exhaled. "I know. I just think we need to do something to stroke her ego."

"Do whatever you think you need to. She's a good client—rather, her parents are." Sara turned from the window and watched Tori packing up. "Listen, I have to go. I'll call you back later."

"I need you to help me figure out how to placate Kristy." Craig was doing a great job covering for her, but when it came to soothing upset clients, he usually expected her to take over.

"We've talked about how to work with difficult clients—it's part of the job. I'll call you later and we'll figure something out, 'K?"

"*Fine.*" He sounded like a whiny teenager, but she knew he was just blowing off steam.

Sara suppressed a smile. "Talk to you later." She hung up and went back to the table.

"Ready?" Tori asked. They'd driven up together in Tori's car.

Sara collected her work bag and her purse. "Yep. Have you heard from Liam or Evan? Or Kyle?"

"Just Evan, but only because I harass him on a biweekly basis." Because she looked out for him. Like Kyle used to do for Sara. "Not a peep from the other jerks. I take it you haven't either?"

Sara shook her head. Though Sara had expected Kyle's lack of response, it still stung. It seemed she was still waiting for him to fix things. And she was beginning to wonder if she would wait forever. "I see what Alex was trying to do—bringing us together," she said softly, the still-painful wound of his death digging into her chest. "Did he really think he had to die to make it happen, though?"

Tori blinked, probably fighting back a tear or two. "And it isn't happening, is it?" She grew quiet and looked at her hands for a long moment. "I wish I knew what he'd been thinking, why he thought death was a better choice than life."

"We'd all like to know that." While they were all coping differently—with anger and sadness and isolation—this was the one thing that united them.

"I hope his letters tell us—not that we'll get them anytime soon." Her tone dripped with resentment. "Next time we meet with Aubrey about the trust and the zoning for the project, I've half a mind to demand my letter."

Sara knew Tori was angry and upset, they all were, but it wasn't Aubrey's fault. Sara felt sorry for the lawyer. Alex had put her in a pretty lousy position. "We'll get them when Alex intended. Doesn't that mean something? Isn't that what we're doing here—honoring him and his last wishes?"

Tori pulled the raincoat from the back of her chair and drew it on over her light spring sweater. "I suppose. But I still think it sucks. Who was that on the phone, your assistant?"

Sara twirled her bracelets with one hand and fingered the edge of her sweater sleeve with the other. "Craig, yeah."

"He doing okay?"

"Just managing a Bridezilla. I'm finding it kind of tough to be away, actually."

Tori straightened her coat and belted the waist. She always looked tailored and fabulous, like she just walked out of Ann Taylor. "Tell me about it. I tried to offload all of my projects to do this—and my boss was really cool about it—but I keep having to go down there and do stuff. In fact, I need to be in San Francisco for a meeting next week."

"Yeah, I should probably do more to help Craig, but it's hard to disengage from everything here."

Tori came toward her and took her hand. "I know. You've been so good with Mom. I honestly don't know what she'd do without you right now. I try to be there, but, well, you're better at that stuff." Mom got along great with all of her children, but the relationship she shared with Sara was extra special. By necessity, she'd spent more time with Alex, Sara, and Evan when they were younger, which had fostered a closeness that the other kids perhaps didn't share. Sara had only realized that in the last few years, since she'd left home, actually. But now she saw the flashes of bitterness and resentment from Tori and even Hayden.

"She loves all of us." Sara gave Tori's hand a squeeze.

Tori let her go. "I know that. But I also know that you and Evan and Alex needed her in ways the rest of us didn't." She shook her head. "She had her hands full, even with Birgit's help." Their old housekeeper, who'd really been more of a nanny, had died over a decade ago, but she'd been an intrinsic part of their childhood.

Sara picked up her laptop bag and pulled it over her shoulder. "And after Birgit retired, Mom managed it all on her own. Now, with Alex gone, I think there's a void she's struggling to fill."

Tori walked toward the door. "That makes sense. Does she talk to you about her therapy appointments?"

Sara followed. "Not really. It's frustrating. I know she's supposed to be taking an antidepressant, but sometimes I wonder if she's really following the prescription."

Tori paused with her hand on the right hand door. "Should we talk to the therapist?"

"They can't share information with us." Sara opened the door on the left and stepped out into the now-sunny late morning. "I'll try talking to Mom again."

Tori slid on a pair of Kate Spade sunglasses. "Let me know if I can help."

As they walked toward the car, Sara's mind was a tumult of too many things: Craig and Bridezilla. Mom. Dylan Westcott.

It certainly looked as though she'd be working with him on this project. It would be…odd, but she could do it. They'd agreed to Vegas Rules, and there was no reason they couldn't be professional. She'd just have to hope her reaction to seeing him today was simply a residual effect of their one-night stand. With everything going on in her life at present, she didn't have the capacity to deal with anything else.

Chapter Five

DYLAN LISTENED TO his mother chatter incessantly about work, his half-sister Brie's latest snowboarding feat, and the trip Bill was planning to the San Juans in their boat—the boat Bill had bought when Dylan was twelve and which Dylan had ridden in exactly twice.

"Dylan?" she said in the tone that indicated she knew he'd drifted off.

"Sorry, I have a lot on my mind."

"Is it work?" Her face crinkled with concern. "Sometimes I wonder why you don't go back to the army. Or why not work for the corps of engineers?"

"I like living here in Ribbon Ridge." Although "here" was currently Newberg where the hospital was located and where Mom was a pediatric nurse manager. It was also where he'd spent half of his youth as a joint custody kid who went back and forth between parents. He didn't like to share too many details with her because she liked to gossip, so he only said, "I've bid on a new job. A big one. If I get it, things will really start to move."

She picked at her salad, looking for the candied pecans. "Sounds great." She found a nut and popped it into her mouth. Then she fixed him with her patented Mom stare. "I worry about you. Work isn't everything. You need to find time to have fun and relax."

No one could say his mother and Bill didn't know how to do that. Their entire life revolved around hobbies and trips. And Brie.

"I do, Mom, just not in the same ways as you. I enjoy fixing up my house or just watching a game with the guys."

She paused, her fork poised over her salad. "You're alone, Dylan—a loner. When are you going to date someone? It's been three years since the divorce."

Dylan endured this line of interrogation every time he saw her, and he always said the same thing in response.

"I see people, Mom. I just haven't found anyone I wanted to date. Ribbon Ridge isn't exactly hopping." An image of Sara Archer rose fast and clear into his mind.

"That's ridiculous. There are plenty of young, single women in Ribbon Ridge and here in Newberg. You should try one of those online dating sites. My friend Deanna, you remember her? She met a really nice man that way. We're taking a trip together later in the summer—a long weekend at the Shakespeare Festival."

While Mom went on about how much she loved Ashland, Oregon's festival, Dylan pushed away thoughts of Sara. Dating her was out of the question. Dating anyone was out of the question because he wouldn't have time when he got this project. And he was *going* to get this project.

Mom crunched another bite of salad and studied him a moment. "Don't let one failed marriage discourage you, Dylan. Your *father*," she always reserved a special intonation for when she mentioned her first husband, "and I didn't get it right. I found Bill, and your *father* found what's-her-name, and everyone lived happily ever after."

Everyone except Dylan.

"What do you think?" Mom persisted. "Will you try online dating?"

"No." He pushed his unfinished sandwich away. "I need to go." He stood and bent to brush a kiss against her cheek. "Say hi to Bill."

"Will do. And don't forget to put Sabrina's graduation on your calendar!"

"I did it right in front of you." Dylan had typed it into his phone as soon as they'd sat down.

She waved her fork. "I guess. You know I don't get how all those gadgets work. Too much effort. Besides, I remember everything."

Dylan smiled at her, knowing her memory wasn't what it used to be but appreciating that she still thought it was. She wasn't the easiest person, but she loved him and he loved her. "See you, Mom."

He headed out of the hospital cafeteria and made his way to the parking lot. Outside, the skies were bright gray. No rain, but no sunshine either.

He slowed as he walked toward his truck. A petite, middle-aged woman stood next to his driver door. She was very still, like a statute, and her stony gaze was locked on some distant spot.

Dylan approached her cautiously. "Hello?"

She didn't immediately register his presence until after he said hello a second time. Finally, she blinked and turned her head. "Yes?"

"Are you lost or something?" Maybe she was a young Alzheimer's patient.

"No." She blinked again several times and then looked around the parking lot. "That is, I might be. I can't seem to remember where I parked my car."

"What do you drive?" Given the woman's disorientation, Dylan wondered if she actually drove a car at all.

"A blue Prius."

He scanned the parking lot for a Prius, but didn't see one. Maybe she was completely out of it and there was no Prius. He studied her for a moment. She seemed vaguely familiar. "Should we go look for it?" He offered her his arm.

She looked up at him, her blue gaze seeming a bit more coherent. She didn't hesitate to put her hand over his forearm. "Thank you. I don't know what's wrong with me. I just had an appointment and it was..." Her voice trailed off, and she pressed a finger to the corner her eye.

Had she gotten some bad news? He steered her toward an area he couldn't see very well due to the trees and finally saw a blue Prius. "That yours?"

"Oh, yes, thank goodness. I'm such a dunderhead."

"I doubt that." They walked toward the car, and the license plate nearly made Dylan trip.

Archer 1.

Now he knew why she seemed familiar. She looked a bit like Sara, which meant she was probably her mother. Yeah, that was it. Dylan had met her a few times back in high school. "I hope everything's all right."

"It's not," she said, her tone frank. "But it will be. Or so my therapist says."

Her honesty gave him a jolt. He'd been making small talk—what did one say to someone who looked like an extra from the set of *The Walking Dead* minus the blood and gore?

They reached the car, and she dug her keys out of her purse. He noticed her hands were shaking, and she was still quite pale.

The keys slipped from her fingers, and Dylan bent to pick them up. "Are you sure you're all right?"

She put her hand to her forehead. "I don't know. Maybe I should call one of my children to pick me up."

Ribbon Ridge was a good twenty or thirty minutes away. She'd be waiting out here alone. He supposed he could wait with her. Or, he could just drive her home and have Cameron bring him back to his car. "I'm Dylan Westcott, Cameron's brother. I'd be happy to drive you home," he offered. "If that's all right with you."

Her blue eyes flickered with recognition. "How silly of me not to recognize Hayden's best friend's brother. I remember you now. But I don't want to be a bother."

"It's no trouble, really."

"What about your own car?" She glanced around. "I know, I'll ask one of my kids to drive you back."

Hell no. Dylan couldn't think of anything more awkward given that he was waiting to hear about the job. Even worse, what if one of the kids ended up being Sara? Double awkward.

"Cameron can take me. Come on, let's get you home." He escorted her to the passenger side and opened the door. When she was settled, he circled back to his side, texting Cameron as he went: *Pick me up at the Archers' in 30.*

As he climbed into the driver's seat, Emily Archer gave him an assessing perusal. "I should've recognized you right away. You and Cameron have the same eyes."

They didn't really, but he didn't correct her. His eyes were an odd color that no one else in his family shared— just another way he didn't really fit in.

He stared at the console. "I've never driven a hybrid before."

"It's not difficult; just don't be alarmed when it sounds like the engine isn't running."

"Will do." He started the car and got them on the road to Ribbon Ridge. He wondered if she was as disoriented as she'd been today when she left her other appointments.

Grief inhabited the lines around her eyes and the creases framing her mouth. She looked tired, and though he hadn't seen her in years and hadn't known her well, he thought she was probably a little too thin. "Thank you for doing this—you're a welcome distraction. Today was a little tougher than usual. I'm used to coming to the hospital on a weekly basis, but always with Alex. To see his lung doctor. Now that he's gone, I'm still going, but to see a therapist. For me. I don't like coming alone."

Why wasn't one of her kids going with her? Or her husband? Their family was huge. Surely someone could take time out of his or her busy schedule to go with her. Annoyance crept up his spine, surprising him. She wasn't *his* mother, after all. And he was supposed to be distracting her. Best get back to that. "I was here having lunch with my mom."

"That's nice of you. Are you close?"

Not particularly. "Close enough to have lunch on a somewhat regular basis." And pretty much nothing else, which was fine by him. "She lives in Newberg."

"I remember now. Didn't you move to your dad's in Ribbon Ridge specifically so you could go to West Valley High School?"

"Yeah, for the football program." It had been one of the best in the state at the time. In fact, they'd won the state championship in Dylan's senior year. "I'm surprised you remember that."

"We were big in the booster club. Rob was president during the sextuplets' senior year." She turned her head and looked out the window, hiding her expression from him. He'd heard the downward lilt of her voice as she'd mentioned her husband.

Dylan pressed his lips together. So far, he wasn't being a very good distraction. "I remember the cookies you used to make—maybe you still do."

She turned her head back, and her voice perked up. "Which ones?"

"Snickerdoodles. My favorite."

"Those were Alex's favorite too." Her tone was quiet, reflective.

Dylan gripped the steering wheel. "I am completely striking out in the distraction department."

"No, you're fine. It's nearly impossible to breathe without thinking of him or the…loss that I live with now."

"Is the therapy helping?" He probably shouldn't ask, but so far his distraction tactics were a complete fail.

"I don't really know. How can you tell?" She laughed, a rusty sound, like she didn't do it often.

"I don't know either. I had to talk to a therapist a few times when I was in the army. It was required after we went overseas."

She shifted in her seat, turning toward him. "Goodness, did you see combat?"

He threw her a reassuring smile. "No, which sort of made the therapy seem unnecessary to me, but it was required so I went. The one thing I took away—not just from the therapy but from the army in general—was to find solace in myself. Trust myself. Believe in myself. Rely on myself. It was the best advice I've ever gotten."

"How so?"

From the corner of his eye, he could see she was watching him intently, completely vested in what he was saying. "Just that at the end of the day we have to be happy with ourselves. That within ourselves we can find whatever strength or direction or inspiration we need. And that the only approval that really matters is our own."

She settled back against her seat and was quiet for a moment. "Sounds very independent. I can't remember the last time I thought of myself in that way. Being a wife and mother is about as codependent as you can get."

This conversation seemed to be veering into an extension of her therapy appointment, and he barely knew her. "Don't underestimate yourself."

"Thank you. I'll work on that."

He did a better job distracting her as they drove the next fifteen minutes to her house, focusing mostly on the new bypass that would divert traffic from going through the small towns on their way to the beach.

At last he pulled into the quarter-mile lane and then into the circular drive that looped around a giant water feature.

"Would you mind driving through the porte cochère?" she asked, pointing to the archway that connected the massive house to a garage.

He did as she directed, and she pressed a garage door opener.

"You'll have to do a U-turn to get in. I park in the garage attached to the house."

The first door was up, so Dylan parked there. "That right?"

"Perfect, thank you." She smiled, but the weariness on her face stamped out any genuine pleasure in her expression.

She climbed out of the car before he could help her. "Come inside so we can figure out how to get you home."

Though he hadn't felt his phone vibrate, Dylan pulled it out anyway, hoping Cameron had texted him back. Nothing. Dylan sent another text.

Emily led him into the house through a mudroom. Dylan noted the hooks with the kids' names. Alex's name was still there, as was Sara's. A black coat hung from her hook.

"Hi, Mom."

Trailing Emily down the short hall to the kitchen, Dylan froze at the sound of Sara's voice.

"Hi, dear." Emily lifted her hand. "Dylan Westcott drove me home."

Sara was standing at the doorway to a small circular room that adjoined the kitchen and looked to be an office. Her blue eyes grew wide. She turned toward her mother. "Drove you home from where?"

"My therapy appointment." She rubbed her fingertips against her temple. "I'm tired. I think I'm going to lie down. Will you drive him back to his car, please?"

Sara glanced at him quizzically. "Um, sure."

Emily thanked him again. "I'll remember what you told me," she said with a forced smile. She looked even paler than when he'd seen her in the parking lot. She walked through the kitchen toward the hall and left. Sara pivoted toward him, crossing her arms. "What happened?"

"I found her in the parking lot at the hospital. She seemed lost or disoriented. Or both."

Sara blinked. "I don't understand."

"She was just sort of standing in one spot and staring off. It took me a couple tries to get her attention."

"Maybe she was just daydreaming."

Dylan didn't want to be blunt, but he wanted Sara to understand that her mother hadn't been in a good place. "I had to help her find her car. She was completely out of it for a bit."

Sara's face crumpled, and she dropped her arms to her sides, her shoulders sagging. "Oh. Well…thanks."

He took a small step forward. "She seemed pretty upset. I wonder if someone should take her to her appointments from now on."

"Is that what she said?"

"She told me she used to go to the hospital every week with Alex, but that now she went alone."

Sara leaned back against the doorframe of the little office. "Sometimes I went with them. I'd meet them in Newberg." It was halfway to her condo, Dylan noted. "Thanks for telling me. And for bringing her home. You didn't have to do that."

She looked at him in question, silently asking why he had.

He shifted, uncomfortable with her gratitude. Their relationship should be business and nothing more. "It was nothing, really."

"It wasn't, but I won't argue with you." She pushed away from the wall and started down the short hall toward the mudroom. "Come on, I'll drive you back." She stopped at the hooks and pulled her coat down. She'd pushed one arm into a sleeve before Dylan got to her and held the garment up for her.

He checked his phone again. Still nothing from Cameron. "I was hoping my brother would come get me. I don't want to put you out."

She glanced at him in surprise. "Like you driving my mom home wasn't a major inconvenience."

He shrugged. "She was so out of it I didn't want her to wait around while one of you came to get her."

"Well, thanks." She eyed him with a mix of curiosity and caution. "Let's go."

SARA CRINGED AS she walked to the garage. She'd used those exact words—*let's go*—when they'd left Sidewinders for their one-night stand. She desperately wished she could take them back. Sneaking a look at him as he followed her into the garage, she wondered if he'd even noticed. Likely, the awkwardness she felt was all one-sided.

What if it wasn't? She was dying to ask if she made him uncomfortable. And if so, why? Did he regret their night together? Did he want another one?

Yikes, where had that come from? She turned and got into the car, long-ago advice from her dad bouncing around her head: *Don't ask questions you don't want the answers to.*

Dylan got into the passenger seat as she started the engine. The temperature in the car seemed to spike. Again, she assumed that was only her perception. He was staring forward, his expression utterly inscrutable.

Great.

She backed out of the garage and turned toward the drive. She punched the radio on, thinking that could help defuse the tension.

"I like this song, even though it's a little goofy. You?" His deep voice cut through her anxiety and gave her a jolt.

"What?" She hadn't been paying a lick of attention to the music and now sought to listen. Catchy tune, lots of radio play, nominated for an Oscar for that kids' movie with the little yellow minion things. "It's cute."

They fell into silence for a few minutes. By the time they reached Ribbon Ridge proper, she couldn't stand it anymore. "What did you and my mom talk about?"

"Not much. Cookies, the bypass, her therapy a little bit."

Her therapy? She hadn't wanted to talk about it lately. "What did she say about the therapy?"

"You know, it really wasn't a lot. Just what I told you about going alone."

"Alex's death has been hard." Her voice hitched a little as emotion welled up in her chest, but she swallowed it back. "Especially for her. She spent so much time with him. He still lived at home, and he worked for Archer."

"Your dad's company? What did he do?"

"He was a writer. He did all of the marketing copy, the website, that sort of thing. He named all the beers. Hmm, I wonder who will do that now." It was just another question that needed answering since he died. It seemed like there was something new every day. Something he touched that now gave them pause. "It's still so weird to say 'was.'" She pulled her sleeves up over her hands so she could rub the fabric between her fingertips and the steering wheel.

"I bet," he said softly. "Your mom's strong though. Maybe stronger than you guys think."

"Why do you say that?"

He shrugged and set his elbow on the door. "She's going to therapy. She's trying to find a way back to normal maybe."

Every time she thought things might actually start to return to normal, something happened to make her realize normal was a long way off. And maybe it was gone forever. Maybe they had a new normal. Her senses started to spin, causing her to seek more sensory input from the ridges on her cuffs.

"I notice you do that with your sleeves." His question drew her to look toward him. He nodded toward her hands. "And judging from the condition of the edges, I'd say it's a little more than a habit."

"A compulsion, you mean?" She felt a jolt of defensiveness. Most people didn't get the things she did to regulate herself—the fiddling, the squeezing and compressing, the lingering in quiet corners. "It's part of my sensory disorder."

"What disorder?"

"You don't remember from high school?" People may not have known the specifics, but she'd been Quirky Sara with her odd ticks and aloofness.

"No. Tell me." He'd been a senior when she was a freshman, so it was likely he'd never been aware of her reputation. In fact, nobody might have been aware of her at all if it hadn't been for Liam, Tori, and Kyle, who'd been insanely popular.

"It's kind of hard to explain." And she didn't really want to get into it, especially with him when she was trying to keep things professional. "Forget I mentioned it."

"I think this is the second time you've brushed this off. If I'm remembering right, you were going to say something about it at Sidewinders."

She cast him a sidelong glance. "Uh-oh, you broke the Vegas Rules."

He laughed. "My bad. I guess we should be pretending we didn't meet each other that night at all."

Should they? That's what Vegas Rules sort of implied and that whole night was supposed to be locked in a vault. Too bad it kept leaping into her head at the slightest provocation. "I don't know about you, but that's pretty hard for me to do. I can separate it from our relationship now, but I can't forget it." *I hope*. She stopped herself before she said anything more, like how great it had been.

She snuck another look at him, saw him watching her, and quickly snapped her gaze forward.

"I get you. Vegas Rules in full effect."

Eager for a safer topic, she asked, "Sounds like you and my mom had a good chat on your drive."

"I don't know if it was good, but it wasn't bad. Actually, I offered to distract her, but I wasn't very good at it."

She sensed from his tone that his heart was in the right place. "I'm sure you tried. It's hard to avoid the subject. It's consuming her."

"I can see that. I gave her some advice from the army. Rely on yourself, find inspiration within."

"That's what the army taught you?"

"Among other things, but yeah. Trust and believe in yourself. All that crap."

She laughed, slowing for a red light. "You gave my mom crap advice?"

"No," he said with a touch of humor. "It *sounds* like crap, but it actually does work. At least for me."

The light turned green, and she pressed the accelerator. "Tell me about the army."

"There's not a lot to tell—bad food, tedious assignments, really boring outfits."

She laughed again, enjoying his company more than she wanted to. It would be so much easier to keep him at arm's length if he weren't charming and funny. "You cared about the clothes?"

"Okay, not that much. But my ex complained about doing the laundry. She stopped doing it after the first year." He winced slightly, as if he wished he hadn't said that.

Sara didn't want him to feel bad—she dealt with enough of that already. He was her light spot, someone she could forget about her troubles with and…be someone different. Wait, was that true? "So she divorced you over laundry? I can see that. I'm putting that in my prenup—each spouse must do his or her own laundry."

"I don't mind that. I actually don't hate laundry. You should see my washer and dryer."

Was that some sort of invitation? Or at least the verbalization that maybe someday she'd have cause to be in his house? Whoa, she was way overthinking. They were having an innocent conversation. No, they were kind of flirting and she should put an end to it. But she didn't.

"You're an odd man, Dylan Westcott. I suppose you cook and clean toilets, too?"

"I try to cook—and sometimes I succeed." He flashed her that disarming smile and she locked her gaze on the road, which is where she planned to keep it. "I'm an ace at cleaning toilets—the army made sure of that."

He liked laundry, could cook, and cleaned a mean toilet. "Why exactly did your ex divorce you? She sounds like a moron."

He laughed and it heated Sara's insides, infusing her with a soothing warmth she hadn't felt in a long time. "I promise you, I have plenty of faults," he said.

They'd somehow entered the outskirts of Newberg in record time. Or maybe she'd just been enjoying the ride too much to notice, which was pretty bad since she was driving. As she pulled into the hospital parking lot, she cast him a sidelong glance. "Like line dancing."

"Ouch. And you broke Vegas Rules."

Sara clapped her hand over her mouth, eliciting another laugh from him.

She parked next to his large, gray truck. "Thanks again for bringing Mom home. I hope she didn't mess up your entire afternoon." She suddenly realized he was maybe supposed to be working.

"It's fine. We're in the middle of a remodel, but the electricians were working today so I stopped in this morning before I had lunch with my mom. She works here at the hospital." He turned to look at her and suddenly the space in the car seemed very, very small. "And it was my pleasure."

Just hearing him say "pleasure" sent shivers up her spine. She glanced away, reminding herself that she'd be better off ignoring her attraction to him and trying to make it go away. They were probably going to be working together, for crying out loud. At least, she was 99.9 percent confident they would. Tomorrow morning, Derek would join them to review the proposals and hear their interview feedback; then they'd make their hiring decision.

She was tempted to tell Dylan he practically had the job, but in the end only said, "Talk to you soon."

His gaze lingered on her for a couple seconds and the attraction she was trying so hard to ignore leaped between them again. "Tell your mom to take care of herself." He opened the door and, just like that, the sparks of electricity dwindled and disappeared.

"Okay. Thanks again."

He threw her a smile and closed the door.

Argh. She had to get a hold of herself. Their Vegas Rules night was long over, and they'd agreed that it was a one-night thing. Besides, it wasn't like she had the bandwidth to start anything more permanent. Her life was in turmoil, and she had no idea where things would be in a week, let alone a month. Beyond that, they were going to be coworkers. She needed to forget about Dylan Westcott in every capacity except as general contractor. But how was she supposed to do that when he'd given her the most memorable night of her life?

Chapter Six

DYLAN PULLED INTO his dad's driveway the following morning to help clean out the gutters. It was early, the temperature crisp, the sky a bright blue with the promise of a beautiful spring day.

He went to the door and knocked. Dad answered quickly with a warm smile. "You know you don't have to knock."

He never felt comfortable just walking in. Yes, he'd lived there, had called it his "primary" residence in high school, but he'd never thought of it as home. It was the place he'd stayed when it had been his father's custodial time.

"Just you and me today?" Dylan asked. "Or is Cameron joining us?"

"He should be here, but you know him. Punctuality isn't exactly his thing." Dad gestured for Dylan to follow him. "Have some coffee."

Angie stood at the island in the kitchen with three mugs in front of her. "Hi, Dylan," she greeted cheerily. She settled her glasses more firmly on her nose. "I have that vanilla creamer you like."

She did try to be thoughtful and was much better about it now than when he'd been younger. Her focus had been on her three sons, and part of Dylan couldn't fault her for that. "Thanks."

"What's new, son?" Dad asked, sipping his coffee, his hip against the island.

"Not too much."

"You can do better than that." Dad chuckled. "Getting information out of you is like pulling teeth. How's work? Any exciting jobs lined up?"

He never told anyone about jobs unless they were done deals. "Maybe. Too early to tell."

"Well, keep us posted. We want nothing but the best for you."

"Thanks." He forced another swallow of coffee before setting the mug on the counter. "Ready to go?"

"Let's do this." Dad set down his mug and led him into the garage.

Dad's house was a split-level, so one half was higher than the other half. They typically started with the high end. Dylan carried the ladder over and set it against the house as Cameron drove up in his ten-year-old Land Rover. Four years younger than Dylan, he bore a fairly strong resemblance to Dylan in height and build even though they were only half-siblings. Their similarities did not extend to their wardrobe, however. Cameron looked like he'd gone to Urban Outfitters that morning to get dressed.

"You do realize we're cleaning gutters," Dylan teased.

Cameron glanced down at his clothes. "These are my work clothes."

"You won't be sad if they get dirty? What will you wear to the club tonight?" Dylan's own clothes were things he actually *worked* in. They had stains and holes, and he'd never dream of wearing them "out."

"Funny," Cameron said. "I don't go clubbing every Saturday."

"No, I guess you have to do your nails and hair sometime." Dylan always gave him shit for his metrosexual habits, which Cameron took in stride.

"Happy to have you join me sometime. I've said it before and it bears repeating, you'd benefit from a manicure."

Dylan's hands, currently covered with work gloves, were as rough and calloused as you could get. And he was fine with that. "You expect me to build shit with baby-soft hands? You're nuts."

Dad came around the house lugging the power washer. "Hi, Cam." His gaze dipped to what his son was wearing. "Did you forget we're cleaning the gutters?"

Cameron laughed. "No, I brought a rain suit." He opened the back of his rig and pulled out the suit.

"You're a dick." Dylan grinned at him.

Dad looked between them, confused. "What? Why?"

"Just stupid brother behavior." Cameron toed his boots off and pulled the rain pants over his jeans.

"The pants should be enough," Dylan said.

"And where are yours?" Dad asked.

"I'll get wet and muddy, so what?" Dylan didn't care—his jeans were pretty trashed anyway. And once he was dirty, he wouldn't have to go inside and have lunch or chitchat.

"I have extra rain pants." Dad was already heading toward the garage.

"It's okay, Dad!" Dylan called after him, but Dad just lifted his hand and kept going.

"Nice try," Cameron said. He'd put his boots back on and joined him at the ladder. "You'll have to hang out for lunch now." Cameron knew his tactics well.

Dylan crossed his arms and waited for the stupid pants.

"What, you have somewhere else to be? I doubt that. Seems like your social agenda has taken a nose dive lately." Cameron looked at him expectantly.

So he hadn't been going out much the past few months. He'd been busy working on his kitchen. "Yeah, so?"

"You should come out with me tonight. Hayden Archer and I are heading into Portland to a new wine bar."

"I'm waiting to hear their decision about the job, so that would be pretty awkward. Thanks for the offer, though."

Cameron grimaced. "Oh, I didn't realize the timing, sorry. But Hayden's cool. It won't be awkward for him, I'm sure. Hey, maybe it'll boost your chances—you're a hell of a wingman."

Dylan snorted. "Real professional, bro. Besides, tonight's the night I sharpen all my tools and polish *my* nails—the kind I drive into wood with a hammer."

"Ha ha, you're a laugh a minute." Cameron leaned closer. "Come on. You haven't been out with me in ages. Don't tell me you've finally shucked your player reputation."

"Hey, I've worked hard *not* to have a reputation. At least around here."

"I know you have, and since I'm inviting you to *Portland*, there's no reason for you to decline. Especially since I know how much you love a good chase."

"Shut up, Dad's coming. Unless you want to discuss our sex lives in front of him. If so, I'm happy to ask you all about your flavor of the month."

Cameron grinned. "You're cruel."

Just then a familiar figure came striding down the sidewalk, her arms swinging in a power walk. She slowed and stopped in front of the house. Hell, it was Monica Christensen, his ex-mother-in-law. He occasionally saw her in passing—at the grocery store or something, but they hadn't exchanged words. She pretty much hated Dylan's guts for "taking her baby away" when he was stationed in the army.

"Morning, Monica," Dad said. "I'll get Angie." He cast Dylan an apologetic glance and went inside.

"Hi, Dylan, it's been a long time," she said.

He worked not to grit his teeth. "How are you?" And because not to ask would be a massively rude omission, he added, "How's Jess?"

"She's great. Wedding plans are coming along."

Wedding? His surprise must've shown. He'd had no idea Jess was getting married again.

Monica put her hands on her hips. "I thought you must've heard. I walk with Angie every Saturday."

Dylan had forgotten that; otherwise, he might've organized today's work party a bit differently. But that was stupid. He was a grown man, and he could handle seeing his ex-monster-in-law. "No, I hadn't heard. Give her my best."

The door opened and Angie jogged to the sidewalk. "Bye!" She waved at them and the two women strode off in full power-walk mode.

Dad scowled. "Sorry about that. I wasn't thinking the two of you might actually have to exchange words. I know you don't get along."

"It's not a question of getting along. She hates me for taking her daughter away."

Cameron's eyes narrowed. "Which is lame, since her daughter ended up leaving you and choosing her stupid family over your marriage." He blinked and shook his head. "Sorry, didn't mean to dredge up old shit."

"It's fine. Ancient history. I'm glad Jess found someone else. She's a good catch." *For someone who didn't mind meddling in-laws and a controlling wife.* His neck prickled uncomfortably. He wasn't jealous, but why was it easier for some people to find happiness than others? He shook off the thought. He didn't care about that right now. He was on a great path—he was going to score this Archer job, and he was going to turn it into something life-changing.

He pulled on the rain pants Dad had brought out. "Let's get moving." He picked up the power washer and climbed up the ladder one-handed with Cameron following behind. At the top, he set the washer on the roof and turned to his brother. "You know, I think I will go out with you tonight." Why not? He hadn't been back out there since Sara, and if he was going to be working with her, the time was ripe to exorcise her from his mind.

Cameron's mouth lifted in a lazy smile. "Feeling a little left out now that your ex has moved on?"

"I figured you'd make it about that. No, maybe I just want to get laid." And he suddenly did. Only, the image in his mind wasn't of some nameless, faceless hottie he randomly picked up. It was Sara Archer's pert nose, sexy blue eyes, and lush pink lips.

"Great. Hayden and I'll pick you up at seven."

Shit, he'd forgotten about Hayden. How the hell was he going to pick someone up in the company of his last one-night stand's brother? Forget that, Hayden was going to be his boss too. He'd meet up with them and then take off on his own. "No, I'll meet you there. Just text me the address."

He was looking forward to a night where he could forget about work, family garbage, and, most of all, Sara Archer.

DEREK FLIPPED THROUGH the last file. Folders and papers cluttered the table in the gathering room. Sara, along with Tori and Hayden, waited while he read.

Dad came into the kitchen and moved toward the table. He glanced down at the papers spread out before them. "What're you kids up to?"

"We're selecting a contractor for phase one of the project," Derek said. "Do you want to join us?"

Dad gripped the top of the chair at the end of the table where he typically sat. "Alex didn't assign me a role for a reason." His tone was clipped, but then they all knew it bothered him that he hadn't been included.

Hayden shook his head. "Nonsense, Dad. We'd love your input. We contacted some of the people you recommended—and we'll be contacting others when we solicit bids for the other phases."

"This phase is just the house renovation? Sara's wedding-space project?"

Sara nodded, glad to see him engaged. "That's right."

"Great idea, you having the wedding there. Your mother just can't handle a big event here." He looked out at the expansive back lawn and the trees beyond. "It's a shame, since we built this place both to raise all of you and to entertain our large and hopefully growing family."

Sara heard the wistfulness in his tone. "Someone's bound to get married here someday, Dad."

He turned a half-smile on her. "Maybe that'll be you, kitten." He looked at Derek. "You're okay with getting married up at the new place?"

"I am. And Chloe is, too. We're just glad to have our family there." Derek's gaze spoke volumes—the Archers were his family, and he treasured it above all else. "But to get there, we need to hire someone. I wasn't able to attend the presentations, but it looks like there was a clear choice, and after reviewing the documentation, I agree."

Hayden flashed him a smile. "Excellent." He leaned back in his chair and looked up at Dad. "Dylan Westcott."

Dad squeezed his fingers around the back of the chair. "Your friend's brother? You sure he's the best, or are you just choosing the guy you like?"

"We chose the best guy for the job," Tori said. "That he happens to be someone we know is just icing on the cake. He's a Ribbon Ridger. I thought you'd like that."

"Here, look at his presentation." Hayden had the folders stacked in front of him. He exchanged glances with each of them before handing the one on top to Dad.

Dad thumbed through it. "He bid on the entire project? Aggressive."

"You typically like that," Derek pointed out.

Dad nodded vaguely. "You're just hiring for phase one right now? He's probably fine for that. But when it comes to phase two, I hope you'll contact McAvoy. He did our last two brewpubs." Dad flipped the presentation folder closed.

"I'm sure we will." Derek took the folder from Dad.

Sara noted the new lines around Dad's eyes and wished he'd find a way to deal with his grief. He just seemed ready to explode. Standing, she went and touched his hand. Physical contact was the best way she knew how to comfort, because it was what soothed her. "You know we appreciate your feedback."

He nodded. "Alex didn't want me to help you. The letter he gave me…He specifically told me to let you all manage everything."

Sara's heart constricted and she saw the same reaction in the pained gazes of her siblings.

"I'm sure he didn't mean for you to stay out of things entirely," Tori said softly.

"Well, we'll never know, will we?" Dad's tone was bitter and dark, like Mom's favorite chocolate. "It's not like I can ask him to clarify."

Sara hugged him, but he only patted her back in response.

He stepped back. "I'll leave you kids to it."

Hayden stood. "Dad, have you thought about talking to someone? Maybe going to therapy with Mom?"

Dad's gray eyes flashed. "Like Alex went to therapy? You can see what good that did."

Tori crossed her arms tightly over her chest. "How will you know if it will help until you try?"

Sara worried the edges of her sleeves. The shirt was one of her favorites, which meant the fabric was frayed and little holes had formed along the seams. She hated seeing her father like this and for the first time she felt a surge of anger toward Alex for being so selfish.

Dad shook his head. "Please don't try to fix me, Tori. Or any of you. I'm doing the best that I can and that's all I can do." He pressed his lips together then turned and left.

Seeing her father so agitated fed Sara's own anxiety and sent her senses spinning. In response, she folded her arms over her chest then clasped her elbows and squeezed. She held her breath while she set her body into a full muscle compression. Her siblings were going to notice and probably say something, but she couldn't help it. She needed to regulate.

Derek, who was at the end of the table, looked over at her. "You okay?"

Hayden's and Tori's gazes swept toward her.

"No, she's not." Tori went to Sara. "Do you want to go down to the gym and swing or something?"

Old therapies Sara had thought she'd grown out of over the past few years. Until the stress of the last several weeks had sent her spiraling backward. She hated being like this in front of them. It only encouraged their overprotection.

"I'm fine. Really."

All three of them looked at her skeptically.

"Really," she repeated. "I get upset—just like all of you— only my stress manifests like this. It's no big deal."

They looked away, and Derek spoke first. "Well, that was…"

Hayden retook his seat and fidgeted with the folders in front of him. "Troubling."

"Sad," Sara contributed. She willed her body to relax, letting her hands drop to her lap.

"Awful," Tori finished. "He really needs to see someone. What are we going to do?"

"I don't know that there's anything you *can* do." Derek exhaled. "I know what this feels like too well." He'd lost both his parents. "He'll get through it."

Tori brushed a knuckle over her nose. "Or he won't."

Derek gave them all a pained look. "I hate to go like this, but I need to meet Chloe in town. Hayden, you'll notify everyone about the decision?"

Hayden nodded. "I'll get in touch with Dylan this afternoon."

"Is there a way we can tell him in person?" Tori asked. "I'd like to see his face."

Hayden laughed. "Actually, I would, too. I'll see what I can do."

"Good enough." Derek stood. "Let me know what you pull together."

"I need to get out of here for a bit," Tori said, standing up. "I'm going for a run."

Sara's phone vibrated in her back pocket. She pulled it out and saw that it was Craig. Ugh, she didn't want to talk to him right now, but he had an event today. "It's my assistant," she said to Hayden.

"Go ahead." He gathered up the folders and stood.

Sara answered the call. "Hey, Craig."

"Hey. What's wrong? You sound upset."

She got up from the table and went into the little circular office off the kitchen that they'd all been using as a sort of headquarters for the monastery project. "Just another day in paradise. What's up?"

"The Carters' wedding is today. The photographer has shingles."

Holy shit. Sara massaged her forehead, trying to banish the anxiety coursing through her. "Who have you called?"

"Everyone who was on their list. No one's free."

Shit, shit, shit. Total crisis. But what was she supposed to do, go take the pictures herself? She'd actually done that once, back when she'd been a newbie. It had worked out, but the event had been a small second marriage and the clients had been okay with that fix. Mrs. Carter-to-be would *not* be okay with that. She would freak out. "Does the bride know?"

"Not yet, but pictures are due to start in like four hours."

"Contact every photographer we know—even those who don't do weddings. Offer them whatever you have to."

"Carter won't be happy if he has to pay more."

"He probably won't. The guy they hired was pretty high end." The bride definitely had champagne wishes and caviar dreams. "But if there's a price difference, we'll eat it." The cost of doing business.

"You want to split the list?" The sound of him typing on his laptop came through the phone.

Sara heard the fridge open behind her and turned to see her mom's legs beneath the open door. "Sure. E-mail it to me. I have to go."

"Wait! Are you going to call now?" His panicked voice was starting to spin her up again. "We need to get this locked down fast."

"I know. E-mail me the list and I'll get started in like five minutes." Ten tops. Had Mom overheard anything that had gone on in the kitchen?

Craig exhaled loudly, forcing Sara to pull the phone away from her ear. "Text me when you start so I know you're working on it." He hung up.

Sara frowned at the phone as she set it on the desk. Their conversations were getting less and less friendly, she'd noticed. More work-focused. Before—last month even—he would've pressed her to talk about why she was upset and tried to make her feel better. She also wasn't calling him just to talk anymore. She'd been talking to her siblings instead.

She couldn't think about this right now, not with Mom standing in the open fridge door. She'd had it open so long it had started to beep.

Sara went to the fridge and poked her head around the side of the door. "Morning, Mom."

Mom turned her head. "Oh, good morning, sweetheart."

Sara put her arm around her and tried to ignore the annoying beep of the fridge. "Can I help you find something?"

"I don't know. I was just looking."

Mom, dressed in a robe and slippers, browsing for food like some college guy? Sara guided her away from the fridge and closed the door. Then she walked her to a barstool and got her situated. "Let me get you some tea. And how about a scone? I baked some last night."

"Lovely, thank you."

Sara set the kettle to boiling water and prepped two Earl Grey teabags in Mom's favorite giant teacup. Then she grabbed a scone from the Tupperware she'd stored them in and set it on a plate in front of Mom. "Apple ginger."

"Mmm. I'm so glad you took on my love for baking. Your sister is hopeless in the kitchen."

Sara forced a smile. It seemed Mom was oblivious to the earlier drama, and Sara preferred to keep it that way. "Pretty much."

Mom nibbled at a piece of scone. She looked so fragile. Sara hadn't talked to her since Dylan had driven her home yesterday. Mom had gone to her room, eaten from a tray Tori had taken her, and gone to bed early.

It would be simple to avoid the topic entirely. It seemed they all tried to take the easy path—and why not? It was *easy*. And everything just seemed so *hard*. She gathered her courage. "What happened at your therapy appointment yesterday? Why did Dylan Westcott have to drive you home?"

Mom picked off another tiny piece of scone. "Oh, that. I was hoping you wouldn't ask." She put the bite into her mouth.

"Of course I would ask. I care about you. I'm here to help you, aren't I?"

Mom smiled. "Yes, you are, and I love you so much for it. I just had a rough appointment. You know how it is. Some days are not so good." Her voice dipped and trailed off as she finished.

"But this seems like more than that. He said you were dazed, that he had to help you find the car." *And you just got lost in the fridge.*

Mom shrugged as though none of this were a cause for concern, when it absolutely was. "I was caught up in my memories." She wiped a finger beneath her eye. "It happens more and more."

Sara realized there was something off about her. More off than normal. She'd been sad, yes, and some days *were* worse than others, but she'd managed. It was like she'd reverted to how she'd been a couple of months ago, right after Alex had killed himself.

The teakettle began to whistle. Sara took it from the stove and poured the near-boiling water into the cup.

She turned the burner off as she set it back on the stove. Grabbing a spoon from the drawer, she pressed the back against the teabags to hurry along their steeping.

As she'd indicated to Tori, Sara wondered if Mom had gone off her meds. "Have you stopped taking your Paxil?"

Mom's hand froze as she was pulling off another bite of scone. "Why do you ask?"

"Because you seem as upset as when Alex died. Once you started taking the pills, you started to feel better. It just seemed logical that maybe you'd stopped taking them."

Mom's brows knitted and her chin lifted. "I'm sorry, but I just can't take something that Alex used to...kill himself." She ground the last two words out through a scratchy, tear-filled throat.

Sara rushed around the bar and hugged her. "Oh, Mom. I didn't think about that." Alex had taken a drug cocktail of antidepressants, sleeping pills, and pain medication, none of which had been prescribed to him. He'd obtained them illegally somehow, and they still didn't know where or how.

"Let's talk to your psychiatrist, okay?" Sara rubbed her back, hating the helplessness she felt. For the first time, Sara glimpsed how it must have been for her mom watching her children struggle with various challenges. Sara knew she couldn't wave a magic wand and fix things, but oh how she wished she could. "There has to be something he can do. How about I call him after breakfast?"

Mom nodded against her shoulder. Sara drew back and gave her a warm smile. "I'll drive you to your appointments from now on. Or Tori. Or Hayden. Or Derek. One of us will go with you." She was ashamed that none of them had thought of it before.

"Thank you, sweetheart. You take such good care of me. Like that young man yesterday. He was very kind. I don't know what would've happened if he hadn't helped me. I suppose I'd still be standing in that parking lot."

"I'm so sorry, Mom. We shouldn't have let you go alone."

Mom patted her hand. "Or maybe I should've asked for help. It's hard for a mother to admit to her children that she's struggling."

"You're still my hero," Sara said softly, admiring her mother so much for all she'd done for them and hating that she now felt inadequate. Again, she felt a burst of anger toward Alex. Mom didn't deserve to feel like this.

"Thank you, sweetheart. That means more to me than you could ever know." Mom sipped her tea and gave Sara a warm smile that reminded her of the way things had been before Alex had died. A smile that gave Sara hope and just a sliver of joy.

Chapter Seven

DYLAN PARKED NEXT to Cameron's Land Rover in the sports bar parking lot in Newberg. It was odd that he and Hayden had chosen to meet up here instead of in Portland, but that was fine with Dylan, provided they didn't try to pressure him into riding with them—he was on his own schedule tonight.

As he climbed out of his truck, he had second thoughts about joining them. He wasn't sure he wanted to spend the evening with Hayden when they hadn't yet made a decision about the Archer job. And if he was honest with himself, he was in kind of a shitty mood since seeing Monica earlier in the day and learning of Jess's marriage. Not because he still loved her—a part of him would always care for her—but because it made his life seem lacking somehow. As if getting married would complete him? Total bullshit. He just needed a beer and a good game of pool. Maybe he could talk them into playing before they headed downtown.

He walked inside and scanned the interior. Spotting Cameron and Hayden in a corner booth, he made his way over and nearly tripped when he saw who was on the other side of the table—Tori and Sara.

"Hey, Dylan!" Tori gestured for him to sit.

Both seats were long enough to fit three people, and since each currently held two, he had to choose—sit next to his brother or next to Sara?

His gaze lingered on her. She'd made eye contact when he'd first approached but now she was studying her drink— another lemon drop. She looked fantastic, the ends of her blonde hair grazing her shoulder blades and her makeup accentuating the lush pink of her lips and the alluring blue of her eyes. He quickly looked at his brother before he could be caught staring and dropped down beside him.

Sara's shot him a look, and Dylan realized he'd chosen poorly. He'd thought to avoid proximity to her by sitting across the table, but now he was looking right at her. And fighting a sudden and overwhelming desire.

Irritated at the direction of his thoughts, he turned to his brother and socked him in the arm. "What's with the blindside?"

"My fault," Hayden said. "Since you're coming out with us tonight, I didn't want there to be any weirdness. And since we've already decided about the job…"

Hell. The job. Of course. "You convened at a sports bar on a Saturday night to work?"

Tori flashed him a grin. "We Archers know how to do things right—plus, we grew up in brewpubs so this feels natural."

"But we didn't want to meet at the Arch and Vine," Hayden said, referring to their flagship pub in Ribbon Ridge. "This at least gets us partway to Portland so we can get our evening started."

Dylan snuck a look at Sara, but she was still engrossed in her drink. That was twice now that Hayden had mentioned them going out. Was that awkward for her to hear? He shouldn't care...they didn't owe each other anything, but he was surprised to find that it bothered him.

"Are you going to tell him or what?" Cameron asked.

It seemed Cameron knew about the job before Dylan. He tried not to let that irritate him even further. He really hated that they'd surprised him like this. His head had been wired for a guys' night out, not a work meeting involving his favorite one-night stand.

Favorite? Hell yes.

"You've got the job," Tori said, smiling.

Dylan felt a surge of adrenaline but tamped it back. "The entire job?"

"Just phase one," Hayden answered, exchanging a brief glace with Tori. "For now. You're definitely not out of the running for the next phases."

Dylan couldn't help feeling disappointed, which was silly. Phase one was a great opportunity, and his guys would have months of work now. Plus, he'd be on-site and could continue to lobby for the rest of the job. And show them how right he and his team were for it.

He glanced at Sara again. She hadn't said a word since he'd arrived.

"Thank you," Dylan said. "I appreciate the opportunity, and I'll make sure you have no doubt that we're the best choice for phases two and three."

Tori lifted her beer. "Excellent. We should toast."

Sara finally spoke. "He doesn't have a glass." She reached over to the empty pint glass sitting beside the nearly empty pitcher and poured him the rest of the IPA. "Here." She slid it over to him.

He took it from her, his fingers connecting with hers and driving a jolt of awareness straight to the pit of his belly. "Thanks."

"To phase one," Tori said.

"To phase one," Hayden answered and they all drank.

Dylan took a long pull on his beer before setting it back on the table. "Do me a favor though; next time you have a meeting, can you let me know about it in advance instead of ambushing me?"

"I told them it was a bad idea," Sara said, casting him an apologetic glance that made him like her even more. *Damn.*

Hayden nodded. "So you did. You're the boss now," he said to Dylan.

"Ha, not really. I answer to you guys." Including Sara.

"Speaking of meetings," Tori said, leaning forward, "I'd like to meet at the site trailer Monday morning at eight thirty to review the plans and permits and whatnot."

The conversation turned to project business for the next fifteen minutes as they finished their beers and

Sara nursed her lemon drop. She contributed to the discussion—clearly taking her job as phase-one manager quite seriously and damn if that wasn't sexy as hell—but Dylan sensed there was something off about her tonight.

Cameron set his empty pint glass on the table. "Enough business for a Saturday night, people." He looked at Hayden and Dylan. "Ready to go? I thought we'd stop in for a bite at Urban Farmer."

"Mmm, yum," Tori said. "I'd invite myself but it's clear you guys are on the prowl and I have a date with a soaker tub." She glanced around. "Who's picking this up?"

Sara pulled her wallet from her purse. "I got it. Business expense."

"Absolutely," Hayden said, looking at Dylan with a gaze that clearly implied, "Let's go."

Dylan stood from the table. "Guys, I think I'm going to pass tonight."

Cameron slid out from the booth. "No, you can't. You have to come. I insist."

Dylan gave him a wry smile. "Insist all you like."

"Come on, dude." Hayden straightened his shirt as he stood. "You just scored a major project—you need to celebrate."

Maybe, but cruising for his next one-night stand had lost its appeal. His gaze dropped to Sara's head. No, it wasn't because of her. He just wasn't in the mood. "Thanks, but I'm good. Really."

"I'll wait here with Sara for the bill," Tori said. "You guys go ahead."

Dylan saw an opening and he took it. "I think I'm going to hang out and play some pool. I'll wait with Sara."

Her gaze shot up, but only briefly so that he couldn't tell what she thought of that.

Tori shrugged. "Cool."

Sara stood so that Tori could exit the booth.

"We'll walk you out," Hayden said to Tori and the trio left.

Sara sank back into the booth. "You don't have to wait with me."

"It's no trouble. I really am going to play some pool. You want to play with me?" What the hell was he doing?

She looked up at him, her blue eyes contemplative.

"It's just pool," Dylan said. "Come on, I'll tell the server we're heading to the back."

Without waiting for her response, he went over to the bar and told the bartender they were moving. When he turned around, she had her lemon drop in hand and was walking to the back of the building where a half-dozen pool tables were ringed by bar-height tables and stools. A handful of large flat-screen TVs were mounted high on the walls and showed either a basketball game or a highlight show.

She set her drink down on a table and scooted onto the barstool, hanging her purse over the back. He joined her.

"I really am sorry about the blindside. Tori and Hayden thought it would be fun, despite my insistence that it wasn't very professional."

"It's okay." Maybe Fate was trying to tell them not to be professional. *Whoa, Dylan, keep that shit to yourself.* "I don't tend to like surprises."

"Why?"

He shrugged. "I like routine. Probably because I didn't have much of one when I was younger. Moving back and forth—weekdays at one place, most weekends at the other."

"That must've been tough. I can't function without routine."

The server arrived at their table with a beer for him and another lemon drop for her.

"I hope you don't mind that I ordered you another drink."

"On my tab?" She laughed.

"Actually, I paid for these already," he said, arching a brow.

She lifted her glass in toast. "Touché."

He set his beer down after taking a drink. "Is this weird? I probably shouldn't be fraternizing with the boss."

"I'm not really your boss."

"Hmmm. You decided whether to hire me. You'll give me direction since you're managing phase one. And you'll evaluate my work. Sounds like you're my boss." He couldn't resist winking at her.

"You put it like that…" She looked down at her drink and twirled the stem between her fingers. They never stopped moving along the glass. He saw a faint ridge along the stem and figured it was a sensory thing. She peered over at him. "Yeah, maybe this is weird."

The boss-employee thing. The one-night stand. His smoldering desire for her. The fact that he'd ditched a guys' night out in favor of hanging with her.

"Not weird." Not fine either. What the hell was it? Excruciating, he decided. Time to change the subject. He really didn't want things to be awkward. Regardless of their past, he liked her and he wanted to be friends—as much as a boss and employee could be friends. "You seemed a little pensive earlier. Is everything all right? Wait, I think I know. You weren't in favor of hiring me, were you?"

"Actually, I wasn't at first." He'd been kidding, and hearing her admit it felt like a kick to the gut. Something must've reflected in his reaction. "No, no. It's not you, it's me." She smiled. "I'm really screwing this up. What I mean to say is that I was worried the… our…that night would get in the way. But I realized that was dumb. We're consenting adults and we both said we're good with this. I think you're going to do an amazing job and I'm looking forward to working with you."

He sat back against the stool in relief. "That's good to hear. I want you to be comfortable with this."

"I am. I'm just preoccupied with my mom and my dad. Things are really tough for them right now."

"I'm sure."

The server showed up again, this time with potato skins and spinach-artichoke dip.

Sara plucked up a tortilla chip and swept it into the dip. "I'm actually starving. And this is my favorite dip."

"But no Archer brew." Dylan nodded at Sara's drink. "Do you only drink the family beer?"

She shook her head. "I rarely drink beer at all. Only if it's got a bunch of fruit in it." She laughed. "Much to my dad's chagrin."

Dylan smiled at the irony. Her father was one of the best microbrewers in the state and she practically never drank it. "I'm a fan of the Nock. And the Longbow. And I really like the Robin Hood in the summer."

She squinted an eye at him. "Are there any you don't like?"

He laughed. "Probably not."

"My dad's always brewing new stuff. You should come over some time and sample the kegs." Her face darkened and she scooped up her glass for a long drink.

He leaned forward, setting his elbow on the table. "What's wrong?"

She looked to the side of him for a moment before answering, like she was gathering her words. "Dad actually hasn't brewed anything in a long time. Not since before…"

Before her brother had killed himself. Sorrow lined her face, and he recognized the expression as the one she'd been wearing when he'd first come to the table. She was sad. Had something happened today? "You don't have to talk about it if you don't want to, but if you ever do, I'm happy to listen."

"My dad was pretty upset this morning. It's hard to watch him struggle like that. You look to your parents for strength…" Her voice trailed off and her eyes shuttered, like she was closing up inside.

He rushed to bring her back from her dark thoughts. "I think you probably have plenty of strength all on your own." How did he know that? He wasn't sure, but he just did.

She glanced up at him as she dipped another chip. "Thanks. Why didn't you go out with Cameron and Hayden?"

He blinked at her, not knowing what to say, which was asinine. He didn't have to tell her the truth—that he'd jumped at the chance to just hang here with her. "I just didn't feel like going out. Some of the clubs they hit aren't my scene."

"I hear you. That night I met you at Sidewinders, my assistant tried to get me to go out to a club in town—totally not my thing."

He was glad she'd gone to Sidewinders, but he didn't say so. In fact, he decided to drive the conversation in a new direction—one that didn't continually remind him of the amazing night they'd spent together. "You aren't the only one who had a rough morning. I found out my ex is getting married."

She put her fingers back around the stem of her glass and stroked the ridge. "Oh. You aren't still…?" Though she didn't finish, the question was clear in her gaze.

"In love with her? No." He shook his head. "I don't think I loved her for a long time."

Where had that come from? He hadn't ever told anyone that.

Sara cocked her head to the side, clearly interested. "Really? Why did you marry her? Or did the falling out of love part happen afterward?"

He couldn't pinpoint an exact time. "We were high school sweethearts who probably should've broken up when we went to different colleges. I should've realized after we took a 'break' during our junior year that we weren't meant for the long haul. But we got married anyway. She hated being away from her family when I was in the military, and that was pretty much all it took to end it for good."

"I still can't believe she walked away from your domestic skills." She gave him a playful smile. "But she knew what she signed up for when she married a military guy, so that's her bad, in my opinion."

He laughed. "I like your assessment. Honestly, I was relieved." He paused. "Wow, that makes me sound like a bit of an asshole, doesn't it?"

Her smile crept back. "No, I think I understand. How'd you find out about her getting married?"

He took another drink and leaned back against the stool. "Would you believe my stepmother is still close with my ex-mother-in-law?"

Her eyes rounded and one side of her mouth ticked up. "*No.* That's awful."

"It's bizarre, for sure. But Jess and I were together for more than ten years, off and on. I guess it's to be expected that they would be friends."

"I suppose. Still weird, though. Does your stepmother realize that?"

"I doubt it. She doesn't realize much." He pressed his lips together. "That's not fair. She's a good person; she just doesn't get too involved in my life. Which is fine."

"I don't know, being BFFs with your ex-mother-in-law seems pretty involved. At least in your former life." Sara sipped her lemon drop. "I'm firmly on your side for this one."

He shifted, unsure of how to respond. He was used to being alone, *liked* being alone. He decided he was over-thinking the hell out of an innocuous statement. He held up his beer. "I propose a toast. To forgetting about our lousy mornings."

"I'll drink to that."

They clinked glasses and dove into the food for a minute or two.

"You know," she said, "I'm getting kind of tired of lousy mornings. Since I went back to live at home, it's like this horrible weight of sadness just hangs over everything. I'm not sure how much more I can handle." She flicked a worried look at him, like maybe she was afraid she was sharing too much. She wasn't. He liked hearing her talk. About anything really, but especially to unburden herself. He sensed she didn't get much of an opportunity to do that right now.

"I didn't realize you'd moved back to Ribbon Ridge."

She nodded. "Not permanently, but for now, while I'm managing the project and to be there for my mom. I go to my condo once in a while, but only for a night here and there. I miss being on my own. Independence was the reason I moved away in the first place."

Dylan thought of his own need to get out of town. "I get you. I couldn't wait to get to U-Dub and then I enrolled in ROTC with the intent of joining the army and getting far away from Ribbon Ridge."

"Why?"

He shrugged. "Restless, I guess. When I went from spending weekdays at my mom's to spending them at my dad's in high school, it was a...weird adjustment."

"How?"

He thought of the awkwardness of intruding on his dad's family, invading their daily routine, which was precisely how it had felt. They loved him, welcomed him, but he was a piece of a different puzzle—one he wondered if he'd ever find. "My room was my dad's office. I slept on the sofa bed. I never really felt like I lived there, but it was important enough for me to go to West Valley High—for the football program—so I put up with it."

"That doesn't sound like fun," she said softly.

He inwardly cringed, wishing he hadn't shared so much. "Is it too late to ask for Vegas Rules again?"

She returned his smile. "Not at all. Guess that means it's your turn to ask me something."

Heat sparked in his groin as the first question popped into his head: *Will you let me make love to you again?* No way was he going to ask that. Since he'd over-shared, he decided to go for broke. "Why did Alex kill himself?"

Her hand flexed, her fingers tugging her sleeve up over her hand. She didn't immediately answer and Dylan worried he'd overstepped. Why had he asked such a personal question anyway? Because he felt comfortable with her—like they were friends. An apology formed on his lips when she said, "Actually, it's a bit of a mystery. None of us saw it coming."

She looked out at the pool tables where a few games had started up. "He was sick. He'd always been sick. He was the one born with the most problems. He was the smallest, stayed in the NICU the longest, suffered several infections, and had terrible respiratory issues that became chronic lung disease." Dylan vaguely remembered this from their reality show, which had detailed their miraculous conception—via fertility drugs—and birth. "He was oxygen dependent and apparently very depressed," Sara continued. "We all knew he was seeing a psychologist, but we didn't understand how bad off he really was. He tried taking antidepressants but suffered a reaction that caused a lung infection. Honestly, he hid the symptoms of his depression really well. Or we were all just too self-involved to notice." She wore a vague frown, almost akin to befuddlement, like she was going over in her mind how they all could've missed the clues.

"Can you talk to the psychologist?"

"She closed her practice and left Ribbon Ridge after he died. Anyway, it doesn't matter now, does it? He's gone and we can't bring him back." Her gaze connected with his for a brief second, but it was enough for him to suspect that she was done talking about this.

He felt bad for asking the question in the first place. She'd already said she was tired of bad days, and here he was dredging up her brother's suicide. Damn, he was really off his game with this one. "I think it's time for that game of pool. Have you played before?"

Her eyes took on an attentive luster. "Yes, but not in a long time."

"It's like riding a bike." He jumped down from his stool and went to select a couple of cues from the wall. He was mildly surprised when she joined him and immediately picked one up. "You know what you want?" he asked, not intending the innuendo, but enjoying the answering sparkle in her gaze.

She ran her palm along the length. God, was she doing that on purpose? He went half-hard and prayed she didn't notice. "Looks good to me." She strolled over to the closest pool table.

He chose a cue for himself, adjusting his jeans while his back was to her, then went back to the table. "Do you want to play eight ball? That's the simplest, and if it's been a while since you played, might be best."

She narrowed her eyes at him slightly. "Are you going easy on me because you feel sorry for me after the conversation we just had?"

He laughed. "Maybe. Should I stop?"

She was quiet a moment. "No, an easy game is for the best, I think."

He gathered the balls and racked them on the table. "Ladies first."

Sara positioned the cue ball and broke. She immediately sank the yellow number one ball. She glanced up at him. "Lucky break."

"Apparently. Do you know what to hit next?"

"I try to put all the solids into the pockets, if memory serves."

"That's right."

She moved around the table, bending to try a shot, but then standing up and moving. "This is harder than I remember." She leaned over again and took her shot, sending the blue ball skidding into a side pocket. Her gaze flickered surprise.

She moved to a new position on the opposite side of the table and took her time lining up for a shot. She hit the orange ball, but it didn't go in. She straightened, though her gaze still studied the table. "Your turn."

He touched her back lightly. "That was a great start."

"Thanks." She retreated to their table and sipped her drink while Dylan contemplated his shot.

He took the easiest angle first, dropping the ten ball in a corner pocket, then sank the fifteen and twelve in rapid succession. He glanced over at Sara, but she was watching the table intently. Should he miss his next shot? He didn't want to trounce her. He also didn't want to give her the game, both because he didn't think she'd want him to and because the competitor in him was alive and well.

He took his time eyeing his next shot, but finally put the nine ball in a side pocket. Sara stood near the table, her hand wrapped around the upper part of her cue, which rested on the floor. Her hip was cocked at a provocative angle that drew Dylan's eye to follow the curve of her thigh up to the sharp indentation of her trim waist and then farther up to the lacy camisole peeking out from the low V-neck of her green sweater.

"You going to play or gawk?" she asked.

He snapped his head up to find her eyes on him in a distinctly hot stare. There was a challenge and a promise in her gaze that nearly drove pool completely from his mind. Reluctantly, he forced himself to take his next shot, but just missed sinking the thirteen ball.

He walked back to their table and took a drink of beer. Sara was already taking her shot by the time he set his glass down. The number three ball slid into a corner pocket. She barely hesitated before sending the four ball into another pocket. Then she leaned down to shoot the five ball. She was shooting them *in order.* And doing a damned good job of it.

Before he knew it, she'd sunk five, six, and seven. Without looking at him first, she set her cue behind the eight ball and shot it mercilessly across the table, smacking the fourteen ball in the process. Nevertheless, the eight ball ricocheted off one side and rolled relentlessly into the opposite pocket.

"I'll be damned," he breathed. "You're a little better than you let on."

She looked at him sheepishly. "Sorry."

He narrowed his eyes playfully. "You lied."

"No, I took an advantage." Her cheeks turned a lovely shade of pink. "You shouldn't have gone easy on me."

He couldn't suppress a grin. "Tell me about it. And though you kicked my ass, I had fun watching you do it. Now it's revenge time. Again?"

Her gaze, alight with joy, found his. "Absolutely."

They played two more games. He won the next, and the last was a hard-fought battle that she managed to pull off.

They sat down to finish their drinks.

"How'd you get so good at pool?" Dylan asked.

She stroked the stem of her glass. "We have a pool table."

"I forgot." Now he remembered playing there a few times in high school.

"And brothers." She lifted her drink for a sip. "Though it's probably George's fault."

"George?"

"He's the bartender at the Arch and Vine. He and Dad have been friends for years and he's quite the pool hound. Played in a league for a long time until his back started bothering him too much."

A dark-haired woman in her thirties tentatively approached their table. "Excuse me, aren't you Sara Archer?" She shot an apologetic glance at Dylan before fixing her attention on Sara. "I don't mean to bother you, but I wanted to ask what's going on with the old monastery. I heard your family is renovating it into a hotel or something? Anyway, I hope I'm not being nosy, but I wanted to ask when it's going to open."

"Not for another year at least," Dylan said, eyeing Sara who seemed a little nervous. "How did you know she was Sara Archer?"

The woman blushed a pale pink. "I used to watch the show, and, well, the Archers are local celebrities, right? Anyway, a friend of a friend used Sara for a baby shower a year or so ago and raved about her." She looked at Sara. "I was wondering if you planned to do events at the monastery. It's such a pretty location."

Sara perked up. "Who's your friend of a friend?"

The woman moved closer to the table, her face lighting up. "Shelby Clark. I'm Jemma Rodriguez."

"Hi, Jemma, nice to meet you." Sara offered her hand and Jemma took it. "We will be offering events at the new facility. I'm not quite at liberty to say much right now, but if you give me your number, I'll be in touch when I can disclose more."

Jemma smiled broadly then dug into her purse. "Here's my card. I'm so happy I saw you sitting here and that I had the nerve to talk to you."

Sara blushed slightly. "I'm glad you did, too, thanks."

"I'll talk to you soon!" Jemma gave a little wave and walked away.

Sara turned and tucked the card into her purse hanging from the back of her chair.

"Does that happen often?" Dylan asked. "People recognizing you from the TV show?"

"It used to, not so much anymore."

"How was doing the show? Surreal?" Shoot, just because he would've found it odd didn't mean she did.

She rolled her eyes, pulling a grin from him. "God, yes. I was pretty uncomfortable. Not filming the show, but with the attention that came from it. We basically had no secrets, and that's hard as an adolescent girl."

He could well imagine how difficult it must have been, particularly for her. "How'd you guys end up on TV?"

"I'm not entirely sure, but it had something to do with an old friend of my parents. He thought our family was inspiring or something."

Dylan polished off his beer. He could go for another, but knew she'd hit her two-drink limit.

"I suppose we should go?" Her gaze connected with his in silent question. He couldn't tell if it was an invitation or an innocent query, like, "I'm up for more if you are." His body most definitely was, but no way was he tapping that again. Two nights could easily turn into three, and then things weren't simple anymore. Dylan preferred—no, he needed—simple, particularly given their work relationship.

"Tonight's Vegas Rules can't be like last time," he said.

She nodded sharply. "Of course not." She pulled her purse from the back of her chair and withdrew her wallet.

He waved at her to put it back. "I got this, remember?"

"I still have to pay for the first round from earlier."

"Actually, you don't. I got that too."

She pursed her lips. "You shouldn't have."

"If I'd known what an independent-minded woman you are, I never would've done it. You can buy next time—and I'll order a giant, expensive steak."

She laughed as she stood up from the table.

He jumped to his feet, grinning. The evening had been fun, casual—even with the undercurrent of attraction simmering between them. Shit, he'd just implied they should do it again. He wasn't sure he could endure another evening like this with her, knowing it was going to end with them apart. "I'll walk you to your car."

She preceded him and he struggled to keep his hand from touching her lower back. Outside, she walked toward her car, parked just a few spaces from his truck in the lot. He was surprised he hadn't noticed it when he'd arrived. She unlocked it with her remote and then turned to face him, her backside grazing her driver door. "Did you change your mind about meeting Hayden and Cameron?"

He wasn't in the mood to hook up with a stranger. Problem was, after spending time with Sara, he wanted to hook up. *With her.* Which he could *not* do. Damn, he needed to sever this attraction once and for all. Maybe he *should* meet them. "Yeah, I think I will."

"Oh." Hell, she sounded disappointed. "Tell my brother to behave."

"No sage advice for me?" He really needed to stop flirting with her. Like *now*.

"Something tells me you don't know how to behave."

"If you only knew how well I was behaving right now, you'd give me a medal." He stepped back before he succumbed to impulse and brushed his thumb over her lips and tasted her mouth. "But like you said, no fraternizing. See you, Sara."

Her blue eyes were dark and intense in the lamplight bathing them. "See you."

She turned and opened the door. With a final, heated glance she got into her car and started the engine. He didn't move until she pulled out of the spot and drove away.

Chapter Eight

AFTER SPENDING SATURDAY night and Sunday at her condo, Sara pulled into the dusty lot at the monastery for Monday morning's meeting. She was early on purpose so she could enjoy a few minutes of solitude. Alex had chosen such a beautiful place—she could almost feel his presence.

However, her plan was foiled as Tori drove in and parked beside her. "Hey," she said, climbing out of the gold Prius their parents kept for when their children visited from out of town. "Where were you yesterday?"

"At home—Mom knew where I was."

"Alone?" Tori's question dripped with insinuation. "Or did you take Dylan back to your place?" Her accompanying wink said she was kidding, but Sara nearly choked considering she'd actually done that not too long ago.

"Yep, that's me. Picking guys up in bars and taking them home." She fought the urge to giggle. Tori would be shocked, and it was almost worth spilling the beans in order to see her reaction.

Except Sara hadn't taken him home. He'd gone out with his brother and Hayden and probably gone home with someone else. She'd moped about it all day yesterday. Even yoga hadn't been able to keep her mind off wondering what might've happened if they hadn't agreed to keep things professional.

It was a silly fantasy. They *had* to keep things professional.

"When's the last time you went on a date, Sara?"

Tori's question drew her attention back to the present.

"What?"

"You know, a date? With a guy? Something romantic?"

"It's been a while. I've been focused on my business."

Tori started toward the trailer. "How's it going without you there?"

Sara walked beside her, slinging her purse over her shoulder. "All right. I miss being there, but I'm actually more into this project than I thought I would be."

"Really?" Tori smiled. "That's cool. I admit, it's different designing something so personal. I'm enjoying it, too." She paused just outside the trailer. "And hey, I get how hard it is to walk away from your life even if it's only a car drive away."

"Thanks, I appreciate that." Sara did miss her cute condo, but she had missed things about Ribbon Ridge—the small-town businesses, the country feel, her family. "How are things in San Francisco? It seems a crime for your condo to sit empty." Though her place was small, Tori had a prime piece of real estate.

"It's okay." Tori unlocked the door to the trailer as Hayden drove into the parking lot. He met them inside.

Six or seven years old, with slightly outdated décor, the office sported two desks, one small that was essentially for Dylan, and one large that Tori had commandeered for the most part, a kitchenette, a couch, and a sorry excuse for a bathroom.

Hayden set his case down on the couch and turned to Sara. "How was pool the other night, sis? I bet you creamed Dylan."

"Naturally. But didn't he tell you?"

"I haven't talked to him."

Dylan hadn't met up with them Saturday night? Warmth spread through her, but she reminded herself he still could've gone out. Maybe he'd tried to find them and failed. Why was she obsessing about this? Dylan Westcott was her employee, not her boyfriend.

The sound of wheels on gravel heralded the arrival of someone else. Sara gravitated toward the window and saw that it was Derek. He hurried over to the trailer and came inside. "Morning. Where's the coffee?"

Tori's mouth dropped open briefly. "Crap, I forgot to set the timer on the pot. I'll get it going."

"Addict," Hayden said.

Sara faced her siblings. "Before Dylan gets here, I wanted to run something by you guys. I was thinking about what to name the hotel and since it was Alex's vision…what do you think of calling it The Alex?"

Tori looked up from the coffee pot and blinked at Sara. Then her lips curved into a smile. "It's perfect."

"Yeah, it is," Derek said.

"Nice one, sis." Hayden patted her on the shoulder.

Sara basked in their approval for a moment—she didn't remember the last time she'd felt like that with them. Maybe never. "I wanted to call the wedding venue something separate—Ridgeview at The Alex."

"Also perfect," Derek said. "You've got a real knack for this. Maybe you should take over naming the beers."

Tori sucked in a breath and went back to making the coffee.

Hayden went to her and put his arm around her shoulders. "Hey, don't be sad. Life has to go on."

"I know, but sometimes it's just…hard."

Hayden wrapped her into a tight hug. "It's okay. We're all doing the best we can." He pulled away, his eyes alight. "As long as we're naming things, let's call the restaurant The Arch and Fox." Every Archer kid had an animal associated with them. It stemmed from Christmas ornaments Mom had given them over the years. Sara's was a kitten and Alex's had been a fox.

Derek nodded. "And we're on a roll."

The sound of another vehicle drew Sara to look out the window again, but it had to be Dylan. They weren't expecting anyone else. He got out of his truck and strode toward the trailer, the light breeze stirring his dark brown hair. He looked like a superhero's alter ego whose sculpted body was covered in nondescript clothing. As if his magnificence could be cloaked.

He came into the trailer and glanced around. "Am I late?"

"Nope, right on time," Tori said.

"Good. I was sure you'd said eight thirty." He flicked a glance at Sara. Was there heat in his gaze or was that her imagination? She tugged the sleeve of her jacket up over her hand and worked the edges.

"We were just naming the hotel," Derek said. He went on to tell Dylan what they'd discussed, then the meeting started in earnest as they reviewed the schedule.

They'd all taken seats around the trailer. Dylan sat behind the small desk that had been designated as his. "We're set to start demo on Wednesday. Any of you going to help out?"

Tori shook her head. "You have fun with that. I have to fly back to San Francisco to deal with some work issues for a few days. Leaving this afternoon. So sorry." Her crooked smile was anything but apologetic. "In fact, I should get going. I still need to pack."

"Convenient," Hayden said as she gathered her bag and went to the door. Tori waved a hand at him that might've had an extended middle finger as she left the trailer.

Dylan looked to Hayden. "Does that mean you'll be here?"

Hayden winced. "Actually, Derek and I have a meeting at Archer, but I'll try to stop by at some point."

Sitting next to Hayden on the sofa, Sara smacked him on the arm. "Also convenient." She turned to Dylan. "Can I help?"

Dylan cocked his head to the side. "I'm sure we can find something for you to do."

"Don't get in the way," Hayden said.

Sara threw him a glare. "Don't be a bossypants. I'm older than you." Not that age had ever stopped him from overprotecting her.

Derek stood up from a chair near the desk Tori had been sitting behind. "I'm older than both of you. Hayden, shut up. Let's go, we need to get to the office. We have a conference call in thirty."

Hayden exhaled. "Never a dull moment. See you guys." Derek preceded him from the trailer, but Hayden paused, his hand on the door. "Hey, this is the second time I'm leaving the two of you alone together. Do I need to be worried? Maybe have Dad polish his shotgun?" He threw Dylan a narrow-eyed stare that evaporated when he cracked a smile.

"Listen to Derek," Dylan said. "Shut up."

"Methinks the gentleman doth protest—"

Sara practically shoved him out the door and slammed it closed. She waited a moment before sneaking a look at Dylan, who was watching her intently.

"You didn't tell them…?"

"God, no. He's just being a stupid brother. You have those, don't you?"

"More than enough." He stood up behind the desk. "Were you serious about helping with demolition?"

"Sure, why not? Breaking things apart sounds kind of fun."

He grinned. "It is. Careful, Archer, a woman who likes to do construction is a bit of a turn-on for me."

And just like that her insides melted. Not good. "Oh, maybe I shouldn't come then."

He looked down and shook his head. "No, you should. I need to stop saying stuff like that. You're just too damn fun to flirt with, what can I say?" He cocked his head to the side. "I don't suppose you have a hard hat?"

His question thankfully jolted her from her own flirtatious thoughts. "Seriously?"

He chuckled. "Guess not. I'll get you outfitted. Just dress for work. Don't wear anything that can't be stained or ripped."

Ripped? Her mind reverted right back to its amorous bent as she imagined him ripping her clothes. Maybe working with him wasn't such a good idea. "Are you sure I won't be in the way?" Ugh, now it sounded like she was listening to Hayden.

"Absolutely not. When it comes to demolition, we can use all the extra hands we can get."

She worked really hard not to look at *his* hands. Or remember what they were capable of doing to her. "I have no idea what to do."

"I'll show you. Like you said, it's breaking things apart. I'm sure you can do that." His gray-green gaze raked over her, heating her from head to toe. "Despite your preference for pink, you don't strike me as terribly girly. You did, after all, kick my ass at pool."

"True." She smiled softly, really warming to the idea of letting out some physical aggression. "I can definitely break things. Just ask my brothers. Taking apart their Legos was one of my favorite childhood pastimes."

"Then you'll be a natural," he said. "We'll start at eight, but don't feel like you have to be here at the stroke of. You're not on the clock."

"Okay. Thanks for letting me help." And because she couldn't think of any other reason to procrastinate her departure, she went to the door. Pausing at the threshold, she looked back. "See you."

"See you," he said, sitting back down at his desk.

She closed the door and stalked back to her car.

Ugh!

He flirted with her. He stopped flirting with her. He gave her vibes that he wanted to repeat their one-night stand. He gave her vibes that he wanted to keep their relationship professional. What the hell?

Wednesday's demolition and the chance to release her frustrations couldn't come fast enough.

AFTER DITCHING HIS brother Saturday night, Dylan invited him over for dinner and to watch the Blazer game Tuesday evening. Cameron arrived with a bottle of pinot noir in hand and sniffed as soon as he stepped inside. "Did you cook?" he asked incredulously.

"Don't act so surprised," Dylan said, "I've been known to cook."

"Actually, I was surprised you didn't ask me to pick up a pizza."

It was true that Dylan typically resorted to take out, especially when he had guests, but for some reason he'd decided to cook. Maybe it was that conversation he'd had with Sara about successfully cooking. He'd been thinking about her an awful lot lately. He should probably knock it the hell off. It was bad enough that he kept flirting with her. He'd stepped over the line yesterday.

Dylan tuned from the door and led his brother down the hallway to the kitchen.

"Damn, that smells pretty good, Dylan. What did you make?"

Dylan crossed back to the stove and stirred the pot. "Chili. I hope it tastes as good as it smells."

Cameron set the wine bottle on the large granite-covered island. "I'm sure it will. I should've brought beer instead."

"I have beer. Help yourself."

"Don't mind if I do." Cameron went to the fridge. "I barely cook, but damn, I have kitchen envy." He traveled a lot for his job as a sales manager for a local winery, so he lived in a small townhome in "downtown" Ribbon Ridge.

"Great, then you can clean it later," Dylan cracked.

"Funny." Cameron popped the top off his beer. "You need another brewski?"

"Not yet." Dylan tasted the chili. Not bad. "We can eat whenever."

"No rush. Game's not for another twenty minutes or so." Cameron pivoted and looked at the TV in the living room, which was on with the volume at half. He went around the island and sat in one of the stools. "How's the project going?"

"Starting demo tomorrow."

"That's the best part."

Dylan pulled sour cream and cheese from the fridge. "Like you'd get your hands dirty." He went into the pantry and snagged a bag of tortilla strips.

"Look at you with all the fancy condiments," Cameron teased. "Has a woman been shopping for you? Sara Archer maybe?"

Dylan nearly dropped the bag as he crossed back to the island. He ripped the top off the package before setting it down. "Why would you say that?"

Cameron shrugged as he took a drink of his beer. "Because you hung out with her the other night. Or did she ditch you?"

Dylan considered lying. He didn't want anyone to know about their…what was it? Connection? Flirtation?

"Uh-oh, you're hesitating," Cameron said, leaning forward with interest. "What happened?"

"Nothing, we played pool. No big deal."

"Then why'd you think about it first? You weren't gonna tell me, were you?" Cameron grinned. "You didn't take her home, did you?"

"I did not." *That night.* "Like I said, it's no big deal. I wasn't hesitating. We played pool, ate some potato skins, and I walked her to her car. End of story." Minus the part where he'd gone home and dreamed about her.

Cameron sat back, looking a little disappointed. "That's too bad. She's cute."

"She's also my boss, so knock it off, Cupid."

"Fine, fine." Cameron took another swig of beer. "But dude, you seriously need to get back out there. Why didn't you come out with us the other night? I was worried you were maybe bummed out about Jess getting married."

Dylan took a couple of bowls from the cupboard and set them on the counter. "Bummed isn't the right word. Surprised, I guess." He grabbed a ladle from a drawer and spooned chili into the bowls. "Which is dumb because it's not like we're friends or anything. I haven't spoken to her since the divorce. It's weird that I never run into her in town."

"No, it's not. You barely do anything in Ribbon Ridge. Sometimes I wonder why you moved back here since you keep such a low profile."

"I do stuff. I went to the Ribbon Ridge Festival last summer."

"Yeah, I guess you did. But you work too much—on the job and here at your house."

Dylan arched a brow at him. "Yet you envy my kitchen, so clearly it's work well spent."

Cameron flashed a smile. "Smartass."

Dylan moved the chili-filled bowls to the island where he'd set out the condiments. "Sour cream?"

"Hit me—all of it. You have any olives?"

"On your chili?" Dylan shrugged. "I guess that could work. But no, I don't have any. See, I clearly don't have anyone shopping for me." He slapped the condiments on both bowls and slid one to his brother. He followed it with a large spoon.

"Looks good, bro," Cameron said. "You going to answer my question about getting back out there? And I'm not talking about picking a girl up here and there. You've mastered that. It's time you find something a little more permanent."

"You're really going to give me advice? The guy who picks up a new babe every time he travels, which is at least once a month."

Cameron stirred his chili, mixing in the sour cream. "I'm younger than you. I have time to sow my oats."

"Oh, I'm approaching middle age or something? I need to hurry up and get remarried before my testicles dry out?" Dylan blew on his steaming chili. "I may never get remarried, and that's fine."

"The hell it is. You deserve a family and some happiness." Cameron held up his spoon. "Don't argue with me. You think you're alone, but you're not. It's time you stopped acting like a loner."

Dylan shook his head. "You sound like my mother."

"Yeah, well, maybe she's right."

"God, please don't ever say that."

Cameron grinned. They tackled their chili for a minute before Cameron spoke again. "I just want you to be happy."

"I am," Dylan said. "I'm really pumped about this job." *And about how much I'll see Sara doing it.* Damn, if he wasn't careful, he was going to develop an obsession for his boss. Not cool.

"There's more to life than work."

Yes, there was. But the more Cameron talked about it, the more Dylan realized what a failure he was at relationships. The only people he saw on a regular basis and whose company he enjoyed were his employees and Cameron—and his other brothers when they were home. And his sister when she wasn't at school. But he even sucked at those relationships, because he rarely texted or e-mailed. He'd learned to keep his focus pretty narrow. There was far less disappointment that way.

Frustrated with the conversation, Dylan let his gaze drift to the TV. "Highlights." He grabbed the remote and jacked up the volume as Cameron turned his head. "Come on, we can move to the table."

Dylan picked up his bowl and beer and went to the table that sat between the kitchen and the living room.

Cameron joined him, shaking his head. "You are the master of deflection."

"And you're a nosy son of a bitch." Dylan finished his beer. "Grab me another IPA."

Cameron bowed. "Yes, sir." When he came back, he started talking about the game, evidently taking the hint that therapy time was over.

But his words stayed with Dylan, and at the back of his mind, he wondered if he really ought to look for something more.

Chapter Nine

ON WEDNESDAY MORNING, Sara dressed in a pair of old jeans and a T-shirt. After a quarter hour of footwear indecision, she'd finally opted for a pair of hiking boots. It was the one thing in her closet that most closely resembled the work boots Dylan had been wearing yesterday.

On her way to the monastery, she checked in with Craig, who'd begun to settle in a little better. It was the first conversation in which he hadn't asked her to do something. As was becoming usual, they barely talked about anything personal, just exchanging cursory "How are yous?" and "Fines."

She pulled into the monastery at eight thirty. The parking lot contained a half-dozen or so cars but not Dylan's truck. She wasn't on time, but was it possible he was late too? No, she was certain he'd be punctual. And sounds of activity carried on the breeze from the direction of the cottage, which sat a few hundred yards away down a dirt track.

Anxious to get over there, she dropped her purse and lunch into the office trailer and locked the door behind her before starting toward the cottage. The sounds of demolition grew louder with each step.

Dylan's work truck was parked at the end of the dirt track. Toolboxes were open and there was a flurry of activity visible through the open front door of the house.

Dylan came outside. "Sara, you're here."

"You doubted I'd come?"

"Nope, just glad to see you." Was he? Her stomach did a silly little flip. "Come with me, I have some stuff for you." He passed by her on the way to his truck.

Sara turned to follow him. "What sort of stuff?"

"Work stuff." He opened the passenger side door and withdrew something then turned around. "Work hat, gloves, and goggles."

She couldn't help but giggle. "They're pink. Even the goggles."

He held them out. "Of course."

She took the hard hat, which held the gloves and goggles in the bowl. "You just happened to have these lying around? I can't imagine you in a pink hat. Or gloves. Or goggles."

He gave her a mock horrified look. "I prefer something in mauve."

She laughed outright. "Do you even know what mauve is?" She'd overseen dozens of weddings and wished she had a dollar for every groom who hadn't the faintest idea what the wedding colors were. They were just "blue" or "purple" instead of cerulean or lavender.

He exhaled as he closed the door of his truck. "You caught me. I don't know mauve from puce. Is puce actually a color? If it is, it must be ugly because, well, just, *puce*. What kind of word is that?" His pale gray-green eyes twinkled in the morning light.

"I agree it's a gross-sounding word. And you're right, it's an ugly color. It's reddish brownish purple. It's actually the French word for *flea* and got its name from the bloodstains left by flea droppings on linen."

His jaw dropped. "That's disgusting."

"Completely."

He chuckled. "Why do you even know that?"

With a shrug, she extracted the gloves and goggles from the hat, then set the pink plastic bowl on her head. "Hopelessly addicted to Wikipedia and other sources of useless information."

Nodding, he led her toward the house. "Good to know. Next time I need to learn about bug dung, I'll know who to ask. Come on, I'll introduce you to the crew."

As he took her inside and introduced her to each worker, she was glad she'd come to help out. His guys were all so nice and so clearly happy to be here working. Warmth spread through her and she felt good about hiring them, even if it meant she was working closely with the guy she was trying to forget.

Forget? Fat chance of that, though she *was* trying.

His right-hand guy, Manny, grinned at her, his dark eyes twinkling. "I like how your hat and stuff matches your shirt."

Beneath her zippered heather gray hoodie, she was wearing a pink and white horizontal-striped shirt. "Actually, your boss got them for me."

Manny flicked a surprised look at Dylan. "Did he?"

Dylan gave him a look that might've held a hint of exasperation. Sara couldn't tell for sure. She needled him a little to see his reaction. "I wish he'd given me some pink boots, too. I doubt they make those in a sturdy enough variety, though."

Dylan's gaze dipped to her feet. "Actually, they do. You can buy them online. I'll send you the link."

She surveyed the men working. Already, things looked different. The kitchen, which had been closed off from the dining and living area, was starting to open up as the crew was hard at work demolishing the separating wall. She slipped on the goggles and tugged on her gloves, which fit perfectly. She snuck a look at Dylan's profile, surprised—and delighted—by his thoughtfulness. "Where do we start?"

"They've got things pretty well handled up here. I was actually going to start in the basement. Have you been down there?"

"Briefly." It contained a laundry facility and some storage space, which they'd use for, well, laundry and storage. "It's hard to tell how much space there'll be for storage since it's broken up into those weird rooms." Besides the laundry room, there were three distinct spaces that looked as if they'd been built out at various times without much thought. One of them was in an odd *L* shape.

"I already took some tools down there," Manny said.

"Thanks." Dylan held a hand out toward the kitchen, where the door to the basement was located. "After you, my lady in pink."

She flashed him a smile and walked into the kitchen. She stopped at the door. "You first. Last time I went down there, I walked into a spider web." She and Tori had spent a lot of time discussing the renovation and they'd had more than one meeting in the building.

"Manny's already been down there this morning."

"No thanks. Manny's not very tall. You first."

He laughed. "Coward."

This was going well. They *could* be friends. He wasn't being overtly flirtatious, and she was doing a good job not thinking about the way he kissed or the way the light gray T-shirt stretched taut over his shoulder blades.

She *had* been doing a good job.

He opened the door and preceded her down the stairs. To the left was the laundry room. Light spilled in from the high windows set into the foundation. To the right was the *L*-shaped room that curved back behind the stairs. It too was illuminated by windows. In front of them were two more rooms, both with a variety of storage features—a word that didn't quite do justice to the closets and ramshackle shelves that looked as though they might fall down.

He led her into the smaller of the two rooms. There weren't really walls—at least no sheetrock or plaster—just bare studs and boards, like they'd carved out this space from the larger room and hadn't finished it. Wood had been mounted between the studs to create a hodge-podge of shelves. Decades of paint, and jars, and boxes of knick-knacks sat here and there.

Dylan moved forward and plucked up two paint cans. "Let's start in here by clearing off these shelves. Just pile everything near the stairs and the guys will haul it up later."

She jumped in and they made short work of emptying the room. "Do we get to demolish something now? I didn't sign up to clean."

He chuckled. "Sure." He went to the landing area and came back with a sledgehammer. "Let's take out these shelves, then we'll do the walls. Have you ever swung one of these before?"

She shook her head as she picked up the sledgehammer. "Wow, this is a lot heavier than it looks."

"Awkward, too, especially if you raise it over your head."

"I'm not sure I can do that."

"No need to for these shelves. Here, let me show you." He came around behind her and put his hands over hers. The proximity of his chest behind her back sent a current of desire shooting through her. *Not good*. She wanted to ask if his physical assistance was really necessary, but didn't want to draw attention to her reaction. He'd given no indication that he had any lingering attraction. And she'd do well to bury hers for good.

"For the shelves, bring the hammer up to dislodge the wood." He guided her hands up, but the bottom shelf only buckled; it didn't come loose. "A little harder." He did most of the work, sending the sledgehammer into the wood. The wood came up then clanked to the floor.

"Nicely done."

She smiled over her shoulder at him. Mistake. He was far too close. And far too handsome.

She turned back around and eased away from him. "Let's do it again."

"All right, then." His tone carried a sheen of admiration. "You try the next one." The room contained probably two-dozen shelves.

Sara moved up to the next shelf and did as he'd showed her. It took three swings of the hammer, but she finally brought the plank of wood down, dancing back in anticipation of it falling to the floor.

He grinned. "Excellent work. I'll just be next door, if that's okay."

He was going to leave? Disappointment skipped over her—not because she needed his help, but because she was enjoying his company. But she didn't tell him so. "Yep."

He disappeared from the room, and she got back to work. By the time she'd finished half of the shelves, she was perspiring. She loved the feel of the hammer hitting the wood. The connection sent a tremor along her arms and up her spine that grounded her in space—something that helped with her regulation. It was fantastic sensory input. Maybe she ought to abandon event planning for construction.

She suffered a guilty pang as she realized she sort of *had* abandoned event planning. No, that wasn't fair. She was doing what she needed to do right now for her family. And for herself.

She set the hammer against the wall and shrugged out of her hoodie. Conveniently, a nail jutted from a stud near the door and she hung it there. The floor was a bit littered with wood and debris, so she took a few minutes to tidy up. When she went to the next bank of shelves she paused, noticing something odd behind it. It looked like there were hinges on one side.

Working efficiently now that she had the hang of it, she took out the four shelves in rapid succession. Yes, they were hinges. Her gaze moved to the other side, looking for a knob or something, but there was nothing. She scrutinized the wood from the ground up and saw a hook-type fastener holding the door closed. At least she assumed it was a door. A cool draft snaked over her. Definitely a door.

"Dylan, can you come here? I think I found something!"

The sound of his hammer halted and he joined her. "Everything all right?"

She pointed at her discovery. "Look, there's a door."

He moved beside her and lifted his hand to touch the fastener. "Should we open it or are you afraid of spiders?" His tone was teasing.

She smacked him in the bicep. "Open it."

His gaze sparkled with mirth. "You have an adventurous spirit despite your arachnophobia." He flicked the hook up and pushed on the wood. The hinges creaked as the door swung open. Cool, underground air rushed at them.

Though it was pitch black past the doorway, it was clearly a room or a tunnel. "Did you have any idea this was here?" she asked. "We didn't."

"No." He looked at her expectantly. "Should we take a look?"

Sara peered into the darkness. Curiosity pricked her neck, but was it wise to wander into some unknown place with Dylan of all people? "Yes." Wise or not, she was in.

"All right, then." He pulled a small flashlight from his pocket. "I always carry one of these on the job site. Never know when you have to peek into dark holes or investigate secret passages. Unfortunately, I don't have a pink one for you."

"It's fine. I have a light on my phone, plus you're totally going first anyway."

He cast her an amused glance. "Right, spider-web removal service. Ready?"

She nodded. He turned and moved into the darkness, his flashlight spreading a wide glow in front of him. She followed him, stepping over the wood threshold and finding soft dirt beneath her feet. The floor began to slope downward. "Is this leading us into some deep pit?"

"What, you mean like hell or something?" The soft timbre of his voice comforted her in the unknown.

"This is like an *X-Files* episode. Maybe it's just the flashlight."

He turned to look at her. "You watched that show?"

"We loved it when I was growing up. Spooky. Tori and I thought Fox was cute."

"Yeah, I was more interested in Scully. And the gross stuff. That one episode, 'Home' is so creepy."

She shuddered, clearly remembering that particular show, which had featured a grotesque family of inbred people. Their current exploration of a house out in the middle of relative nowhere bore an eerie similarity to the show's storyline that she didn't want to think about as she and Dylan descended into the abyss.

A mixture of apprehension and excitement bubbled in her chest. She hurried forward so that she was close to Dylan's back. Then she reached up to clasp his bicep. The contact of her fingers—even encased in gloves—against his thinly clad muscle nearly distracted her. "Are you sure this is safe?"

"Looks like it." He shone the light on the ceiling. "Packed dirt, and there are regular supports." Wooden two by fours went up the sides and met on the ceiling, providing primitive archways along the way.

Sara studied one of the beams and decided it was probably safe enough, especially if Dylan the construction guy said so. "If this falls in on us, I'm blaming you. And relying on you to dig us out."

"Deal." He grabbed her hand and continued downward along the tunnel. His touch surprised her, but she clasped her fingers around him eagerly.

While the basement had smelled a bit damp, in here it was positively dank. The tunnel seemed to reach a plateau. Then it veered sharply to the left. "Where do you suppose this leads?"

"Based on how this turns, I'm guessing we're headed toward the monks' quarters. You all right to keep going?"

"Yeah." Although the farther they got from the house—and an exit—the more her apprehension threatened to quell her excitement.

He squeezed her hand, which did a lot to bolster her courage. It also caused her to repeat to herself, *he's holding your hand for safety, do not read anything into it.*

The tunnel curved a few more times, this way and that. Each time, she slowed down and he didn't rush her.

"This had to have taken a lot of time and energy to build," he said. "Digging, hauling out dirt, hauling in the lumber for these supports."

Just then the tunnel opened into a room maybe forty feet by thirty feet. Racks lined the walls and there was an archway on the other side, presumably leading to another tunnel.

"Whoa." Dylan let go of her hand as he moved into the room. He went to one of the racks and studied it closely. "I can't say for sure, but these look large enough to hold a cask. I wonder if this was built as storage. The monks used to make wine and sell it."

Sara followed him cautiously, sorry that he'd let go of her hand. "I read that, but I thought they made it off-site."

Dylan shined his light around the cavernous space. "They must've stored it here."

"I'm surprised they couldn't find another location. Like you said, this took a lot of work to build."

His light landed on the other archway. "Should we find out where that leads?"

Her muscles had relaxed when they entered the room. She liked the larger space. But she also knew she had to go back into a tunnel to get out.

He turned and flashed his light at her midsection so that the light illuminated her. "You okay?" he asked. "You look a little pale."

"Sorry, sometimes tight spaces make me edgy. I'm good. Let's just hang here for a minute."

He stepped toward her, still wearing that worried expression. "We can go back. I can come exploring with one of the guys."

Not a chance. She wanted to share this adventure with him. Ugh, what was she doing? She had to stop thinking of him like that—in that way that made her stomach flip and her heart speed up.

He flashed his light around again in a slow arc. "You know, this would be a pretty cool underground pub or something."

She turned in a circle, her mind summoning a vision of what it might look like. "You're right. Something straight out of Hobbiton with a round door." She stopped to face him. "Could we do that? I mean, structurally and whatever?"

"Sure. I don't know when this was built, but I'm guessing it's been here for decades, at least." He walked toward one wall. "This could be the bar. And you could have maybe ten tables around. It wouldn't be a huge venue, but that would be part of the charm. And I bet we could install some skylights so it's not completely in the dark. Plus, we'd have to dig out an emergency exit. Actually, I'd recommend a separate entrance straight from here—your Hobbiton door." He flashed her a grin. Desire sparked in her gut. Did he know how sexy he looked? It wasn't fair. "We'll have to map it and see exactly what's above us." He sounded really excited about this. His gaze found hers, then he looked away. "If you hired us to build it, that is."

She almost said, "Of course we would," but she wasn't at liberty to make that decision on her own. She'd lobby the hell out of it though. "Write up a proposal."

"I'll do that." The excitement was gone from his tone.

She went to where he was testing the sturdiness of the wine rack. Again, she touched his arm and relished the delicious jolt the contact gave her. "Hey, it's not entirely up to me, but I'll sell this as your idea and your project, which it is, as far as I'm concerned."

He looked down at her, his gray-green eyes seeming luminescent in the near-darkness. "Thanks."

An electric charge leapt between them. She'd wanted to kiss him in the parking lot at the sports bar, but they'd wisely parted before things could go that way. This was another moment like that one. "I'm ready to keep going if you are. Through the other archway," she added hastily, lest he think she meant something else. *Sara, get over yourself. Of course he wouldn't think you meant something else.*

"You got it." He turned and led her toward the archway. As soon as they stepped through, the change was apparent. This tunnel had walls and some sort of lighting system, given the bulb hanging from the ceiling. "Looks like they spent a lot more time on this one."

"Yeah; that bulb can't possibly work though, can it?" she asked.

He flashed his light along the walls and ceiling. "I don't see how to turn it on." The electrical cord was exposed—it ran from the light bulb down the tunnel away from them. "Let's see where it leads, though my money's still on the monks' quarters."

"Which would be cool. People could come from the hotel to the pub."

He looked back over his shoulder. "And you can still use it as an underground passage system for transporting things from the restaurant kitchen to the wedding cottage if that's necessary."

Though it was dark, she could see his features perfectly, with plenty of help from her mind's eye. She'd thought of him far too much in recent days—his smile, his charm, his sense of humor…She was so busy fantasizing about him, she didn't notice the rock or whatever it was jutting up from the dirt. She tripped, her arms flailing. Her body launched forward and she closed her eyes for impact.

Chapter Ten

DYLAN HEARD HER cry out. He just barely spun around in time to catch her, but the force of her fall was enough to send him sprawling backward in the dirt. He dropped the flashlight and it rolled toward the wall, the light casting in the direction they'd been walking. She'd crashed on top of him.

He gripped her waist. "You all right?"

"Physically, yes. My pride is down for the count, however."

He loved her wit. He'd never met a woman more willing to laugh at herself or expose her flaws. Most women he knew kept their true selves buried beneath a coat of makeup and flirtatious behavior. But then he'd purposely picked up women who wouldn't expect anything from him. Is that what was keeping him from Sara? The fact that she would expect more from him than he could give?

Yes, but she was also keeping herself from him. They both had to admit they wanted each other. Even now, his cock was swelling against her. But who could blame him? Her hips were snuggled against his, and even his toolbelt wasn't providing a decent buffer.

Her hands were on the dirt on either side of his shoulders. This position, her on top, reminded him, erotically, of their night together. He itched to take off his gloves and slide his hands under her shirt, up her sides, and stroke her skin. Without thinking, his fingers dug lightly into her hips.

She ground against him. *Christ*, that felt good. Lights sparked behind his eyes as desire slammed into him.

But then she was moving off him, pushing up to her feet. She hadn't pushed down against him for sexual purposes. She'd done it to get the hell off him. He was such an ass.

He helped her find her footing as he got up himself. "You sure you're all right?" He tried to sound as though the entire interlude hadn't aroused him beyond belief and could only hope he pulled it off.

She bent and picked up the flashlight. "Yeah. I'm fine." Had her voice gone up an octave or were his ears playing tricks? "Here." She handed him the light.

Their fingers grazed each other and it was all he could do to keep from pulling her against him. They were alone in the dark with a ridiculous amount of sexual attraction sizzling between them. Only a saint could refuse that, and Dylan was no saint.

He also wasn't a prick and, for now, she wasn't encouraging anything. And damn, *she was his boss*. Why did he keep forgetting that? Because they'd become friends, damn it, and he liked her more than he'd ever liked any boss or commanding officer.

"Let's keep going. I want to get out of here." Because of what might happen? "The close space is getting to me a little."

Yeah, that. Damn, he really *was* an ass. "Let's keep moving." He resisted the urge to take her hand and turned to lead the way. He blew air from his nose and mouth and urged his body to stand the hell down. Maybe he could keep his mind out of the gutter if they talked about something that wouldn't make him want to rip her clothes off.

"Hold up a sec," she called, and he could tell she was a little ways back.

He turned to see her palms against the wall. It was like she was doing vertical pushups. "What are you doing?"

After she finished, she brushed her hands together to knock the dust from her gloves. "Wall pushes. Uh, it helps me regulate." She wasn't looking at him—her gaze was directed somewhere to his left.

He had no idea what she was talking about. Suddenly a thought hit him like a brick. "You aren't wearing long sleeves. No fidgeting. Your sensory disorder…does this have something to do with that?"

She nodded and looked to the side, looking a little embarrassed.

He didn't want her to feel that way. "Tell me about it."

Her gaze flickered with surprise, but she still didn't look directly at him. "I process sensory information differently. Sometimes I have a hard time regulating myself and I sort of get spun up. It's a bit like wanting to crawl out of your skin or just feeling overwhelmed in a particular situation. It can be auditory, like loud noises or a boisterous atmosphere. Or it can be a space thing—like these tunnels are bothering me a little. It can also be a touching thing. I sometimes touch people without thinking or realizing—that sort of tactile input regulates me."

He started to understand. "Like the sleeves. But what do you mean by 'regulated'?"

She shifted her feet. "People with normal processing can navigate most situations without thinking about it. Their bodies stay regulated with what's going on around them. It doesn't knock them off balance, for lack of a better description. I'm just wired differently so that I occasionally have to think about it. Like with the wall pushes."

That required an incredible amount of self-awareness. "Fascinating." She'd finally looked up and now her eyes narrowed slightly. "No, I mean it. This is interesting. Is this a common thing?" Just because he hadn't heard of it didn't mean it wasn't mainstream.

"Probably more than people realize. I mean, everyone's senses are wonky from time to time. Some people can't stand certain fabrics or tags in their clothes. Other people walk on their toes or sway when they're standing still. We all do little things we aren't even aware of to process our environments. For me, those processes can get messed up or can cause me to slow down. Like I said,

I'm pretty good at managing it now. It's been a long time since I've even talked about it to anyone." Her shoulders hunched and she looked self-conscious again.

He considered touching her, but after their lusty tumble decided it wasn't a good idea. "I'm glad you shared it with me. Sounds like you overcame a lot."

She shrugged. "I guess. I'm really lucky that my parents got me a lot of therapy when I was young. I know that helped." He looked at her in confusion and she added, "Occupational therapy, some speech therapy, other stuff."

"Your family really supports you." He was sure his family would've done the same—wouldn't they?

"That's why I came back for this project and to be here for my mom. Part of the regulation is having people—or a person—who provides a sort of tether. My mom has always regulated me. She's kind of my own personal metronome, if that makes sense." She edged forward. "I'm ready to keep going."

He turned and continued along the tunnel. "You moved away from home, so at some point you managed to regulate yourself, right?"

"Yes, that's part of why I left Ribbon Ridge. I wanted to prove to myself that I could be independent."

He glanced back at her in admiration. "You did that in spades, I'd say."

"Thanks. And I guess I wanted to prove it to my family, too."

He understood that. He'd spent his life proving to everyone that he didn't need his family, that he could be entirely self-sufficient. Damn, he hadn't ever thought of it in those terms before. "Your family is really important to you."

"We drive each other crazy sometimes, but yeah, they're the most important thing. It's why this whole enterprise—Alex's dying wish, this project—is so critical, at least to me."

The floor began to slope upward and he turned to say, "I think we're almost there."

"Thank goodness." Her voice was a mixture of relief and elation. She looked past him and pointed. "I see a door!"

He swung back around and rushed forward, flashing the light against the wood. This one was an actual door, unlike the slab of plywood they'd pushed open earlier. And it had a knob. He reached out and turned it, then frowned.

"Locked?" she asked. He nodded and she answered with a very construction-site-like curse.

"Never fear, I have tools."

She came to stand beside him and took the light. "I'll hold this." She flashed it at his belt and landed on the measuring tape. "Are you going to measure us through?"

"Very funny." He pulled a small screwdriver out and slid it into the doorknob. He jimmied it around and found the release. He turned the knob and the door popped open. He gave her what he was sure was an arrogant look.

She rolled her eyes. "Nicely done."

He pushed the door open. There was a wall directly opposite. He turned and looked for a light switch and then fell back as her body hurled against him.

She groaned into his neck, her warm breath tickling his flesh. "I can't believe I tripped again. I told you back at Sidewinders that I was clumsy."

His spine hit the wall as her breasts crushed to his chest. He wrapped his arms around her to steady her. "Yes, you did." He hadn't meant to sound seductive or flirtatious, but when her eyes found his, he knew that's exactly how he'd come off.

He gripped her hips, but this time he let his fingers stray under the hem of her shirt.

Her palms came down to his shoulders.

The moment stretched and he screamed at himself to push her away, to end this before it became something they'd agreed to avoid.

But then her fingers curled into his neck and drew his head down. He was absolutely powerless to resist. He hauled her more tightly against him, pulling her up. She tipped her head back and her hard hat fell to the floor. He crushed his mouth over hers. He'd meant to be gentle, soft, reverent. But he couldn't. He wanted her. Needed her.

Her mouth opened beneath his and her tongue stroked against his lips, but only for a moment before he opened and met her thrusts. The desire he'd felt in the tunnel exploded inside of him, burning hot and fast. He dug his fingers into her hips, pulling her tight against him and wishing he'd taken his goddamned tool belt off. And his gloves. Then he'd take her shirt off. Then her bra. Was she wearing something lacy and sexy, or had she opted for something more utilitarian for today's work?

He wanted to see her in everything. No, he wanted to see her in nothing at all.

Her fingers wound around his neck and tugged at the ends of his hair. She rotated her hips into him. Blood rushed to his cock. If he turned her, they could just…

With Herculean effort, he wrenched his mouth from hers. "Sorry." He barely heard himself over the roar of blood in his ears and the thundering of his heart.

She eased back from him, her breath coming hard and fast. "Um, where are we?"

Inhaling deeply, he worked to calm his pulse. He took the flashlight from her and pointed it at the wall, finding a switch maybe three feet from the door. He flicked it, but there was no illumination forthcoming.

She bent and picked up her hat. He averted his gaze from the tempting curve of her ass and busied himself with shining the light down the corridor. With another deep breath, he started along it, his body cooling with each step.

The hall ended at a door, which opened into a small office. "We're in the monks' quarters. I was in here last week," he said.

"Really?"

He nodded. "I didn't look behind every door, just checked it out. I assumed this was a closet, not a secret entrance."

"It's pretty cool, isn't it?"

His gaze fell on her. Her eyes were alight, her blonde hair pale beneath the hot pink of her hard hat. She was so beautiful. And so off-limits.

She surveyed the office. "Should we look around some more, or did we solve the mystery?"

They'd been gone awhile and since Dylan was the boss, he supposed he should go back. More importantly, however, he needed to get away from her. Working closely together was bad enough, but traipsing around in darkened secret passages was inviting disaster. He regretted the excursion. And while he was regretting stuff, why the hell had he bought her special pink accessories? He'd gone into the home improvement store, seen a display of everything in hot pink, and immediately thought of her. They'd been too perfect *not* to buy, but he shouldn't have done it. He needed to insert some professional space, *pronto*. "Mystery solved. Let's get back." In fact, they should avoid the dark passages altogether. "Come on, we'll go this way." He strode from the office toward the main entrance.

At the front door, she grabbed his hand. Need coursed through him. He moved away from her before he could do something stupid.

She cringed. "Sorry. I mean, I shouldn't have kissed you. It was totally my fault."

"No, it wasn't totally your fault, but we can't let it happen again. You're my boss…"

"Agreed." She looked at some point behind him, avoiding eye contact. "Besides that, the timing for me is terrible. I need to focus on this project and supporting my mom."

Like any of this mattered. Even if she weren't his boss and her family weren't dealing with a tragedy, Dylan would be keeping his distance. That didn't, however, mean he wasn't wound tight with sexual frustration. Maybe *he* should try a wall pushup. Realistically, he needed a cold shower or an intimate meeting with his right hand. Better yet, he needed to get his game back—the sooner the better.

He opened the door and walked out into the sunshine, which was overly bright. He pulled his hat forward to shield his eyes.

She held her hand up to her forehead. "Yikes, sunglasses would be great right now."

"This way." He turned toward the dirt road that would take them back to the job site.

The silence between them grew into an awkward beast. He refused to battle it. They'd both agreed the kiss was wrong and that it couldn't happen again. End of story.

When the house came into sight, he quickened his pace. A few dozen yards away, the touch of her hand again drew him to stop. He swung around. "Sara, you have to stop touching me."

Her eyes widened. She dropped her hand. "I'm sorry. I didn't realize."

That her slightest touch drove him to distraction? That her scent, her laugh, her insanely soft, luscious lips made him crazy with want? He'd had enough. "You don't? We just talked about not kissing. That has to include touching too."

She looked away, her cheeks growing pink. "Like I said, sometimes I touch people without thinking."

Shit, because of her SPD, not because she wanted to jump him. He was a total asshole. "Sara, I'm just trying to find some boundaries here. I don't want things to be weird—and they're not." The hell they weren't.

Her gaze narrowed and locked with his. "They *are* weird. Worse than weird. Yes, that kiss was a major mistake, and you can bet it won't happen again," she snapped. "I thought we could be friends, but maybe that's too much to expect. Let's just keep this professional."

"Yeah, let's." He avoided looking at her chest, which was rising and falling quite rapidly with her irritation. The motion only made her breasts look even more tantalizing. He had to get a grip. *Real professional, Westcott.* "It might be best if you stayed away from the job site."

She crossed her arms, which also accentuated her breasts. *Damn it.* "Kind of impossible when I'm overseeing the project."

"You don't have to be here every day. I'll send daily updates if that will help." Anything to get her off his turf.

She pulled on her arms, flexing her shoulders. More sensory input? "We have to find a way to make this work, or I don't see how I can recommend you for the other phases."

He sucked in a breath. "Is that a threat?"

She shook her head vehemently. "No, of course not. I'm just trying to be realistic."

"You'd cost me a job—and more importantly, you'd cost my men jobs—because we had a one-night stand?" He'd been frustrated before, angry even. Now, he was furious. "That's hardly fair, particularly since you're the one who insisted it was one and done."

Her eyes widened then settled into a glare that threatened to set his shirt on fire. "Life isn't fair. I don't owe you anything."

"You're damned right you don't." Hayden came up behind Dylan, startling him. Dylan turned, his heart slamming against his ribs as he wondered how much of their conversation Hayden had heard. Given the glower he was leveling at Dylan, he surmised it was far too much.

"WHERE THE HELL have you been?" Hayden's angry question was directed at Dylan, but his gaze strayed to Sara.

She hadn't even seen her brother approaching. She'd been too focused on Dylan and their argument. Even though she was pissed as hell at him right now, she couldn't stop thinking of the feel of his fingers digging into her hips or the ache that was still radiating from her core. But she had to stop thinking of it. This wasn't some lovers' spat. This was two people trying to disconnect themselves from a mistake. Something inside of her crumpled. She could relegate that night to a lot of categories, but mistake just wasn't one of them.

"We found an underground passageway to the monks' quarters," Dylan said coolly. He checked his watch. "We were only gone about forty-five minutes."

Hayden put his hands on his waist, his fingers dipping into the tops of the pockets of his jeans. "You were supposed to be in the basement. We couldn't find you. And you weren't answering your phone."

Dylan pulled his phone from his pocket and frowned. "I didn't hear it."

"There wasn't any service down there." Sara might be angry with Dylan, but it was between them and had nothing to do with his job performance. She would never let their one-night stand—and its fallout—come between him and his career goals, regardless of what she'd said in the heat of the moment. "Did you even look for us in the basement? If you had, you would've seen the door leading to the tunnel."

Hayden looked between them, confused. "Of course I went down there. What door?"

Dylan glanced over at her. "I think it closed behind us. Those kind of hinges don't like to stay open."

And the way it blended in with the rest of the wall, it would be easy to miss. "Well, we're here now and everything's fine." She gave Hayden an authoritative stare.

"You should've let someone know," Hayden said, dropping his hands to his sides. "It's not cool for the contractor to disappear from his job site for such an extended period. And with one of his bosses."

Dylan's eyes were icy as he surveyed Hayden. "It won't happen again."

Just when Sara thought the situation had been defused, Hayden turned on Dylan and glared at him again. "What were you thinking letting Sara participate in demolition and dragging her on some subterranean excursion in the first place?"

Hayden's tone bit into Sara's nerves. She especially detested his talking about her like she wasn't there and as if she were a child. She grabbed his arm and pulled him to look at her. "I *wanted* to do the demolition. You heard me say so."

"I didn't think you were serious." Hayden's fierce gaze lightened slightly as it transferred to her. "It's dangerous."

"Dylan brought me a hard hat." She pointed to her head. "See?"

"That's not enough." Hayden put his hands on his hips. The breeze ruffled his light brown hair. "You shouldn't be in an environment like this."

"What makes you the judge of what she should and shouldn't do?" Dylan moved closer to Sara. "She's a grown woman. If she wants to tear apart drywall and explore secret passageways, that's her prerogative."

Apparently Dylan wasn't so mad at her. Or maybe it was like the family rule: "I can be mad at you, but no one else can be." Which was ridiculous. Dylan wasn't even close to being her family.

She appreciated Dylan's support, but she could stand up for herself. "Dylan's right. Back off, Hayden."

Hayden's lips pressed together, but he didn't say anything.

Sara turned to Dylan. "I'll take it from here. Thanks for the…adventure."

His gaze met hers, and she had a suspicion their conversation, argument, foreplay—whatever it was—wasn't over. Even though they'd both probably intended it to be.

With a final look at Hayden, Dylan stalked into the house.

Hayden watched Dylan walk away, but some of the heat had left his gaze, as well as some of the tension from his body.

Sara punched Hayden lightly in the arm. "Someday, I hope you and Tori and everyone else will stop smothering me. I'm a grown woman. If I want to do something 'dangerous'—though this wasn't—it's my choice. And don't tell me I don't understand the risks. I do. You guys don't understand *me*. I'm not a little girl you need to protect anymore."

He looked at her intently. "You're my sister. I'll always feel the need to protect you."

She moved toward the doorway and he fell into step beside her. "I appreciate that. But there's being a great brother and there's being a meddling jerk."

"Harsh. Do you really think I was being a jerk?"

"You talked to Dylan like he was ten, and in the process referred to me as if I were a similar age and quite helpless or stupid. Yeah, I'd call that being a jerk."

"Yikes." He snagged her elbow and drew her to stop. "Do we do that a lot? Me and the others?"

"Yes."

He exhaled and gave her a sheepish look. "We only ever wanted to make things easier for you, to make sure you're safe and secure. At least, that's all I ever wanted."

His sincerity soothed her irritation. "I know, and I appreciate it. But you guys don't understand that some things will never be easy for me, at least not as easy as they are for you or Tori or Liam. And you know what? That's okay. *I'm* okay."

He put his arms around her for a fierce hug. "I'm sorry. I'll try not to be a jerk. And I'll try to make sure no one else acts like a jerk either. I love you, Sara."

She hugged him back. "I love you, too. You should apologize to Dylan." She probably should too. Again. He was right that she should maybe stay away from the job site—for both of their sakes.

"Yeah, I probably should."

A chime from Hayden's phone broke them apart. He pulled it from his pocket. "Shit. Mom wants me to come home ASAP."

Alarm shot through Sara, tightening her muscles. She wondered if Mom had texted her too. She pulled her phone from her back pocket just as it vibrated. It read: *Come home right away.*

She met Hayden's frown with one of her own and they took off down the dirt road. Her hoodie was still in the basement, but she didn't bother to go get it.

When they got to their cars in the lot, Hayden nodded toward her. "See you there."

After a frantic fifteen-minute drive home, Sara pulled in just after Hayden. They quickly parked their cars and jumped out.

She narrowly beat him to the door and rushed inside. She practically ran down the hall from the mudroom. "Mom? Is everything—"

She stopped short, her heart freezing for a moment at the sight of Kyle seated next to Mom at the island. "Kyle?"

Hayden came up beside her. "What the hell? Mom, are you okay?"

Mom smiled. "Perfectly, as you can see. Kyle's home. To stay."

Sara stared at him in disbelief. After all this time, without any advance notice, he'd just come home?

Hayden asked the question hovering at the edge of her tongue. "What sort of trouble brought you back?"

Chapter Eleven

HAYDEN'S SCORNFUL TONE dripped icicles about the room and froze Mom's smile. Sara rushed forward to touch her hand. "Mom, we're just surprised to see Kyle. You could've said something in your text." She threw Hayden an admonishing glance, which wasn't exactly fair. Kyle's return *was* shocking.

Hayden walked around the island to the smaller island on the other side of the kitchen, which housed the keg tap. He pulled a half-pint and took a long drink. "Listen, I'm sorry if this upsets you, Mom, but Kyle can't just march in here like he didn't abandon his responsibilities when he took off for sunnier climes and zero accountability."

"You could actually say that to me since I'm sitting right here," Kyle said. "You act like I left you in the lurch or something. So I didn't want the job Dad offered me; why does that make me the bad guy?"

Hayden glared at him. "Because he needed someone and you were available. And really, don't you think leaving a note on the kitchen counter and jumping on a plane smacks of running away?"

Kyle's jaw tightened and he looked away. Yeah, he'd run away all right. Sara only wished she knew why.

Hayden leaned his hip against the counter. "So why come back now? It's not like you give a damn about this project. You don't respond to any of the e-mails about it."

Sara almost wanted to join him in lambasting Kyle, but she felt Mom tense. Stroking her hand, Sara watched her warily.

"He's come back to participate, just like I knew he would," Mom said, pivoting to look at Hayden.

Kyle turned his stool toward him. "Alex wanted me to manage the restaurant. I changed my mind. I want to be involved from the beginning."

"Classic. Let's all wait around for Kyle to make up his mind." Hayden set his beer down on the granite counter with a loud clack. "Maybe if you read the e-mails, you'd know we're nowhere near breaking ground on the restaurant."

Kyle crossed his arms and cocked his head to the side, his blue-green eyes chilly. "I *do* read the e-mails, which is how I know Tori is getting ready to draft a design for the restaurant. I'd like to give input."

Hayden flicked a disbelieving glance at Sara. She was as surprised as him. Reaching for her sleeve, she remembered her hoodie was back at the job site. With Dylan. No, she couldn't think about him right now. "You really came back to participate?" she asked. "What about your precious job?" He'd claimed to have found his calling as a beach bartender, which none of them believed or understood. He was a brilliant chef, and concocting tropical drinks was a waste of his considerable talent.

"I left." His eyes narrowed. "Why is it so hard to accept that I decided I should come home?"

"Because you've never showed the slightest inclination." Hayden's pale blue eyes flashed. "Come on, something prompted you to come back. Did you run out of money? Get fired maybe?"

Both of those things had happened back when Kyle had been living in Portland. Which is what made his refusal of Dad's job offer all the more puzzling. Why turn that down and run off to Florida where he had to start over?

"Yes, Hayden, I burned through my entire trust fund." The sarcasm in his tone was razor sharp.

"Stop it." Mom's voice cut through the kitchen with the precision of a cold, steel blade. "I won't sit here and listen to you talk to each other this way. Kyle is home, and he's here to help."

"For how long?" Dad stepped into the kitchen and joined Hayden at the smaller island.

Hayden pulled a pint from the keg and set it on the counter in front of Dad. Then he circled around to the end of the counter.

"Indefinitely," Kyle answered, his gaze turning circumspect with Dad's arrival. Kyle had pissed off a lot of people in the family, but none more than Dad. And maybe Derek. They'd been the best of friends until Kyle had gone to Florida. Something had happened to completely tear their friendship apart—Derek said it was just that Kyle had chosen to run from accountability, but Sara knew it had to be more than that. Did Derek know he was back?

Dad snorted before taking a drink of his beer.

Mom stepped from her stool and angled herself toward Dad. "I'm glad he's home even if you aren't." They always argued about Kyle. Dad was unforgiving about him leaving four years ago, while Mom tried to understand her son's choice.

Dad shook his head dispassionately. "I told you not to buy him a ticket."

"You tell me a lot of things I choose to ignore. And that's my prerogative," Mom snapped, showing a fire she'd kept hidden beneath a layer of sadness since Alex's death. Tension swirled in the room, making Sara want to crawl out of her skin.

"Like seeing a shrink," Dad muttered.

Mom narrowed her eyes at him. "Yes, like seeing a shrink. You should try it."

Sara looked between her parents. What was going on here? She knew things were difficult around the house—the routine they'd had for years had imploded with Alex's suicide—but was it more than that?

Dad shook his head at his beer. "No, thanks."

Mom leaned forward on her stool, her body tight with emotion. "Rob, our son killed himself. You can't bury your head in the sand."

Tears built behind Sara's eyes, and her throat pinched. Her senses thrummed with the need to run or jump or swing—anything to release the tension. "Dad, maybe you could go to the counselor with Mom. I think it would help."

"It sure as hell wouldn't hurt," Kyle said gruffly, as though he was also fighting back some emotion.

Sara had almost forgotten he was there. She ran her fingers along the edge of the counter, pressing against the smooth ridge.

Dad looked down and curled his hand around the base of his pint glass emblazoned with the Archer logo. "Look at what therapy did for Alex." He raised his head and the look in his eyes chilled Sara to the bone. "Absolutely nothing. He killed himself in the end, didn't he?"

A darkness seemed to encompass the room. Everyone went completely still—no movement, no breathing, nothing but shock and emptiness. It felt like the day Alex had died.

Mom's hand went to her mouth. Then she turned and stalked from the kitchen.

"Brilliant move, Dad." Hayden swore violently and left, going toward the mudroom.

Sara wished Hayden hadn't left her alone with the two men she least wanted to spend time with. She looked between them. "You're both Class-A jackasses."

As she turned and walked from the kitchen, Kyle's voice followed her. "Hey, I'm not the one who provoked Mom!"

Maybe not, but his coming home had completely upset the apple cart. Hell, who was she kidding? The apple cart was in irreparable pieces at the bottom of a ravine.

She crossed the house to Mom and Dad's bedroom. The door was closed so she rapped softly. "Mom? It's me. Can I come in?"

She heard sniffing and a muffled response that might've been "yes." Taking that as a sufficient affirmative response, she slipped inside and shut the door behind her.

Mom and Dad's suite was huge—bedroom, sitting room, bathroom, his-and-hers closets. Sara turned to the left and saw Mom in the sitting room perched on the edge of her favorite chair, which was situated near the tall French doors that led to a veranda overlooking the rose garden. A long, cozy couch faced the fireplace. Sara had so many memories of snuggling up there for stories or even to sleep if she'd woken up in the middle of the night. More than anything, she recalled happier times of Mom and Dad sitting there together, their legs propped on the leather footstool where they would play footsie. The vision faded, slipping away like a distant memory. Her heart constricted.

Mom dabbed at her eyes and blew her nose. "Please don't be too hard on Kyle. I know you were upset that he left so suddenly and that he rarely came home to visit."

"So were you," Sara gently reminded, then wished she hadn't. Being right wasn't important here. Helping Mom feel better was.

"I was. I am. I still don't understand why he went." She looked up at Sara. "And yes, I admit I'm surprised he came back now, but I won't question it. Not when having my children around me is the only thing keeping me sane. I'm happy he's home."

And just like that, Sara's heart broke all over again and she wondered if the pieces would ever fit back together.

DYLAN'S FINGERS HOVERED over the laptop keys as he considered how to sign his e-mail to Sara. He'd detailed the demolition of the house, which they would finish today, and plans for removing the roof in order to add on the new second story. In the end, he just typed: "Your hoodie sweatshirt is in the office if you want to pick it up. Dylan." He hit SEND before he could overanalyze anything.

He felt bad about how their conversation had gone the other day, but it was for the best. They couldn't keep pawing after each other, not when neither one of them wanted anything more. A horny voice in the back of his head asked, *But if you both want the physical, why not do that?* And answered, *Because she's your boss, numbnuts.*

He pushed up from the desk just as his e-mail sounded. He sat back down and pulled it up. He ignored the shaft of disappointment when he saw it was from Tori, not Sara. He'd emailed Tori about the underground space and pitched the pub idea to her. He quickly read through her response, which was positive. She'd be back in town next week and asked if they could meet to discuss. Dylan typed in a response, feeling buoyed by the turn of events. Contracting the additional phases seemed closer than ever.

He shut his laptop and stood just as the door to the office swung open. Sara stepped inside and Dylan's body reacted instantly. She looked fresh and beautiful, dressed in skinny jeans and a light ivory sweater with ankle-high boots that made her legs look impossibly long. And sexy.

She glanced at him, but looked away quickly. "Hey, I came by to pick up my hoodie. I left it in the basement the other day."

"It's there." He pointed toward the coat rack to the left of the door. "I just sent you an e-mail."

She pulled the hoodie down and laid it over her arm. "Oh? How's everything going?"

"We're finishing up demo today, but we may have to knock off a little early with the storm coming in."

"Yeah, that's too bad."

The awkwardness of their stilted conversation was making him antsy. He wondered if this was what her sensory disorder felt like. "I'm going to meet with Tori next week about the underground space."

Her fingers stroked the hoodie. "You told her your idea?"

"Yes." Dylan frowned. He didn't want their interactions to be like this from now on. They'd been friends, hadn't they? "Listen, I want to apologize for the other day. I didn't mean to be a jerk. I hope we can go back to the way things were—coworkers and…friends."

She looked at him finally, but her gaze was guarded, skeptical. "Maybe not exactly the way things were."

The attraction. They couldn't go back to that. At least that's what he thought she meant. "I'll keep my hands to myself."

She nodded. "I'll do the same." Still, she didn't relax.

"Is there something else bothering you?" he asked. "I could be your friend, if you need one."

"Family stuff. I don't really want to talk about it."

Probably just as well she didn't want to discuss it. He wasn't exactly an expert in the family department.

Her phone rang—a chime that sounded like falling rain. She pulled it from her back pocket and glanced at the display before answering the call and putting the phone to her ear. "Hey, Craig."

Who was Craig? Dylan wasn't sure if he should wait or give her some privacy, but she was blocking the doorway, so he didn't have a choice but to stand there. Which he perversely realized was fine with him because he wanted to know who the hell Craig was.

"Can it wait? I'm a little tied up." She looked at the floor and toed her boot across a line in the linoleum. "Oh? Uh, okay. I'll be there in a few." She hit the display and stuffed the phone back into her pocket.

The call had sounded important, not anything flirty, which calmed the flash of jealousy he'd felt. Little worry lines streaked across her forehead.

"Everything all right?" he asked.

"I need to go meet with my assistant."

Assistant. He ignored the pulse of relief. "Is there a problem?"

"I'm not sure. He's been running things for me while I've been back in Ribbon Ridge. I thought he'd figured things out, but maybe not." There was a vulnerability lurking in her clear blue eyes, and he had the urge to hug her. "Thanks for bringing my hoodie up. See you later."

She turned and left. Dylan stopped himself before he could follow her and try to soothe whatever was causing her distress. That wasn't his job. They were tentative friends at this point.

What sort of family problems was she having? It could just be related to her brother's death. Dylan knew from losing fellow soldiers in combat that someone's death stayed with you, and he imagined it was exponentially harder when it was your immediate family. He couldn't imagine losing one of his siblings.

He scrubbed a hand over his face to banish the dark thoughts. Which left him dwelling on Sara, something else he needed to stop doing. He needed to get his head on straight—preferably without Sara Archer lodged in the dead center of it. Losing himself in a one-night-forget-fest sounded like an excellent cure for what was ailing him. And this time, he'd damn well go through with it.

After downing an energy drink from the fridge, he strode to the door and swung it open perhaps a little more forcefully than necessary. He stopped short at the top of the pair of steps and blinked. Kyle Archer was standing a few feet away. Dylan hadn't seen him in years, but they'd been on the football team together in high school and he hadn't changed that much.

Kyle smiled and raised a hand. "Hey, Dylan. Good to see you."

"Yeah, you, too." Dylan stepped down from the trailer. "I didn't know you were here." Was this why Sara was upset? Kyle had been AWOL for the renovation project. Maybe his return had caused an uproar at home.

"I came in a few days ago," Kyle said. "I wanted to check things out. Will you show me around?"

"Sure." Dylan walked from the trailer toward the dirt track.

Kyle fell into step beside him. "I was pretty stoked to hear they'd hired you for the gig."

"Just for the house," Dylan kept his tone even. "They haven't hired anyone for the next phases."

"Well, if it's up to me, I'd love to have you work on the restaurant. That's going to be my gig."

The way that the cottage was Sara's. "I'd be happy to do it."

"Yeah, I saw your proposal. I think they should've hired you outright."

Dylan shook his head and looked at him askance. "Too bad you weren't here when they decided."

"I take it they've shared their irritation with me." His voice had darkened.

Dylan shot him an inquisitive glance, not that Kyle could see it through Dylan's sunglasses. "Uh, no. Should they have?"

"They're all pissed at me for not being here." Which probably did explain Sara's mood. Now Dylan found himself annoyed with Kyle on her behalf. Kyle slowed. "The best part? Now I *am* here, and they're still pissed."

Yep, that explained it all right. "Cut them some slack. They're going through a rough time." He was speaking for Sara, but it was true for all of them.

"So am I. My brother died, too." He sounded defensive and sad.

"I don't think it's a contest."

Kyle stopped. "What the hell is that supposed to mean?"

Dylan wished he'd kept his mouth shut. "Nothing. I'm not a great confidant about this sort of thing. Family's not exactly my forte."

"Yeah, I remember. Sorry. You're right that it's a rough time." Kyle started walking again. "How is everyone? Your dad? Your brothers? Your stepmonster?"

Dylan chuckled. He hadn't called Angie that in years. "They're good. Cameron's working for a winery here. Sales. Luke's a vineyard manager down in Napa, and Jamie's working on his master's."

"Bunch of losers, just like I said they'd be. Looks like the army treated you well. I was sorry to hear about you and Jess. I really thought you guys were in it for the long haul."

"A lot of people did. But you remember her mom, right?"

Kyle winced. "How could I forget? She was the worst 'cheer mom' in town. Freaking nightmare." He shuddered. "Is that why you and Jess split? Her mom?"

"Partially." Jess was particularly close to her family, which had made her separation from them difficult. To Dylan, it had simply been another instance of him coming last in a family unit. Kyle had done a nice job deflecting the conversation. Two could play at that. "Why'd you leave Ribbon Ridge?"

Kyle threw Dylan an enigmatic look. "You wouldn't believe me if I told you. Anyway, it doesn't matter since I'm back now."

"I don't think your family feels that way. You said so yourself. If you're going to barge back into their lives, do it with a little finesse. And a lot of explanation." Damn, where had all that come from? He'd already chastised himself for failing to mind his own business. And yet, here he was sticking his nose in.

They'd reached the house. Kyle turned toward him. "Seems like you know quite a bit. I passed Sara on the road when I drove in. Did she say something?"

"No." But now Dylan wanted to ask her. "Forget I said anything. It's really none of my business."

Kyle studied him a minute longer. He let his shoulders relax. "I appreciate you caring, for what it's worth."

Caring about the Archers was something Dylan didn't have time for. He liked them, but his primary objective was to continue their business relationship. To that end, he'd do best to keep his trap shut. "Come inside and I'll show you around."

Chapter Twelve

THE DRIVE DOWN the hill from the monastery—rather, The Alex—could be nausea-inducing enough with its twists and turns. Throw in Craig's demand to see Sara immediately and her already unsettled insides thanks to family drama, and she was ready to hurl by the time she drove into Ribbon Ridge proper.

She parallel parked a block away from Books and Brew and stepped out of her Audi into the darkening day. Locking the car, she told herself that whatever Craig's crisis was, it couldn't eclipse the situation with her parents or Kyle's return. No, she could totally handle whatever Craig threw at her. In fact, it would probably do her good to have some major distraction.

Books and Brew was Ribbon Ridge's only bookstore. It carried every genre and hosted "Meet the Author Mondays" on the first Monday night of each month. The best part of Books and Brew was that the brew referred to beer as well as coffee. They'd arranged a deal with Archer to pour their beers, including a special variety only available there: a strawberry-infused ale called Artemis. It was Sara's favorite beer, if such a thing existed, and she idly wondered if—she glanced at her phone—eleven was too early to drink.

She saw Craig sitting at a table in front of the window, but he was staring at his iPad so he didn't see her approach. A pang of remorse stole over her. Over the past few months, their friendship had seemed to dwindle to the point that it was practically nothing. She wondered if he'd noticed because he hadn't said anything. Maybe they could catch up today.

She stepped into the shop, the bell on the door tinkling as it swung closed.

Craig looked up and offered a smile. "Hey, Sara."

"Hi." Sara hung her purse over the back of her chair and leaned down to hug him. "It's good to see you."

Was his answering hug a bit cool? She decided not to overanalyze and sat down.

"Do you want to get a tea or something?" Craig knew she didn't drink coffee.

"Sure, I'll go order something at the counter in a minute. I was surprised to get your call—that you'd come all the way out here."

He closed the flap over his iPad and set it on the table next to his coffee mug. "I was meeting with a client. That's what I wanted to talk to you about."

They'd taken on several new clients since she'd gone on leave, but none of them were in Ribbon Ridge to her knowledge. Something about his tone and the urgency of this meeting wound her insides into a coil of apprehension. "I'm not sure I'm following you."

Craig looked out at the street. The sun had fought through the clouds for a moment and illuminated the warm brown of his eyes and the highlights he wore in his dark brown hair. When he faced her, those familiar eyes were cool, unreadable. Sara grew even more concerned.

"I wanted to talk to you about the business. The way things are—"

She felt a moment's relief. "I know. It's not great and I really appreciate—"

He cut her off, but then she'd cut him off too. "Let me finish, 'K?"

She nodded in response, her anxiety ratcheting back up. She'd donned her favorite fidget item today—a leather bracelet she'd bought in Hawaii during college—and ran her fingers over the familiar ridges beneath the cover of the table.

He exhaled then folded his hands in his lap. "This arrangement isn't working for me. I'm doing all of the work and I'm still getting paid as your assistant."

She'd planned to give him a bonus. And she should've done it before now. "I was going to rectify that."

His brows arched. "A raise?"

Sara tensed the muscles in her arms. "Retroactive."

"That's a good start," he said. "But I also want coownership."

"What?" Sara couldn't help her reaction. It was like the floor had disintegrated. In fact, she grasped the edge of the table with both hands and squeezed.

"I know this is a shock, but I feel very strongly about it." He looked at her with concern, but his voice was edged with steel. It was a side of Craig she'd never seen before. Gone was the funny, effervescent guy she'd hired and become friends with. He was stoic, serious, borderline jerky now.

"Craig, this is *my* business." She could barely process what he was asking. She'd started the business to prove herself. It had defined her adult life. She didn't want to share it.

"It *was* your business. I've done a lot of work over the past two years."

Sara searched for words. It was like her brain was ten years old again and her senses were so overwhelmed that she simply couldn't think straight. She closed her eyes and focused on breathing for a moment. When she opened them, she saw Craig as she'd never seen him: cold, demanding, his arms crossed over his chest and his mouth pressed together so that his lips disappeared.

She took her hands from the table and clasped them in her lap, squeezing them together. "I'll come back full time. I can't share the business, but I'll give you a substantial raise and a bonus." Though she wasn't sure she wanted to work with him after this—could she even trust him? Never mind the project and supporting her family. Could she walk away from that right now?

Craig shook his head. "I'm not asking for that. I don't want that. The client today—I signed them on my own."

That answered the trust question. "How? Who is it?" If they were from Ribbon Ridge, Sara would at least know of them probably. Why would they sign with Craig instead of her?

"Jessica Westcott."

Dylan's ex-wife? Had she purposely gone to Craig because of…no, no one knew of Sara's hook-up with Dylan. Except Craig. She'd spilled the details to him the day after. "You didn't tell her anything, did you?"

Craig's eyes widened. "What?" Realization dawned and he leaned forward. "No, of course not. She called the business; I returned her call. I would never blab about your personal life." For the first time, she glimpsed her old friend.

Sara let relief flood into her muscles and sagged against the back of her chair. "So she's my client, not yours."

"No, *I* signed her. To Craig Warner Events."

Craig Warner *what*? "You can't do that."

His gaze was probably supposed to be caring, but in Sara's current frame of mind it came off as condescending. "Sara, you're completely wrapped up in your family—and rightly so. Now you can focus on them a hundred percent."

She ran her thumb and forefinger vigorously across the braided leather of her bracelet. "While you steal my business? Fat chance."

"I'm not stealing it. I'll buy it from you."

How generous. "It's not for sale."

"The clients are all loyal to me." He scooted forward and spoke in a sickeningly patronizing tone. "You abandoned them. They want me. They're ready to walk with me."

Sara couldn't believe this was happening. As if things weren't awful enough. "And here I was worried that our friendship was suffering because of me being here. Is that it? Are you mad at me?"

"I'm not that petty." He frowned. "I thought you'd be relieved after you got over the initial shock. I still think you might be." His tone turned coaxing. "Think about it, Sara, you can be here with your mom without worrying about anything."

"Except my livelihood. You're taking my *job*, Craig."

He sat back in his chair and fixed her with a sarcastic stare. "Right, like you need the money."

She'd been shocked the minute he'd asked for her business, but now, hearing him move so easily to spite, she wanted to punch him in the face. "So much for friendship." She reached back and pulled her purse from the chair. "You can't have my business, Craig. And I'll be talking to a lawyer about the clients you stole from me."

"Go ahead. I've already talked to Taylor, of course, and the clients that signed with me are mine free and clear. I'd prefer not to fight you for the others."

She'd almost forgotten his boyfriend was a lawyer. She'd only met Taylor a few times and had been put off by his cool, arrogant ambition and need for praise. "Did Taylor put you up to this?" She could absolutely see that happening.

"He was…encouraging. But this is my decision."

Sara wasn't sure she believed that. Yes, she'd been a lousy friend lately because of her Ribbon Ridge commitments, but Craig hadn't done any better. What was his excuse? The old Craig would've visited her, sent her funny texts, taken her and her mom for mani-pedis.

"You really know how to kick a girl when she's down, don't you? You couldn't have picked a better time to swoop in and snatch my hard work." She stood up and swung her purse over her shoulder, her anger rolling through her like a snowball building mass as it flew downhill. "Tell me, did you target me from the start? Hey, there's a rich girl with a trust fund and a fledgling business. Looks like a gold mine, especially if I can cozy up to her and be BFFs."

He paled slightly. "Don't say that."

She stopped just before she turned. "I'll say whatever I want. Like this: you're fired."

She strode from the coffee shop, her limbs shaking. She'd wanted a distraction. Now she had a full-fledged disturbance. To add on top of all of the other disturbances—her parents' fight, Kyle, Dylan.

She climbed into her car and stared into the distance as the rain began to fall, seeing nothing until Craig emerged from the shop. With a jolt, she started the engine and pulled away from the curb.

Thankfully no one was around when she arrived at home. She went straight to the circular office and called her top clients. The first three went straight to voicemail. As she waited for the fourth to ring, she paced the small space, her body thrumming with the need to move.

"Hello?"

"Amanda!" Relief slowed Sara's pulse and she sank into the chair at the built-in desk. She modulated her overexcited tone. "Hi, it's Sara Archer. I was calling to check on your wedding plans. How's it going with Craig?"

"Fine." Amanda sounded a little uncertain, but she had a very soft, vulnerable-sounding voice, so it may be that everything she said sounded that way. "He's been great."

Normally Sara would've been thrilled. But that had been before he'd turned into Stealy McThiefson. "That's good to hear. I'm not quite sure how to say this, Amanda, but Craig is no longer working for me. I'll be taking over." Sara suddenly realized she had no idea when Amanda's wedding was scheduled, where it was being held, or really anything other than she'd gotten engaged at Christmas.

"Ummm," Amanda sounded really uncertain now. "I don't know if that's going to work."

Sara could practically hear her frown through the phone. "It'll be fine."

"Craig just knows everything, and I really like him." While she didn't know Sara at all.

Anxiety curled Sara's nerves. "Talk to your parents. They'll tell you how capable I am." Capable? She just said she really liked Craig, which was hard not to do since he had a great sense of humor and a terrific eye for taking things from great to spectacular. "And I'm fun." *Really?* "I taught Craig everything he knows." *Better.*

"Oh, I'm sure you're great." There was a long pause during which Sara contemplated dropping on the floor and rolling around, a sensory-processing coping tactic she hadn't had to resort to in years. "Let me talk to my fiancé."

She considered telling Amanda that her contract was with Sara, not Craig, but decided that wouldn't help her cause. Plus, she really needed to talk to a lawyer about the specifics. "Thank you so much. I promise I'll work even harder—and better—than Craig."

"Can I ask what happened? I mean, Craig told me you were dealing with a death in the family—your brother, and I'm so sorry about that. He said you'd decided to let him take over the business."

He'd said what? Sara literally bit the inside of her cheek to keep from losing her composure. Her forced smile was brittle, and unnecessary since Amanda couldn't see her, but it helped her to keep her tone even. "Craig was mistaken. I'm not *letting* him do any such thing."

"I'll get back to you soon. Thanks."

"Thank *you.*"

Sara ended the call and leapt up from the chair. She did a few wall pushes and resumed pacing. Then she pulled up Aubrey Tallinger's number and called her. Unfortunately, she wasn't in. Sara left an overly detailed message and a request for her to call back as soon as possible.

She cradled her phone in her lap, worry eating at her insides. After a long moment, she spun the chair around and gasped at the sight of Kyle leaning against the doorframe.

His blond brows were pitched low and his head tipped to the side. "Everything okay?"

"Yeah, fine," she said tightly.

"Didn't sound like it. Did I hear you say something about your assistant stealing your business?"

"I don't want to talk about it. Especially to you." Sara knew she was lashing out at him, perhaps unfairly, but she was still angry with him and would be until he said or did something to make things right.

"I see." He uncrossed his arms and pushed away from the wall. "Actually, I don't see. You used to tell me everything. I'd like to be here for you."

Sara stared at him, then blinked once. Twice. He was seriously mental. "*Now* you want to be here for me? After years of *not* being here? You think you can just show up and act like things are exactly the way they were when you picked up and left?"

He huffed out a breath and took a step into the office. "No, not *exactly*. Look, I know you're still mad, but I wish you wouldn't be. My leaving had nothing to do with you."

So his pathetically short note had said. "That didn't stop it from affecting me, or didn't you think about that? No, I don't suppose you did, since I'm pretty sure your thoughts don't extend past yourself."

His eyes darkened. "That's not fair."

She leapt up from her chair and it rolled away from behind her. "No, it isn't fair. Your abandoning us— me—wasn't fair. But you know what? Maybe you were onto something. Here I've put everything on hold to help out our family, something you would never deign to do, and now I've lost the life that I built. Maybe if I'd taken your lead and turned my back on everyone, I'd still have my life."

His face flashed with surprise and he reached for her. "Sara."

She recoiled. Her fingers found the leather bracelet and traced the braiding. "Yeah, the more I think about it, the more I think I should've done what you did. What did you lose when you put yourself first? Nothing."

"Not true," he said quietly. "I think I lost you."

His words gutted her. "Yeah, you did." She pushed past him and saw Mom standing next to the island, her face pale and her eyes wide. Sara felt a pang of regret, but she was too wound up to do anything about it. She spun around and ran out of the house, uncaring that the heavens were raining sorrow down upon her.

AFTER PEELING OFF his wet clothes and refreshing himself in a hot shower, Dylan tramped barefoot down the hardwood stairs of his half-renovated farmhouse and padded to the kitchen. He normally didn't cut a workday short due to weather, but the torrential downpour had made pulling the roof off all but impossible.

On the other hand, quitting early gave him the opportunity to clean up and get started on his one-night-forget-fest sooner. He'd have a quick beer and head out.

As he went into the kitchen, his eye caught the boxes of pendant lights waiting to be installed. The weather was especially shitty. Maybe he ought to just stay in and work on finishing the kitchen.

Was he avoiding going out?

He pulled a beer from the fridge and went into the great room to check out sports highlights. As he popped the cap from the bottle, the doorbell chimed.

No one came up here unless they were invited—it wasn't exactly on the Girl Scout cookie sales route. Not that Girl Scouts would be selling cookies this time of year. He shouldn't know that, but his sister had sold cookies for years.

He set his beer on the coffee table and went down the narrow hallway, past the stairs, to the glass-paned door. What he saw on the other side of it took his breath away.

Sara was standing there, her blonde hair dripping water and her clothes plastered to her body.

"Jesus, Sara." He pulled her inside, closing the door behind her. He took her purse and dropped it on the floor. "Stay here."

He dashed upstairs and got a towel from his bathroom, but when he got back to the upstairs hallway, she was there.

He rushed over to her and wrapped the towel around her shoulders. He rubbed at her with the towel, trying—ineffectually he realized—to dry her clothes. "What happened? Why are you all wet?"

Her gaze was pale and fragile. "I...I couldn't decide whether to come in." She clearly hadn't been standing on the porch.

"Why did you come here?" What a stupid question when she was standing there soaking wet and freezing. "I want to hear what happened, but first you need a shower. Come on." No way was he taking her to the crappy bathroom he hadn't renovated in the middle of the hallway. He put his arm gently around her and guided her to his

bedroom. She looked around as he led her through to his bathroom.

"Wow." Her eyes moved from the double sinks set in polished stone to the massive oval soaking tub to the huge river-rock-floored walk-in shower with its plethora of knobs and faucets.

"Just toss your clothes into the bedroom and I'll dry them for you." He went into his closet and pulled out a robe his mom had given him for Christmas the year before last, but that he'd worn maybe twice. He just wasn't a robe guy. "You can wear this." He saw dust had collected on the collar. *Crap.* He swiped it with his hand. "Sorry, I'll clean it up while you're in the shower."

"No."

He stared at her. "No, what?"

"I don't need the robe."

"You can't stay in your clothes."

"No, I'm...I'm freezing." She peeled her sodden sweater off over her head. Underneath, she wore a camisole that stuck to her body with sexy, no-imagination-needed precision.

Dylan's mouth went dry.

Then she kicked off her shoes.

Okay, what was happening? He tried to focus, but damn, it was hard with her stripping in front of him. Right, she hadn't wanted his robe. "Do you want something else to wear?"

"May...maybe later?" Her voice was shaking with cold. She leaned down and pulled her socks off. Then her hands were on her jeans, peeling them down her legs.

He couldn't stand it anymore, even though he hated to disturb the energy coursing between them. "Whoa, what's going on here?"

"I need a shower." She looked up at him with expectation. The frailty she'd displayed earlier was nowhere to be seen. "I think you should take it with me."

And with that, he went fully and completely hard. And lost the ability to speak. And pretty much lost the ability to do anything but watch her kick her jeans to the side and shimmy out of her camisole. Clad in pink lacy underwear and a pink and white bra, she went over to the shower. "How does this thing work?"

He dragged his eyes from the tempting curve of her ass and blinked hard. "What?"

"The shower."

The shower. Right. He went to the shower and leaned in beside her. With a flick of his wrist, he turned on the main spigot.

"What about the others?" She was looking at the rain spigot on the ceiling and the other head on the opposite end of the shower.

He turned those on as well and adjusted the temperature. Though his cock was absolutely raging and he was pretty sure if he didn't at least jerk off he'd have blue balls for a week, he forced himself to say, "I'll wait for you downstairs."

"Why?" She turned toward him and put her hands behind her back. Her bra dropped to the floor. "I invited you to take a shower with me; don't you want to?"

God, more than he wanted anything in his life, but he didn't want to take advantage. Especially not when they'd agreed to a hands-off policy, and the last thing he needed was to further complicate their working relationship.

Her gaze dipped to his crotch and registered the proof of his arousal, which made it extra difficult for him to string words together. "We agreed to put this...attraction behind us, right?"

She stripped her underwear off and tossed them somewhere behind him. Her gaze raked him with lurid intent. "We did, but that doesn't seem very important to me right now. Is it to you?"

Not at all. He was probably going to regret this, but as she said, that didn't seem particularly relevant at present. He snatched her against his chest and kissed her hard, thrusting his tongue into her mouth. She clawed at his back, and he drove her into the steaming shower.

"Your clothes," she muttered into his mouth.

"I don't give a damn about my clothes."

Taking him literally, she ripped his shirt at the neck and tore it straight down his front. Christ, he was going to come without even doing what she asked.

She angled her head and kissed him wildly, spearing her tongue into his mouth.

He shrugged out of his torn shirt and frantically unbuttoned his jeans. Her fingers joined his and they both pulled the garment down his body. While he worked to free his legs, she looped her fingers inside of his boxer briefs and slid them down his thighs. Then she sank down onto the tiled bench and drew his cock into her hot mouth.

With one hand, she kneaded his hip, while she wrapped the other around the base of his shaft. Her mouth worked the tip, sucking and licking him into a mind-crushing haze of lust. Then her mouth closed over him, taking him deep into herself until he nudged the back of her throat. Her tongue and throat muscles worked magic, sucking him off with the sweetest perfection he'd ever experienced. With extreme effort, he just managed to hold off his orgasm.

He grasped her head and pulled her away. "You have to stop." He was breathing heavily, like he'd done sprints up and down his stairs. "I have to get a condom."

He dashed out of the shower and rummaged in a drawer. He slid the sheath on as quickly as his shaking fingers would work and went back to her. With a growl, he pulled her to her feet and set her beneath the overhead spigot. Hot water streamed over her lush body. She cast her head back slightly. Water sluiced over her face and down onto her breasts. He cupped them greedily before taking one nipple deep into his mouth and pinching the other firmly.

She gasped and held him to her breast, twisting her hands in his hair, urging him to suck and fondle her. Breathy gasps and moans rained down on his head, making him hotter than he'd ever been in his life. He couldn't get enough of her. And if he didn't do something about that right now, it was going to be too late.

Shit, he hadn't had sex in a shower since college. It had been slippery and awkward, and he'd nearly lost his dick in a freak accident.

But his shower had a seat. He swung around and sat down, pulling her with him. She understood what he intended and straddled his lap. He slid into her quickly and easily, both of them gasping when he buried himself to his balls.

She immediately lifted and then dropped again, impaling herself. Again, she gasped. He pulled her head down and kissed her. He wanted to devour her whole so that she was forever a part of him.

She clung to him, her fingers digging into his shoulders as she worked up and down on his shaft. He rose up with her, participating in the motion as much as the bench allowed. He was already thinking about how he'd make love to her in his bed later.

He cupped her ass, parting her cheeks slightly as she rose and fell on him. She ground against him with renewed fervor. He moved one hand around and fingered her clit. She shouted and cast her head back in ecstasy, curling her fingers into his shoulders hard enough that it should've hurt.

But he was too far gone. His orgasm rushed over him like the water crashing down on them from all sides. He held her hips and drove into her again and again until he was spent.

"Thank you." Her words crested over him like a caress, filling his heart and mind with their sweetness.

Then she climbed off of him. "Where are your towels?"

Chapter Thirteen

SARA TRIED TO sound nonchalant, but holy crap, what had she just done? She'd never behaved like that in her life. She didn't even know she *could* behave like that. Every educated part of her brain told her she should feel embarrassed, ashamed, but she couldn't find the emotions. All she felt was satisfied. To her very soul.

Dylan stood up from the bench. He was so amazingly gorgeous, especially wet. He looked like a magazine ad with ridiculous abs and the perfect ass, which she checked out completely.

"Why don't you clean up while I get the towels?" He moved past her and stepped out of the shower.

And such a gentleman. Especially after the way she'd just barged into his home and dragged him into the shower. Not that he'd been unwilling.

She washed her hair and body. Dylan had hung a fluffy beige towel on a hook outside the shower. There was no door, just an opening. She figured out how to turn off the water, then wrapped herself in the cozy towel. She was warm and safe. Happy, even.

Which she'd been a million miles from an hour ago. She hadn't come here with seduction on her mind. She'd come here because she'd been upset, and she couldn't think of anywhere else to go. Her condo was too far away, and Dylan's house was much closer. Plus *he* was in it.

She stepped out of the shower and toweled dry. Then she caught sight of his robe, which he'd cleaned up as promised. As soon as her foot left the bath mat, she sighed in delight as heat from the tile floor caressed her foot. With a contented sigh, she donned his robe and deposited her towel in a hamper in the corner. Inspection of his counter revealed a comb, which she used to untangle her hair. The mirror reflected a face flushed with the heat of a shower—and great sex—as well as a sultry little smile that surely didn't belong to her.

Who was this woman?

Dylan, dressed in athletic shorts and a T-shirt, peeked his head in the doorway. "Can I get you something to drink?"

"Wine?"

He smiled. "You got it. Make yourself at home."

He turned from the doorway and she followed him out into his bedroom. He left and went downstairs, but she remained and studied the room. The house was old, probably built in the twenties or thirties; however, the bathroom was straight off of HGTV with its state-of-the-art shower, gorgeous stone and tile work, and heated floor.

And his bedroom was just as luxurious. A king-sized bed with a massive headboard of what looked like repurposed wood. The bedding—shades of gray and blue—was lush and inviting, though it was haphazardly made, which caused her to smile.

There was enough space for a small seating area on the other side of the room, but it looked as though he hadn't bothered to finish decorating. She was surprised he'd done this much. Most guys would probably throw a Seahawks blanket over the bed and call it good. Or maybe she was just that out of the loop when it came to her experience with men.

She cringed. Probably the latter.

He came back in carrying a glass of red wine. "I hope pinot's okay."

"Perfect, thanks." She took the glass, careful not to touch him lest she jump on him again. Though she felt satisfied, she realized she wasn't necessarily *done*. She took a hearty, fortifying drink then went to the wide windows that looked out the front of the house over the valley. "Your view is as beautiful as the wedding cottage's."

"Especially when the sky isn't falling." He came up beside her, but kept a reasonable distance between them. She wished he'd move closer. "I'd like to build a deck out from this."

"That would be incredible." She pivoted and nearly sighed like an idiot at the beauty of his profile. "Speaking of incredible…"

He looked at her, his eyes unreadable. "Do we have to talk about it? Can we just let it be for now?"

She exhaled, relieved by his reaction. She'd totally overstepped and right now she just didn't want to think about it or discuss any repercussions. She spent too much of her life analyzing and worrying. One night of abandon sounded heavenly. "Absolutely."

She sipped her wine and they stared out at the storm for a few minutes. The silence wasn't awkward or strange. It was comfortable, pleasant, *right*. "I'd rather not go home just yet, if that's okay."

"You can't. Unless you want to wear my robe. Your clothes won't be ready for a couple hours. I had to wash them."

She grabbed his arm. "On cold, I hope. My sweater—"

He chuckled. "I told you before that I'm good at laundry. I've been doing my own since I was nine. Yes, they're in cold."

"You can't dry it though, so I'll have to borrow a sweatshirt or something."

"Let's have something to eat and then we'll figure it out." He peered at her, his gaze assessing. "That okay?"

"Perfect. What's for dinner?"

He gave her a half-smile. "I don't know yet. Let's check out the pantry, shall we?" He held his arm out for her to precede him from the room.

She went downstairs and then stepped aside so he could lead her to the kitchen. The entry hall went straight past the stairs to a back area that he'd completely renovated. Directly in front of her was a rustic farm table surrounded by a mish-mash of unmatched wooden chairs. To the right was a family room with a rich, brown leather couch pointed at a huge flat-screen. To the left was a mostly-remodeled kitchen that nearly made her jaw hit the floor. HGTV on steroids.

"You did this?" she asked, moving into the kitchen and smoothing her palm over the speckled, buttery beige granite.

"It's still a work in progress."

"Barely." She took in the huge stainless sink, the Subzero fridge, and the top-of-the-line gas cooktop beneath a hood that would make Kyle weep.

Kyle.

Damn, she didn't want to think about him or what she'd said. Or the fact that Mom had overheard it.

Dylan moved past her and opened the door to a generous pantry. "I don't have a ton of stuff, but I make some pretty mean meatballs. Do you eat pasta?"

"Love pasta. I don't suppose you have angel hair?"

He stuck his head out and grinned at her. "That's all I have, in fact."

She smiled back, absurdly pleased they had the identical taste in noodle shape.

"Have a seat at the bar while I get things going." He disappeared back into the pantry.

Sara turned and moved toward the massive island that separated the kitchen proper from the table. Four backless wooden stools, as rustic as the table, were tucked beneath the counter.

"Would you mind grabbing my beer? It's over on the coffee table."

Sara went into the great room and navigated around the couch to a low table. Issues of *Sports Illustrated* and *Rolling Stone* were stacked neatly on one side, and an architectural book about the Pacific Northwest sat on the other. She picked up his beer bottle and took it back to the bar.

He'd assembled a variety of ingredients on the counter and was now foraging in the enormous fridge.

"You designed this kitchen for a chef. I have a hard time believing you haven't become a world-class cook. Didn't you say you weren't always successful?"

"I thought it might inspire me to cook more."

"And has it?"

"Yes, but I'm still honing my skills." He turned from the fridge and tossed two paper-wrapped packages on the counter. He opened the first package to reveal ground meat of some kind. Italian sausage, she guessed. "You tell me how I'm coming along when you taste it."

Sara nodded. "Will do. What's the other package?"

He opened the second wrapping. "This is ground beef. I like to mix it with the sausage for a richer flavor." He shrugged. "I really have no idea what I'm talking about. Once, years ago, I had a little bit of ground beef and a little bit of Italian sausage and a hankering for meatballs.

So I mashed 'em up together and I've been doing it ever since."

"Then it must be pretty good."

He pulled some spices out of a cupboard and sprinkled them, seemingly at random, over the meat. "I've tweaked the recipe a bit, but I think I've got it down to a science."

She leaned forward to read the labels, but he stashed them away before she could see them. "What are you adding?"

"Trade secret, sweetheart," He winked at her and her insides melted.

She liked flirting with him. No, she *loved* flirting with him, especially when he flirted back. "Is there anything I can help with?"

He filled a large pot of water and put it on the stove to boil. "If you want salad, there's a bagged kit in the fridge. Sorry, my culinary adventures haven't extended to the vegetable realm yet."

She moved around the island to the fridge. "There's nothing wrong with a bagged salad. Fast, easy, usually fairly good for you." Wow, that sounded like a bad pickup line. She paused with her hand on the door. "That didn't come out right."

He laughed. "I like fast and easy. And the fairly good for you part is a bonus. Though I wouldn't call you easy and I sure as hell wouldn't characterize you as 'fairly' good."

Her blood heated at the compliment. She found the bag and closed the door. "Bowl?"

His hands occupied with forming meatballs, he indicated a cupboard with his foot. "Down here." He scooted over so she could get inside the door he'd indicated.

She squatted down and found a suitable bowl. At this level, her head came to just below his waist. She resisted the urge to reach out and touch him, but gave in to standing up slowly and grazing his thigh with her breast. "Sorry about that," she breathed.

"No, you're not." His voice sounded tight. "Temptress."

Oooh, she liked that. Moving around to the side of the island to prevent further temptation, she prepped the salad.

He'd finished with the meatballs and set them aside while he put the angel hair in the now-boiling water. "Kyle came by this morning after you left."

Her hand froze in midair as she was about to dump feta cheese on the salad. "He did?"

He dashed some salt into the pasta water. "Yeah, you didn't see him on your way out? He said he passed you on the road."

She hadn't noticed. She'd been too fixated on meeting with Craig. "I missed him somehow. What did he want?" She added the cheese and tossed in the rest of the items— some crunchy crouton-type things that weren't croutons, cranberries, and hazelnuts.

"Just to see the progress. He's pretty excited about the restaurant."

"He is?" She'd avoided him since Wednesday, which had been fairly easy since he was staying in the apartment over the garage instead of his old bedroom. Which was weird. Both she and Tori were in their old rooms, why wasn't he? Maybe Dad had told him to stay in the apartment—he'd been angry enough that she could imagine him saying that. Yuck, her muscles were starting to tighten just thinking about them.

"What's going on with him? He said you were all pissed at him."

If anyone else had asked, she would've shrugged the question off and changed the subject. Yet, she found herself wanting to talk to Dylan about it. He was such a good listener—whether she was talking about Alex or her SPD. Even her Mom had said he was great. "Pissed isn't the right word. Hurt or disappointed are more accurate."

"What happened?"

She took the bowl and packet of dressing to the table, intending to toss it when the pasta was ready. "He ran into some trouble or something—lost his job and his apartment in Portland. He came home for a bit, but when Dad offered him a job designing the menus and overseeing food operations for the brewpubs, he bolted to Florida."

His brow puckered. "That seems odd. He's a chef, right?"

"A really good one. What's even more odd is that he wasn't cooking there. He was bartending. And boating. And perfecting his tan." She didn't bother curbing her sarcastic tone.

"So he bailed...I guess I don't understand why that's a big deal."

She could see why he might think that, but there was so much more to what had happened. Why did family have to be so complicated? "Dad was really angry with him for turning down the job. It wasn't just a charity offer—he really needed someone in that role and Kyle refused. I think there might be more to it than that, but neither one of them has ever said. For me, it was more personal. When we were younger, Kyle was sort of my guardian. He looked out for me. While Mom regulated me from a sensory perspective, Kyle was sort of the number two guy in that respect. He kept me grounded, made sure I was okay. When he left, I felt betrayed that he didn't even talk to me about it. He just left a stupid note saying he'd come home soon. Which he didn't. I think he came home maybe three times in those four years."

"Ouch. Now I sort of want to kick his ass."

Sara suppressed a smile. "I don't know that anyone would stop you. In fact, we'd all probably help."

"You Archers are dangerous. I thought Hayden was going to punch me the other day, then you hit him in the arm. I might have to start wearing body armor."

She cringed. "I'm not really violent. Sometimes I react physically—without thinking." That was one of the things she hated most about her SPD.

He looked at her with understanding. "Let me guess, it's a sensory thing."

Wow, he really got it. "Yeah." She was so dumbfounded, she couldn't think of anything else to say.

He threw the meatballs into a pan and cooked them up, changing the subject to whether she followed the Blazers (she loved basketball), the Timbers (she liked soccer), and the Hops (baseball was not her favorite thing).

The conversation was easy and fast and definitely good for her.

When they were nearly finished eating Dylan asked, "How was your meeting with your assistant?"

Yet another topic that had wound her up. She finished her glass of wine—her second—and looked at the water sluicing down the outside of the sliding glass door.

"I shouldn't have asked." He must've read her expression. "Forget I brought it up."

Surprisingly, she didn't mind. Maybe it was the wine or maybe it was the comfort she felt being with and talking to him. "It's okay. He totally blindsided me—the douchebag is trying to steal my business."

He coughed, then reached for his beer to wash his food down. "Sorry, your use of 'douchebag' surprised me. What do you mean he's trying to steal your business?"

"He's been managing things while I've been here in Ribbon Ridge—helping Mom, working on The Alex."

"Right." He nodded before throwing back the rest of his beer.

"Because he's doing so much and has established such a close relationship with *my* clients," she didn't bother to hide her bitterness, "he apparently thinks he should own the entire thing. In fact, he's been signing new clients to *his* new business—Craig Warner Events—on the advice of his lawyer, aka his boyfriend."

Dylan's eyes narrowed as he set his empty bottle on the table. "Douchebag might not be a strong enough word."

"No, it's not. He's a total asshat."

"Better word, but I might go even dirtier." He gave her a somewhat diabolical grin. "That's how we ex-military types roll."

Again, she felt a smile coming on. How did he do that? She'd been wound up in knots when she'd arrived and now she was more relaxed than she'd been in ages. Well, since their last one-night stand anyway.

"Feel free to call him whatever you think he deserves." She pinched the stem of her wineglass and turned it on the table. "I don't know what I'll be able to do. I tried calling my best clients, but no one picked up. I suppose I should check my voicemail. Where's my purse?"

"In the hallway, but forget it. You're not worrying about that tonight." He stood up and bussed their dishes. "I need to take care of the laundry."

"No, tell me where it is and I'll do it."

He arched a brow at her. "I told you I was good at laundry."

She laughed. "And I believe you. But you've got your hands full with the dishes."

"Oh, I see how it is. You'd rather do laundry than clean the kitchen."

"Totally."

He pointed toward a doorway halfway down the wall of the great room. "There's a mud room through there.

Sara got up but paused to look at him. "Why'd you start doing your laundry as a nine-year-old? My brothers could barely pick out their own clothes at that age."

"Necessity because of the whole back and forth thing. I never seemed to be on anyone's laundry cycle." He shrugged. "It seemed more efficient to just learn to do it myself. It only takes a few too-small shirts and pink socks to figure out what not to do."

Though he spoke with humor, Sara felt a pang of sadness for the boy who'd had to fend for himself. He busied himself with the dishes, and she let the moment go.

The mudroom clearly hadn't been remodeled, though his washer and dryer were top-notch front-loaders with steam cleaning and drying. She could actually dry her sweater in his dryer. Cool.

She pulled her clothes from the washer and blushed when she found her underwear. It was one thing to jump all over a guy in his shower and another altogether to realize he'd washed your unmentionables. No sign of her bra, but then he'd bragged about his laundry prowess. She turned a full circle and sure enough, it was hanging on a peg on the wall near the corner. It was still pretty wet, but she didn't want to throw it in the dryer with her jeans so she left it where it was. It looked so odd, so *intimate* hanging in his outdated, somewhat Spartan mudroom.

When she returned to the kitchen, he was just finishing loading the dishwasher. "Your laundry room needs an overhaul," she said, eyeing her empty wineglass, which he'd left on the counter.

His brow arched playfully. "Hey, I don't know if you noticed, but I've been working pretty hard on the rest of the place." He shut the dishwasher and leaned back against the counter. "Can I get you more wine?"

She glanced at her glass. She'd already had two, but she still wasn't ready to go home. Her eyes met his. "Sure."

His gaze seemed to sizzle as he comprehended what that meant—which he had to know when he'd offered her a third glass of wine. He grabbed the open bottle, a great pinot from just up the road, and refilled her glass. "I think I'll join you." He got his own glass and poured out the rest of the bottle. He held up his glass. "To rainy nights."

Sara toasted him silently, her blood heating at the sultry look in his eyes.

He came around the bar and took her glass from her fingers. He set both on the counter behind him. Turning back toward her, he reached for her waist and pulled her forward. Then he situated her so that she was sandwiched between him and the island, which hit her lower back. Without a word and with an incredibly intense stare, he lifted his hands to the front of the robe. He slid his hands inside, parting the fluffy terrycloth, and cupped her breasts.

Sara planted her feet on the smooth, scraped hardwood as sensation rocked through her. His warm hands massaged her, his fingers finding her sensitive nipples and coaxing them into stiff, aching peaks. He pushed the robe back farther to expose her flesh. He bent his head and drew one breast into his mouth with a long, hard suck. She gasped, letting her head fall back. He gently bit her nipple, then licked and soothed it.

He lifted her and set her on the edge of the island. She locked her gaze with his, feeling his lustful stare like a searing caress. He parted her legs, the robe separating with the movement. He clasped her knees then slid his hands up her thighs, his thumbs stroking her as he went.

She had to taste him. She clasped his neck and drew him closer as her mouth crashed down over his. Their tongues met in a hot battle of need and passion. Desire arced out from her core. Then his thumbs were there, parting her most intimate flesh. He ripped his mouth from hers and gently pushed her back down on the island until her spine met the granite. His mouth came down on her hard, his tongue flicking her clit. Her orgasm was already right there, threatening to bear her away to some dark and distant place. And she was ready to go— desperate for release.

His fingers thrust inside of her, filling her. Her muscles clenched down as rapture broke over her. She cried out, her head cast back against the cool granite as he fucked her with his mouth and fingers.

Her orgasm was still flooding her senses when he pulled her up to a sitting position. "I want you upstairs," he said.

She nodded. At least she thought she did. She wasn't terribly certain what she was doing or if she was even capable of moving. Her entire body felt like it was made of wet noodles.

He leaned down to her ear and whispered, "Do I need to carry you?" He nipped her earlobe then suckled the flesh. His hand kneaded her hip through the plush robe.

She scooted from the edge of the counter and landed softly on the floor. Then she threw him a seductive stare, crooked her finger, and turned toward the stairs. She slipped the robe from her shoulders, giving him a view of her bare back.

He came up behind her and trailed his hand down her spine. At the base of the stairs, he gave her behind a playful swat. She turned and dropped the robe at her feet.

With a growl, he rushed forward. Sara laughed, a throaty, sexy sound that sounded as though it belonged to someone else, and tore up the stairs. He followed her, his feet slapping against the wood. She reached the threshold of his bedroom before his hands clasped her waist and he pressed up flush to her back. His cock nudged her backside—he must've tossed his clothes off on the way up.

He moved her forward into the room, his hands splaying up over her ribcage to cup the undersides of her breasts. His thumbs and forefingers drew on her nipples, pulling and pinching them hard enough to make her moan, but not to hurt. He steered her toward the bed and kissed her neck. "Can I do this from behind? Your back...it's so sexy."

It was hard to believe, but Sara had never had sex in that position. She felt suddenly shy and a bit embarrassed by her lack of experience.

"And your ass," he brought his hand down and traced a finger over one cheek then palmed the soft flesh, "also very sexy."

He pushed her hair to the side and kissed a path from the back of her neck to the base of her spine, pushing her over toward the bed as he traveled downward.

She fell forward, catching herself on her palms. "You'll have to tell me what to do." She sounded breathless. Lust pounded through her as if she hadn't just orgasmed downstairs.

He pushed her backside. "Kneel."

She scooted up on the bed, bringing her knees up.

"Keep going. Until you can grab the headboard."

She did as he instructed, moving completely up the bed until she could grasp the top of the carved wood.

"Yes, just like that." His voice was dark and rich. It slid over her like a delicious caress. "Part your legs." His hand grazed down the back of her thigh and then up the inside until his finger found her moist heat. He slipped his finger into her sheath and she closed her eyes in ecstasy. He spoke low next to her ear. "My cock will go in just like that." He nipped her neck and then tongued her flesh with hot, lush strokes. He thrust his finger in and out. "Just like that."

She moaned and clutched the headboard. Her hips moved in rhythm with his finger.

"Yes, Sara. Fuck my finger, just like you'll fuck my cock."

She could hardly believe the things he was saying to her, or the way it was driving her completely wild. She wanted more. "Put your cock in me."

He chuckled and bit her neck again. "Hold on." He left her for a moment and she saw him reaching for the bedside table drawer. He pulled out a condom and she heard the sounds of him tearing open the wrapper.

He moved quickly because his cock nudged her opening and then he eased inside of her. He went slowly—agonizingly so, but she appreciated his care. He held her hips until he was seated completely and she felt his thighs flush with the backs of hers. He ground against her, his groin pivoting, but he didn't thrust.

"Aren't you going to move?" she asked, desperate to feel his friction.

He cupped one of her breasts, pulling the nipple downward and giving it a little pinch. "Needy, aren't we?"

"Now you're just being mean."

"If you think for a second that this isn't as torturous for me as it is for you, you aren't paying attention."

"If it's torture, why do it?" She pushed back against him, mimicking his grinding movements.

"God, Sara, you're so…because it's wonderful, exquisite torture." He withdrew almost completely and slammed into her again.

She grabbed the headboard tightly and gasped. "Again."

He complied, pulling out until only the tip of his cock grazed her entrance and then he thrust forward, filling her until she cried out. "Again," she demanded.

Over and over he stroked, with rough, deliberate precision until she finally yelled, "Faster. Please."

"You're killing me." He tugged on her earlobe with his teeth and then kissed her jaw and neck, his mouth hot and open, his tongue fierce and possessive. All the while, he fucked her, his cock moving in and out with an ever-faster rhythm. The orgasm building inside of her made the others tonight pale in comparison. She felt like she was made of a million pieces that were barely held together and at any moment they were going to fly apart.

His hand skimmed down from her breast and found her clit. He pressed and she came hard, a kaleidoscope of light and color exploding behind her closed eyelids. Ecstasy claimed her and she succumbed completely. He continued to move, which only prolonged her orgasm. A moment later he cried out and pulsed into her one last time. His hand gripped her shoulder as his muscles clenched and she felt him go rigid behind her.

"Be right back," he murmured, leaving her.

Sara crumpled onto the bed and snuggled beneath the comforter and sheets. They were so soft. So inviting. She closed her eyes.

She heard him come back to the bed because a floorboard creaked nearby. "I hope you don't mind, but I'm staying the night."

"I never would've given you that third glass of wine if I hadn't expected it."

She opened one eye and looked up at him. "I know."

"I'll be back in a minute after I turn everything off." He leaned down and kissed her softly on the lips.

Sara sighed as he left and burrowed deeper into his bed. It had been ages since she'd felt so content, so…happy.

By the time he got back, she was trying not to doze off. He climbed in next to her and she snuggled back against his chest. His arm came around her waist and held her close.

"You look like you're almost asleep," he said. "I've never seen anyone nod off as fast as you."

She smiled but kept her eyes closed. "It's funny. I have a terrible time falling asleep usually. I almost always take melatonin—it's another part of sensory regulation. It's hard to go to sleep and hard to wake up." She yawned. "But with you, it's no trouble. Like you're magic."

He kissed her hair. "Glad I can help."

She started to drift off, but not before she heard him say, "Thank you." She wanted to ask why, but sleep claimed her before she could.

Chapter Fourteen

DYLAN WAS DOWNSTAIRS brewing coffee when Sara peeked her head in. Seeing him, she stepped into the eating nook and pivoted toward the kitchen. Her smile was tentative with a hint of sensuality. She wore his robe again, looking sexier than anyone had a right to be.

"Morning," she said. "I don't suppose you have any tea?"

Shit, no he didn't. His regret must've shown because she rushed to say, "It's okay."

"Not a coffee drinker?" He asked. She shook her head. "How about orange juice? And breakfast?"

"Sure, that would be great." She perched on one of the bar stools while he filled a glass.

Damn, the last time he'd had sex more than once with a woman—let alone three times in a twelve-hour period—had been his ex. It went completely against his post-divorce coda: keep everyone at arm's length because it's simple and neat. Why then had he been unable to resist Sara?

She looked at him over the edge of her glass after sipping her juice. "Do you regret last night?"

Why not confront the elephant staring them down? He admired—and appreciated—her for it.

If she was going to be direct, he owed her the same courtesy. "Not particularly. Or this morning, either." Sexytime the third had been a slow, seductive, wake-up call that still had his blood humming.

She set her glass down on the counter. "Good. So here's the thing. I know we said we shouldn't do…this. But I have to be honest. My life is pretty full of crap right now and hooking up with you—sorry, for lack of a better description—makes me happy. Is it wrong that I want to hold on to that?"

He wasn't sure where she was going with this, but his guard was firmly in place. Two-night stands were not his thing, but three-night stands had to be verboten. Especially with the dangerously alluring Sara Archer. But he understood that she wanted this, enjoyed this. He couldn't deny that he did too. "No, it's not wrong," he said slowly, judiciously.

She relaxed, her mouth inching up at the corner. "Then I'd like to propose we do this again. Just this—the physical thing. Well, and the friendship because you have to agree we're friends at least."

Yes, he did. Which was odd in itself. He didn't have woman friends. He did, however, have guy friends who enjoyed a "friends with benefits" scenario with some of *their* women friends. And one of them had recently parted ways with his "friend" quite badly. As expected, one of them—her—had developed deeper feelings and when they hadn't been reciprocated, it had all gone to hell. Dylan couldn't risk that, not with his job on the line.

"As much as I enjoy our trysts, I wouldn't want future hook-ups, to use your word, to affect my employment." She *had* intimated that an entanglement could affect his consideration for the future phases.

A spot of red bloomed in each of her cheeks. "It won't. I never should have said that the other day—about you not getting the other phases. I was upset. You get that, right?"

He did. He'd been worked up, too. But trust in a relationship was pretty hard for a guy who typically went it alone. On the other hand, he couldn't deny his crazy, seemingly insatiable attraction to her. Last night, all rational thought had completely vacated his mind, and he'd liked the sensation of losing himself in her.

She interrupted his thoughts. "What are you thinking about?"

He shook his head. "You. This. I'm still not sure."

She leaned forward, displaying her cleavage. "Anything I can do to persuade you?"

He couldn't suppress a smile at her brazen flirtation. "Lots of things. How do we know this won't end badly? I don't want to hurt you."

She sat back and crossed her arms. "You're assuming I'll fall for you and you'll have to crush my little feelings? Get over yourself. I'm the one proposing this, just like

I did back in January. If I get all clingy and weepy, you have full permission to pull out the 'I told you so' card. Deal?"

He opened his mouth to respond, but she held her hand up and cut him off. "No, please don't try to tell me what's best for me or make decisions for me. I get enough of that crap from my family. This is something I get to do. For me."

"Actually, I'd been about to agree. Far be it from me to try to manage your life," he murmured with a small smile before sipping his coffee. He set his mug down. "I have one caveat. This is strictly between us. I don't want anyone to know. Not your family. Not my crew. No one."

"I completely agree. The last thing I need is my family offering their opinions and advice on my love life. Er, sex life," she amended with a grin.

"Excellent. I can't think of anything worse than people knowing I'm boinking the boss."

"Boinking?" Her eyes sparkled with mirth. "Is that what we were doing, boinking?"

He came around the bar to be closer to her. She pivoted on her stool to face him. He lowered his voice. "Would you prefer I called it screwing? Or maybe I should go literary and call it 'making the two-backed beast.'"

Laughter burst from her mouth and she brought her hand up to cover her luscious, kissable lips. "Please don't. I'd rather you called it fucking. In fact, I don't care what you call it as long as we do it again soon."

He leaned down, bringing his lips a mere breath from hers. "Count on it."

She pressed her mouth to his for what should have been a chaste kiss with the absence of tongue, but which stirred him just the same. "I thought you were going to make breakfast."

He kept his lips against hers. "You distracted me with talk of fucking."

She put her hand on his chest and pushed on him until he stood upright. "Cook. Actually, I should probably get home. I disappeared last night and things were…not good." Her features shadowed and for the first time since their shower last night, he saw the return of her anxiety.

"Stay as long as you like. Really." He picked up his coffee and took a sip. "I was going to make bacon and eggs."

She glanced up at him. "Bacon?"

He rounded the island and went to the fridge. "Hard to say no to, isn't it?"

"Impossible. The situation at home will still be there. Unless Kyle's done what we're all expecting and left."

He put the eggs and bacon on the counter and shut the fridge. "Was he the source of last night's problem?"

"Somewhat. It was the stuff with my assistant and then he was home and I just…I just lost my cool. The worst part is that Mom overheard." She blanched and looked down at the counter. Her fingertips slid up and down the orange juice glass. "I told Kyle that maybe I should deal with my frustrations by doing what he did—leaving. I said I'd put my life on hold, with disastrous results given my assistant's takeover play, and that I should've just put myself first like he did."

Dylan pulled out a mixing bowl and started cracking eggs. "Ouch. What did he say?"

"What could he say? He left four years ago and didn't look back. It took Alex's suicide to bring him home. Who knows what actually precipitated his supposed permanent return?"

Dylan's conversation with Kyle rose in his mind. Kyle had been noncommittal, but Dylan had sensed there was something lurking under the surface. He didn't know if Kyle had come home for a reason other than the project or if there was something else entirely. "You don't think he's here to stay?"

She shrugged. "He says he is, but who knows what he really intends? He's worked really hard to stay away."

Dylan actually felt a little defensive for the guy. Maybe he had a good reason for leaving and staying away and for not sharing that reason. Dylan knew what it felt like to be the odd one out and to want to keep things to yourself, because in the end it was easier that way. "You don't think the death of his brother would be sufficient reason to come home for good?"

"Then why didn't he?" She crossed her arms. "He came home for the funeral, *went back to Florida*, and then came back for the revelation of the trust. Then he went *back* to Florida *again* for a few months. Why not just move home immediately?"

Dylan grabbed the milk from the fridge and splashed some into the eggs. "Maybe he had to resolve some things. It's not easy to pick up and move cross-country. I've done it when I was in the military and it takes some planning."

She narrowed her eyes at him. "Are you defending him?"

"Only playing devil's advocate. It's a bad habit." It had been the only way he'd dared to present his own opinions, which often differed from those of his stepfather—by pretending he was just offering an alternate point of view. He'd learned to keep his judgments to himself when it came to family. "You're perfectly entitled to your hurt and outrage," he'd been about to say, *and I told him to come clean with you the other day.* But stopped himself before he embroiled himself completely in their family drama. *Step back, man.*

She slouched on the stool. "Thanks. I have to admit being angry with him is exhausting. But I'm still not ready to forgive and forget. I do need to talk to Mom though." She scrunched her face up. "I feel really bad about that, actually. In fact, I'm going to get dressed while you cook, if that's okay."

"No sweat. I took your stuff out of the dryer and hung it in the laundry room."

She moved off the stool. "Thanks."

"You're welcome." He smiled at her as he pulled a whisk from the drawer. "It's all good. Breakfast will be waiting when you're ready."

She came around the island. He turned toward her. Slipping her hand up his chest and curling her fingers around his neck, she pulled him down for a quick kiss. With a smile, she turned and padded toward the laundry room.

Dylan watched her go and hoped their secret affair wouldn't backfire on them. So many things could mess it up, and in Dylan's experience one of them would. Some day.

He only hoped that was a long time from now.

SARA WISHED SHE could've spent all day or, really, all weekend, at Dylan's, but she needed to make sure Mom was okay. She felt terrible about storming out the night before after saying what she'd said and even worse that she hadn't taken the time last night to at least call Mom and apologize.

After a lingering kiss on Dylan's porch, she'd climbed into her car and glanced at her phone, which had several texts from various Archers and a voicemail from Aubrey Tallinger. Sara put her ear buds in and listened to Aubrey's message, which she'd left earlier that morning.

"Hey, Sara, it's Aubrey. Sorry I couldn't get back to you yesterday afternoon. I was tied up with a client. I know it's Saturday, but feel free to call my cell when you get a chance. Your message sounded like it was pretty important. Hope everything's okay! Bye."

Sara smiled. She liked Aubrey a lot. Hopefully she'd be able to help with Stealy McThiefson. Sara called her cell and scheduled a coffee date for that afternoon.

By the time Sara pulled her car into the garage, her nerves were on edge. She gave her bracelet several calming strokes and then went into the house, bracing herself for impact like a crash landing.

No one rushed her at the door. In fact, things were eerily quiet. She realized, sadly, her childhood home was like that a lot now.

Instead of heading for the kitchen, she turned down the main hall, which intersected the first floor and went toward the opposite wing, where Mom and Dad's bedroom suite was located. She passed the great room without encountering anyone and continued to the end of the gallery.

It wasn't early, but it wasn't the latest Mom had stayed in her room. When Sara reached the door, she took a sustaining breath and rapped somewhat loudly—the suite contained several rooms. "Mom?"

Silence. She rapped again.

Finally, "Come in."

Sara opened the door and closed it behind her. She went into the sitting room and saw Mom in her usual chair. She was dressed, her hair and makeup done. Maybe she'd already had breakfast and had gotten a good start to her day.

"How are you?" Sara asked, unsure how to begin.

Mom turned her head sharply and looked at her. "Please don't tiptoe around me anymore. I don't want that from anyone, least of all you."

No, she wouldn't. Mom had always expected Sara to work hard, to try, to fight to succeed, which hadn't always been easy, especially when she was younger. "I'm sorry, I shouldn't have left like that. You know I was mad at Kyle, not you? I don't regret coming home to be with you."

"I know you don't, sweetheart, and I know you were lashing out at your brother." She turned to look out toward the yard. "He's everyone's favorite punching bag right now."

Sara couldn't help but cringe at that description because she was right. Everyone was angry with him, yet he was here putting up with it. She expected he'd soon grow tired—or irritated—and leave. "He hasn't given us a reason *not* to treat him like that. He abandoned us, Mom."

"He didn't either." Mom sounded weary, but there was a bite to her response. "I realize *you* felt abandoned, and I'm sure he's sorry for that. He shouldn't have left without giving you an explanation. All of that said, he's entitled to make his own choices and we aren't required to like them."

Sara carefully perched on the edge of a second chair— Dad's chair—on the other side of the doors. "Are you saying you understand why he left? All this time I thought you were so disappointed that he went and that he rarely visited."

"No, I don't understand and I hope in time he'll share his reasons with me. And yes, I was disappointed in him, but if I've learned anything from Alex's death, it's that life is too short to wallow in such things." She gave Sara a pointed look.

Sara swallowed. Yes, life was too short. If something happened and she didn't resolve things with Kyle…she turned her head and looked out at the lawn. A hawk swooped low over the trees and then darted toward the horizon.

"I told Kyle the same thing," Mom said, drawing Sara to turn back toward her.

"Thanks."

Mom's gaze dipped over Sara's clothing, her brow furrowing. Yikes, she was wearing the same clothes as yesterday. She quickly stood before Mom could ask anything. "I stayed at my condo last night," she offered lamely. "But I rushed home to talk to you. I think I'll take a shower. Have you had breakfast?"

Mom nodded. "Kyle made me an omelet."

Kyle hadn't been cooking since he'd come home. Sara couldn't remember the last time he'd cooked for them. Maybe he really *was* trying. "I bet it was delicious."

Mom smiled. "It was. What are you up to today?"

Sara thought of her appointment that afternoon, but didn't want to burden Mom with the situation with Craig. "I'm having coffee with Aubrey Tallinger later. We have some things to discuss relative to the project—zoning variances." She rolled her eyes. "Very exciting."

Mom's eyes glistened as she looked up at Sara. "Your involvement in this project makes me so happy. Is it too much for me to hope that you'll stay in Ribbon Ridge permanently? The event space at The Alex could be a nice full-time job for you."

Yes, it could, and given the disaster that was her existing job, it might just have to be. But she'd worked so hard to prove herself, to be independent, to break away from everyone's expectations and assumptions. "I don't know. We'll see what happens." She leaned down and kissed her cheek. "See you later."

After doing yoga, showering, and keeping to her room to avoid her siblings, Sara left to meet Aubrey. Ribbon Ridge boasted several coffee shops and she'd purposely chosen something other than Books and Brew. She hoped Craig hadn't ruined the place for her permanently.

She walked into Stella's Café, ordered a pot of tea, and chose a cozy table near the back. She didn't want to sit up front where any number of people might be tempted to stop and chat. Ribbon Ridge was a small enough town that people often knew each other or at least found nearly everyone vaguely familiar.

A few minutes later, Aubrey walked in. She scanned the interior and upon seeing Sara, raised a hand. She went to the counter and placed an order then joined Sara at her table. "Hi there!"

"Hi, thanks for meeting with me on a Saturday," Sara said.

Aubrey hung her purse and jacket on the back of her chair. Yesterday's downpour had turned to intermittent showers today. "No problem. You sounded pretty upset." She sat down. "How can I help with this douchebag?" She flashed a smile that lit up her face. "To be clear, that was your word."

Sara laughed. "Yes, it was. Couldn't help myself. I hired him three years ago, and he's one of my closest friends. *Was* one of my closest friends. Apparently I was wrong."

"He's been overseeing things while you've been here?"

"Yes, I took a leave of absence, though I've been consulting with him as necessary." In retrospect, she should've given him a raise at the outset, but she'd been too focused on other things.

The server brought a tray with a teapot, cup, a variety of teas, and a selection of condiments. She turned to Aubrey. "What did you have?"

"A mocha."

The server nodded and left.

Aubrey set her elbow on the edge of the table. "Real quick, before I forget, I don't think we'll have any issue with the zoning variance on the property. It just takes time. I would guess it'll be zoned commercial before the wedding is scheduled in August."

Sara hadn't been fibbing when she'd told Mom they'd be talking about zoning variances. "Thanks, I'll pass that along to the others."

"Back to your issue. You had a verbal agreement or something in writing?"

"Nothing formal." Gah, Sara hadn't thought to put anything in writing. "I wasn't sure how long I'd be here, so we just kept in close touch." Which wasn't difficult given that they'd been friends. She selected a lemon ginger tea, ripped it open, and set the bag in her cup. "Is that a problem?"

"No, just gathering the facts. You said he's already consulted an attorney?"

Sara poured the steaming water into her cup. "His boyfriend."

"What's his name?" The server delivered Aubrey's mocha, decorated with a sun design in the foam. Aubrey smiled up at her. "Thanks."

"Taylor Sandridge."

"I'll get in touch with him. You don't have to talk to the douchebag anymore."

Sara was glad she didn't have to communicate with him, even in writing. "Thank you, that's a huge relief. I feel so betrayed."

"I can imagine." Aubrey picked up her mocha and blew on it before taking a sip. She set the cup back in her saucer. "You said he's stealing your clients. How?"

"A couple of ways. He's convinced the clients that I signed to stay with him in his new business. Plus, he's signed new clients since I've been here. Are those he's signed to his business contracted to him and not me?"

Aubrey frowned. "Unfortunately, yes. However, do you know how he obtained these clients?"

"Not specifically. Actually, he said that one called the business number and he signed her that way."

"So that person had the intent to speak with Sara Archer Celebrations—I looked you up—and ended up signing with your assistant?"

Sara added a bit of honey to her tea. "I believe so, yes. Does that mean he broke the law?"

"Not exactly." She pursed her lips in an expression of distaste. "It's certainly unethical, at least in my book."

It felt so good to have an ally. Actually, a second ally. Dylan had been pretty wonderful in his support. "Mine too, the jerk. What about the people who are contracted to me? He can't steal them, can he?"

"He can, but it would require those clients to breach their contracts. I doubt they'll do that. But you have to ask yourself if forcing them to choose is worth it. I mean, if they want Craig and will be unhappy if they have to come back to you to avoid breaking their contract, do you really want to generate that kind of ill will?"

"No." Sara's stomach knotted. None of the clients she'd left messages for yesterday had called back. Did that mean they preferred to stay with Craig? How would they feel if she forced them to use her or pay to break their contract? "I also don't want to roll over and let Craig take this away from me. I worked really hard to build this business. Yes, he helped and I probably couldn't have done so well so fast without him, but it's *mine*. *Sara Archer* Celebrations."

Aubrey's green gaze was kind. "I know, and you absolutely don't have to roll over. You also don't have to give him your business. You can still be Sara Archer Celebrations. He just won't be working for you and you may not have the same clients. But let me ask you something: do you want the business or do you just not want him to have it?"

"I want my business." Mom's suggestion burned in her brain. She *could* have a full-time business running events for The Alex. And that was also something she could build. "I have…options if he keeps the clients. But like I said, I don't want to roll over."

Aubrey's lips curved into a ruthless smile. "If Stealy McThiefson—also your phrase—wants your business, he's going to have to pay for it. Let's talk numbers, shall we?"

Sara still wasn't sure she could be satisfied with this outcome, but she didn't know if there would be another way. She stirred her tea. "Let's."

Chapter Fifteen

DYLAN STROLLED INTO the Arch and Vine in downtown Ribbon Ridge for dinner with Cameron. It was Cameron's payback for dinner last week—but since Cameron barely cooked they were eating out.

He'd been in here a hundred times, but now that he and Sara had this friends-with-benefits thing, the place took on a new light. Shit, if things went sour between them, would he have to go down the street to the dive bar with the karaoke and Lotto? He hoped not. He liked the beer and the food at the Arch and Vine, and he especially liked the atmosphere—laid back and welcoming. He even liked the décor, particularly the mural on one wall depicting a medieval street scene.

The bartender, a grizzle-headed man in his sixties with glasses and a square jaw, met his gaze. Dylan had made small talk with him on more than one occasion and vaguely recalled his name was George. Wait, could this be the George who'd taught Sara to play pool?

"Evening," the bartender said. "You bellyin' up to the bar or lookin' for a table?"

Dylan glanced around but didn't see Cameron. It was typical of him to be a few minutes late. "Table, I'm meeting my brother."

George inclined his gray head. "Go on and seat yourself then. Chloe'll be over to get your order."

More Archer people. He was absolutely surrounded. But then, he *was* in their pub.

George looked past Dylan at the door behind him. "Well, look what the cat dragged in. Kyle Archer, you are a sight for these sore old eyes."

Kyle grinned a wide gleaming smile. Along with his lingering tan and beach-blond hair, he looked like he'd stepped out of a surfboard ad. "Hey there, George."

George stepped out from behind the bar and hugged Kyle. "'Bout time you came home for something other than a funeral."

"Ouch." Kyle smiled at the bartender and clapped him on the back. "Good to see you too. Why haven't you poured my Crossbow yet? You getting slow in your old age?"

"You wish." George went back behind the bar and drew Kyle's beer. "I can still kick your butt arm wrestling."

"Yes, you can. I'll shut up now." Kyle looked at Dylan. "Hey, Westcott. What brings you here? Hot date?" He looked around for Dylan's nonexistent companion.

Dylan kept a smile from teasing his lips up. "Meeting Cameron for dinner. Why don't you join us?"

"If you don't mind." Kyle picked up his Crossbow from the bar. "George, pour my friend here a drink." Kyle looked at Dylan. "What's your poison?"

As Sara had ascertained, Dylan didn't have a favorite, so he chose what sounded good tonight. "Longbow."

George drew the beer and was just sliding it across the bar when the door opened. Both Dylan and Kyle turned as Cameron entered with Hayden Archer on his heels. Damn, dinner was about to get awkward, given the Kyle situation Sara had told him about.

"Yo, bro," Cameron said, wearing a casually stylish outfit that was pretty much on par with what he'd worn to clean Dad's gutters.

"Kyle!" Cameron slapped him on the shoulder. "Long time. You look good. Ridiculous, in fact. Florida is clearly the place to be. Dylan, hope you don't mind that I brought Hayden along."

Kyle glanced at his brother and tension seemed to crackle in the air.

Hayden nodded at Dylan and said, "Hey, Dylan."

"You boys are taking up a bunch of space," George said loudly. "Go get a table."

Cameron turned and led the group toward a booth situated beneath the medieval mural. "Kyle, you're joining us?" he asked as he slid into the booth and saw that Kyle had followed.

"If you don't mind," Kyle said again.

Dylan sat across from his brother. "I invited him."

"Cool," Cameron said as Hayden sat beside him.

Chloe approached the table. "Hi, guys."

Hayden smiled at her. "Oh, hey, Chloe."

She returned the smile. "Hi, Hayden. Kyle, it's good to see you," she added, though she sounded hesitant and Dylan wondered if she *really* thought it was good to see him. That morning over breakfast, Sara had continued the Kyle saga, explaining that he and Derek had once been best friends and that their relationship had imploded when he'd gone to Florida.

"Good to be seen. Thanks, Chloe." If Kyle had picked up on her nuanced speech, he didn't reflect it.

She glanced around the table, taking in the state of their drinks "Can I get some more beer for you guys? A pitcher maybe?"

"Or two," Cameron suggested. He glanced at what Dylan and Kyle were drinking and said, "A Longbow and a Crossbow."

"Will do. Let me know if you want some food." Chloe smiled and went to fill their order.

"Nachos." Kyle got a dreamy expression on his face. "With Tillamook cheese and sour cream. I've missed Oregon."

"You didn't have to stay away for so long if you missed it that much." Hayden's comment carried bite, but there was a hint of brotherly ribbing in his gaze, too.

Kyle didn't respond. He took a drink of beer instead.

"You here to stay?" Cameron asked Kyle.

Kyle shrugged.

"Hold on," Hayden said, his eyes narrowing. "Mom thinks you're here permanently, so you fucking better be."

Kyle held up his hands as if he'd been caught unarmed in a gunfight. "Yes, I'm here to stay. I'm here to help with the hotel project. I'm here to reclaim my Archer status."

Cameron laughed. "Your 'Archer status.' Like it ever goes away. Wealth, fame, ridiculous good looks. You're stuck with all that shit, even in Florida, I imagine."

"Fame?" Kyle rolled his eyes. "Like anyone remembers that show."

"I wish," Hayden said wearily. "A couple of weeks ago some woman came up to me at Home Depot in Newberg. Asked if I was one of 'those sextuplets.' When I politely explained that no, I wasn't, she was insistent that she'd seen me on TV. I finally had to admit that I was the "oops kid," so yes, I'd been on the show, but I wasn't one of the *actual* sextuplets. She wasn't nearly as impressed as she had been."

Cameron laughed. "Poor Hayden. Never quite fitting in. Sucks to be you. *Not.*"

Chloe returned with their pitchers of beer and two more pint glasses. They ordered nachos and burgers.

Hayden elbowed Cameron after Chloe left. "Sometimes it does suck to be me. We can't all be traveling salesmen with girls in every town."

Cameron snorted. "Right, that's me. American Gigolo. But hey, I am *not* a traveling salesman. I sell wine—great wine—and when I travel, I host upscale dinners paired with our wines."

"Sounds like a traveling salesman gigolo to me," Kyle said.

Hayden pointed at his brother and nodded. "Bingo!"

"Hey, I got your back." Kyle poured beer for everyone.

"So my brother is clearly a cheesy manwhore," Dylan said, casting his brother a mock disapproving glance. "What about you, Kyle? You certainly look like eye candy for a bunch of Florida socialites."

Cameron nodded. "Oh, totally." He leaned across the table and speared Kyle with a faux serious stare. "How much time do you spend on a boat?"

Kyle smiled like the cat that ate the canary. "Plenty."

"And since you don't actually own a boat, I'm guessing it belongs to a lady friend, perhaps? Is it safe to call you The Beach Bachelor?"

Hayden busted up laughing and Dylan joined him.

"I can just see you on the beach with your table of roses like that TV show, trying to choose whose boat you're going to take out for the day. Those poor women think you're going to romance them, but you really only care about their horsepower." Cameron roared with laughter.

Kyle looked around at each of them, shaking his head, then laughed with them.

Finally, Hayden said, "So we have a manwhore, a beach bachelor, what's Dylan?"

"The damaged divorcee," Cameron said. "He's a project for some woman to fix. After his marriage didn't work out, he needs comfort and solace. Though he seems to prefer drive-bys, if you get me." He waggled his eyebrows to impart his lewd meaning.

"You aren't telling us anything we don't already know," Hayden said. "His reputation as a player is common knowledge."

Ouch. Did Sara know that? She must if it was that well known. And she'd negotiated friends with benefits anyway. Any lingering concern he had regarding the arrangement faded completely. She'd gone into this with her eyes wide open. He couldn't have asked for a better setup.

Cameron nodded. "I taught him everything he knows."

Dylan rolled his eyes. "Dream on."

"So, gigolo, beach bachelor, and the damaged divorcee," Cameron summarized. "That leaves Hayden. Clearly he's the One-Hit Wonder."

Dylan looked at Hayden who'd dropped his head and was lightly shaking it from side to side. "I don't get it."

Cameron lifted his beer. "Hayden hasn't had a real girlfriend since Bex."

Hayden threw Cameron a dark stare. "Shut it."

"Is that true?" Kyle asked. "Not one girlfriend?"

"Asked the Beach Bachelor," Hayden said wryly. "I date. I'm not a manwhore. Or a player." He glanced at Cameron and shot a look at Dylan then settled his gaze back on Kyle. "Or a bartending Lothario."

Cameron set his beer down. "Hey, there's no proof of my prostitution. Or manwhore-ness. Just your lurid imaginations. You, on the other hand, have left a trail of broken hearts—or at least disappointed ladies—all over the Willamette Valley."

"Because you're still stuck on Bex?" Kyle leaned forward, his mouth slightly open with surprise.

Dylan didn't hear the answer to that question because his attention was drawn to the door opening and Sara walking in. His body thrummed with her presence and it took every ounce of willpower he possessed not to get up and go over to her. Thankfully, Kyle was blocking his way out of the booth.

As if she too possessed radar that signaled they were in the other's presence, her eyes locked with his. Faint color rose in her cheeks. Then her gaze moved right and connected with Kyle. The smile that had curved her lips faded.

Dylan felt Kyle tense. "Sara's here," Kyle said to no one in particular.

Hayden turned his head and looked over the top of the booth. He raised his hand up. "Sara!"

She came toward the table, her gait slow and her posture guarded. She ran her fingers along the strap of her purse, which was slung over her shoulder. "Boys' night out?"

"Sort of," Hayden said. "I crashed Cameron and Dylan's brotherly dinner."

"I guess I did the same." Kyle sounded as reticent as Sara looked. Clearly they hadn't made up since last night. Dylan wondered how things had gone with her mom.

"Well, I won't intrude. I just came in to pick up some dinner for me and Mom. Neither one of us felt like cooking." Her gaze drifted to Kyle but didn't linger.

"Tell her I said hi," Hayden said, refilling his glass.

"Will do." She looked around the table. "You look like trouble. Behave." Her eyes seemed to sparkle when they landed on Dylan.

He felt a surge of desire so strong, he put his hands on his lap and curled his fingers into the tops of his jeans. He drank her in—from the blonde hair knotted atop her head in a thoroughly haphazard but terribly sexy style to the slouchy sweatshirt over a pair of dark gray leggings to the pink, of course, Converse on her feet. She was dressed for a night in of movies and ice cream, but he'd never seen anyone more alluring. The things he could do with that ice cream...

Hayden toasted her with his glass. "See ya, sis."

She nodded, then turned and went to the bar where George greeted her with a smile. The conversation at their table started up again, thankfully about who was going to make the NBA championships instead of their sex lives. But Dylan was only half listening. He was aware of Sara's every move, and when she finally took her to-go order and left, he set his head back against the back of the booth and contemplated how he could see her later.

A minute later his phone buzzed in his pocket. He pulled it out and read the text.

SARA: *Come up with a reason to excuse yourself for a few minutes and meet me downstairs. Go back past the restrooms and take the last door on the right.*

The lust he'd felt earlier doubled back on him with hot urgency. He managed to say, "Pardon me for a few minutes, guys, I need to call one of my crew." He looked at Kyle expectantly.

Kyle slid out from the booth. "Everything cool?"

"Yeah, fine, just following up on some details."

"On a Saturday night?" Cameron asked. He tossed Hayden a mock glare. "I hope you're paying my brother enough."

Hayden chuckled. "Plenty. And he's worth it."

Normally, Dylan would've warmed to such a compliment. He took great pride in his work and in delivering the best. But right now he couldn't think past the invitation on his phone and the gorgeous blonde waiting for him downstairs. Hell, he hadn't even known this place had a downstairs.

He turned and went toward the back before he could sport wood in the middle of the damn restaurant. He passed Chloe as he entered the rear hallway. She carried a tray of food but inclined her head. "Restroom's just there."

He didn't bother correcting her as to his destination. "Thanks."

"Your burgers will be up in a minute."

He nodded and watched her go into the dining area. When the coast was clear, he moved quickly to the end of the hall, past the restrooms on the left and the kitchen on the right, and ducked into the door Sara had texted him about.

He stepped onto a small landing lit from a faint light source at the bottom of the stairs. He made his way down, careful to keep his tread light. What if someone else were down here?

At the base of the stairs, he saw the basement was basically a large storeroom filled with brewing supplies. The brewing portion of the pub was in an attached building at the back, but they clearly kept everything they needed here.

A hand on his elbow surprised him. He turned around and was sure his jaw was about to hit the floor. Sara was standing before him in nothing but a pink lacy bra and panties.

"Jesus, Sara," his voice nearly cracked with want while his cock surged against his suddenly too-tight jeans.

She reached for his waistband and neatly flicked the button open. She slipped her hands inside his jeans and drew him forward. "I thought there was a cot down here but there's only extra chairs. Oh, and couple of small tables. Extra stuff from the dining room."

"I don't need any furniture." He cradled the base of her head between his hands and dragged his thumbs along her jawline. Her eyes were so blue, her lips so damn pink and sweet. He'd had a beer and a half, but he suddenly felt drunk. He sank his mouth into hers, his tongue piercing into her with crazy need.

Her fingers dug into his hips as she pulled him tight against her. He felt her heat through his jeans and then her hand came forward and stroked the ridge of his cock through his boxer briefs. He groaned into her mouth and angled his head, deepening the kiss.

Her hand moved up and down along his shaft, teasing his already fevered body into a frantic state. He steered her backward until she hit the wall that supported the stairs. If anyone came down, they wouldn't be in plain sight—at least not immediately.

The precariousness of their situation gave him a moment's pause. He drew back from her. He already knew the answer but asked anyway, "Is this wise?"

"Is walking away from this wise? Or even possible?" She palmed his thick cock to punctuate the question.

"No, but we should be quick."

"I don't want it any other way. Not now." She slipped his penis through the opening in his briefs and worked her hand up and down in the most exquisite hand job he'd ever had.

He brought his hands up and cupped her breasts. "Jesus, Sara." He was repeating himself, but he didn't care. He closed his eyes, reveling in her touch, in his insatiable need for her.

"I need you inside me," she urged.

He moved his hands to her mound and rubbed her clit through her panties. She moaned softly and he dipped his hands inside the lace and silk. His fingers found her moist heat and she tipped her head back against the wall. "Yes. More."

He pushed her underwear down her thighs and she wriggled until they slid down her legs. "Open for me," he said against her ear and licked a path down her neck where he nipped her sweet flesh. She spread her thighs, giving him better access to her sheath. He pushed a finger up into her and his balls tightened at how ready she was. "God, you're so wet."

"For you."

Her words drove him wild. He put his hands on her hips and lifted her. "Put your legs around me."

She scissored his waist with her taut legs and his cock nudged her opening. He grabbed the base to guide himself home and then froze. "Fuck."

"What?" She sounded as coldly shocked as he felt.

"I don't have a condom."

"I'm okay not using one, if you are."

He was. Surprisingly so. He hadn't gone without a rubber since Jess. "Me too."

"Then fuck me." She smiled up at him sweetly, so at odds with her spectacularly coarse language. "Now."

"The things you say," he muttered, tugging his briefs down and gripping her hips as he thrust up into her. The feel of his bare cock inside of her nearly drove him to his knees. Ecstasy thundered through him and he slammed her into the wall with the ferocity of his need.

She widened her legs, pulling him in deeper. It was good they had to be fast, because he didn't think he could go slowly. He drove into her, his body pulsing with frenetic lust.

She moaned, her hands digging into his shoulder blades as she clutched him for support. "Harder. Feels. So. Good."

Hell yes, it felt good. His orgasm was already threatening to blow him apart, but he kept it at bay. He hammered into her, one hand holding her waist, the other hand braced against the wall next to her head.

With each stroke, she moaned a little bit louder and her thighs clenched him a little bit tighter. He kissed her, open-mouthed, and devoured her cries like a hungry beast. He slid his hand between them and thumbed her clit. Her muscles tensed and he felt her come. He let go and just drove into her with savage thrusts. He went rigid as his orgasm crested over him like a tidal wave. White-hot light blinded him and his harsh breathing filled his ears. Her fingers dug into his flesh, and her rasping joined his.

At last, she loosened her legs and he eased her down to the floor. He pulled out and realized this was perhaps not the best time to be without a stupid condom. "Um, sorry about the mess."

She shook her head. "I have tissue in my purse." She went to the corner where her clothes were piled and dug out her purse. She tossed him a few tissues while she tidied herself up. Meanwhile, he found her underwear and handed them to her.

While she dressed and he readjusted his jeans, he couldn't stop from staring at her ass, her long, gorgeous legs, or the sexy curve of her back as she bent to pull her shoes on.

"I should get back upstairs."

She flashed him a smile. "Uh-huh."

"Thanks."

She straightened. "Thank *you*."

He gave her a long, lurid stare and his lips curved into a very satisfied smile as he turned and started up the stairs. He leaned over the railing for a final look. "You're incredibly hot, you know."

"I do know." She grinned.

He jogged up the stairs and rejoined the guys. If they wondered what had taken him so long they didn't ask.

And he didn't care that his burger wasn't hot. He'd just had mind-blowing sex with an incredible woman. He felt invincible. Spectacular. Content.

A shaft of cold speared through him. What the *hell* was he doing?

Chapter Sixteen

MAY IS SUCH a gorgeous time in Ribbon Ridge, Sara thought to herself as she parked in the lot at The Alex. She stepped out of her car, the day bright despite her sunglasses. She noted Kyle's car and hoped he was in the trailer instead of at the site. She was feeling happy and buoyant, and though they'd adopted a fairly civil relationship, their unresolved issues hovered in the air between them like a swarm of bees.

The familiar knock of hammering and buzz of saws greeted her as she headed down the well-worn dirt track to the cottage.

Things were coming along nicely. She tried not to come out every day, but it was hard to stay away from watching the progress and, probably more accurately, from watching Dylan work. It was warm enough that by afternoon, he typically doffed his shirt and let the sun bronze his back. Sara found she could sit and watch that action all day. But to do that would be to advertise their friends-with-benefits status to the entire universe, something she worried about doing on a regular basis. They managed to keep their hook-ups quite private—like the tryst in the basement at the Arch and Vine or the one the other day in the tunnels under the job site—and had yet to get caught. She worried, though, that it was only a matter of time.

The cottage came into view, and again the progress was evident. They'd framed the entire second floor and tomorrow, she thought, the roof joists would go on. Everyone was thoroughly impressed with Dylan's delivery schedule. He'd worked in an asbestos abatement, but it had taken less time than he'd budgeted, so they were officially ahead of schedule. This made everyone positively giddy, and that was such a wonderful thing to feel after so many months in darkness and turmoil.

Which wasn't to say that things were perfect. There was a lingering strain between Mom and Dad, and Kyle was still Archer-non-grata. Life at "home" was about as tense as ever. Another reason to spend so much time at the job site.

While the second floor of the cottage was coming along, the first floor looked like it had been through a war—the front door and windows had been removed, part of the siding had been pulled off, and the landscaping around it had been utterly trampled. Dylan stepped out through the opening where the front door had been. He was dressed in a dark heather-blue T-shirt and faded work jeans. He slipped his sunglasses on and smiled as he saw her. "Hey, what's up?"

They came together but didn't touch. "I have a meeting with Aubrey in an hour."

"Yeah? What did you decide—fight or sell?"

They'd discussed her options the other night. She could either hold her clients to their contracts or she could sell the business to Craig. "Right now my life feels like it's here, in Ribbon Ridge. I'm going to sell. For a hefty price."

He grinned. "That's my girl."

His girl? She tried not to read too much into his words. Things were going really well between them. The friends-with-benefits situation was working out great. It was one of the reasons she'd also decided to make a permanent return to Ribbon Ridge, but she wouldn't tell him that. Not yet.

"I hope you're making him pay."

Her lips curved up. "Definitely. Aubrey is encouraging me to be ruthless. We're going to write up the sales contract today. He's also not getting any of my assets." Sara Archer Celebrations owned a lot of decorating accessories, and there was no way she was letting him have them. He could buy his own.

"Good for you. Show no mercy." He drew off his sunglasses and his gray-green gaze was intense, or maybe it was just the intensely blue sky behind him. "Particularly when your opponent has demonstrated absolute savagery."

Sara laughed at his hyperbolic characterization. "That's pretty much what Aubrey said. And you're both right. He blatantly went after my clients and robbed me of future income, which Aubrey used to threaten Craig with a lawsuit."

Dylan nodded approvingly, a smile playing about his lips. "Nice."

"Ruthless." She pushed her sunglasses up onto her head and gave him a dark stare. "Does that turn you on?"

"Everything you do turns me on."

"Mmm." Her phone buzzed in her back pocket, and she checked the display.

HAYDEN: *Emergency family meeting tonight at 6.*

Sara's stomach twisted and plummeted into her feet.

"What is it?" The concern in his tone told her he'd read her face.

"Emergency meeting tonight." She shoved the phone back in her pocket, trying to imagine what disaster could rain down next.

"What do you think it is?" he asked.

"I don't know. Hayden sent the text. Could be a lot of things." The last time she'd gotten a 911-type text had been because Kyle had come home. Did it have something to do with him? "I need to get to my meeting with Aubrey."

He brushed his hand against hers. Subtle, but comforting. "Hey, don't freak out."

"I won't. Thanks." She smiled to reassure him, though she felt anything but reassured.

By the time she walked into the gathering room at six o'clock, her feet were leaden and her senses were completely frayed. She'd gone totally old school with her SPD and donned a thick fleece vest with weights in the pockets to try to regulate herself, but it wasn't doing much to calm her nerves.

Everyone was already seated around the table—Mom, Kyle, Hayden, Tori, Derek—except Dad. His absence and the weary expression on Mom's face sparked an even deeper anxiety in Sara's gut. "Where's Dad?" she blurted.

"Right here." His hand clasped her shoulder and she startled.

Then she spun and hugged him. His arm came around her and swiftly squeezed her shoulders. "My little kitten," he whispered against her ear as he pressed a kiss to the side of her head.

Memories of her childhood, of him holding her and soothing her, filled her with warmth. Her senses relaxed a little and she released the tension in her body. Everything would be okay. It had to be. There had already been too much sadness. Too much upheaval.

Dad guided her to the table and held out a chair for her next to Kyle. He took his customary seat at the head, opposite Mom at the other end.

"Who called this meeting?" Dad asked.

Hayden laid his palms flat on the table. "I did." He was sitting next to Mom, and he reached out and covered her hand with his. "There's no easy way to say this, so I'll just say it. I've been offered an internship at a winery in France, and I'm going to take it."

Sara watched for Mom's response, and when there was none, grew suspicious.

"Now?" Dad's voice snapped through the room like a firecracker.

"In a week," Hayden said, still holding Mom's hand.

"You couldn't have said something sooner?" Tori asked, her tone wound with irritation. "Like, I don't know, one of the hundred times we've been working together over the past several weeks?"

Hayden didn't appear affected by Tori's reaction. "I only decided to take it today."

Derek was on Hayden's other side. "How long will you be gone?"

"A year."

"What about your job?" Again Dad's voice shot out, crackling with anger. "You're a vital part of Archer Enterprises and I don't even get the benefit of a proper notice? I'm not just your boss, I'm your father, for Christ's sake."

Hayden exhaled. "I'm sorry, Dad. They had an opening and I had to give them a quick answer. I'll do what I can remotely. Please understand. I can't turn this down."

Dad didn't look convinced.

"Rob, it'll be fine. We'll make it work," Derek said. He looked at Hayden. "This is a great opportunity for you."

It was. Hayden had been making small batches of wine the past few years—it was his secret passion. His job at Archer was just that: his job. The rest of them had pursued their dreams outside of Ribbon Ridge. Why shouldn't he?

"You can't be COO remotely." Dad's tone was clipped. "I'll have to hire someone."

"I'll do it."

Everyone turned to stare at Kyle. Derek looked particularly surprised, and maybe even a little horrified.

Sara couldn't imagine he would look forward to working with Kyle, at least not until they resolved their differences.

"Hey, don't everyone look so shocked." Kyle shifted in his chair. "Hayden's got a few days before he leaves, and he can show me the ropes. And I'm sure he won't leave me hanging if I have questions."

Hayden met Kyle's gaze. "You can count on me anytime." He looked back at the head of the table. "Dad?"

Dad was staring out the window. The trees were green again, providing a thick canopy around the edges of the backyard. Life had continued and marched onward even if everyone in this house was still struggling in the horrid vacuum of Alex's death.

"I don't know," he said finally. He kept his gaze firmly on the outside.

"Why?" The resentment in Kyle's voice skidded across Sara's nerves, bunching her muscles into tight knots of stress.

Dad finally looked at Kyle. "Because you're unreliable."

"You don't know that. Just because I didn't take the job you offered me before doesn't mean I'm unreliable. It's not like I made a commitment and then reneged."

Dad's gaze sharpened. "Do you really want to get into the specifics right here, right now?"

Kyle glanced away. "No."

"Dad…Dad, you're being overly harsh." Sara closed her mouth because she didn't want to reveal the depth of her distress. They'd all pick up on it and then the focus would turn to her. She absolutely did *not* want that.

Mom cleared her throat. "There's one more thing. I'm going with Hayden." She gave him a warm smile. "A change of scenery will be good for me, and it's been years since I used my French."

Hayden returned Mom's smile. "There's no one I'd rather have with me."

Sara's heart ached. She'd never loved her brother more than in that moment. But if Mom left, what did that mean for Sara? She'd come home to be with Mom, to give her what she'd always provided for Sara—love, comfort, support. She'd also abandoned her life and signed away her business. And for what? She closed her eyes and tugged on the bottom of her vest so that the weight of it pulled on her shoulders.

Silence took hold for a long moment. When Sara opened her eyes, everyone was watching Dad. At last he looked at Mom. "You should go."

Mom nodded. "I'm glad you agree."

"But…Mom…" Sara was having a rare moment when words seemed to jumble in her brain and trip along her tongue on their way out of her mouth. This had been a regular occurrence when she was younger, but therapy and practice had all but eliminated the problem. She pulled tighter on the vest and clenched her muscles. She didn't want them to see how badly she was affected. "What about Derek's wedding?" Thank God the words came out all right.

Mom smiled at Derek. "I'd never miss it." Though Derek wasn't her blood son, he was family and the first of them to be getting married.

Hayden nodded, looking at Derek. "Me neither—I'm the best man after all."

From the corner of her eye, Sara caught Kyle stiffening beside her.

Mom returned her gaze to Sara. "You and Chloe will manage things. And I'll only be a Skype away."

This was all too much. Hayden leaving. Mom going with him. Dad shutting down Kyle's offer to take Hayden's place at Archer. Deciding to sign away her business earlier.

Sara shoved back from the table. "I need to go." She left the kitchen via the mudroom hallway, grabbing her purse on her way to the door.

"Sara!" Kyle called after her.

She heard his footsteps in the hall, but didn't stop. He caught up with her in the courtyard as she went to the garage for her car and punched in the code for the door.

"Sara, wait." He touched her back. "Where are you going?"

"Out." The door opened and she went to her car without looking at him. "Kyle, just let me go."

DYLAN GLANCED AT the clock—nearly seven. He expected Sara to come by after her family meeting. His phone rang and he felt a stab of disappointment that she'd decided to call instead. Until he saw the caller ID and it said "Mom."

He was already thinking of how to get her off the phone when he said, "Hi, Mom."

"You picked up." Her tone was dry. "I'm so used to leaving you voicemail."

"I've just been busy. Working long days." Completely true, but he also hadn't bothered to return her messages. He wasn't in the mood for another lecture about how he should meet someone, not when he was quite happily engaged in a fling with the sexiest, sweetest woman in the Willamette Valley.

"I'm calling to remind you about Brie's graduation on Saturday. It's at one o'clock at the college. And it's outside. I really hope it doesn't rain."

He rolled his eyes. "The forecast looks great. Stop looking for things to worry about."

"The party's at six at our house. You don't need to bring anything, though I hope you bring a date."

"I'm not seeing anyone, Mom."

"Surprise, surprise."

He laughed at her sarcasm. What else could he do? There was frustration, or irritation, or his typical reaction—nothing. But he decided maybe it was time to find some humor. Wow, look at him being all positive. He blamed Sara's influence.

"Some of Brie's friends will be there. Maybe you'll meet someone."

Oh, God. Just what he needed—live and in-person matchmaking by his mother. "On second thought, maybe I will bring someone." He thought about asking Sara, but that would annihilate the whole secret thing.

"That would be lovely, dear. I hope you actually mean it." She saw right through him.

Dylan heard a car on the drive. "Sorry to cut this short, but I need to run. I'll see you Saturday." He disconnected before she could argue.

He went to the door and met Sara. One look at her pale face told him everything he needed to know. He reached for her and pulled her against his chest.

Her arms snaked around his waist and he felt her exhale against his shirtfront.

"Come in." He guided her over the threshold and closed the door. "I have wine. Or I can even make you a foofy drink."

"Thanks." She sounded sniffly, like she'd been crying. God, how bad was it?

He kept his hand on the small of her back, applying pressure, as they walked to the kitchen. He sat her on one of the bar stools.

"A foofy drink would be great." She attempted a smile, but it didn't remotely reach her eyes.

He went to the cabinet where he kept his stash of liquor: a bottle of tequila, two bottles of scotch, and fresh bottles of pomegranate vodka and triple sec which he'd use to make a pomegranate lemon drop. He set the bottles on the counter, then got a martini glass and the lemon juicer. As he set to juicing two lemons, he glanced over at her. "You want to talk about it?"

She stared at him. "You're going full bartender here. Wow."

He paused as her words sank in. He was. He'd actually cut out a little early—the days were long and the crew typically worked until eight—just to hit the liquor store and get home and shower before he thought she might show up. In fact, he just realized she'd been taking a chance by coming here at this hour since he was typically still at the job site. It seemed they each had expectations that maybe went beyond friends with benefits.

He pushed the thought away and focused on making the drink. Even so, he couldn't shake the odd feeling he now had—like he was watching what was happening instead of living it.

"Hayden's taking an internship at a winery in France for a year." She said this so coldly that he looked up. "He's wanted to make wine for as long as I can remember."

"Really? I didn't know that." What was he doing working for Archer Enterprises when he lived in one of the best wine countries in the world? "How is this a bad thing?"

"It's not—for him. Mom's going with him."

Dylan grabbed the cocktail shaker from the liquor cabinet and filled it with ice. He still wasn't sure he saw why this was so bad, but he was very cognizant of her fragile behavior so he tried to think of something supportive to say. Or at least something that wasn't 'What's the big deal?' which would've been the F-grade response. "You don't want her to go?"

"No. I mean yes." She rubbed her hand across her forehead. "I want her to be happy. But for her to go away for so long…I know I moved away from Ribbon Ridge, but I was close. She'll be half a world away. And Dad didn't even seem to care. It just seems like nothing will ever be the same."

"You do realize that nothing *will* be the same."

"Yes. That doesn't make it any easier."

No, it didn't. But life was full of disappointments, wasn't it? He poured the ingredients into the shaker and shook it within an inch of its life.

"I'm worried that my parents are having problems. I've read the death of a child is often a huge strain on a marriage—a lot of couples get divorced."

"Yeah, I've heard that, too," he said, trying to find the right words to make her feel more optimistic. "But maybe this is what they both need to heal."

"Maybe. You're so lucky you don't have a big family to deal with."

Lucky. Huh. He'd thought so, but now he wasn't so sure. He was always on the outside looking in, never part of anything. Ice pricked the back of his neck. He went to the fridge and pulled out a beer.

She sipped her drink. "This is really good." Her mouth relaxed into a smile. "Thanks. Really. You're so sweet to go to the trouble to make this for me." She looked at the bottles on the counter as if she was just seeing them. "Did you go to the liquor store? You can't have had pomegranate vodka on hand."

"Guilty as charged." Damn, this was feeling more and more like a real relationship. She'd been here almost fifteen minutes and they hadn't even flirted. He popped open his beer and took a healthy swig. "You're totally worth pomegranate vodka and hand-squeezed lemons." He injected a large dose of playfulness into his tone— time to change this depress-fest up. "What else can I squeeze?" He dipped his gaze to her breasts.

She blinked at him and he feared he'd overstepped. Maybe she needed to talk more. She took a long sip and then swiveled on the stool, crooking her finger at him.

His blood heated at the subtle narrowing of her eyes. He moved around the island and went to stand between her parted knees.

She unzipped her vest and brought his hands up to her chest. She wore a lightweight ivory T-shirt with a V-neck that accentuated the curve of her breasts. "These what you wanted to squeeze?"

He pressed his fingers into her flesh, suddenly desperate to toss her shirt and bra away. "Yep. Way better than lemons."

She arched up and kissed him, her tongue sliding into his mouth and filling his senses with lemon and pomegranate and Sara. He tried to pinch her nipples, but it was almost impossible to get a good grip with her bra in the way. He slid his hands up under her shirt and slipped inside the frustrating undergarment. Her warm flesh greeted him, sent need spiraling to his groin.

She eased off the stool and dragged him toward the couch. The sex was hot and quick, with him driving into her with rough, swift strokes. He collapsed on top of her and tried to move to the side, but she clutched him close. "Stay there. You feel so good crushing me." Her breathing slowed. "I know that's weird."

"It's not weird." He knew why she liked it. From a sensory prospective it was incredibly grounding for her. He also knew that was why she liked their sex hard and fast from time to time.

"Thanks." She kissed his shoulder, her fingers tracing whorls on his back. "I don't know what I'd do without you right now, especially with my mom leaving."

A streak of panic slashed through him. This was becoming dangerously close to overflowing the parameters of friends with benefits. He steered clear of relationships on purpose, and for this one to turn bad would impact so many things.

She kissed him, her lips soft and warm. Her touch soothed the apprehension coursing through him. "I promised to make you dinner the other day—chicken tortilla soup. You hungry?"

He rolled off her and stood up, glad for something else to think about. "Famished." He helped her up. "You good?"

She shrugged. She began to pick up her haphazardly discarded clothes and dress. "For now. I love knowing that while I'm here all of that can fade away and I can just be myself. With you. My family can stay the hell out."

Dylan pulled on his jeans. He was glad he could be here for her, but he couldn't shake the uneasiness that had settled between his shoulder blades. For now they *could* exist in this bubble, but for how long?

Chapter Seventeen

SARA CLOSED THE door gently behind her and tiptoed through the mudroom just after six on Friday morning after crashing at Dylan's. She was pretty sure no one was around, but there was always a chance Tori was up for an early run. Mom, who'd always risen with the sun before Alex had died, would certainly still be in bed. And Kyle was staying in the apartment over the garage so he likely wouldn't be about either. Plus, he was *not* a morning person.

A bottle of water sounded good, but Sara didn't dare go into the kitchen for fear Tori *was* in there having her pre-run coffee. Instead, Sara made her way quietly toward the stairs near the entry.

And ran smack into Mom.

"There you are, dear, I was worried." She hugged Sara.

Sara's arms felt wooden as she hugged her back. "Yeah, here I am."

"Where did you go last night? We were all so concerned."

She knew that because they'd all texted her repeatedly: Mom, Tori, Hayden, Derek, Chloe, even Kyle. Everyone except Dad. "I told you I was fine."

Mom drew back, her blue eyes dark with apprehension. "Did you go to your condo?" She glanced down at Sara's clothes. "You're wearing the same clothes again. Don't you have anything back at your place?"

"Most everything is here, particularly the seasonal stuff." She was desperate to change the topic to something safer. "You're up so early, and you're dressed." She smiled. "It's good to see you like this."

Mom's answering smile was warm and serene. Genuine. It threatened to bring tears to Sara's eyes, but she blinked them back. "I feel good. Better than I have in ages. I think going with Hayden is the right decision." Lines formed around her eyes and mouth. "Will you be okay with me gone?"

"Of course." Sara answered quickly, maybe too quickly. But she wouldn't do anything to alter Mom's course, not when it finally seemed like she was moving forward instead of stagnating in grief. "I'm so glad you're going. And I've got plenty to keep me busy here."

Mom rubbed Sara's arm, something she'd done for as long as Sara could remember but only just realized had been absent the past few months. "Tori said you sold your business to Craig yesterday. Why didn't you tell me you'd decided?"

Sara had texted Tori about it after meeting with Aubrey. "I'd only just made the decision yesterday morning. The deal came together quickly." And then things had gone to hell at the family meeting.

"Are you happy? Is this okay?"

Happy was stretching it, but she was definitely okay. "My bank account will be thrilled."

Mom laughed, and Sara's heart nearly burst with the joy of the sound. "That's good. But you're sure you're all right? I know how too much upheaval can wreak havoc on your system." She moved her massaging to Sara's other arm. "Maybe you should come to France with us."

"No." Again, she maybe answered too quickly. She offered a smile. "I'm too invested in the wedding cottage project. Plus, Chloe and Derek's wedding. I couldn't possibly go."

"Of course, and I'm so pleased. I've talked to Tori and Kyle, and they've promised to make sure you're regulated."

Great, they'd be trying to baby her more than ever. Sara edged back so that Mom dropped her hand from her arm. "That wasn't necessary. I moved away from home and did quite fine."

Shadows of concern dimmed her mother's gaze. "I know, but I still saw you regularly, and now I'll be so distant. I'll call you every day."

Every day? "I'll be fine." It occurred to Sara that maybe Mom needed that. She leaned forward and kissed her cheek. "You call or Skype me whenever you want. You'll be home in just a few months for the wedding. Less than that, really."

"Speaking of the wedding, I've been looking for a house for Hayden and me and I think I found the perfect one. It has an amazing garden that I think you could adapt for the cottage at The Alex. I'll send lots of pictures."

Sara loved hearing her Mom excited about something. It had been far too long since she'd talked about things in that way—with forward thought and hope. "That sounds great."

"Well, I have a lot to do—so much to accomplish before we leave next Saturday."

So soon. But it seemed to be for the best. And Sara was happy for Hayden. It had been hard to gauge his reaction last night, but he had to be completely jazzed to finally be pursuing his dream.

"Will you be around later?" Mom asked. "I want to go over some things with you, Tori, and Kyle. I know you and Tori won't be living here permanently, so I've asked Kyle to oversee some things while I'm gone."

Sara doubted Kyle's trustworthiness, but didn't say so. But since she'd all but decided to come home, she could keep an eye on things. "Now that I've sold the business and plan to work at The Alex, I've been considering moving back to Ribbon Ridge."

"You are?" Mom's eyes lit up. "Maybe I shouldn't go to France after all."

"No, Mom, you should." Sara thought that Dylan was probably right—that it would be good for her marriage too.

"Thank you for understanding and supporting me. I don't know what I'd do without you." With a parting pat on Sara's shoulder, Mom turned and went back toward her bedroom. Since Sara'd been busted sneaking in, she adjusted her course and backtracked to the kitchen.

Tori was standing just inside the door, cradling her coffee mug. Dressed in a stylish black and aqua running outfit, she looked Sara up and down. "Same clothes *again*, huh? What am I missing?"

"Nothing. I just didn't want to bother with the winter clothes at my condo, that's all."

Tori's blue-green gaze was skeptical. "Are you seeing someone?"

Sara was careful this time not to rush to answer. "No, but that might be nice."

Tori laughed. "Then let's make that happen."

"Are you offering to take me out and find me a guy?"

Tori's eyes shuttered, which was not the reaction Sara was expecting. Tori loved to go out and mingle, and people enjoyed her effervescent and witty company. She was the sort of person people liked to be around and in turn she thrived on social settings. "I was kidding. I'm off for a run. Catch you later." She set her nearly empty mug down on the counter, put her ear buds in, and left.

Sara went to the fridge to grab a bottle of water. When she closed it, she jumped. Standing on the other side was Kyle. He must've come in from the garage apartment when Tori had left because Sara had only heard the door shut once.

He rubbed his palms down his faded jeans. "Hey. I was worried about you last night."

Sara bristled. "As you can see, I'm fine."

"Actually, what I see is you fidgeting with the hem of your vest and the tension in your shoulders. I read you better than anyone but Mom."

Damn Kyle for being observant and astute and for still knowing her so well. "If you're trying to score points with me, it's too little too late." She turned to go upstairs.

"Sara, wait." The note of desperation in his voice made her pause. She slowly pivoted. His familiar blue-green eyes, so like Tori's but framed with lighter lashes given his blond hair, were dark with some emotion. "Please stay and listen to me, just for a few minutes. Will you give me that?"

Now he wanted to talk? After all this time? Sara breathed through the anxiety crawling up her spine. "Why should I give you anything?"

He moved toward the gathering room, which was really just an extension of the kitchen. Tall windows overlooked the backyard, and a seat stretched along their length. He stood in front of the window seat with its bright red and yellow cushions. "Will you come sit with me?"

Because they were family and because she was so weary of all of the conflict here, she went to the seat. Her steps were slow, almost reluctant, but she got there eventually. He sat down and she perched a few feet away on the edge. She opened her water and took a few long swallows. The coolness soothed the tumult inside of her. "Say what you want to say."

His lips curved into a self-deprecating smile. "You aren't going to go easy on me at all, are you?"

"Why should I? Not only did you up and leave, you basically cut us off—cut *me* off." She looked away from him, feeling the pain of his desertion all over again. But then pain lived so close beneath the surface that even the slightest scratch opened every wound she was working to repair.

"I know, and I'm sorry. I was selfish." He reached for her hand, but she snatched it away. She wasn't ready for that level of closeness. Not yet. "Sara-cat, I had to go."

He hadn't called her that in years. Dad had called her "kitten" for as long as she could remember and when she'd turned ten, she'd said she wasn't a kitten any longer. That hadn't stopped Dad from calling her that, but it had prompted her brothers to tease her by calling her Sara-cat instead. Once the nickname had lost its bite, Kyle had adopted it as his endearment for her. It was the one thing he could've said to make her stop and listen. *Really* listen.

She turned toward him on the bench. "Why?"

Kyle looked down at his hands, which he'd laid palm-down on his thighs. "It's hard to be me when Liam and Hayden are who they are. And Tori and even Evan. And especially you."

"Me?" She set the water bottle down on the seat next to her and gripped her elbows, flexing her muscles. "Why would I cause you to leave?"

He smiled at her. "Because in so many ways you're far more independent and capable than any of us. You've built a successful business—away from Ribbon Ridge—without a network of people or a support system."

"That's not exactly true. I had Mom and Dad. And Hayden, Derek, and Alex were great."

"Sure, but you've never relied on a group of friends, or people who purported to be your friends." His tone turned briefly dry. "You go full speed ahead on your own power. It's amazing to behold, and makes me look kind of lame."

Sara stared at him, not quite believing what she was hearing. He was jealous of her success? She knew he felt like a bit of a failure next to his siblings. He was the only one who hadn't gotten a bachelor's degree or gone into "white collar" work. He'd been a chef and then a bartender. "You know, we all have something that makes us different from everyone else. Something that makes us feel like the odd kid out."

He exhaled, his eyes drooping a bit. "And no one knew that better than Alex, though I never realized to what degree. I still can't believe he ended his life. I get angry, sad, frustrated, sure, but never in a million years would I consider giving up." He didn't sound judgmental, but like he was trying to process what none of them had been able to make sense of. "What was he like before he died?"

Sara released the tension from her arms and shoulders and dropped her hands to her sides. "If you're trying to find some sort of clues or signs to the depths of his mental illness, there weren't any. I came home almost every week to go with him and Mom to his lung appointments. He was as pragmatic about things as he'd always been." It had been terrible for him to be sick. All of their lives, he couldn't play the sports his siblings played and he couldn't enjoy the same activities like swimming or biking. Even his bedroom was on the main floor because he couldn't go up and down stairs very easily, while the rest of their bedrooms were together upstairs. There'd been a separation between him and all of them that simply couldn't be breached.

Memories assaulted her. She peered over at Kyle who was staring somewhere in the direction of the fridge—or maybe past that toward Alex's bedroom. "Do you remember staying up late in Alex's room?"

Slowly, Kyle's lips curved up. He turned to look at her. "Of course. Watching *David Letterman* or *Saturday Night Live.*"

"Do you think Mom and Dad knew we did that?"

"How could they not?" Kyle chuckled. "Six kids moving en masse downstairs—that has to be hard to sleep through. I'm sure they thought it was great."

Sara could feel the press of her siblings against her as they'd all piled onto Alex's queen-sized bed. A smile overtook her and warmth bubbled up inside. "I need to work harder to remember things like that. Or like the time you took me to homecoming." She watched for his reaction.

His smile broadened. "That was so fun. Everybody came back here for an impromptu pool party."

"And you were homecoming king." She saw him perfectly in her mind's eye: wearing a navy suit, his model good looks seemingly made for a crown perched atop his head. He'd planned to go to the dance with a group of friends—the "in" crowd, including one of the homecoming princesses who had a major crush on him and who was crowned queen alongside him. However, when Sara's date, a friend from her history class, had come down with the flu, Kyle had changed his plans and taken Sara. She'd normally avoided the social groups that Kyle, Liam, and Tori were popular in—it had been just too hard to fit in. For that night, though, she'd felt included and like she *had* fit in.

"Homecoming king." His laugh was a bit harsh sounding. "That seemed the pinnacle back then, but it wasn't anything really. See, I hit my peak at seventeen."

"That isn't true."

He arched a brow at her. "Name one remarkable thing I've done since then."

"You graduated at the top of your class from culinary school."

He exhaled. "Fine. There's that." He looked at her intently, curiosity burning in his gaze. "Why did you work so hard to stay in the background when we were younger? Even in college, you kept to your very small circle and that lame-ass boyfriend of yours."

"Mike wasn't lame-ass. He was just an ass." Sara had been blithely unaware of his periodic bouts of cheating and less periodic drug use. She'd felt like an utter fool once his behavior had finally come to light—thanks to Kyle, who'd seen Mike on a binge in Portland one weekend. He'd told Sara the hard truth and held her while she'd cried. They'd never told anyone what had really happened, just that Sara had broken up with him. "There's a lot that we shared, Kyle. Things no one else knew or understood about me. When you left, it just…hurt."

He reached for her hand again, and this time she didn't flinch. He looked at her, his eyes sad. "Can I?" She nodded, and he squeezed her hand. His touch was warm, comforting. Like home—a home she'd forgotten existed in the last months especially. "I'm so sorry I hurt you. Like I said, I was selfish, and I didn't realize how much until Alex"—his voice pinched—"died."

"He's made all of us rethink, reassess, even change."

Kyle looked at their joined hands. "I doubt I would've come home if he hadn't died. I hate saying that, and I probably wouldn't to anyone but you."

She appreciated his honesty and trust more than he could know. "I think I understand."

"Thanks."

She squeezed Kyle's hand. "What's going on with Dad and you? Is he going to let you take Hayden's place at Archer?"

Kyle ran his free hand through his hair, ruffling the top so it stood up. "I don't know. After you left last night, he said he needed to think and left."

"I don't know what happened when you left home, but clearly there was something with Dad." She injected as much caring into her tone as she could, while still staying firm. This needed to be said. "And Derek. He was your closest friend and now you barely speak. Actually, you *never* speak unless you have to."

Kyle let go of her hand and stood. He turned and faced the windows, gazing out over the yard bathed in bright, spring-morning light. "They're just as pissed at me as you were. They'll come around eventually."

"You need to talk to them like you talked to me."

Kyle gave her a gimlet eye. "You made that so easy. Imagine how they're being."

Sara nodded. "You have an uphill battle. I get it. But you dug your own hole." She stood and he looked at her. "I'll be here for you."

"Thanks, Sara-cat, that means a lot to me. Hopefully I can convince Dad that I'm here to do my part. I can pick up Hayden's responsibilities *and* oversee the next phase of The Alex."

Her heart lifted. To finally have her brother back filled her with joy. "I know you can."

His answering expression was skeptical. "Thanks. Now I just need to convince everyone else I'm not the fuckup they think I am. Or that I'm not the fuckup I was."

"Admitting you *were* a fuckup is step one." She winked at him. "That'll help."

He laughed. "Good advice. Can I make you breakfast?"

"Yes, please! I've been waiting for you to cook me something since you got home." She punched him in the arm.

He massaged his bicep. "Still smacking people, I see. Lay off the yoga or whatever you're doing."

She threw his sarcasm right back at him. "Still have SPD, loser."

He moved into the kitchen and began pulling out supplies. "Tell me what's going on with you. I want to hear all about this douchebag assistant stealing your business."

The use of "douchebag" reminded her of Dylan. As she told Kyle about Craig, she considered also confiding in him about Dylan. In the end, however, she decided she didn't want to break their secret pact.

Right now, she was content to bask in the warmth of her rekindled relationship with Kyle.

Chapter Eighteen

DYLAN LOOSENED HIS tie as he walked into his mom and Bill's house in Newberg. The day was warm and he'd had to hike up the street after parking a quarter mile away due to the excess of cars that were here to celebrate his sister's college graduation. The ceremony had been earlier that afternoon up in Portland where she went to school at Lewis and Clark. Tonight's celebration at the Davies' house was something akin to a wedding reception. It was certainly far more fancy than the barbecue they'd hosted a month after Dylan had graduated from the University of Washington, which had also doubled as a going-away party before he'd left for boot camp.

A handful of people were milling inside the house, mostly in the kitchen, which Dylan passed through on his way outside. The backyard was immaculately groomed due to Bill's OCD when it came to the house and garden. Everything had to be tidy and perfect, pretty much at all times. His high standards had made living there intolerable—another reason Dylan had moved to his dad's for high school.

Mom's eye caught Dylan as he stepped onto the patio. She waved and Dylan waved back. He beelined for the bar that had been set up beneath the pergola. They'd even hired a bartender to dole out wine from Ribbon Ridge as well as a keg of Archer beer. Dylan ordered a pint of the beer and then scanned the yard for his sister.

She stood beneath a string of colored lanterns, a glass of white wine in her hand, laughing with some friends. He took his beer and went to talk to her. She was, after all, the only reason he'd come to the party.

She turned her head as he neared. "Dylan!" She gave him a warm hug and introduced him to her friends. Then she excused herself for a minute and pulled him over to the side. "Thanks for coming. I know these things aren't your fave."

"I'd walk over hot coals for you, Cheese." He used the nickname he'd given her long ago after she'd insisted on spelling her name as Brie, a shortened version of Sabrina.

She laughed then glanced around him. "No date?" At his headshake, she pursed her lips. "You know Mom's going to harp on that. Please, for the love of all that's right in the world, date someone. *Any*one. Just once. Then I can stop listening to her bitch and moan about how lonely you are." She rolled her eyes. "You're not really lonely, are you?"

"No." Particularly not with Sara around. Last night was still bouncing around in his head like a song he couldn't remember all the words to. Being with her felt great, but he couldn't shake the feeling that something was off. "Thanks for the warning though."

"Eh, like you didn't know she'd pounce on you. Watch out, here she comes." Brie made a face. "So glad I'm off to Hawaii tomorrow."

"Brat." He kissed her cheek. "I'm so proud of you."

"Thanks." A slight blush colored her freckled complexion. "Now let me go. I don't want to participate in the Dylan Matchmaking Extravaganza."

"Consider it my graduation gift to you."

"Done." She waved at him, then twirled back to her friends.

Mom's face was deceptively placid when she arrived at Dylan's side. "It's so nice to see you and Sabrina together. Sometimes I think I raised two only-children."

Sometimes it felt like that. Hell, often *it felt like that.* He said nothing.

Mom turned toward him, her dark blue eyes narrowing slightly. "Why didn't you bring a date? I told you to bring a date."

"Oh, and by your command, I should just magically have someone on my arm?" He forced a laugh. "Sorry to disappoint you. I've been really busy with the renovation I'm working on." *And carrying on a secret fling.* God, he couldn't imagine subjecting Sara to his mother's interrogation and judgment, especially not right now.

"There's always something. Dylan, it's not good to be so work-focused." She crossed her arms and gave him an expectant look. "I heard Jessica is getting married again. Is that true?"

Great. He could hardly wait to hear how Mom was going to spin this. "Yeah. I saw Monica at Dad's house a few weeks ago."

The flesh around her mouth pinched as if she smelled something bad. "Angie's still friends with her? Doesn't she realize that when there's a divorce, it's poor form to support the other side?"

Naturally Mom would think of things in terms of sides. Her split from Dad had been intensely acrimonious and though it had mellowed with time, they were still far from friends. Angie's friendship with Monica Christensen bothered Dylan too, but he wasn't going to share that with his mother. "Sides don't really matter."

"I suppose not. It's not as if you and Jessica have any reason to communicate. Not like it was with your father and me—because of you." *That's right*, Dylan thought. He was a nasty reminder of a marriage his parents preferred to forget. The look of distaste on her face sharpened. "You really need to address your personal life, now more than ever."

Dylan refrained from gritting his teeth. "Why?"

She looked at him incredulously as if he should already know. "If Jessica is moving on, so should you."

"It's not a contest." Suddenly Dylan wondered if she'd married Bill in haste after Dad had married Angie. He'd met Angie when she'd substituted at the middle school, and their courtship had been somewhat quick. They'd married within a year of meeting each other. Less than a year later, Mom had married Bill. Dylan realized he still knew so little about his parents' marriage. They'd divorced when he was only a year old, so he had no memory of them as a couple or of the three of them as a family.

"Of course it's not a contest," Mom said with a healthy dose of exasperation. "But it's a good reminder that you're not getting any younger, and it's past time for you to settle down. For real this time."

He took her hand to try and lessen the blow of what he was about to say. "I'm not you or Dad. I didn't marry Jessica because I knocked her up and then split when I realized things weren't going to work out."

Mom sucked in a breath and her eyes widened. "That's not—"

"What happened?" Dylan finished for her. "Maybe not in your memory, but that's the way Dad tells it and I'm inclined to believe him. I'm not trying to be brutal here. I just need you to back off."

She blinked at him and for the first time in…he didn't know when, there were tears in her eyes. "I only want you to be happy. You don't seem happy."

Didn't he? He wasn't *unhappy*. Particularly these past few weeks with Sara. "You don't have to worry about me. Things will happen for me," *or not*, "in their own time. I don't feel lonely or unhappy, so you shouldn't presume that I am."

She sniffed and took her hand away from his to wipe beneath her eye. "Maybe if you spent more time with me and Bill, we wouldn't worry." Like Bill gave a shit what Dylan was feeling. He never had. The kindest words he'd ever uttered had been following high school football games—"nice pass" or "great pump fake." Mom looked at him imploringly. "Will you have dinner with us next weekend?"

Dylan wanted to ask if Brie could come, but she'd be in Hawaii, damn it. He could suffer one dinner, couldn't he? "Sure, but it has to be Saturday. I work late on Fridays." And Sundays were out because Bill hated to clog up his Sunday nights when he had to prepare for the "long work week ahead." Dylan fought to repress the old resentment toward his rigid stepfather and his endless rules.

Mom's face brightened. "Perfect. How about Hazel at six o'clock? I'll make reservations."

Hazel had a fantastic menu, a great wine list, and terrific beers on tap. At least his stomach would be happy. He took a drink of beer, which was fast becoming the best thing about this shindig too. "I'll see you then." He turned to go talk to one of the few people he knew.

"Don't forget to say hello to Bill before you go."

Yeah, he'd get right on that. Dylan shot a look at his stepfather holding court with a handful of their neighbors over near his highly polished barbecue, which wasn't even in use tonight. A catered buffet had been laid out along the edge of the patio.

Bill didn't look at Dylan, and Dylan didn't expect him to. They enjoyed a mutually standoffish relationship, which seemed to suit them both fine. Damn, family was one effed-up beast. He wondered what these sorts of events were like at the Archers with all of those kids. Granted, their family wasn't a broken home like his. He stopped short. Except it was, just for an altogether different reason. And unlike Dylan's parents who'd made a decision to split up their family unit, the Archers had made no such choice. With the exception of Alex. Dylan found himself wanting to chew him out for being so unbelievably selfish.

He shook his head. What the hell was he doing? They weren't his family. Why would he even want to immerse himself in that drama? Being on the periphery with Sara was enough. He thought of last night and how upset she'd been, how she'd depended on his support. Maybe he wasn't even really on the periphery anymore. How long then until he was right smack in the middle?

He shuddered to think.

SARA HAD SPENT the weekend hanging out with Kyle, which had done great things for her heart and soul. Having Kyle back made losing Mom much easier to deal with.

On Monday she'd worked on transitioning a bunch of work-related stuff, including sending parting letters to all of her old clients, inviting them to contact her if they were ever interested in hosting an event at The Alex. She thanked them for their patience and wanted them to know she wasn't angry with them for choosing Craig (even though she might've been a teensy bit bitter). Besides, it was just good business sense to leave people with a good impression.

After three days of not seeing Dylan and only exchanging a few texts, she could barely contain herself as she practically skipped down the dirt track to the cottage. She'd brought her pink hard hat and set it on her head before she moved into the construction zone.

Dylan was standing inside the former living room, which, once enlarged, would be a phenomenal indoor eating space that opened to a covered patio facing the panoramic view of the valley. He was slightly bent as he and Manny discussed the drawings laid out before them over a makeshift sawhorse table. A green T-shirt pulled taut along Dylan's shoulder blades, and his work belt was slung low across his hips. The view was enticingly sexy.

Manny turned from the table and smiled broadly at her. "Hi, Sara."

"Hi, Manny, how's it going?"

He pointed behind her. "Look, a kitchen."

She'd been so intent on Dylan when she'd walked in that she'd failed to notice they'd framed the commercial kitchen at the back of the building, which had formerly been a bedroom and office. "Oh! It looks great. You guys are really coming along."

"The longer days sure do help. Catch you later, boss." Manny touched the brim of his hat in mock salute and winked at Sara before climbing the stairs they'd installed when they'd started on the second floor.

Sara went to Dylan, who'd taken a step back from the table. "How are you?" she asked, unable to read anything about him for some reason. Her neck prickled. Usually he looked at her the way she looked at him—like a decadent Thanksgiving feast.

"Busy. You?"

She couldn't shake the feeling that something was off with him. Maybe it had been his sister's graduation party. He hadn't said much about it, had only even mentioned it in passing Friday night. In fact, he never said much about his family at all. "Same. How was Brie's graduation?"

"Oh, you know how those things are."

She did. She'd attended several graduation ceremonies for her siblings; surprisingly, none of them had overlapped. "And the party?"

"Even more boring."

She fought back a frown at his lack of elaboration. And a stab of resentment that he hadn't asked her to be his date. Which wasn't fair since they'd agreed to a strict friends-with-benefits policy. At what point, though, did they acknowledge that the rules had slowly and subtly changed? Or had they only changed for her?

She was probably overthinking his mood today. Maybe he *was* just busy. She was, after all, intruding at his workplace. Then again, she was his boss, right? She inwardly cringed. No, she wasn't going to think of their relationship in those terms. It was too...cold. "I had a great weekend with Kyle." She'd texted Dylan that they'd made up.

He smiled, and she relaxed slightly. "That's good to hear. He comes around here almost as much as you do."

"Fair warning, I think it might get worse. He's excited to get started on the restaurant phase. We spent a lot of time talking about plans for the Arch and Fox this past weekend."

"Duly noted. Though I won't be much help if he wants to talk about the next phase."

The reason hung in the air between them—because they hadn't made a decision about who was going to be the contractor. "Tori hasn't even finished the design yet. She needs to consult with an engineer."

"I know, but it would be great if you guys included the contractor on those discussions. It would make their job a lot easier."

He had a point. "I'll let them know, thanks. Do you think next spring is too early for me to start booking for this space?" Though Derek and Chloe's wedding would be here in August, there was no point hosting events in the middle of a construction zone. Which was fine since weddings were booked so far out anyway.

Dylan shrugged. "I really can't say since I don't know much about the next phases."

She hated the chill in his tone. Moving closer, she kept her voice low. "You know it's not up to me, right? If it were, I'd hire you right now."

He quirked a smile at her. "Sure you're not just saying that to…you know, get in my pants."

Was he kidding? Of course he was kidding. She was really overthinking now. She dug to find the flirtation they usually shared. "Of course that's why I'm saying it. I haven't seen you since Friday. I'll say whatever I have to."

He laughed, and the familiar warmth she typically felt with him swept over her. "I have to get back to work, but maybe I'll see you tonight." He gave her a hot stare that sent shivers to her belly and far lower.

"You know where to find me."

His gaze fixed on something behind her. She turned to see Kyle in the doorway. He was looking at them with a bemused expression. Shit, had he overheard? No, they'd been talking very quietly and the sounds of construction from upstairs had to have drowned them out.

"See you later, Sara," Dylan said, his voice crisp and formal.

She glanced at him, saw that he was looking at Kyle and not her, and murmured, "See you." She walked toward Kyle, who moved out of the doorway.

"Hey, Sara-cat."

"Hi, Kyle. I'll be in the office."

"See you in a few. Just want to chat with Dylan about a few things."

She nodded, then started off along the dirt path, pondering whether she'd made a huge miscalculation about Dylan. Maybe he was perfectly happy with the rules of their secret affair and maybe she was doing what she'd promised not to—becoming clingy. Suddenly she could see how things could become very, very messy. And wondered—regretfully—if they should've kept to their original agreement.

Chapter Nineteen

DYLAN PARKED A block or so behind the historic home that housed Hazel, one of Newberg's best restaurants. With the weather warming as summer approached, the exterior was a bustle of outside seating, festive lights, and dozens of patrons. The space looked fun and inviting, but Dylan knew their reservation would be inside. Bill hated to dine next to a road because of the smell of exhaust, and the restaurant sat on the main highway through town.

Passing the outdoor seating area on the lawn, Dylan climbed the stairs to the porch at the front of the house. He pushed the door open and was instantly greeted by someone standing behind the bar in the room just off the foyer. "Amy will be right with you."

He nodded and pivoted on his heel to his right toward the dining area. Cubbies of wine nestled into the wall to his left showcased the best the Willamette Valley had to offer. A young woman in a black blouse and khaki skirt came from the dining room. "Good evening. Are you looking for your party?"

"I am. Davies?"

She smiled. "Just through here."

Dylan passed the smaller seating area with the wine cubbies and moved into the main dining room. His own smile froze in place as his eyes landed on the party—of *three*—against the wall. Mom, Bill, and some unknown young woman with bright blond hair and dark-rimmed glasses set on her pert nose. They all saw him at once, but it was Mom who spoke.

"Over here, Dylan."

The hostess went to stand beside his chair and gestured to the menu, which sat beside his place setting. "Here you are."

"Uh, thanks." He sat down, his entire body feeling as though it were crafted of wood. Very hard and brittle wood.

"Hello, dear," Mom said in a sunny voice that made Dylan want to grind his teeth. "This is Tracy Brinkley. Tracy is a new physician's assistant at work."

Dylan had been forced to take the chair next to Tracy so he turned to shake her hand. He might be seething inside, but he could be polite, damn it. "Tracy."

She smiled, her eyes crinkling behind her glasses. The brown shade of her eyebrows hinted that perhaps blonde wasn't her natural color. "Nice to meet you."

A strong, cloying smell, like Nordstrom during their anniversary sale that Mom had dragged him to when he was younger, wafted toward him. He preferred Sara's fresher, more subtle scent.

Dylan picked up his menu and stuck his face in it before he could glare at Mom or Bill. Mom supplied the conversation until the server came by and shared the specials. Bill ordered a bottle of pinot and Dylan ordered a beer just to be contrary. They'd foisted a blind date on him and if the only independence he could claim was his beverage, then so be it. How could Mom do this to him?

"Your mom tells me you're in construction?" Tracy asked. "How's that?"

"It's good, thanks."

"Tracy spent two years in the Peace Corps," Mom said approvingly. "It's almost like you being the army."

Except it wasn't remotely. "I was an engineer and served mostly stateside. I'm sure Tracy's assignments were far more exciting and exotic. And totally unrelated to military operations."

Tracy laughed. "Um, yes. I don't know about exciting, but more exotic for sure. How was the army?"

"Good."

Mom gave him a disapproving stare, which he returned with a "how could you?" glower.

"You'll have to forgive Dylan," Bill said, laughing the fake laugh he used to fill awkward silences. "He's not the best conversationalist in groups. You get him one-on-one and he's more comfortable." Bill didn't look at Dylan as he said this, which was just as well so he couldn't see the disbelief that was surely etched in Dylan's expression. Bill had no idea what sort of conversationalist Dylan was. They hadn't had a meaningful conversation since Dylan was twelve and Bill had told him in no uncertain terms that he was a nuisance to his family and that he only put up with his presence because of his mother.

Mom nodded in agreement with Bill, touching his arm. "It's true. Dylan is so much better one-on-one. After dinner, we'll let you two have dessert alone." She smiled and settled back in her chair, seeming quite pleased with her plan.

The server brought their drinks and Dylan took a heavy pull on the IPA while the wine was opened, sampled by Bill, and poured into their three glasses.

"I told Tracy about your divorce and how you haven't had a girlfriend in ages," Mom said, obliterating any hope that she'd been even a little bit subtle about her matchmaking. *Fucking A, could this evening get any worse?*

The answer was a resounding yes.

Just then a trio of Archers walked into the dining room: Tori, Kyle, and Sara. She stopped abruptly and stared at him. He nearly stood but Tracy took that moment to touch his arm and ask him another question. He dragged his gaze away from Sara to glance at Tracy, not hearing a word she said. When he looked back, both Tori and Kyle were peering at him surreptitiously while Sara stared down at her menu, her hands buried in her lap. If knew her at all, she was rubbing her leather bracelet for sensory input.

Kyle said something to her. She nodded, but didn't say anything.

The conversation at Dylan's table limped along. Mom and Bill laughed at something. Sara stood suddenly, knocking over her water. Kyle jumped up and rubbed his hand along her upper arm.

Sara's face was pale and when her gaze connected with Dylan's once more, he read anxiety and distress.

He pushed back from the table. "Excuse me." He crossed the small dining room. "Sara, are you all right?"

She glanced up at him, but said nothing.

"We just stopped in on our way back from the airport." Tori watched him bemusedly, likely wondering why he'd come over to check on Sara. Damn, he hadn't thought that through at all. "We dropped Mom and Hayden off."

Shit. Dylan had forgotten they were leaving today. After spending Tuesday night with Sara, he'd worked late the rest of the week and Sara had been also been busy, probably helping her mom before she left, now that he thought about it. Their "benefits" were starting to become an expectation, and that wasn't what they'd signed up for.

He was aware of near silence in the restaurant, of more than a dozen diners' eyes fixed on them. And now their *thing* had gone from totally clandestine to ragingly public.

She looked up at him. "What are you doing here?"

"Having dinner with my mom and Bill."

"Aren't you forgetting someone?" Her gaze traveled past him briefly.

He didn't want to have this conversation in front of her siblings. "I didn't bring her, my mother did. Sara, I didn't know."

"Is there something going on here?" Kyle asked, looking between Dylan and his sister.

"Apparently not," Sara said. The hurt in her eyes twisted into Dylan's gut like a knife. She turned to Kyle. "I want to go home."

"No problem." He threw Dylan a look of disgust while he massaged Sara's shoulder.

Dylan stepped to the side in an attempt to catch her eye. "Can I take you?"

She pulled away from Kyle and strode from the restaurant.

Dylan caught up with her on the porch. "Sara, wait."

She paused on the top step, but again was looking behind him. Dylan heard the door open and glanced over his shoulder. His mother.

"Where are you going, Dylan?"

"Mom, I need to leave." He didn't bother masking the anger he'd been stifling since he'd arrived. "You shouldn't have brought a blind-freaking-date."

From the corner of his eye, he saw Sara moving toward the street. Tori and Kyle came onto the porch and pushed past his mom. Kyle shot him another dark look as he started down the stairs.

Fuck, this was an unmitigated disaster. Goddamn families. "Mom, I'm going." He jogged down the stairs and followed the Archers to the sidewalk. Thankfully, they were walking away from the outside seating area so they would hopefully avoid any further scenes.

"What am I supposed to tell Tracy?" Mom called after him.

Dylan didn't bother turning around, just kept moving toward Sara, who was walking quickly along the sidewalk.

"Sara!" He called, running to catch up to her and passing her siblings in the process. He grabbed her hand. "Let me take you home, okay?"

She tried to pull away, but he kept his grip firm, yet gentle.

"Please?"

After a long moment, she nodded.

He knew Tori and Kyle were still behind him, and he turned and exchanged looks with them. They seemed skeptical, but didn't stop him. Dylan put his arm around Sara and walked her around the block to where his truck was parked.

He opened the door for her, but she turned and pierced him with a sizzling blue stare. "I just want to know one thing: Am I your only secret?"

SARA WATCHED THE play of emotions on his face—surprise, distress, resignation. None of them told her what she wanted to know. She knew she didn't have the right to be jealous or upset. They'd agreed to friends with benefits, and there had been absolutely no discussion of exclusivity. Still, she didn't see how he could do the things he did with her, talk with her the way they did, or share the things they'd shared if he didn't care about her as more than a friend. It all felt like a lie, which was why she'd asked the question.

He took her hands and met her gaze with an intensity of his own. "You are my only secret. At least you *were*. A secret, that is."

She nearly smiled at that. The proverbial cat was definitely out of the bag.

She climbed into his truck and waited for him to get in beside her. He put the key in the ignition, but didn't start the engine. Instead, he turned toward her. "Is there anything I can do for you right now?"

She felt itchy and twitchy and completely overstimulated, but there wasn't much to be done right now. She couldn't roll around on the floor or do wall pushups. That left joint compressions and muscle flexing. "You could compress my joints." She held her left hand out. "Put your hands on my wrist and sort of squish the joint, like you're going to pull my hand off, and then push it back."

He looked alarmed. "Pull your hand off?"

"Not literally. Just gently. You'll feel what I mean when you try it."

He put his hands on hers and where his touch usually sparked need and desire, tonight it elicited a sense of comfort. He pulled on her hand and then pushed back. "I see. Is this right?"

She nodded. "Ten times. Then the other wrist. Then you can do my elbows."

He finished with her left and moved to her right. "I'm sorry about what happened back there. My mom thought it would be great to set up a blind date and not tell me about it."

"That doesn't sound fun."

"It wasn't." He finished with her wrist and moved to her elbow.

His hands were rough from his work, and tanned. She looked soft and pale next to him. "You don't talk about them much. Your family."

He didn't immediately answer. When he moved back to her right elbow, he glanced at her face. "There's not much to say."

"Seriously? You have two sets of parents, three brothers and a sister, and there's not much to say?" Why hadn't she broached this with him before? Clearly there was something up with him and his family. "Your mom just set you up without your knowledge. You have to have plenty to say about that. I would."

He finished with her elbow and settled back in his seat. "What would be the point of bitching about it? She won't listen. I'll just be careful not to go out with them anymore. Hell, I knew better than to do that in the first place." He muttered the last part, but she heard him.

She buckled her seatbelt. "So you take the path of least resistance? It's better to ignore them or pretend they don't exist than to deal with the situation?"

He started the truck. "Yep."

Sometimes he could be so damnably uncommunicative. "It really wouldn't help to talk to her?"

He pulled out into the one-way street and got into the right lane so he could turn and double back toward Ribbon Ridge. "I've tried, and it never changes anything."

"Will you tell them who I am? About why you left them to take me home?" She practically held her breath.

He slid her an inscrutable glance. "I'm sure I'll say something."

The sadness over her mother's departure and the shock of seeing Dylan on a freaking *date* bubbled up inside of her and threatened to make her explode. "Let me know what you plan to say so we can keep our stories straight because, unlike you, I'll be giving Tori and Kyle a real explanation for what happened tonight. They likely already figured it out." Her voice had climbed, so that she sounded pissed and shrill. She didn't care.

"I know they did," he said quietly. "Tell them whatever you think is necessary. I plan to tell my mother that you're my employer and that you're going through a rough time. I helped you out tonight."

She turned in her seat and gaped at him. "*What?* My siblings can think we're together but your mom has to think I'm your employer? Are you embarrassed by me?" It had been years—since she'd left Ribbon Ridge—since she'd worried that people thought of her as weird or quirky. And she was. She couldn't change who she was and she didn't want to. Moving away had taught her to accept her differences and even value them.

He cast her a long look as they drove out of Newberg. His brows were pitched low over his eyes, which currently reminded her of the ocean during a winter storm. "No, I'm not embarrassed by you. Why would you think that?"

"Oh, I don't know, because you don't want your mom to know we're fuck buddies?" She'd gone for crudeness on purpose because he was being an ass. "That is what we are, isn't it?"

"Sara, that's not fair. We agreed to keeping this secret because of your family and because of the work situation."

"That's what I thought, but maybe it's secret because you just don't want anyone to know."

He swore under his breath, but she caught it. "My family is completely fucked up. I don't share my life with them on purpose, and that has *nothing* to do with you." He looked over at her. "*Nothing*, okay?"

The ferocity in his tone and the intensity of his gaze made her nod. She was quiet for a few minutes, turning over what he said in her mind. At length she asked, "Why is it so effed up?"

He exhaled loudly, his fingers tightening around the steering wheel. "It just is. I grew up with two families, neither of which felt like a real family to me. It's not like you and your family, how you all have this shared experience. Sure, I'm close to my siblings, but it's different. There are things my brothers shared growing up, experiences my sister enjoyed—all things I wasn't a part of as I was shuffled back and forth."

Sara's heart twisted for him. His voice was full of disdain, but there was an underlying hurt. "That sounds very difficult." She was hesitant to say more, lest she stop him from talking.

"That's why I don't share things with them. It isn't about you. I realize this *thing* between us is more than a thing now. But that doesn't mean they have to know about it."

So he acknowledged their relationship was something more, but not enough to tell his family about her. That should bother her—hell, it did bother her—but she was trying to understand where he was coming from. If he didn't place a lot of value on his family, sharing his personal life with them wouldn't be important. But how did she feel about the lack of regard he had for his family when hers was so critical to her?

She studied his profile as he drove. Looking at him pulled at her heartstrings and she wondered if she might be falling in love with him. She abruptly turned away. That wouldn't help anything right now.

The cab of the truck was eerily quiet as they drove into Ribbon Ridge. As they passed through the main part of town, he adjusted in his seat. "Neither one of us planned for this to grow into something more. This isn't good timing for you, and it isn't really for me either. This job is really important to me and to my crew. My main focus has to be winning the next phases. It will mean everything for our futures."

Wow, this sounded like a breakup speech. Sara gripped the handle on the door and dug her fingers into the leather.

Silence took over again until they neared the long drive to the house.

"You're awfully quiet," he said.

She shrugged, her body still careening out of control. When she got inside, she was going straight for the tire swing that hung in the gym downstairs. Swinging was one of the oldest sensory tools in Sara's experience, particularly rotating instead of being propelled just back and forth. That would slap her back into shape.

He pulled into the circular drive and put the truck into park in front of the stairs leading up to the main door. She noted he didn't turn the engine off, which was fine. She had no intention of inviting him inside.

She opened the door and the gurgle of the water rushing through the fountain in the middle of the circle greeted her. A soothing, familiar sound that took the edge of her frayed senses.

"Can I call you later?" he asked.

"Tomorrow." She didn't want to talk to him anymore tonight—she knew her limits and she was just past them. She stepped out of the truck.

"Sara?"

She turned to look at him and wished she hadn't. Maybe she was already in love with him. "What?"

"Whatever happens, I hope you know I care a great deal for you."

His words should've warmed her, right? She ought to feel encouraged or at least calmer. But she didn't. And maybe that was just the accumulation of everything that was currently heaped on her. "You're right though, the timing sucks. I gotta go." She slammed the door and ran up to the house without looking back.

Inside, she went through the foyer and up the short set of stairs to the central hall, dropped her purse and jacket, and jogged down to the gym. She'd been swinging for a good several minutes and was already feeling better when Tori and Kyle came in.

"Hey there," Tori said, looking around. "No Dylan?"

"He just dropped me off." Sara twirled around in the swing.

Kyle dropped down onto a weight bench. "You want to talk about it?"

"Dylan?" She'd told Dylan what she planned to say, but now she considered his tactic. But no, that wasn't her. "What do you want to know? Am I seeing him? Not formally, but yes, we have a *thing*."

Tori crossed her arms as a smile tilted across her lips. "You lied to me about seeing someone."

Sara dragged her feet to slow the swing. "We'd agreed to keep it secret. It seemed best with everything going on, especially the job."

"Are you happy?" Kyle asked, stretching his legs out in front of him.

"I was. Am." Sara gripped the heavy rope cord that held the swing and ran her hands up and down over the ridges. "I like Dylan a lot." *Too much.*

Tori's smile slipped away. "This makes things a bit awkward for the project."

Regardless of what happened, Sara didn't want Dylan to suffer. "It shouldn't. He's a great contractor. In fact, I think we should go ahead and hire him for phases two and three."

"I don't know if that's wise," Tori said, "now more than ever."

Sara swung herself around again. "I hope it's not because of our relationship. He's the right guy for this. He's already demonstrated he's capable, and it just makes good business sense to go with the guy who's been involved since day one. Plus, he put together a fantastic proposal for the underground pub."

Kyle glanced over at Tori. "She makes a valid argument." He pinned Sara with a serious stare. "But is it going to be a problem if you guys don't work out? What then?"

Sara couldn't answer that. It was already starting to crumble, but she wasn't really letting herself register it. Not today. She had to limit what she let inside or she'd have a total meltdown—or more of one than she'd already had at the restaurant. "Please don't factor my personal feelings into a business decision. I'll handle whatever happens with Dylan. I still think he's the right contractor."

Tori dropped her arms to her sides and moved closer to Sara. "I have to ask, sorry, but are you being objective here? If you have feelings for the guy, how can you know he's the best choice?"

Sara used her feet to bring the swing to a complete stop. Her initial reaction was to snipe at Tori for being unfair, but Sara had learned to measure her responses when she was spun up. She inhaled and fed oxygen to her brain in the hope that she could develop a regulated answer. "I understand why you'd question me, but please don't. I'm being perfectly objective. And I'll manage the situation, okay? Don't be overprotective." She gave both of them stern looks.

They exchanged glances, and that was enough for Sara to be done with this conversation. Needing to be alone, she stood up from the swing. "Thanks for your votes of confidence in my abilities. You both suck."

She strode from the gym and climbed the two flights of stairs, stopping on the main floor to grab her purse and jacket. Her bedroom was at the end of the house, directly above her parents' suite. Sara's bedroom was one of the largest because it housed sensory equipment in a long, somewhat narrow adjoining chamber that ran beneath the front eaves. She flopped down on a pile of pillows and pulled one of her weighted blankets over herself.

She knew in her heart that Tori and Kyle were just trying to look out for her, but she was also tired of being babied. Even Dylan had rushed to help her tonight and maybe only because he'd registered that she was in melt-down mode. She had no way of knowing if he'd been prompted by something more.

Normally she would talk to Mom, but she was en route to France, unavailable. Maybe that was for the best. Maybe it was time for Sara to work through this—really manage things—on her own. She'd thought moving away would give her independence and self-reliance, but maybe this was what it really meant.

The weight of the blanket pressed into her chest and legs, grounding her. She had no idea what was going to happen with Dylan, but she resolved to deal with it head on.

Chapter Twenty

AFTER SPENDING SUNDAY dodging his mom's calls and texts, sending several unanswered texts to Sara, and ultimately spending the afternoon at the job site, Dylan was eager to get back to his weekday routine. He appreciated the nondrama of his crew and the steady progress of working toward their daily goals.

This morning he was more than content to be framing a large pantry in the kitchen of the cottage. However, Sara was hovering at the forefront of his mind. He'd hated how things had gone on Saturday. And since she wasn't returning his texts, he had to conclude he'd absolutely fucked everything up.

He'd meant what he said, that what they shared had progressed past "benefits." He liked her. A lot. Cared for her like he hadn't cared for anyone in a long time. But he also meant what he'd said about the timing being bad. For both of them. Her life was incredibly convoluted right now, and he only added another layer of difficulty. And if he was being honest, he wasn't sure he wanted that added complexity either. Honestly, her family scared the hell out of him. He didn't *do* families. His mom had one thing right—he was a loner and he preferred it that way. He didn't disappoint anyone, and no one disappointed him.

His phone vibrated in his pocket. He slipped his hammer into his belt and withdrew his phone. A shaft of disappointment shot through him when he saw it was Kyle and not Sara.

KYLE: *Can you come up to the office for a quick meeting with me and Tori?*

Now what? Were they going to fire him outright for his dickish behavior? No, he doubted Sara had told them about that. He just didn't see her throwing him under the bus. He texted back, *Be right there*, and he left the cottage. With his and Sara's secret outed, anxiety splintered through him. *This* was why he didn't want a relationship. It overcomplicated everything.

A few minutes later he walked into the trailer. Tori was seated behind her desk while Kyle stood leaning against the counter of the tiny kitchenette behind her.

"What's up?" Dylan asked. They looked circumspect, which only heightened his defensiveness. Was he about to fight for his job?

"We wanted to talk to you about the project," Kyle said.

Apparently, yes. His stomach clenched. His worst fears were realized: that his inability to keep his hands to himself was about to cost him something very important.

Tori coughed as she clasped her hands together on the top of the desk. "It's time for us to hire someone for the next phases."

He assumed it wouldn't be him, but since they were starting with that, maybe he'd at least get to finish the cottage. Wait, they wouldn't really have fired him from the cottage would they? Dylan hated that his heart was speeding up.

"We've talked at length—with Derek and Hayden too," Kyle said, pushing away from the counter and dropping his hands to his sides, "and we've decided to hire you."

Dylan's jaw dropped but he quickly snapped it shut. *Nice one, Westcott.* "Wow, that's great. Thanks."

Tori's eyes narrowed slightly. "You seem surprised."

Was there any point in trying to dodge the issue? "Well, yeah. I'm sure you can imagine why."

Kyle stepped forward until he was standing next to his sister's chair. They looked like a mob boss and her enforcer or something. "Sara. We're concerned about that. We'd actually like to ask you to step back from her while you're working on the project."

"Don't you think that's her decision?" Hadn't he just been thinking that long-term relationships weren't his thing? Now he was being asked to break things off. But not by the person who mattered. The whole thing tasted bad. "What's between me and Sara is just that—between me and Sara."

Tori stood up. "We get how this looks and we sort of feel like a-holes asking, but you don't know Sara like we do. This has been a really tough time for our family, and with Mom gone," she exchanged glances with Kyle who nodded slightly, "it's just a crappy situation. Sara doesn't always know when to step away. It's sort of the nature of sensory processing disorder."

A little of Dylan's ire dissipated. He got that they cared about their sister, even appreciated them for it, but the whole conversation still felt weird. Maybe that was because it was a family-oriented discussion that required him to bare parts of himself or see parts of other people he preferred to ignore.

"We can't control you or Sara—and we don't want to," Kyle said. "But we'd be seriously derelict in our sibling duties if we didn't look out for her."

Dylan wondered what she'd think of that. She'd told him one of the reasons she'd left Ribbon Ridge was to establish her own sense of self, to prove that she could manage things independently. And she'd absolutely nailed it when she'd said her siblings would stick their noses in her business.

Tori nodded. "We love her more than anything, and we'll do anything to protect her."

Dylan got that. He might be the odd guy out in his families, but he loved his brothers and sister and he'd do anything for them too. "I hear what you're saying, but you're going to have to trust Sara to make the best choice for herself. Can you do that?"

They looked at each other. "We can," Tori said. "But if you take this job and things turn ugly between you and her…you have to understand that we'll do whatever is necessary to preserve our family's well-being." Tori blinked as if she were fighting back tears. "It's the most important thing."

Damn, it was so easy to forget they'd lost their brother, an integral part of their family and their lives, not even four months ago. "I understand."

"This isn't a threat." Kyle's blue-green eyes were piercing in their intensity. "It's just a fact. So think long and hard about what's important here, to all of us."

Fuck. If he pursued a relationship with Sara and it tanked, the one thing he counted on for stability and fulfillment, his work, would be an utter disaster. Plus, he will have screwed up her life in the process, which was sufficiently complicated all on its own. Which only left one alternative—calling things off now.

"Thanks for the opportunity. I'll think about what you said." He nodded at them, then turned to go.

"We'll talk later this week about specifics." Tori's voice had lost any semblance of the emotion she'd shown earlier. Back to business. "I need to select an engineer soon, and I'd like your input."

Dylan looked back over his shoulder and summoned a smile he didn't feel. "Sure."

He left the trailer and started back toward the cottage. Of all the things weighing down his mind, one thing stood out: the ferocity with which the Archers loved and protected each other. Did he have that with his families? He hoped so, but because he kept them at arm's length, he realized he'd never know.

SARA WOKE UP Monday morning feeling somewhat refreshed after spending Sunday doing yoga, watching her favorite movies, and painting her toenails. Kyle and Tori had—wisely—given her a wide berth.

Dad strolled into the kitchen and brushed a kiss against her forehead on his way to the fridge. He pulled out a bottled smoothie. "Just finished a nice ride. I was hoping to see you this morning," he said, unscrewing the lid from his drink. "Have you decided what you're going to do now that you've sold your business? I'm so proud of you for the way you handled that."

"Thanks. I'll be managing the wedding venue at The Alex and eventually all of the entertainment when the project is done. And I've actually been thinking of moving back to Ribbon Ridge."

"Really?" Dad's lips split in the most genuine smile she'd seen from him in months. "That's great to hear, kitten."

She turned on the bar stool and patted the one next to her. "What's up?"

He came and sat, his eyes looking more alive than they'd been since before Alex had died. "I'm considering a new project—inspired by The Alex. I've found a property in central Oregon that I'd like to renovate. It's actually an old farm. It'll make a great multipurpose space—bed and breakfast, pub-slash-restaurant, and event venue. It's a great location."

Sara curled her hand around her cup. Was this because he wasn't involved in this project? She felt a pang of irritation that Alex had left him out. "That's a lot to take on."

"Yes, but after nine brewpubs, I think I can handle it," he said wryly.

That was true. He was a real estate developer by inheritance. The Archers had developed Ribbon Ridge, expanded their interests, and owned a great deal of commercial property that housed a variety of endeavors. But at his heart, Dad was a brewer. This sounded like some sort of midlife crisis, which he was absolutely entitled to right now, instead of a business venture.

"Why the sudden interest in this, Dad? Is it because of The Alex?"

He set his drink down and looked at the counter. "In part, I guess. With your mother gone, I just…I just need something to do."

Sara's heart ached for him. Though Mom was visibly the most upset about Alex, Sara wondered if Dad had taken his death the hardest. Sometimes she thought he maybe hadn't faced it at all. "You can be involved at The Alex if that's what you want."

"It's not what Alex wanted," Dad said tightly. He braced his hands on the counter and stared out the windows overlooking the pool and yard below.

She touched his wrist. "Dad. I know this has been really hard for you. Tell me what I can do."

When he turned his head to look at her, his eyes were surprisingly dry. Surprisingly? She had yet to see him cry since the day he'd found Alex. *Oh, noooo.* Why hadn't she ever thought of that? Dad had been the one to find him in his bed that morning. The one who hadn't been able to wake him. The one who'd tried, unsuccessfully, to revive him. "Do you ever want to talk about it?" She said softly, tentatively. "That day."

He looked away from her again and shook his head. "No. That won't help. It's best if I don't think about it too much." He smiled weakly. "You're probably right. I have plenty to keep me busy here, especially with Hayden gone."

"You should let Kyle step in. There's no reason not to." She inwardly flinched waiting for his answer, knowing that Kyle was still a sore subject with him.

Dad's expression turned weary. "There are reasons, but I won't get into them."

"I've made peace with Kyle. It's time for you to do the same. Talk to him. I know he wants to make things right."

"I appreciate that you're trying to help." His features softened. "I'll give him a shot, okay?"

"I don't think you'll be sorry." She hugged him tight. "I love you, Dad."

"I love you too." He pulled back and looked at her. "I'll be in my office if you need me."

Sara watched him go and her phone vibrated on the counter. She reached over to pick it up and looked at the display.

TORI: *Wanted you to know that Kyle and I went ahead and hired Dylan for phases two and three.*

Sara stared at the phone. Had he said something? Done something? She couldn't believe they'd offered him the job after the way they'd tried to meddle the other night.

She didn't know what was going on, but suspected it involved overprotective siblings. Who she planned to punch in the throat.

DYLAN CUT OUT of work early Monday evening after getting a text from his dad asking him to stop by and take a look at his water heater. As the de facto family handyman, Dylan got these sorts of calls all the time. As much as he kept his family at arm's length, he liked feeling needed. Particularly today when he was thinking—too much—about family and his place in it.

When he drove up to his dad's house, he nearly kept going. Parked outside was a car he recognized and strove to avoid: his ex-wife's.

He parked at the end of the driveway and turned off the engine. He sat there for a minute and then jolted to attention as Jessica came out of the house and started down the driveway toward his truck.

He climbed out of the cab and came around. She was dressed in her workout clothes but her hair and makeup were perfect, which meant she'd come from work. She always did her workouts in the morning, before she started her shift as a personal trainer.

"Hi, Dylan." She chewed her lower lip, a telltale sign she was nervous.

"How are you, Jess? Long time, no see."

"Just the way we like it, right?" She flashed a smile. "There's no need to pretend, is there?"

They'd known each other too long and too well to fake anything. "What're you doing here?"

"Dropping off a book from my mom for Angie. Book club."

Angie went to book club with Monica too? Dylan shook his head. "Congratulations are in order, I hear. Who's the lucky guy?"

"You don't know him. He's an alcohol and drug counselor over in Newberg."

At the rehab center most likely. "That where you're going to live?" He couldn't help the feeling of resentment that threatened if her answer was yes. She'd complained endlessly about having to move away from Ribbon Ridge even temporarily when they were married.

"No, we have a house here. In the new subdivision on the east side." Closer to Newberg then. "What about you? Seeing anyone?"

"Sort of." It was as accurate of an answer as he could give.

"Good for you. I hope it grows to more than sort of." She edged toward him and he caught her scent, a tropical, flowery perfume he could never remember the name of. She pushed her long dark hair over her shoulder. "You deserve to be happy, if you can. Did you ever get therapy?"

She'd pushed him to get counseling the last year or so of their marriage. She'd claimed the army had messed him up, but it hadn't been the army, it had been their differences: her need for family involvement and approval and his absolute indifference to it.

"No, I didn't."

She looked to the left, her nostrils flaring. "You're as revelatory as ever."

He leaned back against the hood of his truck, uncaring that it was dirty and radiating heat. "You know, when I divorced you, I thought I was sparing myself from further scolding about my lack of communicating."

She glared at him. "You did. Now I remember why we aren't even friends. Not that I expected anything more given the craptastic example your parents set. See you around, Dylan." She stalked off to her car.

Dylan pushed away from the truck and pivoted toward the house, irritation boiling just beneath the surface. Jessica was the last person he'd needed to see today when he was trying to sort his life out. Why had Dad invited him over if she was going to be here? Why the hell didn't his family close ranks and protect their own the way the Archers did?

He raised his hand to knock on the door and then thought, *screw it*. Dad always told him to just come in, so he did.

Dad came from the kitchen, his face pinched. "You didn't run into Jessica, did you?"

"A little warning would've been nice."

"Sorry, I didn't know she was stopping by. I never would've asked you to come over if I had. Believe me, I know how painful it is to run into your ex."

Jessica's words burned Dylan's chest. "Why is that exactly? Thirty years you and Mom have been divorced, and you still can't treat each other civilly. You guys are great role models."

Dad straightened, his graying eyebrows first climbing then dropping low over his eyes. "What's with you?"

A lifetime of buried hurt erupted to the surface. "I'd like to know why I wasn't important enough for you and Mom to try to get along."

Dad held up his hand. "Dylan, you're plenty important enough."

"Really? Then why did you guys take versions of our family pictures without me in them?"

Dad wiped his hand over his mouth. "That was only a few times. Angie—"

"I know. *Angie*. It was always Angie. You put her before me, just like Mom put Bill before me. That is, when you weren't putting your other kids first." Years of shoving the pain to the back of his mind rolled over him, gathering momentum like a massive snowball tumbling down a steep slope. "I never came first. I have no idea what it feels like to be the most important thing in another person's life. Why the *fuck* is that, Dad?"

"Dylan!" Angie gasped from the base of the stairs to Dylan's left.

He looked over at her, uncaring that he was shocking the hell out of her. He turned back to the right to face his dad. "I'll come back tomorrow to look at the water heater when you're both at work." He had a key.

He turned and left, firing up his truck and speeding away as quickly as possible. He blasted his radio, finding a station that was playing something suitable to his mood. "Shinedown." *Perfect.*

As he drove out of their subdivision toward the hills, he realized he could easily veer west to Sara's. She still hadn't responded to his texts from yesterday, and though he hadn't tried her today, he still wanted to talk to her even if he wasn't 100 percent sure what he intended to say.

He pulled into the Archer driveway and parked in front of the main entry to the house. What if Kyle or Tori answered the door? The hell with it. He marched up the steps and rang the bell.

It took a long minute, but the door opened. Thankfully, it was Sara. All the things he meant to say, all the reasons he'd planned to offer about why they couldn't work out vacated his brain. He grabbed her waist and slammed against her, kissing her with a passion he didn't realize he had.

Clutching at his shoulders, she kissed him back, her mouth hot and open and utterly delicious. God, how he'd missed her. How long had it been since they'd been together? Not even a week and yet he was starved.

She pulled his shirt up and slid her fingertips along his sides, then around to his back, digging into his flesh. He buried one hand in her hair and clutched the other against her ass, which he pulled snug to his hips. She rotated against him, fueling his desire.

She moved backward then stopped abruptly, causing him to nearly knock her over. He pulled back and steadied her. They'd hit the base of a short set of stairs that led up into the massive oval hallway.

Their breath came in heavy pants, creating a rhythmic, animalistic sound that reverberated in his very bones like some sort of primal beat. Damn, he hadn't realized how badly he was drawn to her, how desperately he wanted her. He thought of taking her upstairs or wherever the hell her bedroom was and spending the night showing her how much he'd missed her, but he didn't. The wildness of his need quite frankly scared the shit out of him.

He shook his head. Had to be because of his mental state. He'd completely lost it at Dad's house. He looked at her apologetically. "Sorry."

She smoothed her hair where he'd fisted it while they'd made out. "For kissing me?"

He let go of her and stepped back. "For barreling in here and jumping on you, yeah."

"It was mutual, in case you didn't notice."

He wanted to smile, but didn't. There were too many things to be said. "I noticed. Look, I came here to talk to you because you weren't returning my texts."

"I know and *I'm* sorry. It's been weird adjusting to Mom being gone and my dad is having a tough time—it's all just weighing on me in a big way."

He noted she didn't mention him in her litany of worries. He wasn't sure if that was good or bad. Good, he decided. He didn't want to add to her load. "What's going on with your dad?"

"I'm not sure he's really dealt with Alex's death. Plus, he feels left out of the renovation project. Alex specifically asked him to stay out of it."

Dylan's gut clenched. It was one thing to feel left out, as he did, but to be pointedly excluded in your son's dying wish? He didn't think it got more awful than that. "Your dad's in worse shape than you realized, isn't he?"

"I think so. I'd all but decided to move back here and this sort of seals it. I came back to help Mom and now she's gone to France, but it turns out Dad needs me too."

She was coming back to Ribbon Ridge? The things he'd come to say swam back to the front of his mind. He cared for her. More than he probably understood, but he wasn't sure he was ready for a commitment. Sara deserved a happily ever after, and not only could he not guarantee that, he was pretty sure he was incapable of delivering.

He felt the weight of her expectation, and he couldn't bear the strain. "Sara, I hope you aren't moving home because of me. This thing between us—"

"We should end it." Her eyes were so clear and blue. He wanted to dive into them and float forever. "That's what you really came here to do, isn't it?"

He hadn't been sure. That didn't take the sting from her words. "When you didn't respond to me…"

"You assumed I was done. That's okay; in the absence of communication, you sort of have to make things up, right?" She fidgeted with her bracelet. "Yes, it's mutual. Things are just too complicated right now, and as great as I feel when I'm with you, it's not fair to you that things in my life are such a mess."

Not fair to *him*. She was incredible. He went over to her and brushed her hair back from her face. He gently pressed his lips to her forehead, her cheek, and then her mouth, lightly grazing her soft flesh. "I'm still here for you, as your friend."

"Thanks. I appreciate that." She walked to the door and held it open for him. "I'll see you at the cottage."

"Yeah, you will." He paused at the threshold. "Will that be weird?"

She smiled softly. "Only if we let it, and I'll try not to."

"Me too. See you." He walked out onto the porch and heard the door close behind him.

As he climbed back into his truck, he realized he didn't actually get to do the primary thing he'd come for—rant about his family. The irony that he'd finally been about to open up to someone only to fail miserably wasn't lost on him. If anything, it supported their breakup and cemented what he already knew, that he was a loner and always would be.

Chapter Twenty-One

June

TORI LOOKED UP from the kitchen island where she was reading her iPad and drinking her morning coffee. She took in Sara's white skirt and capped-sleeve teal-colored blouse. "You look cute. Where are you off to today?"

Sara smoothed her hand down her skirt, her bracelets clanging together against her wrist. "Meeting with Aubrey to sign off on the sale of Sara Archer Celebrations."

"It seems like it's taken a while to get all of that settled."

"Yeah, a lot of details to hammer out. Lawyers aren't the fastest service providers."

Tori chuckled. "You're right about that. So you're feeling good about it?"

Sara grabbed a bottle of water from the fridge. "Surprisingly, yes. Thanks." Feeling good was a fleeting thing the last week since she and Dylan had parted ways.

Tori sipped her coffee. "I'm meeting with Dylan later to decide which engineer to hire. I know you haven't been involved with that, but you're welcome to come if you want. I think Kyle might be there too."

Sara had done a good job of avoiding Dylan since their breakup. They'd had one formal meeting to discuss finishes and colors for the cottage, but Kyle had joined them so things had stayed purely professional, which was for the best. Her heart still pulled when she saw him—as did regions further south—but she didn't regret ending things. As they'd agreed, the timing was just terrible. Maybe in a year or whenever, they could try again. That thought gave her very little consolation. She couldn't live in a state of expectation or ambiguity. They weren't a couple, and she wanted to be fine with that. *Needed* to be fine with that.

"I'll see how my day goes," Sara said. "Catch you later." She grabbed her purse and went out to the garage. Fifteen minutes later, she pulled into the small parking lot beside the renovated house that held the law offices of Tallinger and Associates.

Sara ascended the short flight of steps to the wide porch and then went into the small reception area. The receptionist greeted her warmly. "I'll let Aubrey know you're here."

Sara glanced at her phone while she waited.

"Sara?"

Sara turned to see Aubrey standing a few feet away. "Hi, you ready for me?"

Aubrey smiled. "Sure, come on back." She turned and led her down a hallway to her office. Dressed in dark gray pinstriped slacks and heels Sara didn't think she could ever navigate without falling on her butt, Aubrey was the picture of casual elegance.

Aubrey went into her office and sat at a small, round table. She gestured for Sara to take one of the other two chairs. "Here's the agreement." She slid a small stack of papers toward Sara. "You're welcome to read through it again, but it's pretty much the same as the last time you reviewed it."

Sara flipped through the agreement and was surprised at how relieved she felt. It really had been a blessing in disguise. She was excited about building up The Alex, about becoming successful in Ribbon Ridge. Alex had wanted them all to reconnect with their family and with Ribbon Ridge, and she'd done that. She smiled to herself, thanking her brother for this gift.

She quickly signed her name and then pushed the papers back to Aubrey.

"How do you feel?" Aubrey asked.

Sara couldn't have censored herself, even if she tried. "A little sad, but mostly relieved. Okay, and maybe a tad overwhelmed." She felt like she was starting a whole new chapter in her life, and she supposed she was.

"This is a big change. You and your family have had a lot of big changes lately."

Sara took a deep, sustaining breath. "This was just… my thing. The thing that I created that belonged to me. It made me unique and special in my family." She flicked a glance at Aubrey who was watching her intently.

"I'm sure there are lots of things that make you unique and special." Aubrey stood up from the table and went to her desk. Sara didn't watch what she did there, but heard a drawer open and close.

Then an envelope was moving toward her on the table. Her name was scrawled across the front. She recognized the handwriting: Alex's. The breath left her lungs and her heart squeezed. For the briefest moment, it felt as though he were still here.

She reached out tentatively and touched the edge. "Is this…is this my letter?"

"Yes." Aubrey said. "I'm supposed to give it to you at time when you seem truly alone or overwhelmed. I'm not sure how Alex expected me to know these things since I only see you guys once a month when we meet about the trust, but I guess he somehow knew that I'd figure it out."

Alex was like that. He discerned things about people that no one else did. Maybe because he had time to study people because he moved so much slower than just about everyone. He felt like he was left behind, but maybe that had been a gift.

Sara picked up the envelope and stuffed it into her purse.

"If you want to read it now, I'll leave you alone," Aubrey offered.

"I appreciate the offer, but I'll just take it with me." Sara stood. "Thanks again for all of your help."

Aubrey stood too and opened the door for her. "I'll get this paperwork to Craig's attorney. You should have the money in a few days. The wire's still okay with you?"

"Yeah, thanks." Sara was barely listening. Her entire focus was on the letter.

She drove home as quickly as she could and parked in the garage. She hoped no one was around so that she could read the letter in peace. Perhaps she ought to just read it in the car? No, she wanted to read it in his room.

She went in through the mudroom and paused, pivoting to the left. She stared at the door to Alex's room. It was always closed now. She didn't remember the last time she'd gone inside.

With slow steps, she went and opened it, shutting the door behind her as she moved inside. It looked the same. Smelled the same. She half expected Alex to wander in from the bathroom that also opened up to the hallway that led off the mudroom.

But he didn't. And he never would. She set her purse on his desk and withdrew the envelope. Perching on the edge of his bed, she stuck her finger under the seal and split it open. She pulled out the letter—a single piece of paper—and unfolded it. His handwriting stared at her, familiar yet distant, already a memory.

Dear Sara,

First, I want to apologize. I know what I did was selfish and that it affected you in ways I can only imagine. I hope your SPD hasn't been off the charts and that you've been able to manage. I suspect the

*whole family is in disarray and for that, I'm truly
sorry.*

*I wonder if you'll be the first to get your letter, after
Mom and Dad. I sort of think you will. Because of
your strength and capability, you'll be able to move
on from what I've done more quickly and with a
clearer head than just about everyone else. You can do
anything you set your mind to. Who else has gone off
and created a successful business on their own? (Liam
doesn't count—he's a freak, right?) Don't ever forget
who you are and who you can be. For you, there are
no limits.*

*I know you think you're quirky and you worry that
people treat you differently. They don't. Well, I suppose
that's not exactly true. The sibs do sometimes, but you
can't let them get to you, just as you have to remember
our shared experience. They will always remember the
girl who spoke haltingly, who melted down if she felt
too crowded, and who worked twice as hard to achieve
in school. Don't begrudge them wanting to protect
and care for you. It's our—sorry, their—right and
privilege. Of course, I still expect you to kick them in
the ass from time to time because they need it. I hope
you and Kyle find your way back to each other. Your
relationship was so special. Don't be too hard on him.
After all, his leaving was the catalyst for where you are
today, and that, sis, is a beautiful thing.*

*Thank you for taking care of Mom and Dad,
because I know you are. Just remember to put yourself
first. I'm not saying to turn your back on anyone, but*

*when all is said and done, this is your life and you
have to live it. I hope you will. I hope you find love
and have a family—you're going to be the best mom.
One of my greatest regrets is that I won't be around to
see it.*

I love you.

Alex

Her heart pounded a staccato rhythm that filled her
ears. She turned her head and looked at the picture on
Alex's nightstand. It was from the TV show, the photo
they'd taken on the last day of shooting. They were standing together, their arms around each other, Alex in the
center.

He'd been going through a really good patch so he
didn't have his oxygen tank, and he looked more vibrant
than usual. Her gaze moved to Liam who was standing
on the right end. They'd never looked as alike as they did
in that picture. She knew why Alex had kept it next to his
bed, even though it was from when they were twelve. It
reminded him of who he could be, of the heights he could
achieve when he was healthy.

Apparently it hadn't been enough.

She reread the letter and waited for tears to fall, grew
angry when they didn't. Then realized she was angry at
him for leaving.

She looked back at his smiling twelve-year-old face.
"Yeah, that was really selfish of you. I would've helped
you. I would've moved home and done whatever it took
if you'd asked."

But maybe he hadn't because he'd known she needed to fly. And maybe that made him something less than selfish.

At last, she felt wetness on her cheeks. Then she smiled. "Thanks, Alex. I love you, too."

She refolded the letter and put it back in the envelope. She hugged it to her chest and lay back on his bed. The morning passed as she stared at the ceiling—she really didn't know how long she zoned out, but it felt good. Almost as good as she felt when she was with Dylan. It wasn't about the way he made her feel physically—it was the way he supported her, understood her, cared about her. Yes, the timing was bad and things could go to hell, but life was fraught with risk. And that made the reward all the sweeter.

She wasn't giving up on Dylan without a fight.

After a quick lunch, she drove up to The Alex for the meeting with Dylan and the others. As she stepped out into the dirt parking lot, she realized she should've changed—ballet flats weren't exactly the right footwear for the construction zone.

When she walked into the trailer and saw Dylan's reaction to her outfit, however, she was glad she'd kept it on. He sat on the couch set back against the wall beneath a rectangular window, his arm draped over the back. His position was slouchy-sexy and his gaze raked over her, lingering on the necklace she'd worn when they'd met months ago at Sidewinders, with heated approval. So much for breaking up—it seemed he wanted her as much as she wanted him. *Good.*

"Sara, you decided to join us," Tori said from behind her desk.

Kyle sat in a chair he'd pulled up to the side of the desk, which left the couch as the most logical place for her to sit. Beside Dylan.

She set her purse on the floor and sat. He pulled his arm from the back and straightened.

She snuck a look at Dylan, but he was focused on the papers in his lap. "I thought I'd just listen in."

Tori launched into the discussion of the three engineers they'd interviewed. There was one both she and Dylan agreed was out, but the discussion as to which of the remaining two to hire was lively. Dylan and Tori each had a favorite and it came down to them asking Sara and Kyle for their opinions.

"How are we supposed to decide from this?" Kyle said, thumbing through their resumes and portfolios. He handed one set to Sara. "How about rock, paper, scissors?"

Sara laughed. She was in too good of a mood to contain herself. "Or I could pick a number between one and ten."

Kyle chuckled but both Dylan and Tori did not appear amused. "Well," Kyle coughed, "should Sara and I schedule an interview with the other two?"

Sara looked at the papers in her hand. "Wait. I know this guy—Cade D'Onofrio. Sorry, I didn't realize he was the same guy until I saw the picture. I did an anniversary party for his parents a couple of years ago. I like him."

Tori rolled her eyes. "You're just siding with Dylan because—" She snapped her mouth shut. "Never mind."

Sara slid a look at Dylan, but he was angled toward Tori. Was he giving her a death stare? Sara shot her sister a WTF look. Tori made a teensy shrug and looked down at her desk.

"Cade D'Onofrio it is," Kyle said. "Honestly, I would've voted for him based on the paperwork, if it had come to that. His experience is more in line with what we're doing. Besides, he's a nice-looking guy, Tor, maybe you'll hit it off." He winked at her.

Tori's gaze practically threw daggers at him. "Don't play matchmaker. I prefer to keep business matters completely professional."

Ouch. Sara tried to pretend that didn't sting.

Dylan stood. "If that's everything, I need to get back to the site. See you guys." He left the trailer before Sara could tell him she wanted to talk to him, not that she would've after Tori's comments.

Sara turned to her sister. "What the hell was that?"

Tori shuffled the papers in front of her and stacked them to the side on top of a file folder. "Sorry, I wasn't thinking. My bad."

Sara wasn't letting her off that easy. Alex's letter had bolstered her in ways she hadn't known she needed. There was no need for her to take any crap from her siblings. "What did you mean with that backhanded professional comment?"

"Nothing, really." She looked directly at Sara. "Really."

Sara relaxed. There was something lurking in Tori's eyes, something dark and sad. Was she upset about Alex? They all went through bouts of depression about it. Maybe this would cheer her up. "I got my letter from Alex today."

Tori's eyes widened briefly and she sat straighter in her chair. "Where is it? What'd it say?"

"It's at home. He wrote some stuff I needed to hear."

"That's great, Sara." Kyle's eyes shone with genuine warmth.

Tori crossed her arms. "Why'd you get yours?"

Sara grew a little uneasy. Tori seemed pissed. Sara remembered that she'd been upset to learn they had to wait for their letters. "Because I seemed to need it. Aubrey said Alex wanted me to have it when I was feeling overwhelmed."

"Are all of our letters like that? I mean, will I get mine if Aubrey thinks I'm overwhelmed?" Tori sounded hopeful.

"I don't know. I didn't think to ask, sorry. I'm happy to share mine later." She glanced over at Kyle who was watching Tori. "He apologized."

Tori bent to pick up her laptop bag and set it on the desk. She gathered her files and papers and slipped them into the bag. "Good." She stood up and pushed her chair back. Kyle got up and Sara joined them.

"Tori, I'm sure you'll get your letter just when you need it most," she said.

Tori's mouth twisted into a skeptical smirk. "It's hard to imagine I haven't hit that point yet. It's been rough, hasn't it?"

Sara gave her a tight, fierce hug. "We're just taking this one day at a time."

Kyle joined the hug, wrapping his arms around both of them. The embrace reminded her of happier days and felt like just a little slice of normal.

When they broke apart, Tori left. Kyle said, "She'll be okay. You know how she is."

Emotional, yeah. "I do and I hope so."

"All right, I'm outta here. I actually have a, *gasp*, job to get back to."

"How's that going at Archer? With Dad?"

Kyle reached for the doorknob. "Not bad. We stick to business for the most part."

"And Derek?" That was probably the bigger question. Their rift was perhaps wider and deeper than his and Sara's had been.

Kyle blew a gust of air out and glanced at the ceiling. "Don't ask. We try not to talk to each other, but it's kind of hard."

"Um, yeah. You're the COO and he's the CFO. How does not communicating work exactly?"

"I'm not officially the COO," he corrected. "Hayden's on a leave of absence. I'm just a short-term, fill-in lackey. I'm not even sure I get benefits." He winked at her, always trying to make light of situations.

"Are you ever serious?"

He arched a blond brow. "Have you ever known me to be?"

She shook her head at him and released a smile. "Only when your life depended on it."

He gave her a quick hug. "Love you. See you later."

Alone, Sara squared her shoulders. Time to go talk to Dylan. She walked outside and paused, looking down at her rather inappropriate outfit for a construction site. Once she'd made up her mind, she'd wanted to see him right away, but now she realized interrupting his workday probably wasn't the best idea. Best to catch him tonight at home. Altering course, she went back to her car and drove home to wait through the interminable afternoon and evening hours until she could see him again.

BY THE TIME Dylan drove up his driveway, it was full dark. It had been a long, exhausting day, but seeing Sara had definitely been the highlight. He'd missed her over the last week, more than he thought he would and definitely more than he cared to admit. He'd thought of calling her—after all, they'd agreed to remain friends. But he doubted they could do that. They were always tempted to be something more.

He squeezed the steering wheel, wondering if they'd made a mistake. No, failing at a relationship with her, letting her down—that would be an even bigger mistake.

His mind froze as he recognized her car parked next to his house. He shut off his truck and got out, wishing he didn't look and smell like a construction dog. As he carried his lunch cooler up the stairs, she jumped from the porch swing. "Hi. Hope you don't mind that I was waiting for you."

"No, but let me turn a light on." He unlocked the door, set his cooler inside, and threw the porch lights on.

"Thanks, it's pretty dark up here. I had this flashlight in my purse though." She held up a little handheld light that looked as though it doubled as a mini standup lantern. "A guy I know suggested carrying one for safety purposes."

He thought of that day in the tunnels with her. It seemed forever ago and yet like yesterday. "Good plan." He should invite her in, but he was petrified of what might happen. They couldn't keep falling into bed together. It wasn't going to help anything.

She wasn't wearing her hot little outfit anymore, but a pair of jeans and a basic purple long-sleeved T-shirt. She fingered the edge of the sleeve, which told him she was maybe a little nervous. "I wanted to talk to you."

He leaned against the doorframe and crossed his arms to give his hands something to do besides itching to touch her. "Everything okay?"

"Yeah, it's good. Great, actually." She smiled at him. "I think we made a mistake."

Shit. She wanted to talk about *that.*

Her fingers moved faster along the hem of her sleeve. "I think we should try to make this work. In the real world."

Shit, shit, shit. "Nothing's changed, Sara. We still have The Alex, and if things don't work out…"

"I know and I've thought about that. Things are awkward either way. Today with Tori didn't show you that?"

Yes, it had, but there were degrees of awkward. A full-on breakup after a full-on relationship would be a hell of a lot more difficult than what they were currently navigating.

She crossed her arms and flexed her shoulders and biceps. "Now that I've decided to move back to Ribbon Ridge permanently, I'm looking forward to the next chapter in my life. I'm excited about The Alex. About being home again with my family. About a future with you."

He was happy for her, but freaking out about the last thing she'd said. "Sara, I still don't think this is a good idea—us, I mean. The timing is still lousy."

She moved toward him. "When is timing ever good? We're pretty good together, aren't we?"

Better than good. "Physically, yes, but we can't build a future on that."

Her brow creased. "No, but it's also not all we share." She glanced at him and quickly looked away, clueing him that her senses were likely out of whack. "We have friendship and trust. The only thing missing is commitment." She took another step forward, her gaze connecting with his. "I'm ready to make one, if you are."

"Sara, it's so much more than that." He rubbed his hand over his chin, felt the two days of growth there, and bizarrely compared it to the prickliness to this goddamned conversation. "What you're offering is…it's more than I deserve."

Her brows knitted. "What do you mean?"

"You said it wasn't fair to me for us to pursue anything. What I didn't say, and should have, is that it isn't fair to you either. There's a reason I stick to one-night stands. I'm terrible at relationships. Look at my marriage. Look at my family. I'm a total failure. I'd only end up hurting you in the long run, and I can't bear that."

He registered the hurt in her eyes and despised himself for starting things up with her in the first place. She was a spectacular woman with so much to offer—someone else. "It's better to call this quits now while we can still be friends. I hope we can still be friends." He said it to convince himself as much as her because right now he wasn't sure how he could stop thinking of her as his lover.

"I see." She sounded like she couldn't breathe. She'd dropped her head and was staring at the boards of the porch.

God, he was an asshole. But how much worse would this be six months from now? "I'm saving you a lot of heartache."

When she looked up, her eyes were full of fire. "I believe you think that and for now, I don't know how to convince you otherwise. You say you're saving me a lot of heartache, but my heart is aching. Right now. It's too late to protect me from falling in love with you, Dylan. It's done. I'm there. I'm *here*."

Fuuuuuck, she'd said the *L* word. It was like a Mack truck had smashed into him from all sides. Emotion bubbled up in him, but he squashed it down. Loving her didn't matter. He'd loved Jessica too and that hadn't mattered. He'd tried to love his family and that hadn't mattered. If you kept trying something and it didn't work, at some point you had to accept that it was broken. *He* was broken.

"Sara," he didn't know what to say. "I'm…not in love with you." Saying it cut so deeply because he suspected it wasn't true. He thrust the thought away—he couldn't love her. Love was an emotion that just never worked out for him.

She put her hand over her mouth. Then she nodded, turned, and started down the porch steps.

His own heart was aching, but he really and truly thought this was for the best. For her. Better to disappoint her now than later.

As she drove away into the night, Dylan slumped back against his front door. If he was doing the right thing, why did it feel so wrong?

Chapter Twenty-Two

AN HOUR LATER, after taking a scalding hot shower that did nothing to warm his insides and drinking a beer that did even less, Dylan crashed on the couch. He put his feet up and stared at the ceiling, not even registering whatever show he'd landed on when he'd thrown the TV on. Some sitcom.

The sound of his doorbell jolted him upright. He turned off the TV and listened, wondering if he hadn't heard the noise as part of some wishful thinking.

No, he didn't want Sara to come back. He'd done the right thing.

The bell rang again. He considered ignoring it, but decided he wasn't that big of a dick.

With a slow, heavy gait he made his way to the entry hall. Then nearly tripped when he saw his parents—his dad *and* mom—through the window.

He opened the door. "Uh, this is weird."

"Hello to you, too." Mom didn't wait for an invitation, but pushed in past him. "Goodness, you still haven't done anything with that room?" She was looking at the front parlor, which was covered with godawful floral wallpaper and a hideous oak chair rail from the late '80s. Mom hadn't been here since shortly after he'd moved in, what, three years ago?

He didn't say anything, just led them toward the back of the house. He heard Dad shut the door behind him.

"This better?" he said as he moved into the kitchen. He took a small amount of pleasure from Mom's obvious shock.

She turned about, gaping. "It's gorgeous. Why doesn't the whole house look like this?"

"Little things called time and money."

She glanced at him before continuing her visual inventory. "But you do all of this yourself."

"The granite and appliances aren't free, Mom."

She sniffed. "I suppose."

He went to the fridge and pulled out another beer. "Can I get you guys anything?"

"A beer would be great." Dad smiled, but his eyes were dark, like he was a bit apprehensive.

Dylan got a second beer, opened them, and handed one to Dad. "Mom?"

"No, nothing for me." She slid her hand across the countertop. "I can't get over how fabulous this looks. Who designed it?"

"I did."

Her jaw sagged. "Really?"

Dylan nearly laughed at her reaction, but he was too emotionally drained. "Yeah, really. So what brings you guys up here? Together. This is weird." He knew he was repeating himself, but he couldn't help it. He hadn't seen them together since his wedding.

Mom and Dad glanced at each other. Dad took a drink of beer. "We wanted to talk with you. To apologize, mostly. Should we sit?" He half turned toward the great room.

"Suuuurrre." Dylan preceded them and took a seat on the couch. Dad sat beside him and Mom took one of two chairs that were angled in front of the windows. They wanted to apologize? He looked at Dad. "Is this because of what happened last week? I texted you an apology."

"I know, but it wasn't necessary. I'm," he shot Mom a stern look, "*we're* the ones who need to apologize. And it's been a hell of a long time coming."

Holy shit, he wasn't sure he was ready for this. Not tonight. His insides were already pummeled into bits after Sara. "Why now?"

"Why not now?" Dad shook his head ruefully. "I'm so sorry it took you losing your cool for me to open my eyes. I thought we did a decent job, that you were happy. You were so young when we split up, I never imagined our divorce affected you."

"It didn't—at least not in the way it does for most kids, I guess." Dylan shrugged. He had an odd sensation, as though this conversation wasn't really happening.

Mom scooted forward to the edge of her chair. "I know things haven't always been easy between you and Bill."

"He doesn't like me, Mom. Never has." Though how did an adult not a like a kid? Especially when they were married to that kid's mom?

She pursed her lips. "It isn't that. He just…he didn't want to try to be your father since you already had one."

"I'd asked him not to," Dad said quietly. "I didn't think he'd be quite so literal. I screwed up, son. I should've encouraged him to love you and cherish you as much as I did." His voice started to break, and he inhaled sharply. "As much as I *do*."

Dylan's breath rattled around in his chest like it was trapped. He didn't know what to say.

"And I wasn't exactly supportive of Angie," Mom said. "Or of you, Sam." She looked at Dylan's dad. "We should've done more to make this multifamily thing work for Dylan, and I know you tried."

Dylan stood up, the energy coursing through him forcing him to move. He picked up his beer and took a long drink. Then he moved back toward the kitchen.

Dad turned on the couch to look at him. "Dylan, you seem uncertain."

"This is just…I can't get my head around the two of you here together."

Mom got up and followed him. "It's long overdue. When your dad called to tell me what you said…"

Dylan stood in the kitchen behind the giant island he'd built, using it as a defense against them. "He called you?"

She nodded. "I'm glad he did. No, I'm sorry he had to. I know I'm…controlling. I just want you to be happy.

I think I knew, deep down, that you weren't. That it was more than Jessica. You never should've married her." She stood on the other side of the counter and rested her palms atop the granite.

This was too much. Mom had practically pushed him to marry Jessica. "Why were you in favor of it then?"

"I thought it would be good for you. I thought it was what you needed." Dylan couldn't argue with her since he'd thought the same thing.

Dad came and joined them, setting his beer down and looking at Dylan with an intensity that honestly made him a little uncomfortable. "I thought so too. I thought a family of your own would coax you to open up, to *feel*. You're a pretty closed off guy."

"And why do you think that is?" He sounded angry. Hell, he *felt* angry. "Look, this is a great effort. I guess I appreciate it, but it's kind of late. I'm thirty-one years old. I am who I am. I don't like to show how I feel and I sure as hell don't like to talk about it."

Dad held up his hand. "I get it, and no one's asking you to change, least of all us. We just want to do things differently. And we hope, in time, that you'll want to open up and join in with our families—*your* families."

Now they wanted to find a way to make him feel included? "I don't know if that will work. Like I said, I am who I am, and things are the way they are."

"Things are only the way we let them be," Dad said, starting to sound a little stern. "I'm going to do my damnedest to make sure you know how important you are to me. I've already told Angie that Monica Christensen can't come over anymore. She was horrible to you during the divorce. If she wants to apologize, I'll reconsider, but for now, she's not welcome at Rancho Westcott."

Dylan nearly cracked a smile. "Thanks, but that's not necessary."

Dad slapped his hand on the counter. "For Christ's sake, stop discounting yourself, Dylan. It *is* necessary. You've always done that, made your needs and wants so small as to be overlooked, probably because you just wanted to fit in." Dad wiped his hand over his face. "When I think back…" His voice cracked again, and this time Dylan saw the sheen of tears in his eyes. "If banning Monica from my house is the least I can do, I'll do it from the mountaintops."

Everything Dad said resonated with him, made something inside of him break free and take flight. He braced his hands on the counter and stared at the pattern in the granite. When he looked up, Dad was wiping his eyes and Mom was biting her lip.

She blinked rapidly. "Tell us we haven't ruined you."

Earlier he'd thought of himself as broken. But maybe he was fixable. They certainly thought so. And it seemed like they wanted to invest whatever necessary to make him right. "You haven't." He was surprised to hear the gravel in his voice.

Mom came around and hugged him. He put his arms around her, trying but failing to remember the last time they'd done this. When she pulled back, it was Dad's turn. He thumped Dylan on the back a few times. "I'm sorry, son. I hope you'll be able to forgive us someday."

Dylan stepped back. "I already do. I know you tried. And I know I haven't made it easy. I'll try to be better about…sharing." The thought nearly gave him hives.

Dad gave a single nod, then went and plucked up his beer for a long quaff. "Good beer."

Dylan shook his head. "I still can't believe you guys came up here together."

"We don't hate each other. In fact, I honestly can't remember if I ever did." The look she sent his dad was nearly his undoing. There was kindness and even a hint of…love.

Dylan took a drink of beer to stave off the unwelcome rush of emotion, then struggled to swallow it past the lump in his throat.

"Now, tell me what's going on with that girl from the restaurant," Mom said. "That was Sara Archer, wasn't it?"

"What girl?" Dad looked at him quizzically. "Do you have a girlfriend?"

"No." But God, if he let himself accept the emotions battering at him from all sides, he could. He'd been the worst sort of prick. He hadn't been thinking of her, he'd been protecting himself from having to open up and, you know, *feel*. But this…family conference with his parents had opened up some sort of floodgate and suddenly he knew exactly how he felt about her. He'd never felt as alive, as capable, as happy as he did when he was with her. She gave him a sense of that elusive thing he'd wanted so badly but could never seem to find—family. And he couldn't wait to tell her. "I hate to throw you guys out, but I need to go somewhere."

Mom looked at the clock hanging to the side of the doorway to the hall. "Now? It's after nine o'clock."

He laughed. "You guys *just* came up here; clearly it's not that late."

"We waited until we were sure you were home from work and had eaten dinner."

Dinner? He'd completely forgotten that. Not that he wanted any. He was only hungry for one thing, and it wasn't food. He grabbed his keys from the hook on the wall. "I gotta go. Stay, leave, whatever." He went into the hallway and then turned to look at them. "Thank you."

Dad toasted him with his beer. "Good luck with whatever you're doing. And let us know how it goes?" The hidden message was clear: don't keep this stuff to yourself.

Dylan smiled. "I will. I promise."

SARA SAT AT the little table in Dad's office situated in front of the windows that overlooked the drive. Her iPad was propped in front of her as she tried to read the latest Elisabeth Naughton romantic suspense. She was local and one of Sara's favorites, but it was hard to concentrate when the man you were in love with dumped you.

She leaned forward and closed her eyes. Maybe she should've gone to France with Mom.

No, do what's best for you, Sara. Like Alex said: Put yourself first.

She gave up on the book, and left the office, nearly colliding with Kyle in the main hall.

He caught her elbows. "Hey, Sara-cat. I know it's late, but I'm starved. I was about to cook something. You interested?"

Her stomach growled in response. She'd totally forgotten to eat dinner. "Sounds good."

They went into the kitchen just as Dad came in from the mudroom.

Kyle opened the fridge. "I'm cooking dinner, Dad. You hungry?"

Dad blinked at him and glanced at Sara who nodded her head in encouragement—they'd reached a truce for the sake of working together at Archer, but Sara knew they had things to resolve, hopefully soon. "Sure, thanks. I think I'll grab a beer. It's new—I just hooked it up this morning."

Sara followed him to the other counter. "Really? I didn't realize you'd brewed anything." If it was already drinkable, he had to have made it weeks ago.

He shrugged. "Just this. It's a grapefruit base—you might like it." He grabbed two pint glasses from the cabinet behind the island that held the keg and wine fridge.

"Hey, don't I get one?" Kyle asked from across the kitchen.

Dad got a third glass and filled them.

"It's so good to see you brewing again," Sara said, eager to focus on something besides her encounter with Dylan earlier.

Kyle joined them and all three lifted their glasses. "Cheers!"

Sara sat on one of the stools and sipped the brew. It wasn't bad. Not too hoppy, which she hated, with a smooth, sweet finish. "This is pretty good."

Dad cracked a half-smile. "Finally a beer my kitten will drink. I dub thee, 'Kitten Ale.'"

"Why are you all drinking without me?" Tori came into the kitchen too and sat on Sara's other side. She tapped her hand on the counter. "Hit me, Dad."

He turned and got another glass, pulled the tap, and pushed the beer over to Tori. "This is Kitten Ale. Grapefruit."

Tori sampled the brew and nodded. "I don't usually like fruity beer, but this is really good. Nicely done, Dad."

"What a happy accident to have all of you here," Dad said. He lifted his glass again. "To family."

They all drank.

Sara glanced at her siblings, hoping that what she was about to say would be okay with them, but she was sure it would be. "I got my letter from Alex today, Dad. He told me to go after my dreams no matter what. I know he wanted you to stay out of the project, but I've decided my wishes trump his because I'm still here. I think we'd all like it if you'd help with The Alex. Provide input and just be a general sounding board."

Tori nodded. "Absolutely."

Dad's gaze was skeptical as it landed on Kyle. "You agree to this too?"

"I do. You have a lot to contribute to the project, and we're the ones who have the say. We decided to hire Cade D'Onofrio today to engineer the renovation of the church and monks' quarters. Good choice?"

Dad blinked at him. He took a drink of beer. "He's young, but yeah, he's good. Who else did you interview?"

Tori answered and told him whom she would've preferred to hire.

Dad shook his head. "No, D'Onofrio's the better choice." He leaned back against the counter behind him. "Look, I don't want to intrude on this project."

"You're not. I think it'll be great to have you involved," Sara said. "And clearly I'm not alone."

"Actually, I don't know if you should spend much time on the project," Tori said, holding up her glass and studying the liquid inside it. "I've missed your beer, Dad. Maybe you should focus on *that*."

Dad smiled, and it was the most genuine look of pleasure Sara had seen on his face in months. Warmth and joy spread through her. *This* is what they'd been missing. "I can try," he said.

Kyle stood up and walked toward the pantry, which was off toward the mudroom, calling out behind him. "I'm making dinner, Tor, if you're hungry."

"I'm famished." Tori smiled, and Sara thought it was the happiest she'd seen her in a while too.

"Look who I saw lurking outside." Kyle came back into the kitchen and stepped aside to reveal Dylan.

Sara's chest tightened. His eyes were somber, his hands stuffed awkwardly into the pockets of his jeans.

She'd turned her head to look but now pivoted on her barstool.

"You want us to leave you alone?" Tori leaned close to Sara and whispered.

"No," Dylan said, clearly having heard her despite her lowered tone. "I've recently—very recently—learned I need to open up more, so I'm just going to do this in front of all of you." He glanced at Kyle then at Tori and Dad. "And try not to embarrass myself too badly."

Dylan walked slowly toward Sara, pulling his hands out of his pockets. He circled the edge of the large table that sat in the center of the gathering room.

When he got to Sara, he dropped to his knees.

Oh God, what was he doing? Dad was standing right behind her! Her legs turned to jelly and she pulled her sleeves over her hands.

Dylan smiled and took her fingers in his. "Don't be nervous. I came to apologize for being a ridiculous butt-head. I wasn't ready to commit, but now I am."

She didn't understand. "That was like two hours ago. Maybe less."

"I realize that. And I think I knew I blew it the second you walked off the porch. I was just too stupid to say anything."

"Sounds like it," Tori said. Sara sent a sharp glare at her over Dylan's head. Tori held up her hand and mouthed, "Sorry."

"Your family scares the hell out of me." He kept his eyes glued to hers. "Because mine does too. Or did." He ran his hand through his hair. "I told you I suck at this."

"I think you're doing fine," Dad said softly.

Dylan looked over at him and brightened, his lip curving up. "Thanks." He returned his gaze to Sara's and tightened his hold on her hands. "When I said I wasn't in love with you, I was lying. Only I didn't know it. I feel things, I want to do things…and I just push it all away. I just got stepped on so many times…"

She heard the anguish in his voice, something she never imagined she'd hear from him, and her heart broke. She reached out and stroked the side of his face, loving the sensation of his slight beard against her fingertips. "I understand. And I was going to convince you anyway."

He laughed. "I don't doubt it. You're a force of nature, Sara Archer, and I am head over heels in love with you. I don't know what the future holds and I can't promise that I won't screw up on a regular basis, but I'm going to be the best boyfriend you could ever want. You don't deserve any less."

Tears burned her eyes, happy, joyous tears that she hadn't felt in months. "You're the man of my dreams, so of course I deserve you. And you deserve me."

"Oh. My. God. This is nauseating. I was hoping to *eat*." The sarcasm in Kyle's voice made Sara laugh. "You staying for dinner, Westcott?"

He looked up at Sara. "If it's all right with you."

She reached down and wrapped her hands around his neck. "Stay forever."

Epilogue

July 4

"AND THAT IS how I came up with my signature cocktail, the Naked Ginger." Kyle sat back in his chair and took a long drink of beer, his eyes full of mischief.

Dylan laughed. "I call bullshit. No way she let you do that to her on the bar."

Kyle's brows rose. "I tell it like it is, brother."

Brother. They weren't. At least not yet. Dylan glanced over at Sara, who was chatting with his sister, and thought it would come to that though—if he was lucky and she said yes.

He shook his head to clear distant thoughts of engagement from his mind. First they had to make it through Derek and Chloe's wedding and to do that he needed to get the cottage finished on time. They'd gone from ahead of schedule to behind, as construction tends to go. He really ought to have been working today, but everybody had convinced him to come to the barbecue at his Dad's house. So here they were—Westcotts, Archers, and even Davies—enjoying one big happy family event.

Well, maybe not everyone was enjoying it. His gaze strayed to Bill, who was sitting on the periphery and looking very uncomfortable while Cameron chatted his ear off. Dylan would thank his brother later.

"Hey, isn't Rob coming?" Dylan asked. He'd gotten to know Sara's dad over the last month and loved talking beer with him. In fact, he was looking forward to attempting his own batch of homebrew.

Kyle's eyes clouded. "He should be."

The old Dylan would've let the moment go unnoticed, but the Archers had turned him into some sort of family guy. It was disturbing. "Everything okay? I thought you two had reached a civil accord." Kyle and his dad still hadn't patched things up, according to Sara, but their relationship was a damn sight better than it was with Kyle's former best friend, Derek. In fact, suspiciously, Derek and Chloe were out of town today. Dylan noted they rarely socialized together, even in large groups. How awkward was the wedding going to be? Or was Kyle even invited?

"It's fine." He shifted in his chair. "I just need to talk to him about something work-related."

"Hey, why do you look so serious?" Sara asked Kyle as she came and perched on Dylan's leg. "You better not be giving my boyfriend a hard time."

Dylan slid his hand around her waist and drew her closer so he could get a better whiff of her unique Sara-scent—oranges and spice, everything nice. "He's fine."

"We were wondering where Dad is," Kyle said.

"Oh." Sara glanced at Dylan, then her gaze went beyond him. "He just got here. He's over talking to Sam."

Dylan turned his head and saw that his dad was steering Rob toward his barbecue, likely to talk about its various bells and whistles. Was Dylan going to be like that at that age? He squeezed Sara's waist, thinking about the future with her, and hoped so.

Kyle stood. "Time for another beer." He left them alone, and Dylan took the opportunity to nuzzle his face against Sara's neck.

"You smell so damn good. Think anyone will notice if we go inside for a few minutes?"

She wrapped her hand around his neck as he pulled back to look up at her. "Um, probably. Do you care?"

"Not a bit."

She jumped off his lap. "After you, hotness."

His cock started to swell, and he groaned softly before he leaned in to softly bite her earlobe. "Let's go."

She preceded him inside, nodding at family and friends and neighbors along the way. Once inside, he took the lead and pulled her into the downstairs bath-room. He turned and closed the door behind her, locking it. He clasped her hips and pushed her against the wood. Her hands came up his arms and she dug her fingers into his biceps.

He pressed his lips to her neck, just beneath her ear and kissed his way down to her collarbone, edging the strap of her tank out of his way.

"Are you having a good time?" she asked, sounding breathless.

"I am now."

She laughed. "Liar. I saw you outside. You *are* having a good time." She swatted his back. "Don't be a jerk about it. Things are good, right?"

He pulled his head back and looked at her. He clasped her waist tightly. "Perfect." He kissed her, slipping his tongue into her mouth and claiming what she so eagerly offered.

He slid his hands up her ribcage, pushing her top up to her bra. "Front clasp. My lucky day." He snapped the bra open and palmed her breasts.

She moaned softly. "What if someone needs to use the bathroom?"

"*We're* using the bathroom. There's another one upstairs. And another one downstairs." He yanked her top past her breasts and tongued her nipple.

She threaded her fingers into his hair and held him close. "You're so naughty. I never dreamed how much I'd love that. How much I'd love you."

He chuckled against her breast and looked up at her, reveling in the sweet emotion in her eyes. "I never believed I'd have this or you. It was always just a dream."

She pushed at him and moved over to the counter. She shimmied out of her undies and hoisted herself up onto the tile. "I'm real, baby. This is real."

"Thank God. No, thank *you*."

He moved between her legs and bent to kiss her again, but she stopped him. "You just reminded me of something I've been meaning to ask you."

He nuzzled her neck, his lips caressing her skin. "What's that?"

"That first night I came to your house—in the rain. Right before I fell asleep you thanked me. Why?"

He lifted his head and looked at her long and hard, feeling humbled and so damn lucky. "You said I was magic. No one had ever made me feel that important before. I'm sure I was half in love with you then—no, I know I was. I was just too stupid to realize it." He touched her face. "I love you. So much."

She smiled, his love reflected in her eyes. "Show me."

Author's Note

Sensory processing is something we all do. If you twist your hair, tap your foot or leg, sway back and forth when you're standing in line, hum, or make other nonlingual sounds, or can't stand the seam in a sock, you are processing your environment in a way that is unique to you. And that's just the stuff we can see! Most people think of five senses, but there are actually at least two more, and these two can be particularly challenging for people with sensory processing disorder (SPD). Your vestibular sense is your sense of balance and your proprioceptive sense is where your body is in space. Some people have difficulty lying down flat (particularly in unknown places) or jumping off of things, such as into a pool. My own vestibular sense was sort of jumbled when I was younger. I remember my mom taking me to an ear doctor to see if there was something they could do to help me with feeling dizzy on amusement park rides! Conversely, when my daughter was very young, she had difficulty *getting* dizzy, even after spinning round and round with her occupational therapist.

If you're interested in learning more about sensory processing disorder, there are so many great books and resources. I'm a big proponent of educating yourself so that you can make informed decisions about how to deal with or treat something like SPD. It's been an incredible journey with our daughter, who was diagnosed with SPD at age three. Now, ten years later, she manages her environment incredibly well and we know the next ten years will only bring greater maturity and awareness.

For more information on sensory processing disorder, you can check out the Sensory Processing Disorder Foundation at http://www.spdfoundation.net or do an Internet search to find the SPD information that is most helpful to you.

Acknowledgments

I COULDN'T HAVE written this book without the fantastic support system for my daughter, and really our whole family. Thank you, Sarah Kramer at Advanced Pediatric Therapies. You have made (and continue to make) such an impact on our Quinncess. And thank you to Tricia Rogers, an incredible speech therapist who helped Quinn articulate all the thoughts in her head. Those meeting her now would never suspect that she was once a girl of few words! Finally, we can never thank Dr. Margaret MacDonald enough for her support, wisdom, and love. You've given us understanding, information, and acceptance. Thank you from the bottom of our hearts.

I want to thank my wonderful agent, Jim McCarthy, for helping to take this book from good to great. And thank you to my editor, Nicole Fischer, for falling in love with the Archers and guiding Sara and Dylan to an even more fulfilling happily ever after. I'm so excited for what the future holds for Ribbon Ridge!

Thank you Carey Baldwin, the best Moonlight and Magnolias roommate EVAH, for your medical expertise regarding Alex. I so appreciate your help! I also want to thank Leigh LaValle for being an excellent sounding board and helping this story in so many ways. Much, much love to both of you.

Thanks to Erica Ridley for reading and Elisabeth Naughton for reading and plotting and endlessly listening to my angst. Huge hugs to Joan Swan and Rachel Grant for their unwavering support and cheerleading. I also owe a heap of gratitude to the NW Pixies for our annual get-togethers, one of which was the birthplace of Ribbon Ridge. It's truly the highlight of my writing year.

Finally, to my family—you are my light, my love, my life. Thank you for showing me that happy ever after isn't just found in books. It isn't perfect, but I'd like to think it's better. *Love you most.*

Thank You!

Thank you for reading *Only In My Dreams*! I hope you enjoyed your stay in Ribbon Ridge and that you'll come back for *Yours to Hold*, the next book in the Archer family saga. Ribbon Ridge is a fictional town based on several cities and towns dotting the Willamette Valley between Portland and the Oregon Coast. It's pinot noir wine country, very beautiful and picturesque—and a short drive from where I live. My brother actually dwells right in the heart of it in a tiny town with no grocery store or gas station. There is, however, an amazing antique mall in a historic schoolhouse.

Reviews help readers find books that are right for them. I hope you'll consider leaving an honest one on your preferred social media or review site.

Be sure to visit my Facebook page for the latest information, follow me on Twitter (@darcyburke), check out images of the northern Willamette Valley and other things that inspired this series on Pinterest (darcyburke-write), and sign up for my newsletter so you'll know exactly when my next book is available.

Thank you again for reading and for your support!

Don't miss the next Ribbon Ridge novel from
USA Today bestselling author
DARCY BURKE

Black sheep Kyle Archer may find love
in the last place he ever imagined. . .

YOURS TO HOLD

Coming March 24 from Avon Impulse!

Read on for a sneak peek...

An Excerpt from

YOURS TO HOLD

July, Ribbon Ridge

KYLE ARCHER WANTED answers. The elevator chimed as it hit the third floor. He stepped into the corridor, his gaze finding the list of medical offices, and, more specifically, the name he sought.

Psychology, Maggie Trent, PhD, 320

Following the arrow indicating the suite numbers, he turned left and strode down the hall with purpose. Suite 320 was on the right, about halfway down. Without pausing, he pushed open the door and took in the gurgling fountain in the corner, the instrumental music featuring what he thought was probably a lute and a sitar, and the muted lighting. He supposed it was meant to establish a calming environment, though none of it did anything to soothe the frustration that had taken root in his gut over the past week.

He went to the check-in window, which was closed. The glass slid open as he approached. A guy in his late twenties with brown, wavy hair and horn-rimmed glasses looked up at him. "May I help you?" he asked in a quiet, almost tranquilizing tone. His mouth relaxed into a pleasant, rather bland smile. He was probably trained to put people at ease, but he only set Kyle's teeth further on edge.

Kyle forced a brittle smile. "Hello, I have an appointment with Dr. Trent. I'm Cal Drogo." He tried not to smirk as he said the name, but given the receptionist's lack of reaction, the joke was apparently lost on him.

"Yes, Mr. Drogo." He glanced at his computer screen. "No insurance, is that right?"

"Yes."

The receptionist's lips pursed. "The scheduler explained that you'll receive a discount if you pay in full today?"

"She did. And I will." Kyle whisked out his wallet and handed over a hundred bucks. The fifty-minute appointment was ninety dollars without insurance.

Horn-rims gave him change and handed him a form on a clipboard. "You'll need to fill this out—front and back."

Kyle didn't touch the proffered item. "I explained that I didn't want to complete any paperwork before I meet the psychologist. It's part of my…paranoia." He glanced away in an effort to convince horn-rims that he might suffer from some sort of anxiety disorder. Kyle was a lot of things, but anxious or high-strung wasn't one of them.

"I see. No problem." Another patronizing smile to accompany his sugar-sweet tone. "Have a seat, and we'll call you when it's time. Feel free to help yourself to some herbal tea." He indicated a mini-bar in the corner that surely lacked the accoutrements of a typical mini-bar. Bummer. Kyle could've used a stiff shot of something to get through the next hour. If this even took that long.

Kyle stowed his wallet in his back pocket and nodded. "Thanks, I'll check it out."

The tea station had no coffee and no tea with any caffeine. It did, however, have little bags of gluten-free crackers. How hypoallergenic.

"Cal Dr—" The feminine voice cut off. "Cal Drogo?" She sounded skeptical, and Kyle knew this one had gotten the joke.

He turned, smiling, then crossed the empty waiting room to where the young woman stood at an open door with a clipboard in her hand.

"Your name is seriously Cal Drogo? Like that massive guy on *Game of Thrones*?"

He'd needed a fake name and it had been the first thing that had come to mind. Kyle/Cal, they sounded alike. Though he hadn't spelled it the same as the character. That would've been a dead giveaway. He'd take the little bits of humor he could find in life. "Weird, right?"

She laughed. "Totally. You're pretty tall, I'll give you that, but nowhere near dark enough. You look like a surfer dude."

"Guilty as charged." At six-three, he *was* nearly as tall as the actor on the show, but where that guy was tall, dark, and scary looking, Kyle was blond, blue-green-eyed, and in possession of a smile that said, "I'm all about having a good time." So far that had served him pretty well.

They turned a corner and he followed her to a door at the end. Next to it was a shiny placard that read MAGGIE TRENT, PHD. Kyle's gut tightened and just like that, his brief bout with good humor evaporated.

The young woman who'd escorted him smiled warmly. "Go on in, Mr. Drogo."

Kyle didn't spare her another glance as he moved into Dr. Trent's office. The door closed behind him as he stepped further inside. Dr. Trent looked up from where she stood behind her desk. The smile curving her lips froze and her eyes—dark like the TV show character whose name he'd borrowed—widened.

"Your name isn't Cal Drogo."

"What gave me away? I'm pretty sure your assistant, or whatever she is, doubted that was actually my name, but she went along with my joke. Why won't you?" Normally, his tone would be light, teasing. He could scarcely carry on a conversation without injecting some sort of humor or sarcasm. But he wasn't messing around with Maggie Trent and so his words came out hard, clipped.

Her gaze turned wary. "I've seen your picture. You're Kyle Archer."

"Alex showed you pictures of us?" It bothered him to think his deceased brother had talked about them to a stranger, but then that's what one did in therapy, right? Talk about your family? He wished he could ask Alex, but of course he couldn't. Not now. Not ever.

She nodded stiffly. "Yes. This," her voice squeaked, "this is highly inappropriate. I can't talk to you."

Kyle glanced around her cozy office. Besides her desk and the bookshelf behind it, there were windows, a leather couch, and a chair. He assumed the couch was for clients and the chair for her. He sat in the chair. "I figured you would say that. It's why I made the appointment under a fake name and refused to give them any of my information."

She scanned the paper on her desk and frowned. "You told them you were too paranoid to give that information over the phone."

He leaned back and put his feet up on the leather ottoman. "Yep, I did."

Straightening, she crossed her arms. She was more attractive than he'd envisioned. He'd pictured a middle-aged, dried-up hag with a pointy nose. Maybe with a little greenish tinge to her skin. He'd imagined a monster. How else would he see the woman who'd counseled his brother and failed to stop him from killing himself?

However, life was a cruel bitch, and Maggie Trent was quite pretty. She was about Kyle's age—twenty-eight— but had little pleats between her eyebrows that gave the sense she worried too much. Maybe *she* had anxiety.

She blinked—her eyes were the color of Dad's special recipe Christmas stout, dark and rich like bittersweet chocolate. A light freckle dotted her upper right cheek. He couldn't get a good sense of her hair because it was wound up on her head, though it was also dark, and little springy curls grazed the back of her neck.

"If you're done staring, you should go."

"No, I don't think so." He cracked a lazy smile, which didn't reflect the anger roiling inside of him. "The going, I mean. I'm done staring."

She exhaled loudly and dropped her hands to her sides. "I'm not doing this. I'm really sorry about Alex. *So* sorry." Her voice broke and she looked away toward the windows.

A pang of sorrow hit Kyle, and he hesitated. No, he was doing this for Alex.

That wasn't necessarily true. He was doing it for the entire family.

Kyle didn't want to prolong this interview so he got right to the point. "How did my brother get the drugs he took?" He'd taken a mix of antidepressants, sleeping pills, and painkillers. A potentially lethal mix for anyone, but for someone with Alex's chronic lung disease, it was absolutely deadly.

She looked at him sharply, her gaze shrouded with anguish and regret. "I don't know." Her words carried the weight of unshed tears. "I…I cared about him a great deal."

He steeled himself against feeling sorry for her. "He was my brother. And he never should've been able to get his hands on drugs like that, not with his illness. He had to have obtained them illegally."

She shook her head. "I can't prescribe drugs. I'm not a medical doctor."

"I know that." He needed to move. He stood up and walked the length of the couch.

She backed up a step, even though her desk and several feet separated them. "Are you here to accuse me of something?"

"Like what, lethal incompetence? Yeah, I think you have to be a pretty shitty therapist if one of your clients killed himself. *You* have to live with that, though. I just want to know who contributed to my brother's death. What they're doing is illegal, and I'm going to put a stop to it."

Moisture gave her eyes a luminous sheen. "It won't bring him back."

"It'll make a lot of us feel better." He moved forward again. "There's a psychiatrist in this office. Did he give Alex the drugs?"

She shook her head, jostling the curls that grazed her neck. "No one would prescribe them to him—not with his condition. You're right that he had to have obtained them illegally. But I don't know how. He didn't discuss—" She sank down onto her chair. "I can't talk to you about this. It's unethical."

"Why? Are you telling me about his treatment? I haven't asked what you talked about, though I'm sure we'd all like to know. You do realize his suicide shocked the hell out of all of us? My family is a mess. Our parents are barely speaking to each other."

Her expression was pained, those lines between her eyes creased to full effect. "But you're back home. That's a good thing, right?"

Alex must have told her about him and that he'd moved to Florida almost four years ago. Like everyone else in his damn family, Alex believed he'd run away and had wanted him to come home. Kyle didn't think Alex had killed himself to provoke that, though he couldn't help but think it had made it onto his list of pros. As if Alex had sat down and made out a list of reasons to off himself and reasons to live. Even if he had, why hadn't the latter been long enough?

Kyle's chest tightened. "I don't think that's any of your business." He had enough trouble dealing with his family members regarding his return. He didn't need some shrink nosing in too.

"You blame me," she said softly, her hand rising to her chest, where it fluttered briefly before dropping to her lap once more. "I'd blame me too, I think."

Damn, she was making it hard to be pissed at her. With those sad eyes and lips that were an inch from quivering—or so he imagined. He could also imagine kissing them. Now, *that* pissed him off.

He gritted his teeth. "So what are you going to do to make it right?"

She blinked at him and her eyes darkened, which he hadn't thought possible. The emotion around her mouth shifted into something harder. "If you think anyone can make this right, you're fooling yourself. Even if you find out how he got the drugs, it won't bring him back. It won't change the fact that he chose death over life." Now her lip did quiver. Exhaling roughly, she looked away again.

"It's the only thing I can do." Kyle shoved his remorse aside. It sounded like she might blame herself, but so did he. Hell, every person in their family carried a hefty piece of guilt. If he'd been here, maybe he would've seen something to indicate his state of mind. His sister Sara, who *had* been here, insisted that wouldn't have been possible.

"I don't think that's true. I think you honor Alex by coming back here, by rejoining your family." She glanced at him nervously. "*If* that's what you're doing. I don't mean to presume."

"Keep your therapy to yourself. It didn't help Alex, and I don't want what you're selling, *doctor*." He set his hands on his hips, his forefingers dipping into the pockets of his jeans. "I want those drug dealers, whoever they are, to pay."

She stood and crossed her arms across her chest again, as if they could provide some sort of defense against his anger. "I told you already that I can't help you with that."

"Did he talk to the psychiatrist here?"

She shook her head. "I didn't even work here then. I had my own practice in Ribbon Ridge."

"Which you conveniently shut down after Alex died."

"I was devastated." She flicked him an uneasy glance and edged closer to her desk. "I think you should go."

"I'm not finished."

Her gaze turned stoic. "I'll call security if I have to."

"Security? Do you feel threatened?"

She tightened her arms around herself. "I don't feel comfortable."

"Then welcome to our hell." He pulled out the business card he'd stashed in his front pocket. He dropped the creased rectangle on her desk. The Archer logo with its A shaped into a bow and arrow stared up from the face. "Call me when you have information to share—and don't tell me you don't have anything. You talked to my brother—what, every week for nearly a year? I'm sure you'll think of something that can help me." He speared her with an icy glare. "It's the least you can do."

Her look of remorse did nothing to ease his frustration at walking away empty-handed, but he hoped she'd come around. She had to have something that could help him track down the person—or people—who'd provided Alex with the means to kill himself. If she didn't…He refused to go down that path.

He turned and strode from her office, leaving the door ajar as he went. Her assistant was in the corridor. "Finished already?" she asked.

"For now," he said darkly, not bothering to adjust his tone.

A half hour later, he walked into the headquarters of Archer Enterprises on the southwestern edge of Ribbon Ridge. Home to nearly fifty employees, it oversaw operations of nine brewpubs and countless real estate endeavors. The two-story building, designed to Dad's specifications about eight years prior, sprawled at the edge of wine country with epic views. Yet stepping inside never failed to jolt Kyle with uneasiness. He was filling in for his younger brother Hayden while he was on a year-long leave of absence making wine in France. And Kyle was, as everyone liked to point out, no Hayden.

Nodding at the receptionist as he passed, he took the central curving staircase up to the second floor. Hayden's—rather, Kyle's—office was toward the southeast corner, situated between his dad and Derek Sumner, the two people who currently despised him most. Altogether, the work environment was *awesome*.

The executive assistant he shared with Derek looked up at him as he approached. "Hey, Kyle. How was your lunch?"

Natalie Frobish was young, attractive, and worked like a fiend. She was the first person there in the morning and the last one who left at night. She'd only been with Archer two years—since graduating from nearby Williver College—but both Dad and Derek constantly remarked how Archer would be lost without her. Kyle was pretty sure Dad wanted to promote her to his assistant when his retired next year. But it didn't take a rocket scientist to see Natalie had ambition, and Kyle thought her upward mobility at Archer would move her out of the executive assistant category before that could happen.

"It was fine." He hadn't told anyone he'd planned to ambush Dr. Trent. Better to keep his plans to himself until he had something important to share. He *hoped* he'd have something important to share—and soon.

Natalie gestured for him to come around her desk, which was tucked behind a counter at which she greeted those who visited the executive wing.

Since she was being a bit secretive, Kyle glanced around, but the office was quiet. Dad's assistant, Paula, was out to lunch, and Dad's office door was closed. Derek, who was CFO, didn't seem to be about either. Kyle stepped around to where Natalie was sitting. "What's up?" he asked quietly.

Her dark eyes—maybe a shade lighter than Dr. Trent's—found his and she pointed at her computer screen, which showed a large bouquet of flowers. "Paula and I were thinking of sending these to Emily from Rob."

Mom had gone to France with Hayden almost two months ago. Things had seemed a bit strained between her and Dad, and they all hoped this separation would help both of them heal. Alex's death had taken a pretty hefty toll on them. Kyle had spoken to Mom several times and she sounded better, more relaxed. Dad, however, was as tense and short-tempered as ever. It was like he just didn't want to deal with the grief at all, so he shoved it away. Since he was already pissed at Kyle from four years ago, their relationship was as uneasy as ever. Helping Dad find some closure with Alex's death had prompted Kyle to track down how Alex had obtained the drugs he'd used to kill himself. And scoring some points in the meantime wouldn't be a bad thing.

Kyle looked at the beautiful flower arrangement. "It's a nice sentiment, but I wouldn't do it. I'm not sure how things are between them." They'd find out when Mom came home in a few weeks for Derek's wedding.

Natalie nodded. "Okay, it was just a thought."

Kyle moved back around to the other side of her desk. "And a good one. Just maybe not right now." Dad was so uptight all of the time—Kyle and his siblings were all worried about him.

Dad's office door opened. His slate-gray eyes landed on Kyle. "I thought I heard you."

"Hey, Dad." Though they had yet to discuss Kyle's departure four years ago, Kyle knew it was coming at some point. Dad was still pissed that Kyle hadn't accepted the job he'd offered and Kyle was still frustrated with how his Dad had meddled in his life. And if he were truly honest with himself, he was ashamed too. A conversation would happen someday, preferably when Dad was in a more positive mental state.

"Come in here for a minute." Dad turned from the door and went back behind his desk. When Kyle came in, he said, "Shut the door."

Uh-oh, Kyle thought as his dad sat down. Kyle didn't want to sit so he stood in the center of the office and folded his arms over his chest. "What's up?"

Dad glanced at the chair, registered that Kyle wasn't going to get comfortable, and briefly pressed his lips together. "Have you and Derek nailed down the details for our booth at the Ribbon Ridge Festival?"

"Nearly." Though it was taking forever since they were communicating almost entirely by email.

"You know, things might happen faster if you and Derek actually talked."

Probably, but the rift between Kyle and his former best friend was deep. He imagined they would've lost touch entirely if Derek hadn't moved in with the Archers during their senior year of high school when his mother died, subsequently becoming the de facto eighth Archer sibling. Now Derek was as much a part of their family as Kyle. And, like the situation with Dad, Kyle didn't think they could ignore the past forever. But he was fine doing it for now. Better than fine. "Hey, don't blame me."

Dad leaned back in his chair, his gaze cool with skepticism. "So if Derek came to you tomorrow and said, 'Let's start over, forget what happened four years ago,' you'd drop whatever grudge you're holding and move on?"

Derek had betrayed him. He owed Kyle an apology and it was *never* going to come. Fuck it. "We'll take care of it." Kyle's response was clipped. He itched to turn and leave.

"How? I want to know how you're going to improve your working relationship at least. When I agreed to let you fill in for Hayden, I expected you to behave professionally."

Kyle dropped his arms to his sides. "Haven't I? If you have an issue with how I've performed, I'd like to hear it." Kyle hadn't known the first thing really about being a chief operating officer, but Hayden had been very helpful, even from France. Kyle had worked harder than he'd ever worked in his life to try to prove himself, and he was sick of taking the brunt of Dad's grief and anger. "When are you going to cut me some slack?"

"When you're ready to talk about what happened before you ran off." Dad set his forearms on his desk, which had become far more cluttered than Kyle ever remembered it being. "You never even thanked me."

The familiar resentment gathered in Kyle's chest, made him grit his teeth. "Because I didn't ask for your help. I had things under control."

Dad's eyes narrowed. "You didn't, and the fact that you still don't realize that is why I don't cut you any slack."

Kyle threw up his hands. "I guess my coming back and participating in Alex's project and taking over for Hayden didn't earn me any points at all." He turned to go.

"You say you're back, but for how long?" Dad asked quietly. "You need to regain my trust, Kyle. You need to regain everyone's trust. And you're not going to do that if you don't actually engage and really come *back*."

What more could he do? He was afraid he knew the answer, but he wasn't ready for that. Not yet. "I am back, Dad, and I'm doing the best I can. Too bad it's never been enough."

About the Author

DARCY BURKE is the *USA Today* bestselling author of hot, action-packed historical and sexy, emotional contemporary romance. Darcy wrote her first book at age eleven, a happily ever after about a swan addicted to magic and the female swan that loved him, with exceedingly poor illustrations.

A native Oregonian, Darcy lives on the edge of wine country with her devoted husband, their two great kids, and two Bengal cats. In her "spare" time, Darcy is a serial volunteer enrolled in a twelve-step program where one learns to say "no," but she keeps having to start over. She's also a fair-weather runner, and her happy places are Disneyland and Labor Day weekend at the Gorge.

Discover great authors, exclusive offers, and more at hc.com.

Give in to your impulses . . .
Read on for a sneak peek at seven brand-new
e-book original tales of romance
from HarperCollins.
Available now wherever e-books are sold.

VARIOUS STATES OF UNDRESS: GEORGIA
By Laura Simcox

MAKE IT LAST
A BOWLER UNIVERSITY NOVEL
By Megan Erickson

HERO BY NIGHT
BOOK THREE: INDEPENDENCE FALLS
By Sara Jane Stone

MAYHEM
By Jamie Shaw

SINFUL REWARDS 1
A BILLIONAIRES AND BIKERS NOVELLA
By Cynthia Sax

FORBIDDEN
AN UNDER THE SKIN NOVEL
By Charlotte Stein

HER HIGHLAND FLING
A NOVELLA
By Jennifer McQuiston

An Excerpt from

VARIOUS STATES OF UNDRESS: GEORGIA

by Laura Simcox

Laura Simcox concludes her fun, flirty
Various States of Undress series with a
presidential daughter, a hot baseball player,
and a tale of love at the ballgame.

"Uh. Hi."

Georgia splayed her hand over the front of her wet blouse and stared. The impossibly tanned guy standing just inside the doorway—wearing a tight T-shirt, jeans, and a smile— was as still as a statue. A statue with fathomless, unblinking chocolate brown eyes. She let her gaze drop from his face to his broad chest. "Oh. Hello. I was expecting someone else."

He didn't comment, but when she lifted her gaze again, past his wide shoulders and carved chin, she watched his smile turn into a grin, revealing way-too-sexy brackets at the corners of his mouth. He walked down the steps and onto the platform where she stood. He had to be at least 6'3", and testosterone poured off him like heat waves on the field below. She shouldn't stare at him, right? Damn. Her gaze flicked from him to the glass wall but moved right back again.

"Scared of heights?" he asked. His voice was a slow, deep Southern drawl. Sexy deep. "Maybe you oughta sit down."

"No, thanks. I was just . . . looking for something."

Looking for something? Like what—a tryst with a stranger in the press box? Her face heated, and she clutched the water bottle, the plastic making a snapping sound under her fingers. "So . . . how did you get past my agents?"

He smiled again. "They know who I am."

"And you are?"

"Brett Knox."

His name sounded familiar. "Okay. I'm Georgia Fulton. It's nice to meet you," she said, putting down her water.

He shook her hand briefly. "You, too. But I just came up here to let you know that I'm declining the interview. Too busy."

Georgia felt herself nodding in agreement, even as she realized *exactly* who Brett Knox was. He was the star catcher—and right in front of her, shooting her down before she'd even had a chance to ask. Such a typical jock.

"I'm busy, too, which is why I'd like to set up a time that's convenient for both of us," she said, even though she hoped it wouldn't be necessary. But she couldn't very well walk into the news station without accomplishing what she'd been tasked with—pinning him down. Georgia was a team player. So was Brett, literally.

"I don't want to disappoint my boss, and I'm betting you feel the same way about yours," she continued.

"Sure. I sign autographs, pose for photos, visit Little League teams. Like I said, I'm busy."

"That's nice." She nodded. "I'm flattered that you found the time to come all the way up to the press box and tell me, in person, that you don't have time for an interview. Thanks."

He smiled a little. "You're welcome." Then he stretched, his broad chest expanding with the movement. He flexed his long fingers, braced a hand high on the post, and grinned at her again. Her heart flipped down into her stomach. Oh, no.

"I get it, you know. I've posed for photos and signed autographs, too. I've visited hospitals and ribbon cutting ceremonies, and I know it makes people happy. But public appearances can be draining, and it takes time away from work. Right?"

"Right." He gave her a curious look. "We have that in common, though it's not exactly the same. I may be semifamous in Memphis, but I don't have paparazzi following me around, and I like it that way. You interviewing me would turn into a big hassle."

"I won't take much of your time. Just think of me as another reporter." She ventured a warm, inviting smile, and Brett's dark eyes widened. "The paparazzi don't follow me like they do my sisters. I'm the boring one."

"Really?" He folded his arms across his lean middle, and his gaze traveled slowly over her face.

She felt her heart speed up. "Yes, really."

"I beg to differ."

Before she could respond, he gave her another devastating smile and jogged up the steps. It was the best view she'd had all day. When Brett disappeared, she collapsed back against the post. He was right, of course. She wasn't just another reporter; she was the president's brainy daughter—who secretly lusted after athletes. And she'd just met a hell of an athlete.

Talk about a hot mess.

An Excerpt from

MAKE IT LAST
A Bowler University Novel
by Megan Erickson

The last installment in Megan Erickson's daringly
sexy Bowler University series finds Cam Ruiz
back in his hometown of Paradise, where he comes
face-to-face with the only girl he ever loved.

Cam sighed, feeling the weight of responsibility pressing down on his shoulders. But if he didn't help his mom, who would?

He jingled his keys in his pocket and turned to walk toward his truck. It was nice of Max and Lea to visit him on their road trip. College had been some of the best years of his life. Great friends, fun parties, hot girls.

But now it felt like a small blip, like a week vacation instead of three and a half years. And now he was right back where he started.

As he walked by the alley beside the restaurant, something flickered out of the corner of his eye.

He turned and spotted her legs first. One foot bent at the knee and braced on the brick wall, the other flat on the ground. Her head was bent, a curtain of hair blocking her face. But he knew those legs. He knew those hands. And he knew that hair, a light brown that held just a glint of strawberry in the sun. He knew by the end of August it'd be lighter and redder and she'd laugh about that time she put lemon juice in it. It'd backfired and turned her hair orange.

The light flickered again but it was something weird and artificial, not like the menthols she had smoked. Back when he knew her.

As she lowered her hand down to her side, he caught sight of the small white cylinder. It was an electronic cigarette. She'd quit.

She raised her head then, like she knew someone watched her, and he wanted to keep walking, avoid this awkward moment. Avoid those eyes he didn't think he'd ever see again and never thought he'd wanted to see again. But now that his eyes locked on her hazel eyes—the ones he knew began as green on the outside of her iris and darkened to brown by the time they met her pupil—he couldn't look away. His boots wouldn't move.

The small cigarette fell to the ground with a soft click and she straightened, both her feet on the ground.

And that was when he noticed the wedge shoes. And the black apron. What was she doing here?

"Camilo."

Other than his mom, she was the only one who used his full name. He'd heard her say it while laughing. He'd her moan it while he was inside her. He'd heard her sigh it with an eye roll when he made a bad joke. But he'd never heard it the way she said it now, with a little bit of fear and anxiety and . . . longing? He took a deep breath to steady his voice. "Tatum."

He hadn't spoken her name since that night Trevor called him and told him what she did. The night the future that he'd set out for himself and for her completely changed course.

She'd lost some weight in the four years since he'd last seen her. He'd always loved her curves. She had it all—thighs, ass and tits in abundance. Naked, she was a fucking vision.

Damn it, he wasn't going there.

But now her face looked thinner, her clothes hung a little loose and he didn't like this look as much. Not that she probably gave a fuck about his opinion anymore.

She still had her gorgeous hair, pinned up halfway with a bump in front, and a smattering of freckles across the bridge of her nose and on her cheekbones. And she still wore her makeup exactly the same—thickly mascaraed eyelashes, heavy eyeliner that stretched to a point on the outside of her eyes, like a modern-day Audrey Hepburn.

She was still beautiful. And she still took his breath away.

And his heart felt like it was breaking all over again.

And he hated her even more for that.

Her eyes were wide. "What are you doing here?"

Something in him bristled at that. Maybe it was because he didn't feel like he belonged here. But then, she didn't either. She never did. *They* never did.

But there was no longer a *they*.

An Excerpt from

HERO BY NIGHT
Book Three: Independence Falls

by Sara Jane Stone

Travel back to Independence Falls in Sara Jane
Stone's next thrilling read. Armed with a golden
retriever and a concealed weapons permit, Lena
Clark is fighting for normal. She served her
country, but the experience left her afraid to be
touched and estranged from her career-military
family. Staying in Independence Falls, and finding
a job, seems like the first step to reclaiming her life
and preparing for the upcoming medal ceremony—
until the town playboy stumbles into her bed . . .

Sometimes beauty knocked a man on his ass, leaving him damn near desperate for a taste, a touch, and hopefully a round or two between the sheets—or tied up in them. The knockout blonde with the large golden retriever at her feet took the word "beautiful" to a new level.

Chad Summers stared at her, unable to look away or dim the smile on his face. He usually masked his interest better, stopping short of looking like he was begging for it before learning a woman's name. But this mysterious beauty had special written all over her.

She stared at him, her gaze open and wanting. For a heartbeat. Then she turned away, her back to the party as she stared out at Eric Moore's pond.

Her hair flowed in long waves down her back. One look left him wishing he could wrap his hand around her shiny locks and pull. His gaze traveled over her back, taking in the outline of gentle curves beneath her flowing, and oh-so-feminine, floor-length dress. The thought of the beauty's long skirt decorating her waist propelled him into motion. Chad headed in her direction, moving away from the easy, quiet conversation about God-knew-what on the patio.

The blonde, a mysterious stranger in a sea of familiar faces, might be the spark this party needed. He was a few feet away when the dog abandoned his post at her side and cut Chad off. Either the golden retriever was protecting his owner, or the animal was in cahoots with the familiar voice calling his name.

"Chad Summers!"

The blonde turned at the sound, looking first at him, her blue eyes widening as if surprised at how close he stood, and then at her dog. From the other direction, a familiar face with short black hair—Susan maybe?—marched toward him.

Without a word, Maybe Susan stopped by his side and raised her glass. With a dog in front of him, trees to one side, and an angry woman on his other, there was no escape.

"Hi there." He left off her name just in case he'd guessed wrong, but offered a warm, inviting smile. Most women fell for that grin, but if Maybe Susan had at one time—and seeing her up close, she looked very familiar, though he could swear he'd never slept with her—she wasn't falling for it today.

She poured the cool beer over his head, her mouth set in a firm line. "That was for my sister. Susan Lewis? You spent the night with her six months ago and never called."

Chad nodded, silently grateful he hadn't addressed the pissed-off woman by her sister's name. "My apologies, ma'am."

"You're a dog," Susan's sister announced. The animal at his feet stepped forward as if affronted by the comparison.

"For the past six months, my little sister has talked about you, saving every article about your family's company," the angry woman continued.

Whoa . . . Yes, he'd taken Susan Lewis out once and they'd ended the night back at his place, but he could have sworn they were on the same page. Hell, he'd heard her say the words, *I'm not looking for anything serious*, and he'd believed her. It was one freaking night. He didn't think he needed signed documents that spelled out his intentions and hers.

"She's practically built a shrine to you," she added, waving her empty beer cup. "Susan was ready to plan your wedding."

"Again, I'm sorry, but it sounds like there was a miscommunication." Chad withdrew a bandana from his back pocket, one that had belonged to his father, and wiped his brow. "But wedding bells are not in my future. At least not anytime soon."

The angry sister shook her head, spun on her heels, and marched off.

Chad turned to the blonde and offered a grin. She looked curious, but not ready to run for the hills. "I guess I made one helluva first impression."

"Hmm." She glanced down at her dog as if seeking comfort in the fact that he stood between them.

"I'm Chad Summers." He held out his hand—the one part of his body not covered in beer.

"You're Katie's brother." She glanced briefly at his extended hand, but didn't take it.

He lowered his arm, still smiling. "Guilty."

"Lena." She nodded to the dog. "That's Hero."

"Nice to meet you both." He looked up the hill. Country music drifted down from the house. Someone had finally added some life to the party. Couples moved to the beat on the blue stone patio, laughing and drinking under the clear Oregon night sky. In the corner, Liam Trulane tossed logs into a fire pit.

"After I dry off," Chad said, turning back to the blonde, "how about a dance?"

"No."

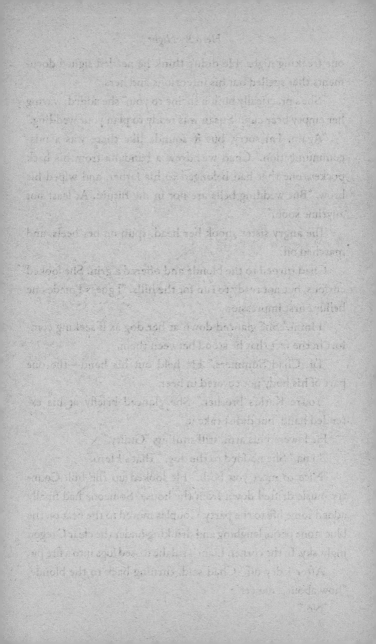

An Excerpt from

MAYHEM

by Jamie Shaw

**A straitlaced college freshman is drawn
to a sexy and charismatic rock star in this
fabulous debut New Adult novel for fans
of Jamie McGuire and Jay Crownover!**

"I can't believe I let you talk me into this." I tug at the black hem of the stretchy nylon skirt my best friend squeezed me into, but unless I want to show the top of my panties instead of the skin of my thighs, there's nothing I can do. After casting yet another uneasy glance at the long line of people stretched behind me on the sidewalk, I shift my eyes back to the sun-warmed fabric pinched between my fingers and grumble, "The least you could've done was let me wear some leggings."

I look like Dee's closet drank too much and threw up on me. She somehow talked me into wearing this mini-skirt—which skintight doesn't even begin to describe—and a hot-pink top that shows more cleavage than should be legal. The front of it drapes all the way down to just above my navel, and the bottom exposes a pale sliver of skin between the hem of the shirt and the top of my skirt. The fabric matches my killer hot-pink heels.

Literally, killer. Because I know I'm going to fall on my face and die.

I'm fiddling with the skirt again when one of the guys near us in line leans in close, a jackass smile on his lips. "I think you look hot."

"I have a boyfriend," I counter, but Dee just scoffs at me.

"She means *thank you*," she shoots back, chastising me with her tone until the guy flashes us another arrogant smile—he's stuffed into an appallingly snug graphic-print tee that might as well say "douche bag" in its shiny metallic lettering, and even Dee can't help but make a face before we both turn away.

She and I are the first ones in line for the show tonight, standing by the doors to Mayhem under the red-orange glow of a setting summer sun. She's been looking forward to this night for weeks, but I was more excited about it before my boyfriend of three years had to back out.

"Brady is a jerk," she says, and all I can do is sigh because I wish those two could just get along. Deandra and I have been best friends since preschool, but Brady and I have been dating since my sophomore year of high school and living together for the past two months. "He should be here to appreciate how gorgeous you look tonight, but nooo, it's always work first with him."

"He moved all the way here to be with me, Dee. Cut him some slack, all right?"

She grumbles her frustration until she catches me touching my eyelids for the zillionth time tonight. Yanking my fingers away, she orders, "Stop messing with it. You'll smear."

I stare down at my shadowy fingertips and rub them together. "Tell me the truth," I say, flicking the clumped powder away. "Do I look like a clown?"

"You look smoking hot!" she assures me with a smile.

I finally feel like I'm beginning to loosen up when a guy walks right past us like he's going to cut in line. In dark shades and a baggy black knit cap that droops in the back, he flicks a cigarette to the ground, and my eyes narrow on him.

Dee and I have been waiting for way too long to let some self-entitled jerk cut in front of us, so when he knocks on the door to the club, I force myself to speak up.

"They're not letting people in yet," I say, hoping he takes the hint. Even with my skyscraper heels, I feel dwarfed standing next to him. He has to be at least six-foot-two, maybe taller.

He turns his head toward me and lowers his shades, smirking like something's funny. His wrist is covered with string bracelets and rubber bracelets and a thick leather cuff, and three of his fingernails on each hand are painted black. But his eyes are what steal the words from my lips—a greenish shade of light gray. They're stunning.

When the door opens, he turns back to it and locks hands with the bouncer.

"You're late," the bouncer says, and the guy in the shades laughs and slips inside. Once he disappears, Dee pushes my shoulders.

"Oh my GOD! Do you know who you were just talking to?!"

I shake my head.

"That was *Adam* EVEREST! He's the lead singer of the band we're here to see!"

An Excerpt from

SINFUL REWARDS 1
A Billionaires and Bikers Novella
by Cynthia Sax

Belinda "Bee" Carter is a good girl; at least, that's
what she tells herself. And a good girl deserves
a nice guy—just like the gorgeous and moody
billionaire Nicolas Rainer. Or so she thinks,
until she takes a look through her telescope
and sees a naked, tattooed man on the balcony
across the courtyard. He has been watching
her, and that makes him all the more enticing.
But when a mysterious and anonymous text
message dares her to do something bad, she
must decide if she is really the good girl she has
always claimed to be, or if she's willing to risk
everything for her secret fantasy of being watched.

An Avon Red Impulse Novella

I'd told Cyndi I'd never use it, that it was an instrument purchased by perverts to spy on their neighbors. She'd laughed and called me a prude, not knowing that I was one of those perverts, that I secretly yearned to watch and be watched, to care and be cared for.

If I'm cautious, and I'm always cautious, she'll never realize I used her telescope this morning. I swing the tube toward the bench and adjust the knob, bringing the mysterious object into focus.

It's a phone. Nicolas's phone. I bounce on the balls of my feet. This is a sign, another declaration from fate that we belong together. I'll return Nicolas's much-needed device to him. As a thank you, he'll invite me to dinner. We'll talk. He'll realize how perfect I am for him, fall in love with me, marry me.

Cyndi will find a fiancé also—everyone loves her—and we'll have a double wedding, as sisters of the heart often do. It'll be the first wedding my family has had in generations.

Everyone will watch us as we walk down the aisle. I'll wear a strapless white Vera Wang mermaid gown with organza and lace details, crystal and pearl embroidery accents, the bodice fitted, and the skirt hemmed for my shorter height. My hair will be swept up. My shoes—

Voices murmur outside the condo's door, the sound piercing my delightful daydream. I swing the telescope upward, not wanting to be caught using it. The snippets of conversation drift away.

I don't relax. If the telescope isn't positioned in the same way as it was last night, Cyndi will realize I've been using it. She'll tease me about being a fellow pervert, sharing the story, embellished for dramatic effect, with her stern, serious dad— or, worse, with Angel, that snobby friend of hers.

I'll die. It'll be worse than being the butt of jokes in high school because that ridicule was about my clothes and this will center on the part of my soul I've always kept hidden. It'll also be the truth, and I won't be able to deny it. I am a pervert.

I have to return the telescope to its original position. This is the only acceptable solution. I tap the metal tube.

Last night, my man-crazy roommate was giggling over the new guy in three-eleven north. The previous occupant was a gray-haired, bowtie-wearing tax auditor, his luxurious accommodations supplied by Nicolas. The most exciting thing he ever did was drink his tea on the balcony.

According to Cyndi, the new occupant is a delicious piece of man candy—tattooed, buff, and head-to-toe lickable. He was completing armcurls outside, and she enthusiastically counted his reps, oohing and aahing over his bulging biceps, calling to me to take a look.

I resisted that temptation, focusing on making macaroni and cheese for the two of us, the recipe snagged from the diner my mom works in. After we scarfed down dinner, Cyndi licking her plate clean, she left for the club and hasn't returned.

Three-eleven north is the mirror condo to ours. I

straighten the telescope. That position looks about right, but then, the imitation UGGs I bought in my second year of college looked about right also. The first time I wore the boots in the rain, the sheepskin fell apart, leaving me barefoot in Economics 201.

Unwilling to risk Cyndi's friendship on "about right," I gaze through the eyepiece. The view consists of rippling golden planes, almost like . . .

Tanned skin pulled over defined abs.

I blink. It can't be. I take another look. A perfect pearl of perspiration clings to a puckered scar. The drop elongates more and more, stretching, snapping. It trickles downward, navigating the swells and valleys of a man's honed torso.

No. I straighten. This is wrong. I shouldn't watch our sexy neighbor as he stands on his balcony. If anyone catches me . . .

Parts 1 – 7 available now!

An Excerpt from

FORBIDDEN
An Under the Skin Novel
by Charlotte Stein

Killian is on the verge of making his final vows
for the priesthood when he saves Dorothy from a
puritanical and oppressive home. The attraction
between them is swift and undeniable, but every
touch, every glance, every moment of connection
between them is completely forbidden . . .

An Avon Red Impulse Novel

We get out of the car at this swanky-looking place called Marriott, with a big promise next to the door about all-day breakfasts and internet and other stuff I've never had in my whole life, all these nice cars in the parking lot gleaming in the dimming light and a dozen windows lit up like some Christmas card, and then it just happens. My excitement suddenly bursts out of my chest, and before I can haul it back in, it runs right down the length of my arm, all the way to my hand.

Which grabs hold of his, so tight it could never be mistaken for anything else.

Course I want it to be mistaken for anything else, as soon as he looks at me. His eyes snap to my face like I poked him in the ribs with a rattler snake, and just in case I'm in any doubt, he glances down at the thing I'm doing. He sees me touching him as though he's not nearly a priest and I'm not under his care, and instead we're just two people having some kind of happy honeymoon.

In a second we're going inside to have all the sex.

That's what it seems like—like a sex thing.

I can't even explain it away as just being friendly, because somehow it doesn't feel friendly at all. My palm has been laced with electricity, and it just shot ten thousand volts into him. His whole body has gone tense, and so my body goes tense, but the worst part about it is:

For some ungodly reason he doesn't take his hand away.

Maybe he thinks if he does it will look bad, like admitting to a guilty thing that neither of us has done. Or at least that he hasn't done. He didn't ask to have his hand grabbed. His hand is totally innocent in all of this. My hand is the evil one. It keeps right on grasping him even after I tell it to stop. I don't even care if it makes me look worse—*just let go*, I think at it.

But the hand refuses.

It still has him in its evil clutches when we go inside the motel. My fingers are starting to sweat, and the guy behind the counter is noticing, yet I can't seem to do a single thing about it. Could be we have to spend the rest of our lives like this, out of sheer terror at drawing any attention to the thing I have done.

Unless he's just carrying on because he thinks I'm scared of this place. Maybe he thinks I need comfort, in which case all of this might be okay. I am just a girl with her friendly, good-looking priest, getting a motel room in a real honest and platonic way so I can wash my lank hair and secretly watch television about spaceships.

Nothing is going to happen—a fact that I communicate to the counter guy with my eyes. I don't know why I'm doing it, however. He doesn't know Killian is a priest. He has no clue that I'm some beat-up kid who needs help and protection rather than sordid hand-holding. He probably thinks we're married, just like I thought before, and the only thing that makes that idea kind of off is how I look in comparison.

I could pass for a stripe of beige paint next to him. In here his black hair is like someone took a slice out of the night sky. His cheekbones are so big and manly I could bludgeon the counter guy with them, and I'm liable to do it. He keeps staring, even after Killian says "two rooms please." He's still staring as we go down the carpeted hallway, to the point where I have to ask.

"Why was he looking like that?" I whisper as Killian fits a key that is not really a key but a gosh darn credit card into a room door. So of course I'm looking at that when he answers me, and not at his face.

But I wish I had been. I wish I'd seen his expression when he spoke, because when he did he said the single most startling thing I ever heard in my whole life.

"He was looking because you're lovely."

An Excerpt from

HER HIGHLAND FLING
A Novella
by Jennifer McQuiston

When his little Scottish town is in desperate
straits, William MacKenzie decides to resurrect
the Highland Games in an effort to take
advantage of the new tourism boom and invites
a London newspaper to report on the events.
He's prepared to show off for the sake of the
town, but the one thing William never expects
is for this intrepid reporter to be a she . . .

William scowled. Moraig's future was at stake. The town's economy was hardly prospering, and its weathered residents couldn't depend on fishing and gossip to sustain them forever. They needed a new direction, and as the Earl of Kilmartie's heir, he felt obligated to sort out a solution. He'd spent months organizing the upcoming Highland Games. It was a calculated risk that, if properly orchestrated, would ensure the betterment of every life in town. It had seemed a brilliant opportunity to reach those very tourists they were aiming to attract.

But with the sweat now pooling in places best left unmentioned and the minutes ticking slowly by, that brilliance was beginning to tarnish.

William peered down the road that led into town, imagining he could see a cloud of dust implying the arrival of the afternoon coach. The very *late* afternoon coach. But all he saw was the delicate shimmer of heat reflecting the nature of the devilishly hot day.

"Bugger it all," he muttered. "How late can a coach be? There's only one route from Inverness." He plucked at the damp collar of his shirt, wondering where the coachman could be. "Mr. Jeffers knew the importance of being on time today. We need to make a ripping first impression on this reporter."

James's gaze dropped once more to William's bare legs. "Oh, I don't think there's any doubt of it." He leaned against the posthouse wall and crossed his arms. "If I might ask the question . . . why turn it into such a circus? Why these Games instead of, say, a well-placed rumor of a beastie living in Loch Moraig? You've got the entire town in an uproar preparing for it."

William could allow that James was perhaps a bit distracted by his pretty wife and new baby—and understandably so. But given that his brother was raising his bairns here, shouldn't he want to ensure Moraig's future success more than anyone?

James looked up suddenly, shading his eyes with a hand. "Well, best get those knees polished to a shine. There's your coach now. Half hour late, as per usual."

With a near-groan of relief, William stood at attention on the posthouse steps as the mail coach roared up in a choking cloud of dust and hot wind.

A half hour off schedule. Perhaps it wasn't the tragedy he'd feared. They could skip the initial stroll down Main Street he'd planned and head straight to the inn. He could point out some of the pertinent sights later, when he showed the man the competition field that had been prepared on the east side of town.

"And dinna tell the reporter I'm the heir," William warned as an afterthought. "We want him to think of Moraig as a charming and rustic retreat from London." If the town was to have a future, it needed to be seen as a welcome escape from titles and peers and such, and he did not want this turning into a circus where he stood at the center of the ring.

As the coach groaned to a stop, James clapped William on the shoulder with mock sympathy. "Don't worry. With those bare legs, I suspect your reporter will have enough to write about without nosing about the details of your inheritance."

The coachman secured the reins and jumped down from his perch. A smile of amusement broke across Mr. Jeffers's broad features. "Wore the plaid today, did we?"

Bloody hell. Not Jeffers, too.

"You're late." William scowled. "Were there any problems fetching the chap from Inverness?" He was anxious to greet the reporter, get the man properly situated in the Blue Gander, and then go home to change into something less . . . *Scottish*. And God knew he could also use a pint or three, though preferably ones not raised at his expense.

Mr. Jeffers pushed the brim of his hat up an inch and scratched his head. "Well, see, here's the thing. I dinna exactly fetch a chap, as it were."

This time William couldn't suppress the growl that erupted from his throat. "Mr. Jeffers, don't tell me you *left* him there!" It would be a nightmare if he had. The entire thing was carefully orchestrated, down to a reservation for the best room the Blue Gander had to offer. The goal had been to install the reporter safely in Moraig and give him a taste of the town's charms *before* the Games commenced on Saturday.

"Well, I . . . that is . . ." Mr. Jeffers's gaze swung between them, and he finally shrugged. "Well, I suppose you'll see well enough for yourself."

He turned the handle, then swung the coach door open.

A gloved hand clasped Mr. Jeffers's palm, and then a high, elegant boot flashed into sight.

"What in the blazes—" William started to say, only to choke on his surprise as a blonde head dipped into view. A body soon followed, stepping down in a froth of blue skirts. She dropped Jeffers's hand and looked around with bright interest.

"Your chap's a lass," explained a bemused Mr. Jeffers.

"A lass?" echoed William stupidly.

And not only a lass . . . a very pretty lass.

She smiled at them, and it was like the sun cresting over the hills that rimmed Loch Moraig, warming all who were fortunate enough to fall in its path. He was suddenly and inexplicably consumed by the desire to recite poetry to the sound of twittering birds. That alone might have been manageable, but as her eyes met his, he was also consumed by an unfortunate jolt of lustful awareness that left no inch of him unscathed—and there were quite a few inches to cover.

"Miss Penelope Tolbertson," she said, extending her gloved hand as though she were a man. "R-reporter for the *London Times*."

He stared at her hand, unsure of whether to shake it or kiss it. Her manners might be bold, but her voice was like butter, flowing over his body until it didn't know which end was up. His tongue seemed wrapped in cotton, muffling even the merest hope of a proper greeting.

The reporter was female?

And not only female . . . a veritable goddess, with eyes the color of a fair Highland sky?

He raised his eyes to meet hers, giving himself up to the sense of falling.

Or perhaps more aptly put, a sense of flailing.

"W-welcome to Moraig, Miss Tolbertson."